# The Neapolitan
# Sisters

Also available by Margo Candela

*Good-bye to All That*

*More Than This*

*Life Over Easy*

*Underneath It All*

# The
# Neapolitan
# Sisters

◆ *A NOVEL* ◆

## MARGO CANDELA

alcove
press

Published in the United States by Alcove Press, an imprint of The Quick Brown Fox & Company LLC.

Alcove Press and its logo are trademarks of The Quick Brown Fox & Company LLC.

Library of Congress Catalog-in-Publication data available upon request.

ISBN (hardcover): 978-1-63910-084-2
ISBN (ebook): 978-1-63910-085-9

Cover illustration by Niege Borges

Printed in the United States.

www.alcovepress.com

Alcove Press
34 West 27th St., 10th Floor
New York, NY 10001

First Edition: August 2022

10 9 8 7 6 5 4 3 2 1

*For my sister Martha*

# · 1 ·

# MARITZA

"*MAMÁ*? HOW DOES THAT song go? The one that's always playing on the radio when you're washing the dishes? The one about the girl and her party." I set another stack of wedding magazines on the dining table and sit opposite her so we both have enough space from each other. "You know which one. Where she's crying and it's her party. *Her* party. You know the one I'm talking about. Don't you, *Mamá*?"

My mother is pretending she can't hear what I'm saying. This is just another one of her little games, but I can outplay her, or at least keep playing until she quits.

"Anyways, what's the biggest, most important party of any girl's entire life?" I'm wasting my time asking her because, like always, it's me who's going to have to answer my own question. "Her wedding! Right, *Mamá*? And since it's *my* wedding, I can wear what I want to. So why shouldn't I wear white?"

*Mamá* won't answer me because she wants me to not wear white, and she doesn't want to tell me to not wear white. She thinks if she waits long enough, my question will go away. It won't. I won't.

My mother rubs her forehead like she does before she gets one of her migraines. I'll change the subject for now.

"I need to be at my nail salon at four fifteen." Every third Sunday I do exactly the same thing. She knows this, but she'll forget on purpose if she thinks she can get away with it. "We'll eat when I get back. Make sure Daddy doesn't drink any more beer until then."

If it wasn't for me, she'd let him have all the beer in refrigerator. This was sort of okay until what he did last year. After that happened, even she had to admit it wasn't normal for Daddy to have Budweiser with his breakfast instead of coffee. And it's not like he can't drink any beer—he can, just not as many as before.

"He gets so impatient when he has to wait," Mamá says.

"So?" I tell her. Her hand goes back on her forehead, but I don't have time to be nice about this. "It won't kill him to wait."

I don't understand why she's making this an issue. I already have more than enough to worry about besides keeping track of how many beers Daddy drinks. And it's not like she wants him walking around with pee down his pant leg again. That was so embarrassing. All the neighbors saw him, but Daddy says it never happened.

"Maybe, Maritza, if you go now, we can eat—"

"It's just a color change, no fill this time. I want to try a new shade before my wedding. I'll get my pedicure on Wednesday when I go to the bank."

Mr. Kim, my boss, will complain about me being gone from the office for so long, but he always does that. To Mr. Kim, complaining is like breathing.

"It's Sunday, Maritza. Why do you have to go so late?"

My mother says this as if she and Daddy have some-where to be tomorrow morning. I'm the only one who has anything real to do Monday through Friday. My mother has never worked, and Daddy's retired now, so what's the problem with having dinner an hour or so later one or two Sundays a month?

"Because they close at five, and I want my nails done by Mr. Ngo." I can pretend just like her that we haven't had this exact same conversation million times before. "He's fast and doesn't make mistakes, especially since he wants to go home."

I've learned enough Vietnamese at my job, so Mr. Ngo and the other manicurists can't get away with talking trash about me like they do with their other customers. And they don't waste my time with hand massages or by suggesting extras like paraffin dips and stupid designs. Maybe, though, I'll do something special for myself, like a facial, before my wedding.

"*Mamá*? Don't you think it would be wrong if I didn't wear white? I mean, it's my wedding, not some sort of funeral. People expect a bride to wear white. You did. Didn't you, *Mamá*?"

My mother looks at me but doesn't say anything. She can't. She wore a white dress when she got married even though she was already pregnant with my sister Dulcina.

Not that she and Daddy could've gotten married at St. Mary's even if she hadn't been pregnant. Daddy's not Catholic or Jewish even though he's both.

Our last name is Bernal because Daddy's dad was Jewish and his mom was an Italian Catholic named whose maiden name was Renzi. And it's even more confusing because Daddy speaks Spanish like a Mexican even if he doesn't look like one except for how he dresses. Mrs. Gonzalez took Daddy in after his parents died in a car accident when he was in junior high. His three older brothers had all moved away to start their own families and Daddy didn't want to leave his friends.

I always thought it would be easier if we used my mother's last name, Suarez. Sometimes people ask rude questions about what I am and they don't believe me when I tell them there used to be a lot of Jewish and Italian people in Boyle Heights. They just assume everyone from here has always been Hispanic because that's what they are now. Now with my wedding really happening, maybe I'll change my last name, but not to Auggie's. I don't like his at all. If his, Acevedo, is my only choice, I'd rather keep Bernal.

Anyways, Daddy's never cared about being any type of religion even though Mamá has always wanted him to be Catholic. All she can do is go to church enough for both of them, but I only go with her to the first morning mass on Sundays.

"Okay, sure, my wedding might not be at St. Mary's—and that's not my fault and it won't be fair if Father Gabriel doesn't change mind—but I'm still the bride. I should at least get to wear what I want. Right, *Mamá*?"

My mother pinches the bridge of her nose and leans away from me. This is how she is about everything, even with simple stuff that's not worth stressing out about.

What time does she want to go to Target? Later? Right now? Maybe tomorrow? What does she want to have for dinner? Pollo Loco? King Taco? Leftovers? How many beers are in the fridge? None? Some? What number is some?

Sometimes I just want to yell at her when she gets like this, but that would be disrespectful, like my sister Claudia is. Claudia never asks, she just does what she's decided to do. Kind of like Dooley with her problems, but Claudia is worse. She's always acted like she's too busy to have problems of her own, but she's never too busy to point out what everyone else is doing wrong or could do better. She loves to show up here at the house, boss everyone around, and then disappear back to her practically empty Studio City townhouse.

And neither of them has ever had to drive Mamá to Costco for toilet paper or reprogram the universal remote for Daddy. Claudia's fancy job keeps her *so* busy. And maybe

Dooley will never get herself together. So who's going to take care of Mamá and Daddy forever?

Me, that's who!

And since I will, I want my mother to tell me I deserve to wear white. I want my answer and I'll wait for it. I'll wait forever if I have to.

Mamá hides behind a two-year-old issue of *Bride* before she says, "Whatever you decide to wear is your choice, Maritza."

"Exactly! If I want to wear a rainbow tube top and acid-washed jeans with the knees and butt all shredded and walk down the aisle to Def Leppard's 'Pour Some Sugar on Me,' that's what I'll do."

She looks at me like I'm crazy, as if she really thinks I'd do something so tacky. It annoys me that this is what gets her attention. I force myself not to show how mad I am.

"I'm wearing a white dress. Super white," I say to her. "With a long veil and a train. I don't care what anyone says. It's *my* wedding."

"Okay then, Maritza." She flips through the magazine, stopping every so often when something catches her eye, which seems to be everything but wedding dresses. "You know what's best."

"How about this one?"

I slide an even older issue of *Bride* in front of her. I've been collecting wedding magazines for a few years, and the dresses are beginning to show their age. The dress is atrocious. The bottom is like a birdcage with crushed up cotton balls stuck all over it, and it has only one sleeve. I wouldn't even wear a dress like that for Halloween.

"What do you think, *Mamá*?"

"It's very dramatic." She looks away quickly, as if it's a picture of a squashed bug. "More for a very big wedding maybe, but not so much for—"

"For what?" I ask. She stares down at the magazine, twisting her hands in her lap. "Not for what, *Mamá*?"

I don't need her to remind me that she thinks my second wedding shouldn't be a big deal. If she had it her way, all I would get is a five-minute ceremony at city hall and dinner at El Torito. Then we would pretend none of it ever happened, just like after the first one.

That wedding was big, at St. Mary's and almost exactly like I dreamed it should be. No one could question my wearing a white dress then. But I couldn't stay married to that person, and she's never going to let me forget it. I was barely eighteen. How could I have known about that kind of stuff?

"What does Augustino think?" she asks, like it matters. "He might want to see you in something different."

Yeah, a thong and stripper heels. That's exactly what he likes. How else would I know what "Pour Some Sugar on Me" sounds like?

"Augustino agrees with me. This is my wedding, and we deserve to have what I want."

Mamá has never liked to make a fuss over things like graduations and birthdays. Once we were old enough, me, Claudia and Dooley had to arrange our own special days, or else it would be just us and a Betty Crocker cake in a flavor none of us liked with never enough frosting.

We're all summer babies, born one right after the other—August for Dooley, July for Claudia and June for me but only because I was born six weeks early. When we were little, we looked so much alike, people thought we were triplets. No one would think that anymore.

"Are you looking at the dresses, *Mamá*?"

I've made it easy for her by marking the pages of the ones I like best. Even so, my mother isn't saying anything about the dresses I want her to have something to say about.

"Yes, Maritza, I'm looking." Her words all run together, her voice traveling up and down almost like she's singing.

My mother mostly speaks English to me, but she still has her accent. She wasn't born here, like Daddy was. She came to East Los Angeles as a teenager and she only knew Spanish, so Mamá decided not to talk for the longest time. Even now, she doesn't like to answer the phone or order her own food at restaurants. Her accent isn't too bad, but it's obvious she was born in Mexico. Me, Dooley, and Daddy sound like where we're from, Boyle Heights.

But not Claudia. She changed everything about herself the minute she left for college. After she was done, Claudia moved back to L.A., but has always lived on the Westside on purpose. Dooley went to San Francisco for art school, but she stopped going to classes after her first semester. It's too bad because she's really talented. She used to draw me pictures of whatever I could think of and they always turned out even better than I imagined.

Claudia says Dooley hasn't done her art in while, but it doesn't mean she won't go back to it someday. Maybe she will, but I don't know. I've never gone to San Francisco to visit her, and she hasn't been here in a couple years because of her problems. Claudia is only fifteen miles away and she hasn't come by since Thanksgiving. She didn't even stay to eat because, supposedly, there was another thing she *had* to go to. Then she ended up having to work over Christmas or, at least, that's the excuse she gave my mother and Daddy.

I grab another magazine. It's from April 1997. I bought it after my first date with Augustino and he proposed six months later. It's too old to be useful, but I'll keep it since it was a sign.

I check my cell phone to see if Auggie has answered the text I sent him after Mamá and I got back from church this morning. I want him to choose our first dance song. He has to pick either "You Sang to Me" or "This I Promise You."

One or the other, it doesn't matter to me. We're not doing a choregraphed dance, just something easy so he doesn't embarrass me too much.

Nothing from Auggie, not even a stupid ;-). I hate that winky face. What is it even supposed to mean?

Fine. We'll dance to "You Sang to Me." My mother likes Marc Anthony, so at least this will make her happy.

I set my phone aside. Once he gets back to me, I'll make him wait. Maybe I'll make him wait so long we miss the movie we're supposed to see. He'll still drive over from Glendale, but he's not going to get what he wants from me. I check the time. It's already 3:36. He definitely doesn't deserve anything for making me wait this long for a stupid text message. I look toward the front window and sigh, but my mother doesn't ask me what's wrong.

Outside, there's the usual Fickett Street noises of traffic, kids yelling, and neighbors blaring music from boom boxes on their porches or car stereos. Coming from our backyard, I can barely hear the steady *thunk*, pause, *thunk*, pause, *thunk* as Daddy works his shovel into the dirt.

I woke up really early yesterday, giving up my Saturday morning, which is the only day I get to sleep in, to go buy rosebushes at Home Depot. When I saw how much they cost, I decided on a mix of light pink and white flowers the plant guy promised would last through the month. They're pretty and close enough to the right colors. Anyways, I don't have time to wait for roses to bloom and I can't dig them up and take them with me after my wedding. I already spent hundreds of dollars on sod for the backyard because I refuse to let my special day be ruined by patchy grass. It's not like I can roll it up like a carpet and take it with me either.

My mother looks up when there is an extra-long pause from the backyard. If she goes to check on Daddy, it'll be almost impossible to get her back to the table.

She's worried he'll have a heart attack or hurt his back, but it's not like him spending his Sunday afternoon watching soccer, eating pistachios, and drinking Budweiser is any less dangerous. At least this way he's getting some exercise. And she's the one who suggested I should have my reception here instead of a banquet hall like the first time. What she didn't consider is what I've had to spend to get the house to look halfway decent. It's my wedding account, not Daddy's back or heart, that's in danger.

"Don't you think a gazebo would look pretty in the backyard?" I ask to bring her attention back to where it's supposed to be. "I'm thinking of renting one for my wedding."

"Rent a what?" Her eyes are on the kitchen door. She doesn't look away until we hear the sound of my dad digging again. "A gus sey bo? What is that?"

"Gah-ZEE-bow! And you know what one is. If Father Gabriel doesn't change his mind, we can say our vows and have our first dance on it. We can even set up a small table for me and Auggie so we're away from everyone else. Then we can put the cake there to cut it." In my mind, it looks perfect. With lots of white Christmas lights and some of those paper lanterns— very romantic. "We'll just get rid of some of the tables and chairs to make room. People can stand during the ceremony and then take turns sitting when it's time for the food."

I didn't budget for a gazebo because I just thought of it, but that doesn't mean I don't have a plan. I know exactly what I'm doing. I always have.

"I don't know, Maritza." She looks out toward the doors, front and back, as if she expects someone to bust in and save her from whatever her problem is. "People expect to sit down and there's not—"

"How about this one?" I interrupt her and show her a strapless dress with a full skirt and lots of beads and lace. It's very white and costs almost $10,000. "Isn't it pretty?"

She wrings her hands together. Mamá has arthritis, but she still won't stop doing it. She just sits there and twists them around each other and doesn't say anything or even nod.

"If I want to spend all my wedding money on that dress, I will." I never seriously considered that dress, but that doesn't mean I shouldn't be able to have it if it's dress I want. Not that I do, but still. "This is my wedding. Mine."

"It's a beautiful dress, Maritza." She doesn't even try to sound like she means it. "Maybe we can find something like it in ivory or cream? You look so nice in ivory—"

"Wedding dresses are white. Not cream or ivory." I hold up a picture of a bride in white and a guest in a light blue dress. "Wedding dress. Party dress. Big difference."

"Okay, Maritza," she says, giving up. "If it's the dress you want, it's the dress you should choose. Okay?"

I hate it when she does that—tells me what she thinks I want to hear so I'll shut up. But not this time. If I listened to her, I wouldn't even be having a wedding. I wouldn't have my job or a fiancé and I definitely would never have my own house. I'd be stuck here forever while my sisters are off doing whatever they want with their lives. It's time I did something just for me, and it has to happen on May 31 because it's not fair I lost out on those extra six weeks.

My phone vibrates, making us both jump. Auggie's answered my text. I leave it where it is. He can wait. I hand my mother this month's issue of *Modern Bride*. My dream dress is on page 179. It's not marked with a tab. I want to see if she finds it on her own.

"Will you call Claudia and tell her to call Dooley?" I've already asked her once, but with Mamá I have to tell her what to do at least three times before she gets around to it. "I can't deal with either of them right now. I'm so busy with everything else I have to do."

"I will," she says, but we both know she won't do it today.

As long as it happens by the end of the week, it's fine with me. I don't care if it gives her a migraine. My mother can have as many as she wants after she does this one little thing for me. I'm the bride, I shouldn't have to do everything.

# • 2 •

# CLAUDIA

I CUP MY HAND over the microphone of my Bluetooth headset and take a sip of my $3 custom-blended, elixir-in-fused tea which is supposed to promote clarity and serenity. What it definitely does is make me pee like a racehorse. I take a moment to marvel at the absurdity of spending so much money on something I'm just going to flush away, but so what. It tastes good, I can afford it, and $3 tea is better for me than Xanax.

I'm very careful with those little pills and should throw them out or, at least, stop refilling the prescription, but I won't. I need to not want them and being afraid to have them would mean I need them.

So what's my problem? Why don't I just drink my damn tea, pee it out, and pop a Xanax when I feel like not feeling like any other normal person? Because I'm not and I can't. Nothing about me or my life is normal, and it's all my fault.

Clearly, my $3 tea is not living up to the serenity part of its promise.

"Claudia? Are you there?" Mom says.

This is all I'm going to get from her. She wants me to fill in the rest, to say what she can't and to do what she won't. This is why she's called me.

"I'm here," I answer in Spanish.

I keep my voice low and measured, wishing I'd closed my office door before taking her call. No one can understand what I'm saying, but it's still obvious I'm taking a personal call at my desk. As far as my boss and colleagues are concerned, I don't have a personal life in any language. This used to be mostly true, but it isn't now and the last thing I want is for anything about me other than how well I do my job to be a topic of conversation around here.

"Will you call her?" She's asking but not really.

"If Maritza wants . . ." I switch over to English. In Spanish, I sound as annoyed as I am with her and this conversation. ". . . if she wants Dooley to be there for this wedding thing of hers, then Maritza can pick up the phone and call her herself."

We all came out of the same uterus, but Maritza's from a different planet. Planet Princess. With her, everything has to be perfectly unrealistic no matter how much of a pain in the ass it is for everyone else to make it real. It's annoying. She's annoying. They all are.

And I'm a bitch.

I love Maritza, but she's an almost-thirty-year-old woman who lives with our parents and believes marrying a thirty-three-year-old man who also lives at home will be the answer to, well, anything. Augustino is a huge mama's boy in the worst way. One of the reasons they've been engaged for so long is because his mommy can't stand the thought of losing him to another woman, especially if that woman is Maritza. Not that she can stand for much of anything—Perla is a gouty diabetic who smokes like a chimney. Auggie's two sisters, Dani and Gabi, dislike Maritza just as much as their mother does.

Maritza has complained to me about all of them for years, and yet she's still going to marry the guy. Why? Just for the wedding? I wouldn't put it past her and it would confirm how bonkers she is.

"Claudia, don't be like that. We all have to do our part." Mom's voice barely carries over the sound of running water in the kitchen sink and the radio playing oldies in the background. "Maritza needs our help."

"I completely agree, she really does need to get help," I say, unable to keep this most obvious of observations to myself. "And this is her second wedding, so it's not like she doesn't know what to do."

A familiar stab of contrition hits me straight in the chest. Sarcasm is an industry-related malady I willingly suffer from in abundance, but my comment was gratuitously unkind, even by my own standards. Mom doesn't say anything, which of course makes me feel like an even bigger bitch and worse daughter and horrible sister. In other words, exactly who Mom and Maritza think I am.

"Sorry, Mom."

My apologies to her are frequent, almost automatic. Most of the time, I don't feel remotely sorry. It's more that I feel, or, rather, what I feel is . . . I really don't know. I've had more than one therapist tell me not knowing what I feel is, in itself, a perfectly valid feeling.

Fuck feelings.

"Claudia, you have to do something," Mom says quietly, as if she's worried my sister will somehow overhear her from where she is miles away at work in Long Beach. Maritza has a nose like a bloodhound and ears like a bat just like Mom. "She has all these ideas. Can you maybe say something to her, Claudia? You've always had a way with her."

I frown down at my tea, annoyed with her lazy manipulation. I don't want to reminded that I have "a way" with my sister. What I want is for Mom to be, well, a mother.

Mom was a beautiful woman, still is, and always fragile like a porcelain figurine that should have stayed in its velvet-lined box. My sisters and I were lucky to inherit her clear, pale olive skin and thick, dark, wavy hair. We had to learn what to do with what we got from Dad—our height, intelligence, left-handedness, wispy mustaches, and aggressive unibrows over big hazel eyes. Mom made us feel like we were supposed to ignore puberty, just as she was desperate to. We weren't supposed to grow breasts or have periods, but we did—one right after another like nesting dolls who suddenly grew too big to stay safely tucked away on a high shelf. This is when the hand wringing started.

All of a sudden, we were taller than everyone else, wearing the wrong-sized bras, and sporting matching unibrows. My sisters and I accepted we were on our own and pooled our meager knowledge and resources. We shared tubes of pimple cream and boxes of maxi pads and tampons. We learned to bleach and shave hair from all sorts of places. Dooley, Maritza, and I took care of each other up until we chose to go in different directions. Dooley had her art and her anger, I decided college would be my escape, and Maritza watched one Disney movie after another when she wasn't reading romance novels.

I turn back to my computer screen and start scrolling through emails that have arrived since she called me.

"What's there to talk to her about, Mom? It's her wedding, and she's paying for it. I have to give her credit for that at least."

Mom and Dad already gave Maritza her dream wedding. It was all too pink and poufy even for an eighteen-year-old who kept reminding everyone that Princess Diana was ancient at twenty when she bagged her big-eared prince.

The man Maritza married was almost twice as old as she was and seemed even older. I met him a week before the wedding and all it took was one sweaty handshake to confirm he was a creep. By that point, though, there was no talking any sense into Maritza. Nothing and no one, especially not me, was going to keep her from wearing her white-as-snow hooped dress and too-long veil. I wasn't at all surprised but a lot relieved when she moved back to the house a couple months after the wedding. It was a mess-and-a-half that took most of my sophomore year to sort out, but I still made the dean's list.

I resent Mom for expecting me to once again fix the unfixable and have been waiting for exactly this task since Maritza announced last weekend that she'd be getting married at the end of the month. She has twenty-nine days left to pull a wedding out of her ass. And now I have to pull our eldest sister out of mine.

"I told her it was too much to do so fast. She should wait until next year, but you know how Maritza gets." Those last few words are as close as Mom will ever come to acknowledging my sister has issues. "Claudia, she keeps talking about renting a gazebo and taking away chairs for people to sit on. You have to tell her she can't do that."

"If you don't want her to plop a gazebo in the backyard, then she can't. It's your yard, not hers." Annoyance wells up and instead of swallowing it, I let it pour out of me. "The problem is you and Dad only tell her what she wants to hear. You're not doing her any favors. This is why she is how she 'gets', Mom."

Both of us are quiet for a moment. Mom to punish me for not playing along and me to prove to her I've had too much therapy to be manipulated by her silence.

"She's running out of time, Claudia. Things need to be arranged, and your sister needs help," Mom says, pulling a mom card while cutting my punishment short for the sake of staying on Maritza's schedule. "She's busy with her job and planning this wedding."

"I'm busy too." I look up to see if anyone's caught me whining.

She sighs like I'm the one who's the cause of all her problems. Great. Now I'm on her shit list because one of my sisters is being difficult. Nothing new there.

I sigh right back at her since I don't have the option of hanging up on her. I want to, but I won't.

"Your father is going to have a heart attack with all the work he has to do in the backyard," she says, slapping down another mom card. The only one she has left is her winding up in an early grave. "He's not so young anymore, Claudia. Neither am—"

And there it is.

"Okay, Mom, okay, I'll call Dooley." We both know it's the only option I ever had, but both of us need to go through the motions of being displeased with each other to make it feel right.

"It's not too much trouble?" she asks, practically daring me to be honest with her. "You must be busy with your work."

I look at the watch on my wrist not to see what time it is but to just look at it. It's a very nice watch and it's not mine, but who it belongs to pretty much is.

"I'm always busy and I already said I'd call her."

I've learned just how far I can push the line of disrespect by simply being blunt with Mom. I'm positive my most recent ex-therapist would disapprove of all of this. He'd say I was resorting to tactics that didn't work when I was a girl and which, as an adult, I shouldn't expect to make any sort of difference now. Wrong. Some of what I learned as a kid is exactly what makes me so good at what I'm now able to make happen.

I'm patient, I notice everything, and I always anticipate the inevitable while running at least three other concurrent scenarios in my mind. I've learned how to tell a loser from a wannabe from a has-been from who might be the next big thing. I read everything, listen to everyone, and forget nothing. And, if everything goes right, a movie happens. But my family is not my job, they're just a lot of work. They also don't understand    what I do or how much responsibility I've created for myself. I don't expect them to. When I'm with them, I'm just a daughter or a sister. Nothing more, nothing less.

"Make sure to tell Dulcina she can stay with us. Or maybe she could stay with you?" she asks.

This is Mom's way of checking in on my love life. As in, do I have one I'm hiding from her because it's what I've always done.

"I'll call her, Mom." I sound like I'm twelve and have been tasked with fetching Dooley from a neighbor's house.

"She listens to you, Claudia."

I'm sure Mom thinks she means this as some sort of compliment, but it's her way of trying to make herself feel better about making me responsible for the most stressful task on Maritza's wedding to-do list. I have no idea if Dooley will listen to me or if she'll even take my call. I don't even know if I can track her down in time.

"Not always," I warn her.

"You can make her understand," Mom says as confidently as she can.

With this settled, she moves on to the rest of Maritza's plans. I can tell she's on the verge of being overwhelmed, but I keep my comments to myself and jot down notes in shorthand.

I took a course in high school at the suggestion of my guidance counselor, Mr. Gleason. Girls who weren't pregnant and showed a modicum of ambition were encouraged by him to aim high and become secretaries. When I got into

Princeton, I made sure to send Mr. Gleason a thank-you note for all his help and encouragement. I wrote it in shorthand.

My new assistant, Julie, a recent USC graduate who's already eyeballing my job, appears at my office door. She's holding a cup of coffee and has a sheaf of papers tucked under her arm, but she manages to point to her watch without spilling either. I have a production meeting in ten minutes, and I'm already sweating through my silk blouse. Careful not to tip over a stack of memos, scripts, and press kits, I reach into my desk and pull out a bottle of prescription-strength antiperspirant. It singes my armpits but will keep me dry for seventy-two hours straight—a small price to pay for looking like I'm in control.

"Yeah. Okay. Got it." I cut Mom off as she begins complaining about Dad.

"Don't forget about Saturday. Maritza has her appointment for her dress. She needs you there." Mom pauses. I can almost see her looking around to make sure Maritza hasn't driven from Long Beach and back to the house just to catch us in the act of talking smack about her. "She needs your eye, Claudia."

"Yes, okay, totally doable," I say for Julie's sake. "Not a problem."

"Don't forget to call Dulcina," Mom reminds me before she hangs up.

Julie takes a generous step into my office. I wave her off, stopping her where she is. Last thing I need is any sort of caffeine. I'm already jittery and will have to excuse myself from the meeting at some point to go to the bathroom and get a grip. Julie knows this. Any good assistant will find out what her boss's weaknesses are and then compensate or exploit them as needed for her own advantage.

"Claudia? Are you still on the phone?" Julie mewls like a cat looking to be let in from the rain.

During our obligatory welcome lunch, Julie informed me USC's extensive alumni network practically runs this town. As far as my assistant is concerned, her future of endless successes is inevitable. She's not wrong. Connections matter in the movie business, which is why Julie is amazed at how far I've managed to get with just a degree from Princeton and the determination to make something of myself. She also believes the only reason I have my job is because I'm a Latina.

I've kept my Jewish and Italian heritage quiet, deciding to follow Dad's example even if for very different reasons. He's never made any sort of big deal of being anything other than what he is—a proud amalgamation of Boyle Heights.

I've learned it's easier to be vague about where I come from with a surname like Bernal and looking like I do—too much and too little of three things to be one or the other or the other. I identify as as Latina, but there's only so much diversity this business is willing to tolerate especially from a woman.

I won't take her out to lunch again, but I'll have to do something for her birthday. Ever helpful, Julie has programmed the date into my calendar. I've set aside a random gift certificate from a kiss-ass gift basket some PR blow-up doll sent me last month. Julie will be suitably insulted by a regifted gift bag castoff, but she'll still redeem it.

Besides schooling her on the realities of being my assistant, my second job is keeping her away from my phone and email when I'm not at my desk. She goes through everything she can get her hands, ears, and eyes on. I did the same thing when I was starting out.

Julie will go far, but not today or tomorrow. For now, her job is to pick up my dry cleaning, get my $3 tea in the morning, my $9 salad at lunch, and take care of whatever other crap work I choose to dole out to her. I would feel badly about it, but some of the assistants around here have it a lot worse. I'm not a screamer, and I don't throw things. I want to, but I'd never do either.

I cup my hand over the microphone so we can both pretend I'm interrupting my call to deal with her. "Yeah?"

"Meeting in eight, Claudia. I can totally sit in and take notes for you." Julie doesn't want to take notes. What she wants is to put her face in front of my boss, also a USC alum. "Should I go on ahead?"

"No."

"No?" It's as if she's never heard the word before. "Maybe I can sit in until you're done with your . . ."

I stare her into silence to make it clear I have no intention of repeating myself. When I say yes or no, I mean exactly yes or no. Never maybe. A maybe is nothing but a simultaneous weak no and a cowardly yes and always open to pointless interpretation.

Fuck maybes.

"These need to be cleared off my desk." I point to a thick stack of rejected scripts.

"Uh, sure." Julie's expression is one of naked disappointment.

I'm sure it's the same look she laid on her parents when they told her they were going to buy her a used Jetta instead of the new white BMW convertible she'd set her heart on for her graduation gift. It might have worked on her mommy and daddy, but it's dead in the water where I'm concerned.

I don't give a fuck what she drives to fetch my tea and salad.

"Um, Claudia?" Julie isn't prepared to give up so easily. How boring of her. "I was thinking, maybe, if I sit in on the—"

"Before you start shredding, I need you to messenger over these scripts." It's rude of me to cut her off, but it spares us both from her wasting any more of my yeses and nos. I gave her my answer, and it stands as is. "They have to go out before noon. Thanks."

What I'm asking of her is exactly what I had to do when I did my time as an assistant. And while I may never say please, I do thank Julie for doing her job.

"These?" Julie asks, pointing to pile of scripts she knows she's supposed to shred.

She's quick as a ferret and dumb as an ox when it suits her, but she'll never screw up on purpose. Julie has enough ambition to knock a circus elephant into a coma. She reminds me of how I was at her age, but I was motivated by a fear of failure, not fueled by vast reserves of entitlement like she is.

"Other way around, Julie. When you're done, I need coverage for these." I hand her a couple of scripts I've already decided to pass on, but they'll serve as a bone for her to gnaw on. "Tomorrow morning will be fine. Close the door after you. Thanks."

"No problem, Claudia! I'll get right on it." She sets the cup of coffee on my desk.

I wait until Julie and her big ears are out of my office before dialing what I hope is a working number for Dooley. Every so often, my sister will leave me a message with her latest phone number.

It rings and rings. While it does, I take a sip of coffee, hating myself and Julie for it. Mostly Julie. The coffee tastes off, not like it usually does. I spit it back into the cup and wonder if Julie spit into it before I did.

"Leave a message." My sister has a husky, voice having been a smoker since she was just a kid. Considering everything, I hope it's the only thing she's doing these days.

"Señorita Dulcina Bernal, it's your bitchy sister. No, the other one. Guess what? Maritza is getting married. Again and for reals. Saturday, May 31, 2003, sometime in the afternoon at the house. There might be a rented gazebo and, knowing who she's marrying, most definitely a *piñata*. Call me back, Dooley. . . . Please."

# ♦ 3 ♦

# DULCINA

I STARE AT AMBER'S freshly pierced nipples, unsure if I should pat her on the shoulder or offer to buy her a one-way ticket back to Nowhere, Minnesota. Amber has been looking for an excuse to show me her boobs, pierced or not, since we were introduced a month ago, which was about two weeks after she moved to San Francisco.

The sight of them, and her, is just a huge yawn. I look past her nakedness to gauge what kind of night we're in for. It's slow right now, but it's not going to stay this way. On an average Friday, The Clap Trap serves a steady stream of lesbians, wannabe lesbians, people curious about lesbians, and, as of late, the tech boys who are still hanging on and around after the dot-com bubble popped in their faces.

"You think I made a mistake. Don't you? Just tell me, Dooley."

"It doesn't matter what I think, Amber." I wince when she twists each of the rings between her fingers. "Maybe don't do that."

What girl—and this is what she is at twenty-one—hasn't done something dumb like indulging in trendy self-mutilation on the road to reinventing herself? I can't blame her for being stupid. I was once like her and still might be, but without any more holes than the ones I was born with.

"The piercing guy suggested a clit ring and offered me a discount." Amber buttons up her shirt, and for a second I'm afraid she's going to pull her jeans down. "He says they make like, sex, like, really awesome. Should I go for it?"

"I think he's trying to charge you for getting to look at your *chocha*. The ring itself is incidental."

"Huh?"

I pick up a glass and towel, hoping she gets the hint that I'm done talking about her boobs and bean even if she's not. The glass is barely warm. I like it best when they're straight out of the Hobart, almost too hot to touch. After a glass is run through a wash cycle, everything that's happened to it is scalded away. It's almost like new, or as new as it'll ever be again. I wash everything in hot water for the same reason. Hot is the only way to go with dishes, clothes, and showers. Everything else is a waste of time.

"It's sort of raining. Do you think it'll be slow tonight?" Amber leans her hip on the bar right next to the stack of glasses we need to polish and shelve. "Maybe Curtis will let me go early if I ask him?"

She won't ask him. She wants him to ask her even if he has no idea he's supposed be asking her anything. That's the way it was with the Minnesotan boys and men she grew up with. If she wises up, she'll realize pretty only goes so far and lasts only so long well before her looks start to fade. Amber won't wise up, but she's definitely going to get her bean pierced.

"Tell him you're on your period," I suggest. For a pervert, Curtis is pretty vanilla. "And it's really heavy."

"I can tell him that?" She rubs her nipple through her shirt. "I mean, it's not a lie. I really am on my period."

"Well, of course you are, Amber." I laugh, which just confuses her. "You want to help me out with these glasses?"

I'll have to repolish hers, but there's no way she's going to get out of doing some actual work on my shift.

"I don't see why we can't use them like they are. They're just going to get dirty again," Amber whines as she arranges dishwater blond hair so it draped right over her newly ringed nipples.

When Curtis asked me what I thought of her as a bar tender, I told him the truth. She's not cut out for much else besides standing around being blond and looking sort of pretty. It's why he hired her and why she won't last. I've worked for Curtis on-and-off for years, and he's always had a job for me when I've needed one. In the past, I may have shown up hungover, but I always worked my full shift. Curtis trusts me, even when he shouldn't have, leaving it up to me to prove him right.

This is why I've been bartending for the last year or so at The Clap Trap instead of waitressing again at any one of his half dozen restaurants in the city. After knowing each other for more than a decade, we both can trust me.

Oddly enough, bartending makes sense to me. Horny people who can't get laid drink. Unhappy people too cheap or scared to see a therapist drink. Bored people who can't stand themselves drink. I don't judge because I can't. I used to be all of them, which makes me an excellent bartender who has enough sense to know my own sobriety will never endear me to anyone who's hauled themself to The Clap Trap to not be sober. So I keep my own trap clapped, stick to seltzer water, and remember their preferred topics of conversation along with what they like to drink.

"Hey, Dooles. What's shaking?" Todd asks as he slips out of his dead dot-com branded hoodie.

He only comes in when he knows I'm working and has no problem with slapping a fiver on the counter for a two-buck beer. Todd sold his gambling-porn-semilegal music downloading website for an obscene amount of money just before everything fell apart. He's moved on to another start-up that's going to make him even richer and less happy. The poor guy is doomed to fail upward for the rest of his life and he knows it.

"Hi, Todd! Hi!" Amber, betraying her junior varsity cheerleader days, calls out.

"Hey . . ." He's forgotten her name, and she's is too much of a dumb bunny to realize it. ". . . girly."

"Speaking of which! I'm going to the little girl's room, Dooley. Okay?" She says this like she really expects me to tell her she can't go change her tampon. "Dooley?"

I nod but don't look at her, keeping my face turned toward the stack of glasses we're both supposed to be polishing.

"Hey, Dooles," Todd says again. I ignore him. Again. "You look pretty tonight."

This earns him a glance. From the white wifebeater over a black push-up bra, faded Levi's to my scuffed Doc Martens— the look I've settled into is more of a cliché than pretty.

"Don't call me Dooles, Todd, unless you want me to spit in your beer, which you probably do. Same thing you drank last time you were here and the time before that?"

I toss a cardboard coaster in front of him, not bothering to wait for his answer. I know what he wants and also know he'll drink whatever I decide to give him without a word of complaint. Being mean to Todd is a bad habit, but one that's safe enough to indulge in. It comes natural to me, being mean, but it was way easier when I was drinking.

"Moody tonight, Dooles. You on your period?"

"I bet you'd like it if I was." I grab an unpolished glass for him. "Wouldn't you, Todd?"

"Yeah, you know it," he says. He's dead serious.

I look at Todd, really look at him for the first time since he started coming to The Clap Trap. He might not be as vanilla as I assumed he was. Interesting.

He watches me pour his beer, waiting for just the right moment to say his usual line. "Just like I like it, Dooles, with plenty of head."

"Charming." I make sure some of his beer slops over the rim of the glass and onto the bar. "As always."

He wads up a couple of cocktail napkins and wipes down the area around his coaster. He knows from experience I'm more than happy to let him sit in a puddle of stale beer.

"Slow tonight." Todd looks around, taking in the sparse crowd. "Guess the lesbos are staying in and munching carpet."

"Where's your girlfriend and her carpet?" I lean in over the bar, close to him, staring him full in the face. Todd, eyes half closed, is ready for a kiss I almost want to give him. I pull back and start polishing glasses again. "You must have been a very good boy for her to put some slack in your chain."

"We broke up," he says with an indifferent shrug of his shoulders but ruins the effect by taking a long pull on his beer and burping. "Excuse me."

"Tell me all about it." I focus on the glass in my hand so I can pay attention to what he's saying without having to absorb any of his heartache. "But skip the boring parts."

I already know all about his cold mother, his dead father, and his disapproving stepfather. I also know his ex-girlfriend looks like his mother and seems to be a lot like his stepfather. Todd could never admit this about her—it would destroy him.

"Not much to tell. She moved out." He says this in a way that gives me the impression he's conflicted about not being more upset than he actually is. "We wanted different, uh, we had different plans."

"Mm-hmm?" This and the raising of one eyebrow is all I offer him while admitting to myself I'm not completely indifferent about his breakup.

His ex-girlfriend came by the bar last week. She ordered an expensive mixed drink, introduced herself as Todd's girlfriend, and told me *her boyfriend* was depressed and *her boyfriend* was letting opportunities slip through his fingers. She asked if I thought *her boyfriend* was drinking too much and spending too much time at The Clap Trap. What she really wanted to know was if I was messing around with *her boyfriend* and, if I was, how much of a threat I was to *her* becoming the future Mrs. Todd whatever his last name is.

Even if I had been giving him the kind of sex he'll remember for the rest of his life, he was still going to give her a big fat engagement ring. The only one who was in denial about it was Todd. Instead, she broke up with him, a blatant tactic to force his hand, and now he's exactly where she didn't want him to want to be in the first place. Dumb bunny.

"Dooley? Phone call." Curtis pokes his head out from the back room. "Where's Amber?"

"Here I am!" she calls out from the other side of the bar.

Amber, cramps forgotten, boobs bouncing under her shirt, descends on Curtis. He ducks back behind the door to avoid the avalanche of her enthusiasm. I hand her a glass and towel to stop her from moving. She's making me seasick.

"Don't kill yourself before I get back, Todd." I reach under the bar for a fresh bowl of nuts to keep him busy while I'm gone.

"You're a saint, Dooley," he says, and, to his credit, he doesn't crack a lame joke about the nuts. "You did something to your hair. I like it."

I walk over the springy rubber mats that carpet the floor behind the bar and make my way into the cramped office where Curtis oversees his mini empire. He prefers the drunks in the Mission to the Noe Valley super moms who've taken over his creperie with their book clubs and expensive strollers.

Curtis has his face pressed close to the flickering computer monitor he refuses to get rid of. He's convinced it makes more fiscal sense to increase his glasses prescription instead of buying a new one. Curtis has always been cheap where it doesn't make sense, but sentimentally generous to a fault.

"Hello?" I say trying to figure out who would call me here as opposed to just showing up.

"Dooley! For Christ's sake."

"Oh, hey, Claudia." I roll my eyes at Curtis, but my heart picks up a beat or two. My sister only calls when she has a reason to. I turn my back to him for some privacy. "What's shaking?"

"What's shaking? Are you drunk?" she snaps, followed by a sharp intake of breath. "Sorry, that was—"

"Don't worry about it," I cut her off, my voice icy. Curtis gets up and scurries out the door, clutching his cheap adding machine and receipts to his chest. "What do you want?"

"Did you get my message?" Her voice is calm, but I can hear the guilt she's feeling for accusing me of drinking.

"Nope. I left the mobile phone you sent me somewhere between here and wherever." My shoulders are tensed up to my ears. I roll my neck to try to ease away my half of our collective guilt. "Sorry."

"Yeah, I figured that was the case." Claudia says.

My sister is very persistent, but knows when to back off. She never gives up. Ever. I've given her thousands of reasons to give up on me and she hasn't.

I catch sight of my watery reflection in the mirror above the sink in the corner. I pull my Chapstick out of my pocket and slick on a fresh coat. It's soft. When I get back to the bar, I'll stick it in a glass of ice cubes. This time, I'll put it on a high shelf so Amber doesn't use the glass to serve someone a badly made whisky sour.

"What's up, Claudia?"

"Maritza is getting married. Again. And we get to be bridesmaids. Again."

"Yeah, right." I love my sister and want to talk to her, but I'd have to shed my behind-the-bar persona. This would ruin my ability to serve up drinks and sarcasm for the rest of the night. "I have to get back to work."

"Wait, Dooley, don't hang up. It's really going to happen."

"What do you want me to do about it?" I narrow my eyes at my reflection, practicing the look I'll give Todd when he asks what he should do about his love life.

"Well, there is one thing. Hold on . . ." I hear a series of beeps like when a car door is opened, and the keys are still in the ignition. She mumbles a few words and then turns her attention back to me. "Dooley? You there?"

"What do you want me to do about it?" Again with the attitude. Claudia must be so exhausted by me. I would be if I was her.

"You already fucking said that, Dulcina," she says, losing her patience with me.

She won't apologize this time. She doesn't have to—we both know that one was on me. Claudia is also still trying to figure out if I'm drunk or high or both. I can't blame her. It's been a year and half since I have been, but maybe no amount of time will ever be enough for her to stop worrying about me.

"This wedding is going to happen. And since Maritza wants to get married before she turns thirty, she's dead set on May 31. We're supposed to pretend it's not why she's rushing it, but whatever. Typical Maritza. Typical everyone, including me. Are you there, Dooley?"

"I'm here. Where are you?" I ask, stalling for time. There's a lot of background noise—cars, breezy conversations, more cars. Wherever she is, it sounds very L.A. "Standing in the middle of the 405?"

"I'd rather be. I'm outside The Ivy. It's a restaurant."

"I know what The Ivy is, Claudia. My gynecologist gets *People* magazine." My cheeks go pink at acting like the unattainable bartender with the one person in this world who knows me better than I know myself.

"I'm thrilled for you and your pop cultured vagina, Dooley . . . Wow, that was bitchy, even for me. Sorry." She sounds embarrassed.

We should be even now, her apology canceling out mine, but we're not even close to it. Not when she pays for my medical and dental insurance, not after everything else she has done for me.

"Why are you there?" I ask, wanting to pretend it's possible for us to have a normal conversation about things like the weather, traffic, anything but our baby sister getting married. Again.

"I'm meeting with an actress, or as my boss says, an actor with tits. No one you've heard of yet. I have to convince her that agreeing to a nude scene, if not two, isn't gratuitous T&A but art with a capital A as well as tits. And since we have tits and ass in common, my boss thinks this particular production note will be less creepy coming from me."

"How exciting." And it is, but I sound like a jerk. "Sorry, Claudia."

"No, it's me who should be sorry. This, what I'm about to do, is scummy and a typical part of my job. And Dooley? I'm really good at my job. So about that other thing . . . if you need me to spot you for—"

"No, I'm good. I have to get back to work. Bye, Claudia." I light up a Marlboro and take an extra-deep drag.

"Wait! Don't hang up." Her voice cracks.

She's under stress but trying to hide it. Our mom made her call me because Maritza made our mom call her so Claudia would call me. It's absurd, but this is how it is with us when it comes to things like this. Things like me.

"You're going to need a dress. You haven't gotten fat have you?"

"Nope." I let out a steady exhale, not bothering to cover the mouthpiece of the phone as I go stand in front of the sink. The puff of blue-gray smoke makes everything look bleary and slightly glamorous. "Not fat."

"I thought you were going to quit." As hard as she tries, Claudia can't stop caring.

"Quit smoking? What! And get fat?" I make myself laugh, and it feels good when she joins in.

"I'll just get your usual size. Nothing too hideous, I hope, but you know how Maritza can be." She says this as if I've already agreed to be there. "She's really excited you're coming. We all are."

"Right. I'll call you soon." I hang up before she can say anything else.

I drown my cigarette under a stream of water, watching it absorb the liquid until it falls apart, and toss the rest of the pack into the trash can. Rinsing my mouth out, I avoid looking in the mirror. And then I do. I stare at my face staring back at me and just like that, what I need and want to do are one and the same.

I step back out into the bar where Amber is showing Curtis her newly accessorized nipples. He has the same look on his face he gets when he's counting the receipts after a particularly good night. Instead of taking up my usual spot between them, I head straight for Todd.

He turns to me, surprised, and opens his mouth to say something. Before he can, I grab him by the neck of his

T-shirt and kiss him, making it clear I'm not joking around. After a few seconds, he touches his tongue to mine just as I break it off so we don't start to compete for attention with Amber's half-naked neediness. Still holding the front of his T-shirt, I move my lips next to his ear.

"It's your lucky night, Todd." I give it a lick and nip at the lobe. His whole body shudders. "Nod if this is what you want."

He does. I link my arm through his and tug him to his feet.

"Dooley . . ." Curtis says, but then he just smiles. He knows what's happening and has been waiting for it to happen for a while now. I smile back at him.

Amber stands there slack-jawed, pierced nipples still on display, as he opens the till. Curtis counts out a stack of tens and twenties and more than a few fifties and secures them with a thick rubber band. When he gives me the roll of money, he holds on to my hand for a long moment before letting me go.

"Curtis, please," I gesture toward Amber, "don't even think about it. And thank you. Thank you for everything."

# ◆ 4 ◆

# CLAUDIA

Instead of taking a Saturday morning kickboxing class, sleeping in, or cramming in some semblance of a personal life in the few hours a week when I'm not working, I'm in Torrance at David's Bridal watching Maritza preen herself silly in a blindingly white, extra poufy gown she can't possibly think Mom will allow her to wear without a doctor's note and a dispensation from the Pope.

This dressing room isn't big enough for the three of us and the gown, which is an entity unto itself. Feeling the smallness of the space, I break out in a cold sweat and start swallowing like I do when I don't want to throw up. Forcing myself to calm down, I sip my Starbucks chamomile tea while hiding it from the salesgirls as they pass by.

We've been here for almost two hours, and Maritza's no closer to choosing a dress. In the parking lot, as we waited for the doors to open, my sister declared she'd already fallen in love with "the one" and had it on hold. But she didn't even try on "the one," dismissing it on sight with a wrinkle of her nose and quick shake of her head.

I love Maritza, but what I'd really love to do right now is cram the yards of rejected tulle, chiffon, and machine-made lace down her throat.

This game of dress-up is a waste of time. Somewhere deep inside her where logic and reality go to die, Maritza is well aware she has to buy off-the-rack, which means an as-is, discontinued or canceled dress. My sister has been planning this spectacle from the moment she squeezed a proposal out of Augustino five and a half years ago, but she left buying her wedding dress to just weeks, not even a month, before the actual day she's going to wear it. Maritza is being quintessentially unrealistic, but even I don't have the balls to point it out to her. Especially not now, since the dress she's wearing is between me and the only way out of this room.

Maritza stares at herself in the mirror, making her fashion-model face—pouting her lips and narrowing her eyes—unaware of how her utter and complete devotion to her own reflection is making me and Mom squirm.

"What do you think?" Maritza asks her reflection as she reaches into the bodice to hike up her cleavage so there are just a few centimeters of covered skin before we see her nipples.

"It looks like you've been dipped in Cool Whip from the waist down." I try to sooth the anxious tickle in my throat with another sip of tea. "And you could carry a tray of champagne flutes on your cleavage."

I'm feeling a bit under the weather. This is what my lock-jawed Connecticut dormmate would call it when she staggered back to our room after a night of heavy drinking and vaguely consensual sex. I'm not hungover, but I did get laid very late last night, and again this morning, and it's never been anything but sensual. Remembering this, him, causes my breath to catch in my throat for an entirely different reason.

"Claudia." Mom gives me the look that used to freeze me in my tracks when I was a kid. Unfortunately for her, I haven't been a kid for a long while. "*Por favor.*"

"Okay, fine. You look delicious, Maritza." I look over at Mom. Happy now? Does she even understand what happy is? That would be a no and a hell, no.

Mom turns her back on me as she refocuses on the problem at hand—my sister and that dress. "Maybe a more simple one? To show off your face?"

How anyone is going to make Maritza understand that wearing a strapless ball gown with layer upon layer of snow-white tulle will look out of place at her own wedding is beyond me. Oh, wait. This is why I'm here—the bitchy voice of reason. But I have to leave the bitchy out of it.

Maritza fluffs out the skirt, does a half twirl, and steps on me with one of her Nine West stilettos.

"Damnit, Maritza!"

I rub my foot, making sure to shove my shoe under the seat so no one can see the distinctive lettering on the insole. I don't want to answer any questions about how much a pair of black Prada heels cost. Not a little, and I can well afford them along with the three other pairs I've stockpiled at my townhouse.

"It *does* show off my face," Maritza says to Mom. "And a wedding dress isn't supposed to be boring like Claudia's shoes."

"Okay, Maritza, okay," Mom says, sounding defeated as she looks down at the one boring shoe I'm wearing.

"What I think Mom means—" Tea bubbles up from my belly and my throat closes around it. I swallow and swallow again, very aware that both of them are now watching me. "—by simple is a silhouette that's elegant and not as overdone as a ball gown. Is that what you mean by simple, Mom?"

I have no qualms throwing her under the bus. It would be nice to have some company down here for once.

"What do *you* mean by elegant?" Maritza asks with an edge to her voice. She's already burst into tears once this

morning, and no one wants to be subjected to a repeat performance. "You don't think I look elegant?"

"Of course I do." An outright lie she's forced on both of
us. She doesn't want to know what I think. My sister wants
me to confirm what she believes. "But what if we consider
another option?"

I squeeze my way over to the gown I asked the assistant to
bring in after I got a look at her princess bride selections. It's
an off-the-shoulder fitted sheath with a lace overlay. I hold it
up so the hem barely touches the floor, standing slightly lopsided since I'm only wearing one boring shoe. The dress pools
in my hand in waves of ivory "silk", light enough in color
to make Maritza happy, but not so white as to cause Mom's
arthritis to flare up from pointless hand wringing.

The dress isn't perfect, but it is absolutely appropriate, in stock, and on sale. I don't dare say this to my sister.
Maritza is awake dreaming the Disney movie she's been
starring in since her second grade class took a field trip to El
Capitan Theater to see a rerelease of *Cinderella* in 1983. This
wedding is part two of her dream, the sequel to the one we
don't talk about. And just like with her first wedding, we're
all dutifully playing our roles to make sure she continues to
exist in her cartoon romance novel bubble.

It's all so fucked up, but it'll be even more so if buys the
tub of Cool Whip topped with tits of a dress she has on.

"Why that one?" Maritza wrinkles her nose and frowns.
This particular expression of hers has always made me want
to pull her hair. "Hmm?"

I've been told enough times that it's not my responsibility to fix my family and firm, clear boundaries are not
only healthy but mutually respectful. But none of my past
therapists and psychiatrists understood my responsibility to
my sisters, especially Maritza. I escaped to college, where
I had a chance to create my own identity, and, for better

and for guilt, to live my own life. The only way this could have ever happened was for me to leave the house and Boyle Heights. While Maritza's never articulated her resentments, they seethe just under the surface of every interaction and conversation we've had since I opened my first college acceptance letter so many years before.

Maritza has everything she wants—her job with Mr. Kim, the bedroom we'd shared all to herself, a man-boy who's willing to marry her—and has decided what she has is what she needs. She just wants more of it and for it to be different enough so it seems like it's not the same thing she already has. She's essentially remained the same person, the same girl, she was when I left her behind. She is who she was. There's been no character arc, no third act. If anything, she's more entrenched in her Maritza-ness than ever.

"This is a gorgeous dress, Maritza, for an accomplished *young* woman who has an amazing set of tits and an even better-looking ass." I hold it up against me and smile. It's a forced, very fake smile, and it's the best I can offer her under the circumstances. "Trust me, I see a lot of quality T&A in my line of work, which makes me a very specific kind of expert."

"You don't think it's *too* simple?" Maritza wavers slightly. She's beginning to see there just might be an alternative to parading around like a poufed, cartoon, faux-virgin, extra-sexy princess on her wedding day.

"It's a beautiful dress!" Mom knows Maritza's window of reason will only be ever so slightly open for a fraction of a second. She charges headlong into it in an act of self-de-fenestration. "You look like a movie star and . . . and . . . and—"

"Exactly, Mom. It's classic and elegant. Very sophisti-cated, modern yet undeniably bridal." I pile it on as my per-sonal cell phone vibrates against my work issued BlackBerry.

I talk louder and faster, the compounded noise unnerving me. "I'd be so lucky to ever get a chance to wear a dress like this. But I probably won't since I'm such a massive shrew and married to my job. Well, damn, now I'm so depressed, I could adopt some cats."

Mom frowns at me to let me know to cut it out before Maritza realizes we're manipulating her into choosing a dress that suits both her age and the occasion, such as it is.

"I'll try it on," Maritza says. "Just to see."

She presents her back to me so she can be unlaced from the Cool Whip gown. Mom pushes me aside when I don't move fast enough for her liking.

"Yes, try it on," Mom says, visibly relieved, her hands practically tearing at the ribbons of the ball gown's corset top. "Claudia! The dress!"

"This one?" I ask, playing dumb.

In another life, the one I sometimes allow myself to live without a second thought, I could be kickboxing away the lobster ravioli I thoroughly enjoyed last night instead of slowly melting under the florescent lights and forced happiness of David's Bridal while behaving like a total brat.

"*Yes,* that one!" She jerks the dress out of my hands and helps Maritza shimmy into it without looking at me.

I sit down on the lumpy tufted chair in the corner and put my shoe back on. I'll have to make amends, but not today. I already have a list of people I need to pacify, and Mom is nowhere near the top it. That spot is reserved for the man I snuck out on this morning.

"Claudia? Did you call Dooley?" Maritza asks from underneath the dress.

"Yes." I need more tea. More sleep. More time away from my family. More of who I left sleeping in my bed. "I talked to her last night."

"What did she say?" Mom asks mildly, trying not to raise any alarm with Maritza, especially not now when she's cooperating.

"Nothing much," I shrug. I stare down at the tote bag where I've stowed away my purse and now silent cell phone to keep one out of sight and the other out of mind. "She sounded good."

"Yes, Claudia, but what did she say?" Mom asks, impatient with my vague but accurate answers. "About the wedding."

"She knows about it." I give up pretending I don't care and pick up the tote bag, open my purse and peek inside. There's a missed call and a couple of texts. From him. Ethan. "I'll take care of it. I always do."

"Hello?" Maritza has been ignored for too long.

"Oh, Maritza, you look so beautiful!" Mom touches her hand to her mouth as if she's on the verge of being overcome with emotion that's something more than just pure relief. "Doesn't she, Claudia? Doesn't your sister look beautiful?"

The salesgirl pokes her head into the dressing room. She pretty much called it quits after the first hour and eighth dress. I wave her in. "It's safe to come in now."

"This dress looks like it was made for you. It's in one of our smallest sizes." She pinches a bit of extra fabric at the waist so Maritza can see how the dress will hang when it's perfectly fitted to her. "You hardly need any alterations. We can turn it around fast."

"How fast? I'm on a tight schedule and need it as soon as possible," my sister says in a voice that would put the most pampered actor with tits to shame.

"If you buy it today, we could get it done by next Friday, but there's an extra charge to put it at the front of the line."

"End of the coming week is perfect. My sister is knocked up with triplets and her fiancé is being deported."

I feel a little sick at the thought of Maritza becoming some-one's mother. Lord help us, but especially that poor kid.

"Who's pregnant?" Mom's alarmed voice comes up from the floor where she's fussing with the hem.

"No one is," Maritza and I answer in unison.

"Jinx!" she yells and pinches my arm. "Now you have to be my slave for the rest of the day."

"I can't today. What if I just pay for the alterations?" Whatever it's going to cost me will be worth every damn penny. Hell, if it could be ready today, I'd stay here while it's altered, and hand deliver it to my sister in Boyle Heights. I'm way overdue to show my face. I've been very distracted these last few months. "I'm so jealous of how good you look in this dress, Maritza. If you don't wear it on your big day, you'll never forgive yourself."

It's only half a lie but one that wholly pains me. Manip-ulating her is the only way she'll leave here with a wedding dress she won't regret for a marriage she definitely will.

"Augustino will be so impressed," Mom adds. In her mind, it's all about pleasing the man, no matter how much of a mama's boy he might be.

"It makes your *tetas* look so fantastic, people will assume they're fake." I reach over and grope Maritza's cleavage. "Auggie will be all over you."

"Yes, he'll like it, Maritza," Mom says. She's annoyed with me but also cautiously relieved. We're so close. So close. "He will be . . . *impresionado*."

"Beyond impressed. When he sees how great you look in this dress, Auggie's going to pitch a tent in his rented tux."

Out of sheer boredom and simple pettiness, I continue to bait Mom into scolding me for being crude. If she does, she'll be acknowledging her porky future son-in-law has a dick, a dick he's most certainly porked Maritza with. Mom glares at me. I smile back her, bitterly pleased with my own obnoxiousness. For a moment, it's enough to distract me from the slight rolling feeling in my belly.

"He'll walk funny the entire—"

"I think I like it. I think . . . I love it!" Maritza declares to her own reflection as she turns around, admiring herself from every possible angle. "It's the perfect dress for my wedding."

I stand up quickly, my heading swimming not only from lack of sleep and food, but from how draining it is to be here with them. I steady myself, look over my shoulder at the sales attendant and give her a quick nod before I turn my attention back to my sister's mirrored reflection.

"I couldn't be happier for you, Maritza," I tell her. "If I was, I'd barf all over you. That's how happy I am."

## ◆ 5 ◆

# DULCINA

I STARE UP AT the ceiling and go over what I remember from the night before. Doing this sober means I remember a lot. More than a lot. Everything. Yeah, everything. I give up trying to do any more other than just being where I am, and where I am is on the floor of Todd's bedroom.

He lives in a fake loft, all new construction meant to look industrial, in what was once an industrial part of lower Potrero Hill. I burst out laughing when he pulled his black BMW into his assigned parking space and saw his car was sandwiched between two other black BMWs. Todd laughed too, but in a worried way that made me laugh all the harder. When I saw the triptych of Robert Longo Men in the Cities prints above his platform bed, I almost peed my pants.

Todd wasn't laughing anymore and had the beginnings of a confused puppy-dog look on his face. I went down on him and let him come in my mouth but didn't swallow. He stroked my hair and babbled on about how amazing I was as he handed me a wad of Kleenex to spit into. As soon as my mouth was emptied, I suggested he feed me actual food instead of compliments. He ordered in from my favorite Thai restaurant and, after we ate, we had sex on his dining room table.

Then he gave me a tour of the rest of his place, unable to keep himself from pointing out what his ex-girlfriend had picked out. He then asked if I wanted to take a bath. With him. I didn't even bother to tell him no. I just straddled him on the couch his ex-girlfriend special ordered from Z Gallery and grinded the suggestion right out of his head.

During a lull as we caught our breaths after changing positions, Todd commented on my lack of tattoos and piercings. He was surprised I didn't have any, and I didn't feel the need to explain the why of it as there isn't any why—I just don't. Before he could tell me about the meaning of the tattoo on the inside of his forearm, I got back on top and finished us both off. His eyes rolled back as he came, and he called out, "I love you, Dooles!" I pretended for the both of us he hadn't and patted his shoulder as I used his T-shirt to wipe our sweat and his saliva off my breasts.

We showered, separately, and then got into his bed. He tried to talk to me about his mother, his ex-girlfriend, his dead father, and all the pressure he's under. I sat on his face to shut him up. I came hard, and he looked so triumphant, I couldn't help but give him a kiss on his cheek before we fell asleep. Or at least he did. Of course, Todd's a spooner. As soon as I was sure he wasn't going to wake up, I made my way onto the rug beside his bed with a blanket and one of the decorative pillows his ex-girlfriend picked for looks, not comfort.

Here, on the floor, I can think. More than think, I can feel. And what I feel is good as well as surprised at being able to feel good. It's been a while since I've had sex and even longer since I've been completely sober and had sex. No. Not true. I've rarely, if ever, had sex while sober.

The last time I had any sort of sex was right before I checked myself into the hospital. I met a couple at a party, or it might have been at a bar. A party at a bar. Someone's birthday. Maybe even mine. Either way, I was drunk and more than a little high. We went back to their place, and I took off as soon as we were done, passing on the shower and the getting-to-know-you-after-the-act drill.

By then, I had been exclusively sleeping with couples— those Noe Valley super moms are also super wives to their just as coddled husbands. Everyone got what they wanted, no strings, no promises, no pointless drama. I always made it clear I was there just for the sex and never had a problem with disappearing if things started to get serious.

I ran into the woman of the last couple I'd slept with while wasted earlier this year, and I couldn't for the life of me remember her name, much less his. Honestly, I don't think I knew either of their names in the first place. I didn't ask her if they were still together and didn't pretend I had any interest in sleeping with either of them again. When I walked away, I didn't look back.

After nearly two years without sex, I'd convinced myself I was okay if it never happened again. Now I realize I was trying to deny this part of me like I have to when it comes to drinking and using. No, I'm not done with sex and am more than a little relieved that sex isn't done with me. I'll have to be careful, though, and not just with myself.

Considering everything I've done and who I've done it with, Todd is officially not only the first man I've ever had sex with while completely sober, but he's also the first man I've ever spent an entire night with even if it was on his bedroom floor. (Rosie B. in eleventh grade was my first everything else, and she always will be.)

I expected Todd to be a single-gear humper and was fully prepared to leave after the first go around. Instead, he proved to be not only good but also very giving. He made sure I was into it, watching my face, adjusting his tempo and how he touched me, taking his cues from my breathing and the other sounds I made without me having to tell him what to do.

He also has an attractive penis—proportional length to circumference with a plump round head and a pair of fairly symmetrical balls. My exact thought, when I got a look at him, was, "Good job on that junk, Todd's cold mom and Todd's dead dad." Remembering this makes me want to laugh. I don't, just like I didn't last night. Not being able to be mean to Todd is another reason why he'll never see me again.

He grunts softly, rolls over, and settles back into sleep. His foot hangs just over my head. There's a faint tan line at his ankle from whatever he does to keep fit.

I stand up, naked except for the leather cuff bracelets I always wear on each of my wrists and make my way to the bathroom. I pee with the door slightly ajar to keep an eye on him. Todd's shoulders twitch and I freeze until he settles down again. I let myself finish and flush, cringing at the noise.

I tiptoe across the heated marble tiles to the shower. It's huge, tricked out with half a dozen nozzles, spouts, and a big showerhead that feels like rain. After twisting my hair into a knot, I step inside, fiddle with knobs until water is coming out from every direction, and then open bottles of bath gel to find the one that smells the least like Todd's ex-girlfriend. I use his razor to shave my legs and under my arms and then sit on the floor and let the hot water pour down on me, not caring if my hair gets wet.

Feeling clean and relaxed, I wrap a towel around myself and snoop inside his medicine cabinet. Todd's prescriptions—Paxil, Luvox, Zoloft, Effexor, Prozac, Wellbutrin— are lined up in a neat row and all of them are more than half full. After swiping on some of his deodorant, I close the cabinet, drop the wet towel into a laundry bin, and grab a fresh one, folded hotel-style, from the open shelf and wrap it around my hair.

At the house, our mom won't let anyone have more than one towel at a time and it has to be used three times before she'll allow for a fresh one. The Christmas before I left, Claudia gave me and Maritza each our own monogrammed set of towels. It was not only a practical and thoughtful gift, but also funny and twice as disrespectful. My sister Claudia in a nutshell. I still have the washcloth, have never used it, and fully intend to keep it forever.

In his walk-in closet, Todd has an impressive collection of concert T-shirts, all pressed and hung on heavy wooden hangers. He's also framed some of his ticket stubs, including the one for the T-shirt I pull on. Nirvana, June 13, 1991, at the Warfield. Funny. I was there too. It was the first time I dropped acid.

Todd is still on his stomach, arms out in a wide T. I tap his shoulder, and he lets out a long, soft breath. He's blissfully dead to the world and I envy him for being able to sleep so deeply. I walk out of his bedroom, gathering up my clothes along the way. At the foot of the stairs, I pull on my jeans, not bothering with my underwear and bra, and set the rest of my stuff by the front door before venturing into the kitchen for something to eat.

The sum total of Todd's refrigerator is an almost empty carton of rice milk, an expired carton of plain soy yogurt and a half-eaten burrito wrapped in foil.

"Hello?" Todd's ex-girlfriend stands in the open space between the kitchen and living room holding a couple of coffees and a white paper bag. I'd gladly bet a month's worth of tips that inside the bag there's a saucer-sized bran muffin for them to split.

She is, as I remember, okay enough looking. Skinny but bottom heavy, with long, straight, blond hair. She's wearing just enough makeup so she doesn't look washed out and is carefully dressed in cropped khaki pants and a crisp white button-up shirt under an ivory-colored cardigan sweater. She's the human version of plain soy yogurt.

I shut the refrigerator door and reach up to pull the towel off my head. If I'm going to get into a cat fight, I don't want to look stupid. When she doesn't toss the food aside and charge at me, I figure of the two of us, she's the one who's feeling pretty stupid. I would be if I were her.

"Looks like Todd's not a regular milk and Cheerios kind of guy." I gesture toward the closed fridge with the towel.

"He's lactose intolerant." Her voice is flat and automatic, her eyes wide with disbelief but still calculating. She's trying to figure out what the what is.

"Well, of course he is." I walk over to her, take the food out of her hands, and set it on the counter. "He's upstairs. Asleep."

"Oh."

She flushes, and her mouth thins. The expression on her face is stuck somewhere between hurt and anger. She's disappointed in the way a woman is when she offers her man a threesome just to test him and, predictably, he fails her test by being more than down for it.

"Oh," she repeats.

I look through the cabinets and pull out a tea caddy and a jar of honey. I won't help myself to one of the cups of coffee like I did to the guy she broke up with, who she obviously still considers to be her boyfriend.

"Tea?" I don't look up as I fuss with the packets, pretending to debate choices.

"Oh . . . okay." She sits on one of the stools and puts her head in her hands, still holding her keys.

I put the kettle on and set two mugs on the kitchen island before taking a seat opposite her. I may have just spent the night banging Todd's brains out and am now wearing his T-shirt and smell like his soap and deodorant, but I can listen to her. Not because I care about what she has to say, but to get myself out of this situation with as little residual attachment to either of them as possible.

She'll appreciate this but it'll be a lot harder on Todd. He didn't have enough time to really enjoy her having left him, which is something he's wanted for a long time and will always want for as long as they're together.

She picks up the empty mug, turning it in her hands as she talks. Her fingernails are freshly painted, reminding me of Maritza.

My baby sister is a trip.

She still sleeps in our childhood bedroom, has been engaged to the same guy for almost six years, has worked the same job since high school, and has filled the only decent-sized closet at the house with her modern-day version of a bride's trousseau. Maritza either truly believes there is such a thing as a happily-ever-after or she has her head so far up her own butt, she'll never see daylight. Maybe, for her, those two things are one in the same. One thing Maritza would never do is break up with her boyfriend to get his attention. Bluffing is for drunks and dummies. Maritza might be delusional, but she's definitely no dummy.

This chick? She was banking on the comfort of the familiar becoming acceptance of the inevitable. Instead, Todd went on with his life and, last night, had the best time of his life. He told me so. Twice.

"Todd's never come off as much of a player or liar so . . . yeah," I say to get her started.

"No, he's neither of those things." She clears her throat. She has something she needs to admit. "I moved my stuff out just to scare him. I told him it was over unless he proposed, but I didn't think he would take what I said so . . . seriously."

"He did."

There's no need to rub it in, but I won't sugarcoat it for her either. After giving Todd her ultimatum, one she didn't mean, she now has to take him as he is. She'll worry about this part of him, which she'll never get back if she ever even had it in the first place. This part of him now belongs to me, and I'll be taking it with me, along with his T-shirt, when I leave.

I go to the stove and shut off the burner right before the kettle has a chance to whistle and wake Todd up. I pour water into the cups, plopping tea bags in each without bothering to care what they are. She takes a deep breath, bringing the cup to her mouth but not drinking. The water is still clear, the tea bag floating on top. She puts it down and adds a squirt of honey.

"Did you guys . . . ?" She swallows hard, trailing off.

"You gave him a legit out and he took it." I dunk my bag in and out and watch her face to see what effect honesty has on her. "You can't really blame him. Or you can. It's up to you."

She looks at me hard, her eyes bone dry. She's pissed, but it won't do her any good with me. And it definitely won't get her what she wants from Todd. She's the one who shouldn't be here and she knows it.

"I can't do this," she says, giving up on trying to figure out how to come out on top of a mess of her own making. "I can't."

"You can." I push away my mug of tea. "And Todd will go along with it."

"What do you mean?" She's desperate enough to want me to have an answer for her.

"Come back in fifteen minutes. I'll be gone, and he'll just be waking up. Don't go up into the bedroom, wait here in the kitchen. Don't tell him we talked or that you saw me here. Don't ask him what he did last night. Don't say anything when he strips the sheets off the bed and puts them into the wash. The rest is up to you. You can apologize, suggest couples' therapy, go for a hike, spend a weekend wine tasting in Napa. Whatever it is you need to do to get things back like they were before. And Todd will fall back into line. He can't help that about himself."

In however long or little it takes Todd to convince himself he's happy with his plain soy yogurt girlfriend/fiancée/wife, he'll go to his meticulously arranged closet looking for the T-shirt I'm wearing, find it's gone, and know I took it. He'll show up at The Clap Trap and ask about me. Curtis will tell him I've left but not where it is I've gone to and will make clear it's all Todd can expect to find out about me from him.

He'll trudge back to his faux loft feeling guilty for letting himself imagine we could have been together forever, or at least gotten together again for more good sex. Todd will masturbate to his vivid memories of our night while in the shower. He'll come all over the expensive tile and end up feeling sad rather than satisfied, but he'll find some happiness in being able to at least feel something. These moments, when he can relive the best time of his life, will be enough for him to get on with pretending his actual life is exactly as it's supposed to be.

"And you're just going to go?" She doesn't believe me.

What she does believe is that I'm capable of milking Todd for all he's worth just like she plans to. But her plans also include marriage, moving to Marin, a couple of kids, and a new Range Rover every three years. She'll even offer him a threesome but only to see if he'll disappoint her by responding with a "Yes. Please. Thank you". Mostly she'll provide him with predictability down to the inevitable divorce once their youngest is "old enough." This is a life perfectly in keeping with how they were both raised and she wants it enough for both of them to make sure it happens.

What do I have to offer Todd beyond upending his life by encouraging him to be the man he's afraid he'll never become and equally afraid to be? Maybe that's what he wants? From the looks of what's in his medicine cabinet, it's what he's looking for. Honestly? The idea of this, of Todd, is slightly appealing. I do sort of like him, but not enough to consider taking him on much less being with him. That would be bad for both of us, but mostly for me.

"Yes," I tell her and myself, "I'm just going to go."

"Can I give you a ride somewhere? Get you a cab?" She wants me gone and gone now.

"No, thanks." I get up and upend our cups of weak tea into the sink. "I'm good."

# ♦ 6 ♦

# MARITZA

MY MOTHER GRIPS THE steering wheel with both hands, her shoulders hunched up to her ears. She wanted me to drive, but I have too much to do. My wedding planner is digging into my lap, and I'm a little car sick, so it's not like this is fun for me either. Anyways, it's not like traffic is *that* bad. It's really not. A little stop and go, but when isn't it?

When we get home, she can lie down and rest. Daddy will have to watch his soccer with the volume off, but he can have an extra Budweiser.

"Did Claudia look tired to you?" my mother asks. "Maybe she's working too hard."

She's always worried about Claudia. And Claudia makes it worse by telling her there's nothing to worry about. They always play this game and have since forever.

"It's not like I'm not working hard, and, oh, yeah, planning a whole wedding." I sound annoyed because it's exactly what I am. If she wants to worry about anyone, it should be me. "Maybe you should ask me if I'm tired. Which I am, by the way."

I flip to the back of my planner where I've stapled pictures of wedding cakes and flower arrangements. I mark most of them with an X with a black Sharpie. The smell makes me a little dizzy, but in a good way.

There are some old pictures in my planner, from way before I got together with Augustino. It's interesting to see what I used to want and how different I am now. Much more sophisticated, like the dress I decided on. It's a great dress, the perfect dress. Elegant and sexy. And it was on sale and only needs minor alterations.

"She hasn't said anything to you?" my mother asks again. Like always what I tell her isn't good enough because it's not what she wants to hear. "About what she's doing to make her look so tired?"

"Why don't you ask her, *Mamá*?" My mother always wants to know more. Claudia never tells me anything, but she loves to tell me what to do. "If Claudia looks tired, it's because she's tired."

My sister thinks she's so good at keeping her business to herself, but I know something's up. I won't say anything to my mother because she'll just give herself a pointless migraine from worrying about Claudia, who doesn't even care what she puts Mamá through.

I need Mamá to focus on helping me with my wedding. Phone calls have to be made to guests so they understand an RSVP means they have to reply and that, no, they can't invite anyone and assume there'll be enough beer and refried beans for whoever shows up. My mother can make these phone calls for me. She hates telling anyone no, but I really need her to do this for me. I can't deal with people right now.

"Is Augustino coming for dinner?" Mamá asks, staring ahead and not paying enough attention to her side and rear-view mirrors.

She likes Augustino. He acts all polite and respectful and tells her she looks young enough to be my sister. Sometimes he brings her flowers, and he talks soccer and baseball with Daddy. She doesn't know the other sides of him or how much work it is for me to make it seem like he's the person he pretends to be in front of her and Daddy.

It's me who has to remind him to be on his best behavior, who tells him what presents to buy so it looks like he put more than one second of thought into what he's giving. Because of me, Augustino is way better off—better job, better car, better everything than he would have ever been able to manage on his own. He owes me for everything I've done for him. He owes me my wedding. It's finally my turn to be the center of attention. Not his mother or his sisters or anyone else. Just me.

"Tell him to come over for dinner," Mamá says. "Your father wants to barbecue. He always makes too much food."

"I'm busy." I hold up my list for her to see out of the corner of her eye. "I'll never get half of this done with Auggie around."

I'm not going to waste my time holding his hand and batting my eyelashes at him. If I invite him over, he'll assume everything is okay, and he'll expect something else from me. I don't have time for that kind of stuff. Plus, I'm so mad at him right now, maybe I'd bite his thing off. Not off, but I could bite it. Hard.

"Is he being helpful?" my mother asks.

"Augustino is useless. Worse than useless, he's stupid. He wants to have a *piñata* at my wedding. And I'm not talking to him until he tells his fatso mother and fatty-fat sisters to fall in line about my bridesmaid dresses. All of them are so fat. If it wasn't for me, Augustino would be too, like when we first met. Remember? He looked like a giant, hairy, fat baby."

"Don't say that, Maritza. His family is going to be your family soon."

She's always so quick to come to his defense, like he's the victim. She doesn't disagree about them all being fatsos, though. Even she can't deny what's right in front of her eyes. There's just too much of them for her to be able to do that.

"Anyways, it's not a party. It's my wedding. So no stupid *piñata*." I look out the window. "And there's not going to be any wedding at all if these hundreds of things I have to do don't get done."

Traffic is completely stopped up ahead. Probably a car accident or someone got a flat tire. Stupid people don't know how to drive. How hard can it be to not be stupid? I've been driving since before junior high and I've never, not once, gotten into an accident, *and* I know how to change a flat tire.

"Maybe his sisters could help you out a little bit? I'm sure Gabi and Dani would, if you asked them. Maritza?"

The last thing I need is those two cows sabotaging me. Mamá is just suggesting this so I'll point out how awful they are without her having to say it. When I do, she'll tell me I'm being mean. It's just another one of her traps.

"I have it under control," I tell her, but what I really want to do is scream that she's supposed to be on my side, not theirs. "Everything is going to be perfect. Beyond perfect."

"Maybe you need more time?" My mother's answer to everything is to put off as much as possible for another day, another month, year, or lifetime. "Maritza?"

More time isn't going to change anything about Augustino. My wedding is to happen whether she likes it or not.

"Everything is fine, *Mamá*. Augustino is fine." I go back to updating my to-do list. I have it all worked out, and everyone just has to do what I tell them to do. Why is this so hard for them to understand? "I'll find something for Auggie's sisters to do since it's so important to you that I make *them* feel special."

They can help with the favors. I'll buy double the Jordan almonds to make sure there's enough for them to pig out on and still put twelve into each of the little organza bags I ordered. Who eats Jordon almonds anyways? They're gross, but it's what everyone expects. People are stupid, but it's not my problem if they want to crack their teeth eating hard-as-rocks, not-even-good candy. Are Jordon almonds even candy? Whatever. I don't have time to think about this. My mother is just wasting my time.

"Okay, Maritza," Mamá says in a tone of voice that sounds like I've done something wrong. "I was just wondering because Augustino said—"

"What? What did he say?" I look at my mother. Now she has all my attention. I know they talk, but I never thought they talked about anything I should care about. "What could he possibly have to complain about?"

"He wasn't complaining, Maritza." My mother takes a deep breath and grips the steering wheel. "Just that things were going fast, but not like that, not complaining, just commenting. He said it like time was passing quickly . . . and the date was so . . . soon."

"Fast? Soon? He's wasted almost six years, my best years, and now he says things are going too fast?"

My blood feels hot and sour, my face is tight like when I want to cry but can't. This is typical of my mother, to start this kind of drama when I have so much other stuff to deal with. I try to calm down. There's no use getting mad at her when it's Augustino who I need to deal with. He needs to fall in line, just like his mother and sisters and everyone else too. Especially Dooley. She better be here for my wedding. I'll never forgive her if she isn't.

"He's just excited and nervous. It's normal, Maritza." She sounds guilty as she tries to backtrack. "I'm sure you're nervous too."

"I don't have time to be nervous." I look back out the window. I don't want to be upset. There's no point. My mother doesn't know what's she's talking about. She just wants me to worry because *she* loves to worry. "I think I will invite him over for dinner and then we can go to the movies."

"Good! Yes. Have a nice time together." She turns on the radio and begins to hum off tune.

I roll my eyes but keep my face turned away from her. My mother can be so backward sometimes. Things are not like they were when she and Daddy *had* to get married. I'm a working woman, a career woman, with my own money. I don't need Augustino. He should just be grateful I'm with him. If anything, I'm the one who should be complaining, not him. He's getting everything he wants, and all I want is for my wedding to be perfect. That's not too much to ask, is it?

# ◆ 7 ◆

# CLAUDIA

I NSTEAD OF DRIVING TO my townhouse, I stop almost exactly halfway between Torrance and Studio City, which just happens to be the Beverly Center. As I wait behind a line of cars for my turn at the valet stand, I mentally calculate the worth of my outfit. A little more than $1,400 for my dark navy, almost black, silk jersey Donna Karan wrap dress, Ethan's black Persol sunglasses, a pair of small gold hoop earrings, and the aforementioned Prada heels.

That's not counting my purse. It's a Chanel 2.55, and I still can't believe I had the balls to put my name on a wait-list and then follow through with buying it. The thought of how much I spent on something I didn't really want but wanted to prove to myself I could have makes my stomach flip over onto itself.

"Get a grip, Bernal," I repeat to myself a few times while holding my phone up to my ear so I won't look like a crazy person who has to give herself a pep talk while waiting for the valet attendant at the Beverly Center.

It's just a dumb purse, not something essential or consequential like a car or a mortgage. Still, not being able to forget why I bought it always makes me feel weird about carrying around keys, stray tampons, a Target wallet I make no apologies for, gum, and my phones in it. This is why

I use it most days of the week out of pure spite to convince myself it only exists to serve me and not the other way around. As soon as it stops giving me heart palpitations, I'll set it aside, and once the idea of it taking up space in my closet annoys me, I'll give it to Maritza.

My most recently fired therapist—whose Beverly Hills office was almost impossible to reach on time—would have found this very revealing about how I feel and think about myself. It's exactly why I didn't share this little piece of personal trivia with him. I saw him once a week for four months. I didn't tell him shit, but I told him plenty of bullshit, especially once I started up with Ethan. I regret the wasted time as much I like to kick myself over the money I spent on this particular game of mine. I could've bought myself another stupidly expensive purse to have anxiety attacks over.

I smile at the valet as he opens my door and leave it at that. We might have been born in neighboring zip codes, but we're not necessarily in this together. While I haven't forgotten where I came from, I'm well aware of exactly how I got to where I am. So is he. Greeting him with an *"Holá"* would just make me an assholá who should be parking her own damn car.

He steps back as I expertly climb out of my car.

I may have a degree from Princeton—double major in Comparative Literature and Economics—and have a career no one in my family could have ever dreamed of, but one of my greatest personal achievements has been mastering a graceful exit from a car. I learned this skill the hard way after my first red carpet attempt. I was a nobody, but flashing my panties to the paparazzi got me more attention than I've ever wanted or ever want again.

I take the valet ticket, tuck it into my purse, and force myself to walk away without looking back. He might interpret it as a gesture to force familiarity on each other or, worse, he might think I don't trust him with my car. Not looking back might also come off as me being dismissive of him as a person. I lose in all those three scenarios, which is why I always tip well, but not too well. Tipping is an entirely different but related set of agonizations.

The sliding doors open and a warm puff of expensive air washes over me as I walk toward Bloomingdale's. I'll buy something that I don't need or want to prove to myself, but mostly to the person behind the counter, that I can. This is also something I would never tell anyone I do, especially not someone like a therapist whose job it is to help me figure out why I do what I do to myself.

If I had to admit why I'm really here, it has something to do with having spent the morning with Mom and Maritza. Mostly, I'm here because I don't want to go back to my place to face Ethan and resume our conversation from last night. Round and round in circles we went until I felt so dizzy, I wanted to throw up. Only then did Ethan let it drop, only after I threatened to vomit on him.

Of course, I proved him right by sneaking out this morning as soon as he fell back asleep after we had sex. And I still don't want to talk to him about why I avoid talking to him about what I don't want to talk about. Ugh. Another pointless circle, this time all on my own. No boyfriend needed.

*Boyfriend.*

This is the first time I've acknowledged Ethan is my boyfriend. No, he's much more than just boyfriend. The ground seems to tilt underneath my feet at the thought of him and I pretend to be interested in the window display of a jewelry store so I don't fall flat on my face. As soon as I can, I resume walking, wishing I'd kept Ethan's sunglasses

on instead of leaving them in my car and had something
more than just chamomile tea for breakfast.

Inside Bloomingdale's, the air is so thick with perfume, I can almost see it. My stomach knots up and I
stumble again, this time scuffing one of my heels on the
tile floor. To play it off, I study an array of bottles and jars
filled with empty promises while everything turns in
woozy circles.

A pair of salesgirls stop talking and check me out, top to
bottom. After some whispering, one acknowledges me. "Is
there anything I can help you find?"

"No," I say with the barest of smiles. "Just looking."

As soon as they turn away from me, I head toward the
shoe department. I don't even bother to browse but walk
right up to the shoes I've come for—barely-there strappy
high heel sandals in ballet pink, and a pair of pointy-toe stilettos in ivory tulle, both by Jimmy Choo. The sandals are
for me and Dooley, the stilettos for Maritza. Dani and Gabi
can buy their own damn shoes.

The floor manager gives me a once-over. After deter-
mining I'm not someone who is someone, but someone
who knows her shoes, she nods to the man standing beside
her.

He's slim and tidy, dressed in an impeccably cut suit.
Hands clasped in front of him, he hurries toward me. He
has to make a good impression on his manager. If he doesn't,
he'll never make enough commission to pay off the suit he
wears so well.

"Hello. Welcome to Bloomingdale's." His forehead is a
bit shiny, as if he's been sweating or is about to start.

"Hi." I know from experience I'll get better service if I
act as if I expect it, but not like I deserve it. "How are you?"

"I'm great, thank you for asking. I love your shoes.
Prada?" he asks.

Before I can confirm that, yes, they *are* Prada, I feel myself wobble as if I were on roller skates and each skate has decided to go in different directions. I dig through my bag for something to distract me and come up with a fresh pack of Big Red. Maritza is going to complain about the Chanel smelling like cinnamon gum once I give it to her.

"Are you . . . is everything okay?" The salesman looks over to the stockroom to see if his manager is watching.

I try to smile at him as I carefully unwrap a piece of gum but can only manage to nod my head as I put it in my mouth. I want some water, but what I need is something to eat and to get out of here.

"Everything is great," I lie.

I worked here, in this department, the summer and fall after graduating from Princeton, right before I landed my first paying job at a small production company in Culver City. The first thing Stephanie, the anorexic training manager who was starting to show her age, drilled into us was that we'd never know who we were helping, so we had to be helpful to everyone.

*"They might be somebody, sleeping with somebody, married to somebody, or a potential somebody."* Stephanie sat and we stood as she lectured us in the break room. *"So pay attention."*

If she wasn't on the sales floor, she always had a pack of Gitanes clutched in one of her hands. All she ever had for lunch was a couple of those cigarettes and ginger tea. Her hands were all knuckles and sinew. There was nothing warm or soft about them or her. When I found out she had kids, I imagined they were like just-hatched birds—bald, scrawny, and always hungry.

*"Some of these actresses look like real plain-Janes, dogs even. All of you stay away from the big names. Senior staff will take care of our preferred customers. Understand?"* She stared us down until

*we nodded, too cowed to ask any questions. "Your job is really easy. You treat every customer like a star and mind your own damn business."*

He's looking at me, trying to figure me out. I wonder what he's able to discern from what I allow others to see.

I'm attractive, even beautiful like my sisters, but so are a lot of women who shop here. I have good taste and the money, or at least credit, to afford nice things, but I'm not wearing a ring or any significant jewelry. I'm here by myself, no high-strung assistant or hulking bodyguard hovering near me, no bored-out-of-his-mind boyfriend yawning as he hands over his gold Amex. Most importantly, I didn't automatically flip the shoes over to look at the price.

He's confused by me but sticking to his training.

"I can get you a bottle of water from the back. It's no problem." He's desperate for something to do that will let him back away from me until I can pull myself together.

Instead of answering him, I reach into my purse again for my cell phone. He takes a discreet step back. Sometimes I'll call my voicemail and pretend to consult a friend, making sure the clerk is nearby and listening.

I'm well aware how stupid this meaningless performance is. And it's all for the sake of making some sort of impression on a salesclerk who couldn't care less. I've convinced myself this contrived pantomime of mine makes salespeople more inclined to take me seriously as a customer. This is what I tell myself each time I do it even as I hate what it reveals about me to myself.

I set my purse back on my shoulder and hand him one of the stilettos. I fumble with it and drop it as another wave of dizziness sweeps over me. I sit down so heavily on one of the tight leather chairs, I bounce. It would be funny if I didn't feel so lousy.

"Are you okay? Miss . . . Ms.?" He asks nervously, picking up the shoe and reaching to pluck the other one from my hand.

I wave him off and take deep breaths.

*"Tip off the paparazzi while on the clock and you'll be fired."* Stephanie jabbed a skinny finger at us. *"I don't care if the Pope himself comes in here drunk, high, and naked as the day he was born. As far as you're concerned, it never happened."*

"Miss? Would you like that water now?" he asks a little louder. "You're a little pale."

I look up and give him my best professional smile. It doesn't show too much tooth and never reaches my eyes. It's a smile that politely warns the world it better think twice about fucking with me.

"It's nothing," I say belying the obvious wrongness of me. "I'm okay."

*"If you are caught trying to pass a headshot, script, or even your home number to a customer, you will be fired. Immediately and on the spot."* Stephanie's face cracked into the only smile I ever saw her attempt. *"Do your networking on your own time. You're here to sell shoes, not land your big break or snag a boyfriend. If I find out you are asking customers for favors or advice, I'll personally fire you myself."*

"Are you sure?" He looks over at his manager. She's hovering over a mother and daughter who are arguing about the practicality of suede boots for a twelve-year-old. She's oblivious of the mini crisis her subordinate is trying to handle on his own. "I'd be happy to get you some water. Or something from the snack machine?"

Stephanie shrugged her bony shoulders when I gave her my notice.

*"There a thousand more girls just like you,"* she said. To her the women in her department were girls, while the handful of men she supervised were salesmen. *"Don't expect me to give your job back when things don't work out."*

It took two years for me to work up the nerve and income to come back here. Stephanie had to stand there while I debated one pair of shoes after another. I did this a couple times a month until Stephanie quit or got fired. Now I only come to Bloomingdale's when I have a real reason to or when I don't want to face my real life.

Today, right now, it's a doubleheader.

"Size eight." I point to the shoe in his hand. "Two pairs, same color, same size. This one, same size, just a single pair. And a bottle of water would be great. Thank you."

He rushes off, relieved I'm not going to pass out at his feet.

I quickly walk to the bathroom, hurrying into the first open stall and throw up. It's quick, all chamomile tea and a single piece of cinnamon gum. Not messy, but I flush twice and wipe down the seat out of habit, one I thought I'd discarded years ago.

At the sink, careful not to look like I'm avoiding eye contact with anyone who might have heard me be sick, I rinse out my mouth, press a damp paper towel to my face and neck, and allow myself to be shocked at how pale I am. Then, after a deep breath, I get over it, fix my hair, pinch some color into my cheeks and shove two pieces of gum into my mouth.

"Everything is just fine," I silently tell my reflection before I look away, too embarrassed to see the truth staring back at me.

I'm back in time for the salesman to present me with shoes and a tiny bottle of water. He asks if I want to try them on. I shake my head, sit down, and hand him my gold Amex, still too wobbly to follow him to the counter.

"Would you like another water?" He looks at me with genuine concern, which means I must still look as pale as I did in the bathroom. "Do you want something else?"

What I want is to crawl into my bed and start my day over again.

"No, thank you." I reach into my stupidly expensive purse for my phone, excusing us both from this small drama. "Just the shoes."

# DULCINA

Outside Todd's loft with yesterday's bra and underpants tucked into the pocket of my jacket, I head left, toward SoMa. I'm in no hurry to be anywhere in particular, so I might as well take my time going nowhere. It's typically overcast, but weirdly muggy. It's the kind of weather that makes the streets stink and people move slower than usual even for a lazy Saturday.

I walk past a café full of attractive, sweater-wearing couples. Without letting myself think twice, I double back, go in, and wait for my turn to order.

I've never set foot on Alcatraz and have stayed away from cafés. At first, it made me feel different from the tourist I was and then, later, the refugee from somewhere else that I became. Honestly, it was just smug pride that kept me off of one and out of the other. No one else needed to be impressed by this little feat of self-denial except for myself.

Today is a day of firsts and lasts and, since there's no way I'm going to Alcatraz, this café will have to do the job of showing me the dumbness of my ways.

It's not so bad inside, not nearly as self-satisfied as it seems from the street. The smells are a pleasant mixture of hot brewed coffee, warm baked goods, and, oddly, newsprint. People chat or just read, the music isn't too loud, and there is just the right amount of eclectic art by locals hoping someone has an extra $375 to burn on a painting of the back of some chick's head. The chairs are purposely mismatched, and the menu, written on a chalkboard, is complicated and full of unnecessary choices.

"Hi! What can I getcha!"

The cashier is a plump gal with lifeless dyed black hair and requisite nose ring. Her fingers are poised over the register, lightly tapping the keys. She's had her share of on the house caffeine this morning.

"A coffee, black, and a muffin." I dig through my pockets and pull out a wad of bills. "Anything but blueberry."

"We have *amazing* apple, banana, and cranberry muffins. The banana is the most *amazing*."

Remembering cranberry juice can ward off a UTI and hoping the effect is still the same in baked form, I hand her a ten-spot. "I'll take a cranberry."

"The cranberry is *amazing*. For here or to go?"

I look around. It's crowded but not packed. It would be stupid to flee with my muffin and coffee as this is the one and only time I'll sit in a San Francisco café.

"For here. Thanks."

"Cool!"

She hands me my change, her eyes slightly dipping off to the side where the tip jar sits. I drop the coins into it and move to where a hanging sign reads "Pick Up".

"Coffee, black. Muffin, cranberry," calls out the cashier's counterpart.

Suddenly, standing there holding my food, I feel out of place.

"Excuse me?"

A guy sitting by one of the big front windows waves at me, obviously trying to get my attention. I ignore him.

"Hey!" he says louder, standing up so there's no doubt as to who he's talking to. People look back and forth between us.

Resigned to see this part of the experience through, I weave my way over to him, carefully stepping around Timbuk2 messenger bags and rolled-up yoga mats. I stop a few feet away, holding my impressively large mug of coffee and the muffin on a plate balanced on top.

"Hi." I keep myself from adding, "What do you want?" This would've been okay at The Clap Trap, but might come off as slightly hostile here.

"I don't know if you heard, but that muffin is *amazing*. Have a seat."

Without waiting for me to agree, he begins to gather up his neatly folded newspaper sections, setting them on the floor by his feet.

I try to gauge his game. Maybe he doesn't have game? Maybe he's just offering to share his table and willing to go from there. Still game, but at least it's an honest one. I sit down and pull off my jacket, remembering too late I don't have a bra on. My nipples are hard and visible through the soft cotton of my purloined T-shirt.

His eyes don't dip from my face. Interesting.

"I noticed you don't carry a purse." He takes a sip of coffee, speaking from behind his mug. He's obviously straight and attractive enough. Still, he's surprised I agreed to sit with him, but confident enough to go with it. "Why is that?"

"Excuse me?" I feel my back stiffen as if I've just been accused of something.

"Apologies. I'm a writer." He holds his hands up, palms facing me to show he means no harm. "And I have a habit of noticing things that will freak out beautiful women."

"I have pockets. If something doesn't fit in one, I don't carry it with me." I shrug and have a piece of muffin, choosing to ignore that he called me beautiful and admitted he was a writer in the same sentence. "You carry a purse?"

"It's called a murse." He smiles, relaxing into whatever this is. Confidence is outmaneuvering natural shyness he's worked hard to overcome. "Man-bag sounds too suggestive."

"A murse. My new word for the day." The smell of coffee fills my nose as I lift the mug to my mouth. I have to use both hands to hold it. "I'm going to go ahead and assume the coffee is amazing."

"Black, no sugar." He points at my mug with his spoon.

"I'm hardcore." I look over my shoulder and realize we could be any another couple. There's nothing interesting or extraordinary about us at all. "In most things, but especially when it comes to coffee."

"Is that so?" He smiles at me again, and I realize he thinks I'm flirting with him. Maybe I am. "What other things are you hardcore about?"

"The usual stuff. What kind of writing do you do?" I might as well ask since it's what he's waiting for. Everyone loves to talk about themselves. Especially men. "Books? Newspapers? Toilet stall graffiti?"

"Magazine features. I freelance. Movies, music, book reviews. I was on staff at a website that reached its peak with a Super Bowl ad a couple years ago. Cushy gig before it came to an end. Now I'm back to hustling for assignments while working on my first novel." His right pant leg is cuffed up over the top of his sock. He must have ridden a bike here. "You're used to asking the questions, huh?"

"Force of habit. Up until last night, I was a bartender." I put some more muffin into my mouth to stop myself from talking.

"A bartender? I bet you met all sorts of people." He sits back, giving me some space. "In college, I was an orderly at a convalescent home. Lots of lonely old people and overworked staff. Yeah, that was a job I was happy to be fired from."

"I wasn't fired. I quit."

"Did you?" he asks. "Is that why you're smiling?"

"Am I smiling?" I ask right back.

"You are." He fiddles around with the dishes in front of us, using his fingertip to rearrange them on the table. "It's a nice smile. Do those braids in your hair hurt? How much longer is it when it's all loose?"

I ignore his compliment and question and take another drink of my coffee. It's strong, expensive tasting, and just bitter enough to remind me who I am and why I'm here. I shift back into bartender mode.

"What's your book about?"

"Life, love, and the pursuit of the elusive giant squid," he says, the well-practiced line rolling off his tongue.

"I bet that's what you tell all the girls." I rotate my muffin, turning the pinched side in his direction. It's been a long while since I flirted with anyone, and I'm not sure I'm doing it right. "Do they fall for it?"

"No. Especially not the ones I really want to impress. So why did you quit?" he asks without hesitation.

That it's none of his business and maybe a little rude of him to ask doesn't seem to cross his mind. He's not being rude, though, just blunt. I don't mind blunt. If anything, now that I'm sober, I really appreciate it.

"My little sister is getting married, and . . ." I hesitate, not used being the one who does the talking especially about myself. His expression is open, interested, so I continue, ". . . I haven't been there in a long time, and . . . I'm done with San Francisco."

"For good?" He raises his eyebrows and looks disappointed. A romantic. Poor bunny.

I lean forward and realize not only do I want to tell him what I've been thinking, but I also need to hear myself say it out loud. Once I do, it'll be real and true, not just a vague feeling I want to ignore but can't.

"It's kind of like a relationship that's run its course. If I hang around any longer, I'm going to start to hate San Francisco. All of it. Especially everything that reminds me of why I've stayed for as long as I have."

"Too bad for San Francisco, but I think I understand what you mean." He looks at me straight in the eye as he says this. He's not trying to feed me a line, but really wants me to hear what he's about to tell me. I respect this and allow myself to listen. "This is a beautiful city to get lost in, which is why it's full of people who are looking to find themselves."

"That's a good way of putting it, guy." I take a drink of my coffee, using the cup to hide how his sad observation makes me feel very seen. "I should get going."

"Hold on." He reaches into his bag and hands me his card. "My name is Wyatt, or Wy, whichever you prefer."

"You weren't lying about being a writer. It says so right here on your card. Wyatt Bremmer, writer. How official of you. And you have a website. That's extra fancy."

"I'm guessing none of that will buy me any points or more time?" he asks, returning my smile, but his is a little melancholy.

He's disappointed I'm bailing and not putting up a front about it. Yeah, not much game with this guy.

"Sorry, man." I stand up and slip his card into my jacket pocket, the one without yesterday's underwear in it. "Good luck with your book and enjoy San Francisco for me, Wyatt."

"Wait!" He stands up, but he won't come after me. It would be out of character for him, and he's smart enough to know I'd respond very badly to being chased. "What's your name and where's 'there'?"

I decide to tell the truth. "Dulcina Bernal. Or, if you prefer, Dooley. There is L.A."

"I don't mind Los Angeles, Dooley," he says. "I hear the weather's nice this time of year, as it is most of the time. Can't hold the weather against Los Angeles, can you?"

"L.A. has its faults, but the weather is the least of them. Maybe I'll let you know how nice it is once I get there." I pat the pocket where his card is.

He takes his seat again, his head tilted back as he looks up at me, open and vulnerable. "I really hope you do."

I look at him but see myself even more clearly than I did the night before in the that streaky mirror at The Clap Trap.

There isn't a bar and sarcasm to hide behind. No pen and order pad, sketchbook and pencil, canvas and brush. No drink, pill or the distraction of bare skin. There's just me—the woman I've become despite all the odds as well as because of them and my still broken heart.

"Goodbye for now, Dulicna Bernal," he says.

I smile my goodbye instead of saying it, take my dishes to the counter, and walk out of my first and last San Francisco café.

# ◆ 9 ◆

# CLAUDIA

I DRIVE INTO THE underground garage of my Studio City townhouse a little faster than I should and have to over-correct my turn to keep from clipping the pillar that separates my side from the neighbors. The only thing we have in common is the fireproof wall that runs right down the middle of our places, which are mirror layouts of each other. Theirs had been vacant for more than a year—bankruptcy issues of some sort with the absentee owner—before being sold to Megan and Bryan Cleaver, newlyweds, a month ago. I regret not buying it for no other reason than to have kept it empty.

Neither of them are home—both their spots are empty. He drives a ridiculous yellow Hummer he can barely maneuver in and out of the garage, and she zips to and from her Pilates classes and waxing appointments in a silver Boxter.

I call them the Beaverless Cleavers—a nickname coined when Megan confided in me that she's "totally bare down there," as is her husband, and that their pube-free sex is "absolutely mind-blowing."

She told me this a few days after they moved in, here in the garage, while I was weighed down with a tote bag full of scripts and the hottest container of tom kha gai I've ever held. I merely nodded, which gave her the idea that their lack of pubic hair and the quality of their fucking were appropriate topics of conversation for one complete stranger to inflict upon another.

Megan wants to be an actress, but she'll settle for becoming famous. When she found out I'm a producer, with credits to prove it, she launched a full-frontal assault to become the best friend I've never wanted. She picks up my mail and brings it by within minutes of me setting my car keys and purse down on the hall table. She's always just poured herself a glass of wine and never fails to offer me a sip as she tells me about her day and tries to get me to do the same. She's also invited me to so many lunches, dinners, Sunday brunches, mid-week drinks, and early morning Runyan Canyon hikes, I can only assume she believes there are more than seven days in a week.

I decline her sips, share absolutely nothing about myself she can't glean from my junk mail and always have other plans I can't possibly get out of. She's starting to realize she should be offended by my perfunctory attitude toward her. I have no interest in being her friend—I'm just her neighbor, and only because I have to be.

I deal with people like Megan every day. Like her, they're opportunists with flexible ethics and adaptable morals. Mrs. Beaverless Cleaver likes to flash her diamond rings and talk about how great it is to be married, but she'd drop down to her knees without hesitation to get what she wants. Since I don't have a dick for her to suck, she'll keep trying to suck up to me, thinking this will get her what she wants.

Her nuclear level of chumminess was already glowing hot before she found out who owns the well-used Jeep that regularly parks in my second spot. When she did, Megan was so nice to me I warned Ethan to stay away from her or I'd cut off his dick and pickle it along with his balls. He laughed and kissed me. I wasn't joking. He kept kissing me, everywhere, and promised I'll never have to worry about pickling his junk.

I glance toward the buzzing coming from my purse. I don't have to look to know Ethan is calling me again. I've already hung up on him twice since leaving Bloomingdale's. In my side mirror, I see him standing up from where he was sitting on the steps that connect the garage to my place.

"I never took you for a runner, Bernal," his closer-than-he-appears-to-be reflection says to me.

Ethan leans his shoulder against the pillar. He's not completely blocking my way, but I'll have to brush past him once I get out of my car. He's dressed in a pair of jeans, a plain black T-shirt, and his usual scuffed brown lace-up boots. He wears a custom-made tux with the same casual grace of a man who has always been at home in his body.

Ethan is tall and lanky, still finely muscled like the competitive swimmer he was when he dropped out of Ohio State. He came to L.A. fifteen years ago for a bit part in tired horror movie franchise that he made him a star. He's as painfully handsome as he looks on-screen but even better in real life. His smell, his taste, and the feel of his skin is addictive. At least to me. I always have the urge to lick him and bury my nose in the pit of his arm and inhale. Sometimes I do, and he's happy to let me, expecting nothing more and nothing else.

He half smiles, his blue eyes crinkling at the edges. His dark blond hair is short for his upcoming role as an undercover cop. The week before, it had been long enough for me to wrap around my hands as I came. His hair is the only thing I've admitted I like about him other than his cock.

When I first saw him, post-haircut, I yelled at him and then got angry at myself for being upset over something as stupid as his beautiful hair. After six months of this thing between us, my reaction to a professionally obligated haircut made it impossible for me to ignore that the way I feel about him has changed while I haven't changed enough to admit this to him.

Ethan took me into his lap, tucked my head under his chin, and promised to have his agent include a clause in future contracts that any haircuts will have to be approved by me. He was kidding, but he also wasn't. I told him to shut up, straddled him, and kept my realizations to myself.

"Aren't you going to say hello?" He leans into the open window of my car, his hand braced on the either side. "Or, how about sorry for sneaking out on me and not taking my calls? I've been waiting down here for an hour for you, Bernal."

"Are you stalking me?" I try for sarcasm that isn't there. Ethan is too good-looking for his own good and for my peace of mind. He's also so completely in love with me, I can't help but not trust him and his motives. "My lover, my stalker, my Studio City garage. How very TV-movie-of-the-week."

I stare at him, at once amazed and annoyed that this man is here for me. Mostly, I just feel tired. Tired of fighting with him and tired of how I've been behaving. I can't help it. Something isn't right. Not as in wrong not right, but different not right. I haven't given myself the time to figure it out, and I can't bring myself to admit my confusion to Ethan. He would set me on his lap, tuck my head under his chin, and it would be all over for me.

"Yes, Claudia, I'm stalking you," he says.

He's ready to make amends even though he doesn't have anything to apologize for. Ethan knows the difference between a stupid fight and an honest argument. To me, everything is instinctively a battle. I don't know if it helps or hurts that he's so easygoing while also being incredibly persistent. He's had to be both with me as I haven't made this easy for him, for either of us.

Ethan's learned not to send flowers. He had a beautiful arrangement delivered to my office the same afternoon we first met in passing at some industry thing my boss sent me to in his place. I gave the flowers to the receptionist but did agree to a dinner to discuss a possible project.

Dinner was at an out-of-the-way ramen bar on the fringes of Koreatown where the owners make sure he isn't bothered. He asked if I liked the flowers, and I told him the truth—flowers are so easy, Hitler probably sent Eva Braun a bouquet or two. I hadn't meant it as a joke, but he laughed, really laughed. Like, threw his head back and put his hands on his lean belly and laughed. Then he looked at me like I was the most delightful creature on the face of the Earth. At the end of the night, all he got from me was a firm handshake and a tepid committal for a possible second dinner. I was confused as to what he wanted from me—I still am—and dodged his calls for a couple of weeks.

I only called him back after he threatened to send me an even bigger bouquet of flowers and deliver it himself. He got straight to the point and asked if I was free the coming Saturday and, if I was, to drop any pretense it would be anything other than a real date. That Saturday, he rang my doorbell, presented me with a potted miniature cactus, told me we had reservations at Nobu, and, after dinner, we would be taking a walk on the beach. I thanked him for the cactus and proceeded to talk him out of all of his plans as well as his pants.

After we'd been seeing each other for a month, him always coming here, us never going out, he started to give me tasteful, vintage jewelry. Lately, he's also been giving me art. He has the guy, the one who hangs his pieces for him, come by while I'm at work. Lucky for Ethan, the walls in my place are empty. Lucky for me, Ethan has exceedingly good taste in art.

I could pretend these are just expensive gifts from a very rich man who is foolishly indulgent, but I understand that for Ethan the art, jewelry, and everything else is an investment in me, in us.

Now, because of him, what's inside of my townhouse— on the walls and stashed away in velvet cases along with the shoes, purses, and clothes—is probably worth as much as the place where it's kept. Probably more. I don't like to think about this. Where I live is not a home to me, but I've never felt more comfortable here and it's because of him. This is also something I've avoided thinking about, but I should at least up my insurance policy and buy a safe.

Ethan pushes away from the car window, his eyes on my face, giving me some space as studies me and decides what he's going to do.

I don't have a chance to open the door. Ethan does it for me, holding out his hand for me to take. I ignore his hand, especially the gesture behind it, easing myself out, letting my dress fall away from my thighs, before standing up. I turn my back to him to reach for the shopping bag with the wedding shoes.

"Be that way, then, Bernal." His voice is very close, his breath on the back of my neck. The warmth of his body and the smell of his skin fill my senses. He hasn't touched me and yet I can feel him everywhere. "I was going to help you, and with the rest of the stuff you have in the storage room, but I'll let you lug it all upstairs by yourself."

He's not angry. I've never seen him angry. Annoyed, yes, but never more than that. This is why I try so hard to piss him off.

"Yeah, I am that way, and fuck you very much," I mumble under my breath.

"What was that?" Ethan's question sounds like a challenge because it is one. I don't feel apprehensive, more like thrilled for what is about to happen. "Did you say something to me, Bernal?"

"You heard me." I feel my shoulders tense up, but I don't turn around to face him. Ethan would never hurt me. He's confident, not aggressive, with a firm, steady hand I respond to in ways I never thought I was capable of allowing myself to. "Don't pretend you didn't."

"I believe I heard you ask me to fuck you very much." He moves in closer, his hips pressing into mine, his broad shoulders cocooning me.

"You wish," I snap but don't move away.

He takes hold of my waist, keeping me in place as he touches the tip of his tongue to the side of my neck. My breath leaves me in one long exhale, my body undulating with sensation from his touch.

"I love you, Claudia." His hands skim up my rib cage and reach over to cup my breasts. His eyelashes brush against the side of my face. "Claudia, I love you."

I press back against him. He's hard. I'm wet. By now, he knows this is my way of telling him I'm sorry. I rarely say the actual words, but it's the best he can expect from me. For now, it's good enough for him.

"I love you," he repeats with each kiss to my neck.

He rolls my nipples between his fingers, not hard, but with enough pressure to make me want more. I push my ass against his cock, caressing it, and feel the muscles of his belly clench in response. I turn my head just enough so we can kiss, deep, hard, his tongue on mine, mine on his, until I'm gasping for breath and unable to stand on my own.

He turns me around, lifting me so I'm level with his face, one of his big, strong hands under my ass. My legs automatically open and wrap themselves around him. He brings me up against the concrete pillar, cushioning my back with his other arm.

"Tell me what you want," he says.

"Fuck me, Ethan. Please." I feel his smile under my lips. I kiss him harder to keep him from saying anything else.

He unties the knot of my dress, pushing it open, and groans when he sees my sheer black bra and panties that might as well not be there. I never play fair. He knows this and lets me get away with it.

Ethan kisses me, putting his whole body into it. The muscles of his back ripple under my hands as he presses me into him and against the pillar. I tilt my hips toward his hand as it finds its place between my legs, his fingers brushing over my panties before pulling them aside and out of the way.

"I love you, Claudia." His forehead is against mine, his eyes open, watching me as I shiver at his touch, at his words. "Claudia, I love you."

I can't say these words back to him. He knows this too.

I undo the front of his jeans, pushing them down past his own hips while shoving his T-shirt up so I can feel as much of his skin against mine as possible. My fingers dig into his shoulders as he slides into me with a deep, long stroke. I let him set the pace, let him look at my face instead of hiding against his neck and shoulder.

For a moment, I open my eyes and watch him watching me, the crash of intimacy jarring a rush of tears to my eyes.

I blink them away and arch my back so the crown of my head is against the pillar. He puts his mouth on my breasts, pulling my nipples lightly between his teeth before licking one and then the other. I focus on him, his smell, his skin, and allow him deeper inside of me than he already is.

I'll think about what's confusing me later. Right now, all I want to do is feel.

# • 10 •

# MARITZA

I STARTED WORKING FOR Mr. Kim the summer before my junior year at Roosevelt. Dooley was gone and Claudia only cared about running away to college so I had a lot of time to myself. Mr. Kim had an ad in the neighborhood paper for a part-time office assistant and since I didn't want to work at the Monterey Park Mall, I answered it.

I was full-time by my second week, and neither of us said anything about my job being over once the summer ended. When school started, I arranged my schedule to have a free sixth period, and I came in on weekends too.

After I got married, I was supposed to quit because that person expected me to be a housewife. At first, I thought I wanted that too, but then I didn't. I asked Mr. Kim for my job back and adjusted my hours to be at home in the morning when that person left and back exactly where he'd left me in the evening. On weekends, I told that person I was visiting Mamá and Daddy and spent those days catching up on work. As soon as I filed for divorce, Mr. Kim gave me a raise and told me the code for the security system. The day the divorce was official, he gave me access to the safe and bank accounts.

Everything went back to the way it was but it took a long time to forget about what happened with that person. Sometimes, when I'm not careful, I forget to not remember. Anyways, all that mattered was that I had my job, the Malibu, and the bedroom at the house all to myself. The only thing that's really changed since then is I drive a Hyundai Sonata now instead of the Malibu. It's a nice car, my Sonata, and I own it. Claudia's Audi is leased.

Some people might think working for Mr. Kim for so many years is dumb, but I'm proud of what Kim and Kim International Beverages Company is today. I would never throw away all my hard work to start over somewhere else where they wouldn't appreciate me. Plus, Mr. Kim and Mrs. Kim treat me like their daughter since they don't have kids of their own.

Mr. Kim comes to stand by my desk. He's short and round, and his hair is dyed too-black and combed like he works at a bank. Today he's wearing green track pants, a white counterfeit Ralph Lauren polo shirt that's a size too small, and black dress socks. We leave our shoes by the door, but I put on a pair of special inside shoes. He doesn't. He spends our workday in his black dress socks. One time he wore shorts to the office with those socks. I laughed so hard when I saw him, I almost peed myself.

"ABC Market—" Mr. Kim starts.

"They paid on Friday, Mr. Kim. I went to pick up the check myself. It should clear sometime today or tomorrow."

"Good. Okay. Very good . . . What about—"

"The shipment is delayed, their fault. I made sure they took a percentage off. No use babying them, Mr. Kim. We're going to have to look for a new supplier. For real this time. I'm not playing with them anymore."

"Okay, okay." Mr. Kim walks back into his office with nothing to do but wait until he can think of something else to bother me with. "Okay, bossy girl, Maritza."

KKIBC is the third biggest distributor in Southern California of soft drinks from Asia, but not directly from countries with dictators—too many regulations and headaches. We sell, wholesale, Binggrae banana milk, Calpico lychee drink, Botol sweet tea, and lots more and lots of it.

We're very successful, but we can do even more. I convinced Mr. Kim into expanding KKIBC into snacks and packaged foods. I'm always trying new things, meeting new people, and dealing with all sorts of shipping issues, regulations, import taxes, and typhoons.

Claudia sometimes invites me to movie premieres and gives me the fancy stuff she doesn't want anymore. A row of cans of Sagiko soursop juice at Nam Hoa Market in Garden Grove isn't glamorous, but at least my job isn't full of people who are phonies and jerks.

I watch Mr. Kim in the reflection of my monitor as he picks through the stack of papers on his desk. Everything on there is in the computer system. I have to print him copies because if it's not on paper, it's not real to him.

It took me years to convince him it was okay to shred documents from the 1980s after I scanned every single one. I got so many paper cuts, but it was worth it to get those boxes out of here. Now we're up to 1997. My goal is to keep only a year's worth of paper records here in the office. If he wants to hang on to more years than that, he'll have to agree to rent a storage unit.

Last year, I told him it was time to redecorate our office. He said no, so I pretended to look for another job. I printed a copy of my résumé and left it on the fax machine. Mr. Kim agreed really fast after he saw it. The leather executive chair I got him makes a rude noise each time he sits down, but he's happy enough with how it all turned out.

Mrs. Kim thought she should have been in charge decorating again, but I was done with gold-and-red paisley wallpaper, fake wood furniture and weird table lamps. Now it looks like a legitimate place of business with nice desks, the right kind of chairs from Office Depot, dark gray carpet and light gray walls. Before, it was like working in a South Korean whorehouse. And I know that's exactly how they look. When I went to Seoul with Mr. Kim and Mrs. Kim two years ago, their nasty nephew took me to one of those places. I slapped him twice and made sure the second time was harder than the first. He didn't bother me anymore after that.

A call comes into our general line, so both my and Mr. Kim's phones ring. I answer it before he can. I've told him we have to be more professional and him yelling "Kim!" into the handset gives people the wrong impression.

"Kim and Kim International Beverages, Maritza speaking."

"Maritza! Mr. Kim at work?"

"Yes, Mrs. Kim." I know not to ask if she wants me to transfer her. If she wanted to talk to him, she'd have called his extension or his mobile.

"Ah, good."

She hangs up without saying goodbye, and I go back to the spreadsheet I've made to track my wedding expenses.

I haven't told Mr. Kim about it. He got all paranoid after Auggie proposed, but he stopped asking when it was going to happen years ago. I guess he thinks my engagement ring is just jewelry now. I don't want him to worry because there's nothing to worry about. I sent Mrs. Kim the invitation, and she won't tell him either. This is how it is with them. She'll set out his suit on the thirty-first and yell at him to hurry up and get dressed. Mr. Kim won't know whose wedding he's going to until he sees me in my dress, and then it'll be too late for him to get mad at me.

"Mrs. Kim call here?"

He stands in front of my desk in his knock-off white Polo and new gold Rolex. He bought it from his niece. She manages a jewelry store in Hawthorn and gave him a good price on it. I asked him for the old Rolex and keep here in my desk. It's too good of a fake to toss in the trash.

"That her? She call here? Mrs. Kim?"

"Nope." I click off my spreadsheet before he can see what I'm doing.

The door buzzer sounds, and we both look up. We don't get many visitors here. Mostly we do our business over the phone, at stores, or down at the warehouse that's a few miles away near the port.

"That delivery guy is here again." Mr. Kim sounds a little like Daddy when he comments on my showers being too long. Mr. Kim buzzes him instead of walking the few steps to the door.

"Happy Monday, Maritza!" Rolando is our usual UPS guy. He carries my packages over to the table next to my desk without me having to ask him to. "Mr. Kim, I haven't seen you in a while."

Mr. Kim grunts and puffs out his cheeks, ignoring Rolando. Mr. Kim isn't friendly to Rolando, not because Rolando is Black—he's actually Dominican—but because Mr. Kim only likes people he knows. He's never gotten to know Rolando and says he doesn't want to. Rolando and his wife, Kara, are invited to my wedding. They can all get to know each other then.

"What's on your plate today, Maritza?" Rolando asks, ready for one of our regular talks. "Do anything fun this weekend?"

I hand Rolando a cold tangerine soda from the fridge we keep in the office. I also let him use our bathroom whenever he needs to so he doesn't have to hunt one down when he's making his rounds. I hope he doesn't say anything about my wedding in front of Mr. Kim, but I'm going to take his advice and not let Auggie and his groomsmen wear patent leather shoes with their tuxes. He told me his got really dusty, and it's all his wife sees when they look at their wedding pictures.

Mr. Kim makes a big show of inspecting boxes he knows aren't for him. Mr. Kim would never pay extra to have something delivered by UPS. I've explained it costs almost the same as going through the post office and takes less time, but all he cares about is that it looks like it costs more than it should.

"No fun for me this weekend, just errands and stuff. How about you? Deliver any more suspicious packages? What happened with the FBI?"

When Mr. Kim isn't here, Rolando will sit on one of the guest chairs and enjoy his soda. Sometimes he eats his lunch here and tells me funny stories about what he sees during his workday. Rolando isn't trying to get with me; he really loves his wife even after they found out she can't have babies. We're just friends even if Mr. Kim can't understand why or how something like this is even possible.

Mr. Kim's desk phone rings. If he doesn't answer, it'll kick over to mine. It's Mrs. Kim, and she'll hang up as soon as either one of us picks up.

"Maritza. The phone." Mr. Kim gives Rolando a dirty look. "Work time now, Maritza."

"See you tomorrow, Rolando." I roll my eyes at him and wave him out the door.

I connect to Mr. Kim's extension and watch him go back to inspecting the labels on my packages. I pick up the handset but don't bother putting it to my ear. I just wait a second for Mrs. Kim realize it's not ringing on her end anymore before I put the handset back into the cradle.

"Mrs. Kim hung up, Mr. Kim. It's safe to go back to your desk now."

"I pay you too much." Mr. Kim holds up one of the boxes and shakes it.

"Maybe you do, maybe you don't. But if you want to pay me more, go right ahead, Mr. Kim."

I snatch the box out of his hands and open it. It's the pair of shoes I ordered for my going-away suit. They looked better on my computer. I set them aside. Anyways, Auggie and I won't be going anywhere. I don't want to take the time away from work. Since he's leaving all the planning to me, Auggie won't be able to complain about us not having a honeymoon. Maybe later, after typhoon season. I've always wanted to go to Disney World and it isn't going anywhere.

"How much those cost?" he asks.

He's not being nosy. It's just how he is. Mr. Kim and Mrs. Kim aren't cheap, they're just careful with money and have taught me to be the same.

"A lot, but way less than retail." I tell him. Too bad they're not exactly what I want.

He digs the invoice out of the box and scans for the total. "Too much!"

"They're Charles David, not Payless, Mr. Kim. It's a very good price. When was the last time you bought yourself a pair of shoes?"

"Mrs. Kim's job." He tosses the invoice back into the box. "I make money. She spends it."

"I think it's time you went home, Mr. Kim. Mrs. Kim will make you something to eat with plenty of her kimchi. Extra spicey just the way you like it."

"Smart-mouth girl, Maritza."

Mr. Kim goes back to his desk, and I open the rest of my packages, separating what I'll keep and repacking what has to be returned. Another pair of Charles David shoes will be going back for sure. They're not at all the right shade of ivory for my wedding dress. Maybe I can catch Rolando before he leaves the business park.

"What is this?" Mr. Kim waves a piece of paper in my face. "What is this?"

"Hold it still so I can see it." I grab it and put it on my desk. It's an unpaid invoice for a delayed shipment of Royal Tru dalandan soda from the Philippines. "Mr. Kim, go home! Mrs. Kim wants you to."

"No, she don't. She hasn't made kimchi in a month. She wants to force me eat the stuff from the jar like if I don't have wife. Never!"

Mr. Kim and Mrs. Kim are having one of their fights. Mrs. Kim always gets her way. Always. I've learned a lot about winning fights from her.

"She just called me and asked if you were still here. She misses you. Don't do that!" I snatch the invoice from his hand and shove it into my desk so he can't get at it again.

"Mrs. Kim don't bother to pack my lunch today." Earlier he'd told me he left for work before Mrs. Kim had gotten out of bed. "She wants me to starve."

"She's mad at you, Mr. Kim. She wants you to say you're sorry." I print a return label for the shoes. "Say you're sorry and she'll start cooking for you again."

"No. Mrs. Kim is the one who should say sorry."

The phone rings, and I put it straight through to voice-mail. Last thing I need right now is some mini-market owner yelling at me in Tagalog about his dwindling supply of dalandan soda.

"Go get us some Panda Express. It'll give you a reason to drive your fancy car." I pick up the phone and dial.

"I get a heart attack eating that junk. Then Mrs. Kim would be sorry. How can I work and make money if I'm in the hospital with a clogged heart?"

"I'd like to place an order for pickup." I cover the mouthpiece with my hand when I'm put on hold. "Your heart would feel much better if you just told Mrs. Kim you're sorry."

"Sorry? Sorry!" He continues his complaints in Korean as he heads back to his desk, grabs his car keys, and stomps out the door. "Sorry for what?"

"Don't forget straws! Mr. Kim? You always forget the straws," I yell after him. "Hi, yeah, an order for pickup . . ."

The girls at Panda Express know me by name and order. Orange flavored chicken, mixed vegetables, white rice, and a large Diet Pepsi. Same for Mr. Kim. When it's one of those days, I'll get an extra side order of orange chicken for us to share. But not this time—I have to fit into my dress.

Mrs. Kim will be offended that he ate Panda Express, but she'll make sure to get up at the crack of dawn tomorrow and send him to work with lunch until their next fight. As soon as I hang up, I speed dial the florist Mrs. Kim likes and order her a bouquet of lilies. No card because they're supposed to be from Mr. Kim, and I ask for a rush delivery. Once she gets them, Mrs. Kim can get started on a fresh batch of kimchi. They'll have to wait almost a week before it's fermented enough to eat, but that's what they get for being so stubborn.

I pull out my wedding planner and try to catch up from this morning. I cancel the patent leather shoes at the tux shop, and change them to the matte black leather style. It costs more, but as long as I get what I want, it's okay with me.

Auggie should buy a pair of good shoes instead of renting. He has a real job now, not one where he can wear sneakers. He works for insurance company in Pasadena and has to dress way nicer than when he was the assistant manager at the Glendale Galleria Foot Locker. I leave a message for Claudia with that nasty assistant of hers, and am about to call for an update on the alternations on my dress when Mr. Kim comes stomping back in.

He hasn't taken off his shoes, which means he won't be staying. Good.

"Mrs. Kim call?" He dumps the steaming plastic bags of food on my desk. "What's that?"

"None of your business." I throw my planner into one of the boxes next to my desk. Styrofoam peanuts fly up everywhere. "And yes, Mrs. Kim called. She wants you to come home right away."

"Silly woman. I eat lunch first."

"No, not here. Go play cards with the guys in the warehouse, eat there. And don't even think about drinking any of that Japanese beer. Mrs. Kim will get mad at me for that and the Panda Express too."

"Bossy bossy, Maritza. I'll be back tomorrow. Early." He takes one of the bags and drinks and leaves, double locking the door behind him.

I fill out some paperwork, send some faxes, and pick at my lunch.

Through the glass door of the office, I can see Mr. Kim is sitting in his new Mercedes eating his food and waiting to catch me not working. Maybe he thinks Rolando is coming back so we can *do it* on his desk. This makes me laugh and choke on a mouthful of orange flavored chicken. I spit it out into a napkin and put it inside the bag. We don't throw away food in here because of ants.

As soon as Mr. Kim drives away, I pull my planner out of the box and flip through it. It makes me feel good to see there are more check marks than not. As soon as I find the right shoes for my dress, I can relax and start enjoying being a bride.

# ◆ 11 ◆

# DULCINA

I HAVEN'T STAYED IN Boyle Heights for more than a few days at a time since I was 18. When I did visit, I always went with a need for them to want me gone. This was the only way I knew how to justify leaving all over again.

The last time was at the house was two years ago for our dad's sixtieth birthday. I wasn't going to go, but Claudia insisted. She'd promised them I'd be there, and she's always kept her promises. Even the bad ones. It was the worst possible time for me to be around my family. I showed up drunk and high, got more of both and was exactly the pathetic, raging embarrassment they were afraid I was always going to be.

Our dad was also drunk, but it was his party. Maritza danced and flirted with all of Augustino's friends and argued with him about it. And our mom sat at one of the tables twisting her hands while frowning and . . . that's about it.

Claudia took charge, and we let her.

After she got things under control with our dad and Maritza, she drove me back to her townhouse and put me to bed in her guest room. As wasted as I was, it was still obvious she'd fixed up the room for me since the rest of her place was basically empty. There was a new queen-size bed, matching nightstands, and a dresser with a round mirror over it. The bed was made up with sheets that were still creased from the package they'd come in.

She pulled off my boots, pried my eyes open and patted my check to make sure I understood there was a bucket beside the bed, as well as a bottle of water on the night-stand. A little later, she came back in with a blanket and pillow and stayed with me to make sure I didn't choke on my own vomit.

Once I did get sick, in the guest bathroom over a toilet she hadn't ever used, she held my hair away from my face and pressed a damp washcloth to my forehead like she used to when we were growing up.

She stood there while I rinsed out my mouth, not say-ing a word, just watching to make sure I wouldn't vomit again. I crawled back into bed and waited to pass out. She cleaned up the mess I'd made for her, then she went back to the place she'd made for herself on the floor next to me. By the time she woke up the next morning, I was showered, dressed, and as sober as I was going to get. She didn't say a word to me about what I'd done, how I'd behaved, or the fact that I was leaving less than twenty-four hours after arriving.

At the airport, she paid to have my ticket changed and handed it to me along with some cash. Then she walked with me to the security line, hugged me, and left. No lec-tures, no disappointed sighs, and, worse, no goodbye. I'd never felt so ashamed of myself in my life.

Right now, at this moment, I'm once again letting someone down but feel nothing but annoyance, and it's because of who is literally standing between me and my leaving.

"What do you mean, you're going?" Velma is in the doorway of the room I sublet from her. She looks exhausted but wired. She must have called in sick with plans to sleep off whatever she did the night before. Now, though, she's not going to give it a rest. "After what happened between us? I can't believe you, Dulcina."

Velma works at a hair salon on Clayton and Grove that smells of incense and armpit. Last week, I sat in her chair for hours as she worked my waist length hair into hundreds of tiny braids. When she was done, I kissed her, quickly, on the lips. It was the kind of innocent kiss my sisters and I give each other and that I've given to the few good friends I've been lucky to have in my life.

Velma is not my friend. She never was or will be.

"Nothing happened between us, and yeah, I'm leaving." I sort through my clothes, refolding everything into neat piles. Underwear, T-shirts, jeans, socks, and bras. The color palette ranges from black to faded black. "I've paid through the end of the month, and I'll give you half for next month."

She picks at a scab just above her elbow until it starts bleeding. "What do you expect me to do?"

Velma usually keeps it together around me, but she's mad now. And when she gets mad, things tend to happen. She brags how her landlord hasn't raised the rent in years because he's afraid of her. He also hasn't bothered to make any repairs, so this place is really rundown.

I'd done my time in rehab and halfway houses and I wanted a normal life, which in San Francisco means living with roommates. Velma had a spare room I could afford to rent, in cash, no lease, and it was in the Haight, just about the only area in San Francisco I hadn't yet lived in. She'd also been on her most mellow behavior when I met her.

"I know a couple of people who are looking for a place. I can give them your info if you want." The only thing I plan to do is forget all about Velma as soon as I walk out the door.

She steps inside my room. It's the first time she's been in here since right after I moved in, when she tried to get into bed with me. I made it extremely clear why she should never try that again and I installed a lock on the door the next morning.

"I can find my own fucking roommate, Dulcina. But thanks a lot for the offer, you fucking bitch."

"No problem." I stop folding and start shoving clothes into my duffel bag.

Velma is almost as tall as I am but so skinny, she almost disappears when viewed from the side. She's also jealous and possessive. The day after she braided my hair, she declared her undying love for me, as well as her willingness to get my name tattooed anywhere on her body. I've been avoiding her since then and was looking for a place to move. Now I'm just going to leave. Claudia's phone call came at the right time for a lot of reasons.

"What about all the shit you told me about your family?" She rubs her hand on her shirt, leaving a smudge of blood on it. "How they don't understand you. How they don't want you around? What about that?"

I'd hoped Velma would have been too wasted to remember what I said one night when I was feeling particularly sorry for myself and fed up with sobriety. As soon as the words came out of my mouth, I regretted trash talking my family for cheap sympathy from someone I never even liked just because she was there, paying attention to me.

"I'm moving out, Velma," I say, clearly and calmly. "Today. Right now. Sorry for the short notice."

"You're some piece of work, Dulcina," Velma spits out.

"Coming from you, that means a lot." I want to laugh, but I shouldn't have even answered her.

"Is this about the drugs?" Her voice is starting to sound desperate, raspy. She takes a few more steps inside, closer to the bed. She is sweating, and her pupils are dilated as big and flat as winter-coat buttons. "Because I don't keep anything here. You don't have to worry about that."

I could easily say, "Yes, it's about the drugs," but it would be an excuse. I should have cleared out a while ago. I should have never moved in. I shouldn't have let her braid my hair or kissed her. The wrongness of that kiss will haunt me for a long time if not forever.

"I can stop. I swear." We both know Velma has no intention of stopping, but she'll try to be more careful. "I'll stop. I promise."

I've said these exact same words, and now I realize how insulting it is to be on the other end of the lie.

I don't want her excuses or promises. I just want Velma to let me go and move on. What she can't understand and I won't bother to try to explain is that I'm absolutely certain I'm not supposed to be here in this room, in this place with her because all of it is wrong. I don't want to be some loser hanging on by her fingertips looking for a reason to mess up her life because it's easier to stay than to leave. I'm not that person anymore, I'm not like Velma.

I reach inside the pocket of my jacket to make sure Wyatt's card is in there. I haven't taken the time to ask myself why I haven't thrown it away, but I'll hold on to it until I decide what it is I want to do with it.

"I'll go to those meetings with you," Velma says, revealing that she's been following me.

Of course she has. She did the same thing to an ex of hers. A couple of times, I tagged along for lack of anything better to do.

"I have no idea what you're talking about, Velma," I tell her.

After dropping me off at the airport, Claudia stopped talking to me. I had the terrible habit of calling her when I was at my drunkest. One morning, the thought of starting my day with yet another bottle of gin made me want to slit my wrists open next to the scars that are already there. I took the 9 to the emergency room at SF General and told the intake nurse I'd been drunk for weeks and was pretty sure I was going to hurt myself.

I was tired of waking up and not knowing where I was or who I was waking up next to. I was tired of money slipping through my fingers like water, and tired of friends who never seemed to be around when I needed them but were always there when I had enough in my pocket to pay for a round of drinks. Mostly, I was just tired of myself.

After the longest week of my life, I focused on getting myself out of the psych ward instead of dealing with why I was really there. My social worker found me a room at a halfway house and a psychiatrist with a sliding scale. I stopped seeing the shrink after she said it wasn't worth her time or my money to listen to me lie for fifty minutes three times a week.

Getting fired from therapy left me with more time and cash to do what I'd always done, but it didn't work. No matter how much I drank, how much sex I had, or how much of everything else I took, I couldn't manage to forget what I thought I'd forgotten.

Claudia found me. I have no idea how she managed to track me down, but she did. She literally picked me up off the floor, cleaned me up, fed me and drove me to a private rehab facility near Napa. My sister held my hand as we walked in, filled out the paperwork for me, and hugged me like she's never hugged before. Then she left.

There, the doctors and nurses weren't underpaid and overworked, so it was a lot harder to fool them. They were genuinely invested in me, the person they saw underneath all the anger and pain I'd been wearing like a second skin for most of my life. With their help, I was able to get out of my own way. It was awful, painful, and scary. It's also the bravest thing I've ever done.

Claudia paid for everything, but whenever we talked on the phone, our conversations rarely touched on where I was or why I was there. I understood she didn't want to get her hopes up if she even had any left. I also understood that if I messed up again, I would be lost to her forever and she to me. That's what kept me going and what still does.

"Don't go, Dulcina."

Velma claws at her arms. She does this when she's tweaked out on speed. Her arms and legs are covered in scrapes and scabs she hides under long sleeves and pants.

"I'm leaving." I realize I've filled my duffel bag with clothes I wasn't planning on taking with me.

"What about me?" Velma raises her voice. It sounds as thin and scratchy as she is.

"What about you? I'm not on the fucking lease." I lose it for a moment. This what she wants—some sort, any sort, of reaction from me. "You always knew this was month-to-month. It's what we agreed to. Get over it and deal with it like an adult."

"You're so fucking cold!" She grabs my duffel bag and empties it on the floor like a toddler upending a bowl of cereal.

I stare down at the mess she's made anger rising up inside of me. I'm sick of her endless need for drama, her late-night binges on speed, tempered by days spent in a haze of pot and vodka. Plus, Velma never puts a fresh roll of toilet paper on the holder. Right now, I don't know which of these habits I find more enraging.

"I'm leaving, Velma." My hands shake as I reach down to grab my clothes off the floor.

"You're not going anywhere!" She screams so loud my ears ring. Velma is skinny, but strong and fast. I know enough to take a step back.

"Cut it out, Velma." I don't raise my voice, trying to appear calm for the both of us.

"Fuck you!" Velma comes at me, all bony fists and fingernails.

Instead of moving out of the way, I push her clear across the room. She hits the wall with a satisfying thud and slides to the floor. I yank her up ready to really hurt her if she dares come at me again. Her eyes are desperate but with an edge of excitement.

She's getting off on this.

Seeing this and feeling my hands on her makes my skin crawl. I shove her away from me and keep pushing so we're stumbling down the hallway, through the living room, and toward the front door.

"I swear, Velma, if you even look at me, I'll kill you. Get out of here before I toss you out a window."

"Dulcina, please . . ." She moves toward me, not able to keep herself from trying one last time.

"Get out!" I scream at her until she backs away from me. I push her onto the stairway landing, toss her purse at her, then lock the door and slide on the chain.

I'm shaking so hard my teeth are chattering, but I feel like laughing and never stopping. I run back into the room and shove everything into my duffel bag. In the bathroom, I gather up my toothbrush, deodorant, and shampoo.

I'm drenched in sweat, and my heart is pumping so hard in my chest, it feels like it's going to turn itself inside out. I give myself a moment to run cold water in the sink, splash it on my face, and dry off with the hem of Todd's T-shirt before tucking it, damp, into the waistband of my jeans.

I leave some money and the keys on the coffee table, undo the chain, then double back and go out the kitchen door, down the rickety stairs that lead into the overgrown yard and jump the fence between houses.

It takes many blocks for me to calm down, for my heart to beat in a normal rhythm, for it to feel safe enough to put one foot in front of the other without having to keep myself from breaking into a run. I focus on this feeling as I cross Market Street and head toward the Mission.

# ◆ 12 ◆

# CLAUDIA

A S POINTLESS AS IT is, sometimes I let myself wonder what my life would be like if Mom and Dad had been hippies who encouraged me to go to yoga class and meditation retreats, or at least just summer day camp. Instead, it was catechism and church, Mom using our allowance as leverage.

No St. Mary's? No money for Fun Dip or RC grape soda and especially not for the school book fair.

If either of them could have been even a modicum unlike how they were and as they still are, I could possibly be a well-adjusted adult by now. Instead, I still struggle with childish grievances I can't seem to extricate from the deepest parts of my mind. They're always there, those thoughts and memories, barely under the surface of my meticulously crafted façade, ready to burst out of me in a scream.

I don't scream.

I exercise. I see my acupuncturist twice a month. I drink $3 elixir tea and have willingly forked over $65 to hear a therapist tell me pretty much the same thing a $120 psychiatrist said but with a prescription for pills I get filled but refuse to take.

I'm tired of hearing myself talk and not say anything, of pretending I'm telling the truth when what I'm really doing is seeing how far away I can get from it without resorting to lying. And I like therapy, I really do. I'm just sick of talking about my insufferable self.

This is why my new thing has become a particularly brutal hot yoga class in West Hollywood. Other than a few minutes of trendy spiritual platitudes by the teacher at the beginning of class, everyone here is much too self-absorbed to engage in anything other than good-natured whining in the changing room.

As far as I'm concerned, it's the best kind of therapy. The heat, the contorted poses, all to be endured and celebrated for ninety minutes for a "gratitude donation" of $11, which really means $15 if not $20—no one wants to be the jerkwad who asks for their change. After the final "Om," I always feel exhilarated to have made it through without passing out or vomiting. It's an accomplishment well worth $15 if not a full $20.

So here I am, wearing a sports bra and tiny shorts, standing on my left leg, my right straight out in front of me, leaning over to grasp the bottom of my foot with both hands. I've done this pose so many times and have gotten so good at all of them, I can do the whole class with my eyes closed, my breath steady and slow as sweat drips off my body.

Not this morning, though.

I feel worse than after my first class, when I did vomit and had a headache that lasted for two solid days and nights. When I asked if this was normal, the headache, the nausea, and the nightmares, they told me my body was releasing toxins.

This made sense to me, so I started coming Monday, Wednesday, and Friday mornings at six. I also take kickboxing and bootcamp classes. Sometimes, when Ethan is away, I take two different classes in one day and three on weekends. I don't swim or jog. I like to be told what to do when I exercise, but only by women. I've walked out of classes when the last-minute sub turned out to be a man. I'm sure this isn't normal. It might even be something I should try to figure out. For now, I've decided it's okay to only want to be told what to do by women when I have my ass in the air and am sweating my balls off.

And thinking of a sweaty ballsack . . . why marry Augustino? Where's the logic behind what Maritza is doing? What's her thought process? Is there any? Is she going through with it because it's what she's decided is going to happen?

This wedding thing of hers reminds me of the time I found in our bedroom closet with a jar of maraschino cherries. She was seven, old enough to understand what she was doing was wrong and it was why she was hiding. She refused to give me the jar, and I didn't even bother to ask her where she'd got it from. Accepting there was nothing I could do to stop her, I watched Maritza eat every single cherry. She even drank some of the syrup. As soon as her greed started to get the better of her, I frog-marched her out of the house and got Dooley off the roof where she was smoking one of Dad's Marlboros and avoiding Mom so she wouldn't have to run errands for her.

We hotfooted Maritza over to the public restroom at Evergreen Park where she barfed her guts out for a solid half hour. Dooley went back to the house and snuck out a change of clothes for her. I had to toss what she had been wearing in a trash can after trying to rinse out the maraschino gunk in the sink. Throwing her clothes away felt wrong, and it was what I was afraid I'd get in trouble for. That's what would have pissed off Mom—the waste of a perfectly good dress from Sears, not the myriad of reasons behind why it had to be trashed.

Seeing and smelling a steady stream of chunky, bright-red vomit cemented my lack of a sweet tooth, though barfing was a hobby of mine for a while when I was in college. Once I graduated, I decided to hate vomiting.

It's weak, and I am not weak.

Ugh. This is the exact type of bullshit I'm supposed "check at the door" along with $15 of gratitude. I release the pose and look around. People are standing in pools of their own sweat, their faces twisted into expressions of blissful pain.

The room is oppressively hot and muggy, and I can't seem to get enough water. I'm so thirsty, but drinking is giving me cramps. The instructor comes over, bringing with her a stale cloud of sage and Palo Santo smoke. My stomach turns over on itself.

"You might want to cut back on the water. Just take tiny sips," she whispers in my ear.

I nod, holding my breath. As soon as she moves on to another student, I roll up my mat and walk into the women's dressing room, leaving sweaty footprints on the tile floor.

I turn on one of the showers and step under the spray of cool water, still wearing my sports bra and shorts. I inhale and exhale deeply, humming in the back of my throat, thinking about anything except how I feel. My body has its own ideas. I run soaking wet to the toilet stall and throw up before my mind can catch up with what's happening.

For what seems like a long time, I stay there, on the tile floor. I don't want to move, but I also don't want anyone to find me here like this.

I force myself to stand up, peel off my bra and shorts, and throw them away in the trash can and toss my mat in there too. I shower and dress, not bothering to put on makeup. My wet hair has soaked the back of my dress by the time I walk out of the studio.

Across the street, there's a Starbucks. I order a mint tea and a cranberry scone just because I've never had one before. I allow myself the time to sit, and not scroll through work emails and texts on my BlackBerry. I don't even check my personal phone. Instead, I stare out the window at the passing cars and few people walking by. When I'm done with my tea, I wrap the scone in a napkin and head off to work, feeling much better than I have in days.

I may not be ready to accept what's really wrong with me, but I'm absolutely certain I'm done with hot yoga.

# ◆ 13 ◆

# MARITZA

THE RECEPTIONIST, NOTHING SPECIAL except for her dyed blond hair, flirts with some guy like I'm not even there. This is an escrow company office in Thousand Oaks, not some skanky club, but she's acting like it is.

I'm not her boss, so I can't tell her how she should be doing her job, but I might tell her boss how she's not doing it. I'm pretty sure they expect their receptionist to not pick up guys while she's at work when there are clients she should be offering a cup of coffee or bottle of water while they wait. Those are basic receptionist job duties.

I look out toward the parking lot to where my car is. I wish someone had come with me. I could have asked Claudia, but she's already helping me with my wedding. Sometimes, though, she makes things more complicated than they have to be. And she's always asking questions, and when she doesn't, it's because she's already figured out her own answers and has decided that's what's going happen.

Like with the bridesmaid dresses. Claudia says there has to be a whole special appointment for Dani and Gabi even though I've already picked out their dresses. This way, she says, it'll make them think it was their choice and they'll be happy with what they have to wear. I don't get why they have to be happy at all. I'm the bride. My happy is the only happy that should matter.

I look over at the receptionist. She's still ignoring me while she flirts. Maybe she thinks I've just wandered in from the street and have taken a seat on one of her cheap visitor chairs for fun. But I have a reason to be here.

I'm buying a three-bedroom, two-and-a-half-bath house in Bellflower. Bellflower is almost the same distance between Boyle Heights, Mr. Kim and Mrs. Kim's condo in Torrance, and KKIBC in Long Beach. Bellflower is also far enough away from Glendale so Auggie's mother and sisters won't be able to just drop by when they feel like it.

I haven't told anyone about my house. They would want to know where I got the money from, especially Claudia. How much money I have or where it came from is none of anyone's business. Not even Augustino's. Maybe, it sort of might be. Legally, I don't think so.

Since right after we got engaged, I've been collecting $75 once a month from him to put into a savings account for my wedding. Augustino is so bad with money. He spends it on the dumbest stuff, like tickets to boxing matches and video games, and he gives way too much to his mother and sisters.

He says it's rent, what he gives to his mother, but she'd pay him to live with her forever. And, if it is rent, why does he go to her for money when he needs it? This is not how rent works. That's an allowance! Like he's some sort of little boy instead of a thirty-three-year-old man. It's better I should set aside those $75 instead of letting him waste it.

On the day he gives me the money, we go out to eat and, usually, to a movie. If Augustino hasn't annoyed me too much that month, we'll get a room at the Double Tree. Then I'll shower, making sure not to get my hair wet, and he drives me home because I can't sleep anywhere but in my own bed.

One time, about a year or so after we got engaged, Augustino complained it was too expensive to fuck me. Those were the exact words he used. To me. His fiancée. For five months, I took his money, let him take me out to eat and to the movies, and he didn't get so much as a kiss on the cheek from me. Nothing until he understood what getting fucked really meant.

Around then, Mrs. Kim invited me to the investment group she belongs to with ladies from her church. While they gossiped and ate fried dumplings, I asked questions and learned about what they were doing. Then I started reading everything I could about stocks, bonds, mutual funds, all that kind of stuff. I opened my own E★TRADE account and started investing separate from the ladies' group.

I've always had a knack for numbers. My high school guidance counselor, Mr. Gleason, told me to be secretary for an accountant, but I already had my job with Mr. Kim so it wasn't very helpful advice. Anyways, the stock market made sense to me. I started really small, just a few hundred dollars at most and I made some really good calls.

I more than doubled what I invested during my first year because I stuck with companies I knew about and I still do. Every time Daddy drinks a Budweiser, it's like he's putting money in my pocket. And, I figured, if I can get not only my Barbara Cartland novels but also shoes from an online store for cheaper than at the mall, it's a company I should own stock in.

I waited until it went down to a price that made sense to me before I bought 893 shares of Amazon at $5.91 on October 1, 2001. I used numbers that are lucky in Korea instead of rounding up when I put my order in. Now I wish I would have gotten a thousand shares, but it was such a sad time with all that was happening. I wasn't really thinking as clearly as I could've been.

As of close yesterday, Amazon was at $30.88, which means what I own was worth $27,575.84. That's a lot of money, but I still lost out on $3,304.16 because I didn't round up to buy those extra 107 shares when I should have. I'm not going to sell anytime soon. I don't need to. I'm so good at it now, at investing, I was able to use dividends from my portfolio for the down payment on my house.

Auggie never asks about the money in the wedding account. He just assumes that once he gives it to me, I deposit it in the bank, and nothing happens with it. That's basically true except for one time, right at the start, when I had a bad run and had to borrow just little bit. I paid my wedding account back within the week, and I haven't made any big mistakes since then. I'm the only one who gets the bank statements so Auggie will never find out and we don't talk about that kind of stuff. As far as he's concerned, the money for my wedding has always been there earning fractions of pennies in interest and that's just fine with him.

Not telling him about my money is not the same as lying about money. It's just easier for both of us to not involve him in things he can't understand. If anything, I'm doing Auggie a favor. He doesn't have to worry about catering costs, wedding favors, stocks fluctuations, money market valuations, losses, gains, or tax codes. It's a lot of stress for me, but it would be worse if he started involving himself. And it's just $75 a month, not even $100, which I should have upped it to when he got his new job at the end of last year. I lost out on $125 that could have gone to something useful, like those rosebushes I had pass on at Home Depot.

Now money is more important than ever. Buying a house is a big life event, maybe even bigger than my wedding. And just like with everything else, I have to do it all on my own. And . . . and. . . .

I hate Thousand Oaks. I really do. I hate this place!

That person, the one who married me when I was eighteen, lives a few miles from here in the moldy, potpourri-smelling house he inherited from his mother. I thought it was going to be great, having my own house and being a wife, but it was the exact opposite of what he'd promised me. His mother was dead, but it was still *her* house. He wouldn't let me change anything, not even the gross towels in the powder room. When I discovered the real truth about him, what he had tried to hide and lied to me about, I left that same day with only my purse. Everything else—including my wedding gifts—stayed there because he had contaminated all of it.

The lawyer Claudia found suggested an annulment, but when he explained it to me and what I would have to reveal to get one, a divorce made more sense. That person agreed to a settlement so we didn't have to go to court. I could have gotten way more, including that stinky house, and I could have ruined his life like he tried to ruin mine, but then everyone would have found out why I couldn't stay married.

I hardly think about that person anymore. I never let myself wonder how my life would be now if I hadn't gotten away from him. Mostly, it's like it never happened, but now it's why Father Gabriel says I can't have my wedding at St. Mary's. It's so unfair of him to hold the divorce against me, especially since he's only too happy to ask me to donate cases of soda that they sell for $1 can at fundraisers for the church. What a hypocrite.

Anyways, Bellflower makes sense to me because of where it is, and I found a nice house that, with a little work, will be even nicer. It'll also appreciate in value while lowering my tax liability. I made sure to find out about the big stuff like the roof, electrical, and pipes before I made my offer. Then I got concessions, including credit for the termite tenting, which happened last week.

Today I sign the papers and it's officially mine. I'll consider putting Auggie's name on the deed and the mortgage after my wedding but only if we have a joint account for his paycheck to be deposited into. No more Bank of Fat Mommy for him. I don't have to decide right now. I'll ask Claudia what she thinks before I do anything.

"Your 10:30 is here, Hamid," the flirty receptionist says.

Hamid, who I've only talked to on the phone, is standing by the reception desk smiling at me. He's wearing a suit and tie like he should be. He's taller, younger, and better-looking than I imagined. And he has nice teeth, straight and white but not too white. Good teeth are important. If a man doesn't take care of his teeth, you can't really trust him to take care of anything else.

"Maritza, hello. Sorry to have kept you waiting."

"Hello, Hamid. Good morning." I tuck my planner into my bag and stand up to shake his hand. He smells like nice cologne. I check and see there's no wedding ring on his finger. Maybe I'll ask him what the name of his cologne is. "You're right on time. I was a bit early."

"Your agent isn't here yet? Do you want us to wait for her?" Hamid leans on the front desk where the receptionist is now pretending to be working. "I don't have anything until after lunch, so no rush, Maritza."

"Oh, she's not going to be able to make it," I tell him, which isn't really a lie. The truth is that I didn't tell her I'd be signing today, so there's no way she can show up here. "We can just get started, if that's okay."

I hate my real estate agent, Gena. I especially hate that she has to get a commission when I did all the work. I found the house, I negotiated with the seller's agent, I went through all the checklists and asked tons of questions and then asked about the answers they gave me. Gena wanted me to accept the home inspection from a previous offer that had fallen through. I told her I wanted a new one, with a different inspector. She tried to talk me out of it—it was a waste of money, it would delay the sale, the sellers would back out, and everyone would think I was difficult to work with.

So?

If I had listened to her, I would've gotten stuck with having to pay for draining and capping a just-about-to-fail septic system they'd pretended not to know about. I got the price adjusted for that and other things too, like mold removal from the pantry area and the termite tenting. Gena's lucky I don't report her to whoever is in charge of her. She's really bad at her job and a terrible person too. A giant PFC, like Claudia says about women like her.

"Would you like some coffee or water, Maritza?" Hamid asks.

"Tea would be great." I look directly at Hamid, not the receptionist. "Chamomile or mint. With honey if you have it."

"I think we can manage a cup of tea." He looks over at the receptionist, who nods her dyed blond head of hair as we pass her by. He opens the door to a conference room and stands to one side so I can go in. Auggie doesn't open doors for me anymore. He hasn't for a while. "I promise to make this as painless as possible, Maritza."

He's said my name four times. A man who goes out his way to say a woman's name is interested in her. This is a fact. We sit down at a table, and he hands me a stack of papers. He moves his chair so he's closer to mine and, since I'm left-handed, we're definitely going to touch arms. This is also a sign that he's interested in me.

"It's all pretty standard language, including the addendums for the termite tenting and other agreed on contingencies," he says, smiling at me and showing his very nice teeth. "It looks like a lot of paperwork, but it's because of the second much more thorough inspection. No surprises or tricks are buried in there, I promise. Just stop me if you have any questions."

I nod, but I won't have any. I've read everything there is about buying property. I know the laws and ordinances. I even know how far away my new house is from the San Andreas fault.

The receptionist hasn't moved from her desk to get me my tea. I look from him to her as he goes through the papers, using his capped pen to point to where I have to sign or initial. I sigh, annoyed with the receptionist and with Hamid for not noticing I'm annoyed.

"There's no reason to be nervous, Maritza. It's a good investment property, you should have no problem renting it out to a family."

"I'm going to live there. I'm engaged. My wedding is on the thirty-first. That's why it had to be such a short escrow."

I hold out my left hand with the ring I negotiated for at a downtown jewelry store off of Broadway while Augustino complained he was hungry. He just wanted to go to Clifton's Cafeteria for lunch and didn't care about my ring. If I'd left it up to him, I'd be stuck wearing something twice as small and just as expensive. He's really so dumb with money, he doesn't even understand what a Roth IRA is.

Hamid looks down at my ring, but he doesn't take my hand. "Congratulations! Where is the lucky man?"

"He's at work. This is a surprise." I smile at him, but he doesn't smile back at me right away.

"It's a surprise?" He's not able to hide the look on his face. It's the one I bet Claudia will give me when I tell her about my house.

"He loves surprises," I say. What business is it of his? He still gets his fee whether Augustino is sitting next to me or not. "It's not an issue, is it? They've already accepted my offer and agreed to everything."

"No, of course not." Hamid looks at his watch as he starts to flip through another packet, this one about flood plains and earthquake zones. "We're almost done here."

He hasn't said my name since I told him I was engaged.

"Hamid?" I put my left hand on his arm to stop him and so he can see my ring again. "Wasn't she supposed to get me some tea?"

# · 14 ·

# DULCINA

I F I HAD A cigarette, I'd blow smoke rings at the fire alarm of the room I'm in. It has a red light that blinks every so often. I've been staring at it for the last half hour and can't figure out any sort of pattern. This annoys me. Maybe I'm just annoyed because I can't smoke a cigarette I don't even have in a room I'm not allowed to smoke in.

Our dad caught me smoking when I was about eleven, and asked why I was doing it. I told him I liked the way it made me feel and the smell reminded me of the time when Maritza turned the dial on the toaster all the way to the right because she thought it would cook the bread faster. He didn't tell me I was bad or what I was doing was wrong and I should never do it again. He just patted my head, sent me back to my homework, and smoked the rest of that cigarette without me.

Not too long after this happened, he quit. Not because he wanted to set a better example for me and my sisters but because the simple cold he caught at work turned into double pneumonia. He wound up in the hospital, and it took him months to stop coughing after he got out. He didn't stop drinking and was never careful with his beer. When I started sneaking his beer, he was onto me from the get-go, but he never said a thing.

I turn on the TV and flip through the channels not to find something to watch, but because I don't want to think in silence. I haven't figured out how I'm going to get to Los Angeles, but it won't be by plane. I have a shoebox full of cash and don't want to answer any questions from some overeager TSA agent about why. Plus, I hate to fly and have never done it sober. I'm going to cut myself some slack for those two reasons.

The late-morning news comes on. The stories flow from one to the next: a house fire in the Sunset, a man with a kitchen knife mugged an elderly couple at a bus stop in the Tenderloin, the homeless living in the shadow of City Hall, sunny and breezy for the next couple of days before the skies go gray and quiet again. I stare at the newscasters and listen to what they say with a detached sense of under-standing that none of this, especially the weather forecast, will mean anything to me within a few hours.

I look out the window at what's going on below and feel a little sad. I met some good people here, like Curtis, and some truly awful ones, like Velma. She left me with a parting gift in the form of a black eye. What bothers me is I can't pin down the moment when she got a punch in. I always took her for more of a scratcher.

I spent the last couple of days at a motel on Valencia Street hoping the bruise would fade. Last night, I gave up and walked over to the Walgreens by the Mission BART station. I was just going to get a stick of concealer but ended up adding more and more stuff to the red plastic shopping basket. I spent most of last night sitting on the bathroom counter, my feet in the sink, painting my face, wiping it all off and starting over again. It was fun to feel pretty, to see myself in different ways. Then, around three in the morning, it became an uncomfortable game I wasn't sure why I was playing.

It feels wasteful, but I toss all the makeup into the trash, even what I didn't open. I put on my usual Chapstick, check out, and walk out onto Valencia. For a moment, I feel very self-conscious but remind myself that a woman with a head full of tiny braids that fall almost to her waist with a black eye who also happens to be carrying a duffel bag is not such an odd sight at any hour in this city.

I'm not going to hide behind makeup today, not when it's cost me so much to be able to look at myself without flinching. San Francisco has seen me look a lot worse and only has to deal with me for just a little longer. I stare straight ahead and walk toward where I need to go before I can leave.

There are a lot of people I don't need to say goodbye to. Some of them will find out I've left through Curtis at The Clap Trap and others through psycho Velma. They'll wonder if I owed them money, forget it was me they owed money to, and then have another drink, toke, or pill. There are other people, though, people who I won't pretend aren't important to me.

I come to a stop across from the Women's Building and stare at the murals that cover the facade while thinking about not smoking a cigarette. I've been coming here every week for the last year and a half for group therapy. I've kept to myself, for the most part, and discovered that other people's problems are a valuable point of reference for my own. I was able to figure out a lot about myself by just listening to the other women talk.

We don't meet for another twenty minutes, but I'm here early not just out of habit but because I want to make sure I catch Wendy, the therapist who leads our group, before she goes inside. Any other Wednesday, I would have come even earlier, using it as an excuse to kill time by sitting in on one of the seminars or taking a drop-in class.

Once, back when I first started coming to our group, I spent an entire morning dancing with a bunch of other women. We moved around a candle, a rose in a Dixie cup, a pile of colorful feathers, and a pair of dice as a barefoot hippie Chicana in a long patterned skirt and tank top wafted sage smoke at us and encouraged us to hum and move along with the new-age tribal music playing on the enormous boom box that must have been a pain to lug up the stairs.

I wasn't sure why I was there, but I felt relaxed, almost buzzed. Then she handed out paper and crayons and asked us to draw a picture of what we were feeling. I watched as the other women, women I'd probably seen on the bus on my way to work or passed on the street as they carried plastic bags full of groceries with their kids trailing behind them, sat on the floor with their crayons and paper. They were all really into it, and all I wanted to do was head for the door. I drew a picture of a flower, and when I noticed the others were still working, I added some grass and clouds but stopped short of a smiling sun. I drew it with my right hand instead of my left and refused to think about why I was doing what I was doing.

The hippie Chicana with good, straight teeth that showed her parents understood the value of orthodontics looked at my picture and then stared into my eyes.

"You have a lot of blockages. Here." She cupped her hand over my heart and then pressed her fingertips lightly on my forehead. "And here. We meet every other week. You're very welcome to come back."

I smiled, nodded, and, since then, I've had to duck into an empty room whenever Miss Heart and Head Obstruction is in the hallway with her giant boom box and sandwich bag full of feathers.

"Hey! Wendy!" I call out as I crush a phantom cigarette with the heel of my boot. She waits for me as I jaywalk across the street, not caring that there's an SFPD cruiser double parked on my right.

"Hi, Dooley. You can help me set up."

Wendy hands me a box to carry, and we climb up the staircase together. I follow her into the conference room we use and set the pamphlets, emergency number cards, and boxes of generic tissue on a wobbly card table next to the coffee maker.

"Avery won't be coming. Her ex put her in the hospital again."

"How can he be her ex if she won't break up with him?" I ask, feeling sorrier for myself than I do for Avery.

I'm missing my cigarettes, and the lack of nicotine has given me a headache. Even if I was to smoke an entire pack of Marlboros, Avery's chronic inability to get out of her own way would still annoy me.

"Show a little sisterly solidarity, woman," Wendy says. "Nice shiner, by the way."

"Yeah, I did it myself for a little sympathy," I say, still feeling irritable. "I should have expected Avery would once again take the shine off of me."

Wendy shrugs off the last kicks of my tantrum as I start setting up folding chairs in a perfect enough circle, leaving off one chair that's meant for me and a second that would have been for Avery.

Wendy keeps one eye on the coffee maker—it'll either stop working or work fine within the next minute. "It's just Avery who isn't coming. Put one back."

"I'm not staying." I drop a box of tissue next to every third chair.

"You want to tell me why?" She's asking but she doesn't sound surprised.

Wendy has been doing this kind of work long enough to recognize the difference between spiraling and moving on. Like Curtis, I think she's been expecting me to leave for some time now, if not just disappear.

Last month, our group lost someone. Rio. She had a boyfriend, really more of a pimp, who she was desperately in love with and just as afraid of. A cop came to the door and stood by the coffee maker until Wendy noticed that we had a visitor. I caught the look on her face before she made herself go blank. It was just a second, but her doubts, frustrations, and sadness had been exposed.

We'd all seen each other fail, battle through rough patches, but Rio dying—no, she was murdered—was a whole lot of perspective even for those of us who were barely hanging on. On that day, we realized we weren't dead and how much this counted for something.

"I'm going back to Los Angeles," I tell Wendy, and for the first time those words sound not only real, but right. "To Boyle Heights where I grew up."

"Do you want to say goodbye to the group?" Wendy puts her hands on her hips and stares at me.

"Why bother?" I shrug, unwilling to let myself give in to sentimentality. "It's not like I've ever much."

"If you don't want to say goodbye, own up to it and don't make excuses." Wendy pulls the plug on the coffee maker. If she leaves it on, it'll burn the coffee and she'll have to start all over again. "It's your life, woman. Live it like it is."

"I just wanted to let you know so you wouldn't wonder about me." I take a step toward the door and can hear the other group members making their way up the staircase. "Or worry something happened because nothing has. I'm fine."

"You act so tough, Dooley, but you're a lot stronger than you give yourself credit for." Wendy points a finger, pinning me to the spot where I'm standing. "I believe in you, Dulcina Bernal, I always have."

"Thanks." I pick up my bag and swivel too hard on the polished floor so the rubber sole of one of my boots makes a loud, mood-killing squeak. "Okay, so . . . bye."

"Hey! Guess what?" Wendy calls out. I turn back toward her before realizing she isn't talking to me. "Ladies, our Dulcina is leaving us today. She's going home."

One by one, they hug me. Some cry. They wish me well and twice the luck. I know them all by name and about the horrible things that bring them here, but it's not until this moment that I realize they care about me as much I do about them.

Wendy puts her arm around my shoulders as she walks me to the door.

"You may have not said much, Dooley, but you listened. Most people can't do that. And just between the two of us, Avery is a pain in the ass. She's going to miss you too. We all are."

I nod, not trusting myself to speak. My chest feels tight, like it's trying to squeeze all the blood out of my heart. Wendy closes the door and leaves me alone on the other side of it. I stand there for a minute, crying just a little as I listen to their voices.

When I'm ready, I head down the stairs, exchanging a friendly nod with the Chicana hippie chick who's lugging her boom box up in the opposite direction. Outside, I take one last, long look at those murals before I walk away.

# ◆ 15 ◆

# CLAUDIA

I SIP MINT TEA from a Hermès mug, a gag gift from Ethan. He made a big show of presenting it to me a few weeks into this thing of ours while I was in bed, naked, sweaty, and still trying to catch my breath. He watched my face as I unwrapped it, which made me a little nervous as to what I was going to find inside. When I realized it was nothing but an absurdly expensive mug, I laughed so hard, I gave myself a stitch in my side that left me holding on to him as he tried to massage it away. Then he ruined the joke by admitting he was in love with me and had been from the second we'd met.

That sneaky fucker.

I'm supposed to be working, but all I've managed to do is delete emails I have no intention of reading, much less replying to. It's past noon and I'm still celebrating my divorce from hot yoga with breakfast food, but only the cranberries. The scone itself, which I had a few bites of out of curiosity, tastes like sugary flour to me.

I'm not sure what I'll replace hot yoga with. I could hike Runyon Canyon and get in some networking. Nah, no thanks. I've made it this long and this far without hiking, I refuse to do so now for my health or my career. I could get more sleep. I wish I could go to sleep right now, just for a few minutes.

I drop a cranberry down the front of my dress and glance behind me where Julie is sitting on the floor cleaning out file drawers to make room for newer files. Despite the myriad laptops and computers everyone relies on, there's still a surprising amount of paper in this business.

"Oh. My. God . . . OHMYGAWD!"

I look over at Julie again, startled by the guttural sounds she's making and immediately wonder if I stashed something private in one of those drawers and forgot about it. But it's not anything she's found but rather the someone who's found his way to my office doorway.

Ethan.

Behind him, there's a nonchalant stampede of assistants and execs emerging from their cubicles and offices to get a look at him. I pull off my headset and stand up while still digging the errant cranberry out from my cleavage. Julie, now silent and open-mouthed, is staring at a smiling Ethan. I stare at him too, not smiling.

"Julie," I say to her, my eyes locked on Ethan's, "you can finish this up later."

"But . . ."

Julie had complained about having to do this task and now she thinks I'm going to let her hang out in my office while I . . . what? What am I going to do to Ethan? Something, that's for sure.

I glare at her, making it clear I want her to get the hell out of my office. If she's dumb enough to emit another "But . . ." I will drag her out by her hair. She makes a show of standing up so her ass is in Ethan's direction. It's both gross and funny, but mostly pathetic. I keep my lips pressed together. Laughing at her will give Ethan the impression I'm not going to ream his own ass as soon as we have some privacy.

I watch as she slithers past him, staring up at all six feet four inches of him as if he were a tree she wants to climb, taking a rest halfway up on his proportionally sized perch as if her entire life depended on Ethan being able to hold her weight. He can—he easily holds mine. Ethan moves out of her way even as she veers toward him as if he were magnetized.

"Thanks, Judy. . . . Can I come in?" he asks me as he takes a generous step inside. Ethan taps the nameplate on my office door with a rolled-up script. "Claudia Bernal. Room enough for a hyphen if you want to go that way. Or you can just go with Jacobs. What's mine is yours, Ms. Bernal."

"What are you doing here?" My voice is raspy, my breath quick and shallow.

"I'm taking you out for lunch." He tilts his head toward what's left of the demolished scone. "A real one."

I'm about to tell him to fuck the fuck off when I notice Julie, slack-jawed and glassy-eyed, is watching us. "Close the damn door, Ethan."

Not taking his eyes off my face, he takes a long step back and kicks it shut with the heel of his boot. He comes toward me as I move toward him. His hands on my hips, he pulls me in and kisses me. I open for his tongue as warm waves of desire and my ever-present need to be close to him have me molding my body into his despite myself.

He groans and keeps his mouth on mine when he speaks. "You left way too early this morning. Where is it that you go?"

"Church."

I push away from him, but he tightens his hold around my waist, both of his hands resting on the top curve of my ass. My hips press into him instinctively and I feel him getting hard against my belly.

"You can't kiss me like that in my office In fact, you can't kiss me here at all." There's not much sting to my words as my body is telling him exactly what he wants to hear. "And you definitely can't just drop in on me."

"I already did so . . . oops." Ethan smoothly maneuvers us around the stack of files and boxes and sits on my chair. He pats his thighs with his free hand, not releasing his hold on me with his other, not taking his eyes off mine. "Have a seat, Bernal."

"I'm not sitting on your lap." I run my hand down the front of my dress hoping it skims over the scone that's turned into a lead weight in the pit of my belly. "This is my office with my unhyphenated name on the door. I don't sit on anyone's lap in here."

"Then I'll sit on yours."

He watches me carefully, his expression both curious and determined. I recognize this particular look, the set of his jaw and unwavering gaze. I've seen it before. The first time we met. The first time he kissed me. Last night when I only managed to get away from how exposed he makes me feel by pushing his head between my thighs.

"Fine." I grab on to his wrist with both of my hands and pull him out of the chair. I sit down and pat my own lap. "Have at it, Jacobs."

He does.

Before I have a chance to laugh, there's a knock on my door. In one smooth, quick motion, Ethan is up from my lap and leans his hips against the console table that sits under where a window would be if I were important enough to have one. He's not at all out of breath. Instead it's all very casual, as if he's been there the entire time, his long legs crossed at his booted ankles, his broad shoulders relaxed and an inviting smile on his face. It takes me a moment to realize he's also picked up the rolled-up script he dropped on my desk. The man knows his marks and that the right props make a scene that much more believable.

I'm still processing what just happened, the fluidity of it, when my door is opened by my boss, Milton Wasser, president and chairman of Wasser Entertainment. I'm surprised it took it took him this long to get in here. He can smell real celebrity a mile away, and Ethan Jacobs is 100 percent bankable celebrity. It says so on this month's cover of *Vanity Fair*.

My boss is very smart and so aggressively unattractive inside and out, there was no way he wasn't going to become a successful movie producer. He gets away with being such an ugly prick because he makes good movies that also make lots and lots of money.

"Claudia. You've got company," says the full-body boner that is the man who signs my paychecks.

This is the first time he's ever set foot in my office. He barely spoke to me after I was hired and, when he did, he kept calling me Nadia. I corrected him at my first all-hands company meeting by telling him, "Just so we're clear, Milty, my name is Claudia. Not Nadia. And my last name is pronounced Burr*NAWL*, not *Berr*Null. Thanks."

"It seems that I do, Milty." I sound somewhere between amused and annoyed because this is exactly what I am.

My boss looks me over, reassessing everything he thought he knew about me. He doesn't know much more than I've been willing to share with anyone here, which is close to nothing. Milty will be calling Julie/Judy into his office as soon as he can to rectify this. She, unfortunately, knows a little bit more because it's her job to be all up in my business.

Ethan doesn't move from where he is, though he does lean forward and extend his hand for Milty to shake. His long reach closes the distance between them and stops Milty from getting any closer to me.

"It's nice to see you again, Milton. Or is it okay if I call you Milty?"

"Only Claudia calls me Milty," he says with an overly pleased smile. Discerning if Ethan Jacobs really has found it nice to see him again is going to keep my boss up for a few nights. "It's our thing. Isn't it, Claudia?"

"It is our thing, Milty," I agree, not smiling back at him, "and it's not because I like you."

Ethan laughs, but I hold back as Milty tries to figure out if he should join in. Ethan has sense enough to understand I've overstepped onto my boss's very sensitive toes. He stops laughing and starts schmoozing.

"I was just telling Claudia how impressed I am by what you guys are doing here. George and I were on the court the other day and we got to talking—"

"Clooney?" Milty pants.

"Is there any other George worth knowing in this town?" Ethan grins at him. "As I was just telling Claudia, you can't argue with solid reviews and even better box office."

"I love what you guys are doing too," Milty says as he takes quick steps toward my desk, frowning at the scone and then at me. "Word has it you're going to have to build a new case for all the awards coming your way."

"Awards are nice, but it's all about who you work with. A smart producer who's willing to take a chance on a new voice or even an old one, that's who you want on your team. A producer with this kind of instinct, like Claudia's, is hard to find." Ethan taps the rolled-up script on his knee, drawing Milty's eyes away from me and my desk. "Tell me I'm not right about that, Milty."

The script he's holding is merely his cover for him being in my office. I take meetings in here all the time, but he's Ethan Jacobs. Him coming to me automatically raises suspicions, which will give rise to rumors, which, in our case, will prove to be true if—no, not if, but when we're found out.

"She's been my best hire," Milty says through his very white teeth. "We're all very impressed with our Claudia."

He had nothing to do with my being at Wasser Entertainment. As far as Milty was concerned, I checked two diversity boxes at once as a Latina and it's beside the point that I've proven myself to be a good producer. The only reason he's showing any interest in me right now is because he suspects Ethan Jacobs might be checking my box.

"Yeah, Claudia's a keeper, and she owes me lunch." Ethan takes a few steps to where I'm sitting and reaches for me, taking my elbow to encourage me to stand up and grabbing my purse off the hook behind my desk at the same time. He ushers me out the door, keeping himself between me and my boss. "Let's do dinner, drinks, you name it, Milty."

"I'll have my assistant call your assistant," Milty says to our backs as Ethan quickly walks me through the office and past all the staring faces.

As we wait for the elevator, I can feel the heat from all the buzzing going on behind us. People naturally feed off of gossip, and, for the near future, I'll be the main course. Ethan keeps his hand on my elbow, staring straight ahead at the closed elevator doors. He knows I'm pissed and can't do a thing about it.

"Claudia!"

We both turn around to see Julie trotting over to us, obviously on orders from Milty, who's lurking by her desk.

"What is it, Ju . . . Julie?"

Ethan snickers as I trip over her name. I yank my elbow out of his hand and take a step away from him.

"Um, what time will you be back?" Julie turns her big cow eyes toward Ethan. "Should I, um, cancel your afternoon meetings?"

"Why don't we just play it by ear?" Ethan answers for me. He grins at Julie, stunning her into another stupor of open-mouthed silence. The elevator dings, and Ethan guides me inside with a hand on the small of my back. "Nice meeting you, Julie."

I wait until the door closes before pulling away from him. "Why the hell are you here, Ethan?"

"I want to us talk, and since you won't talk to me in private, I'll take you out to lunch to the godforsaken Ivy or even Joan's so you'll have to, or else people will start talking about us not talking over lunch." He scratches at his chin. Besides having to cut all his hair off, he's also growing out his beard for his upcoming role. "I may not have graduated from Princeton with honors, Ms. Bernal, no hyphen, but I'm smart enough to figure out what the what is."

"What 'what' is there to talk about?" I could never convincingly play dumb and feel like a fool, a cruel one, for trying to play one now.

"Lady, you've got some fucking nerve. Aren't you supposed to be the one who wonders what my intentions are?" Ethan pushes the Lobby button and then shoves his hands into his pockets. "How things are between us? And what is it that we're doing and where it's going?"

"Things are fine." I reach for him, touching my hand to his side, all lean muscle and warm skin under the softness of his T-shirt. I feel a little woozy as the elevator starts its descent and tighten my hold on him to steady myself. "Right?"

"There it is! A little vulnerability." Ethan leans toward me, relaxing slightly. He takes my hand in his, intertwining his fingers with mine. "That wasn't so hard, was it?"

"Vulnerable? Me?" Despite being annoyed by him cornering me, I find it hard not to smile. I also feel sad. This is two too many feelings, if not three if I could admit that, yes, I do feel vulnerable. "Maybe all I want from you is lunch. But not at the Ivy—I'm sick of that place too."

"Claudia . . ." He looks down at our hands, comparing the difference in size before he runs his thumb over my bare ring finger. "I'm all in. I have been from the start. Are you?"

"I'm not sure what you're asking me, Ethan, but I do know you're asking me this in an elevator." My confusion and discomfort causes me to frown at him. I can even hear it in my voice. "Shouldn't we be reclining on a picnic blanket in a meadow for this type of . . . thing?"

"Answer my question, Claudia."

I can't take this conversation seriously, the one he wants and needs to have, but I also don't want to hurt him any more than I probably already have. Ethan is a patient man, but not a fool. I can only push him so far, and every day I keep pushing him a little more and a little harder. It's like I'm playing a one-sided game of relationship chicken to see which one of us will blink first. So far Ethan hasn't taken his eyes off me, and I don't know whether to love him or hate him for it.

I look up at him and all I can do is sigh, feeling, above all else, so tired I won't try to hide it with a joke or any other type of distraction. I wish I could fall into him and let him absorb some of the heaviness that's been weighing me down. I wish I could give him all that he deserves for being such a good man to me.

"Please talk to me, Claudia." He smooths my hair away from my face, his hand cupping the back of my head. "Tell me what's going on in there."

There's a twinge somewhere deep in the pit of my belly. I take a breath and order myself not to think. As I open my mouth to say what we both need and want to hear, the elevator arrives at the lobby.

Ethan releases his hold on me as the doors open, leaving us both exposed. Outside, on the sidewalk and street, there are paparazzi waiting for him, surrounding his Jeep. Ethan gives me a panicked look, as if he expects me to leave him on his own to deal with the consequences of his fame.

"Drive around the back, I'll hop in at the loading dock," I tell him.

He looks so grateful that I'm not going to bail on him, I almost burst into tears.

"Claudia? Are you okay?" Concerned, he steps toward me, but I wave him off before he gets any closer. "Claudia? What is it? What's wrong?"

"Nothing. I'm fine. We're fine, but . . ." I signal to one of the security guards as I step off to the side, out of camera range. ". . . sometimes it really sucks that you're Ethan Jacobs, Ethan Jacobs."

## ✦ 16 ✦

# DULCINA

OUR DAD ONCE TOLD me that if he hadn't married our mom, he would have been a professional stock car racer. Instead, he worked his way up to general manager of a foundry in South Gate. After work, our dad exiled himself to the porch where he drank can after can of Budweiser and smoked one Marlboro after another. He'd only come inside for dinner and then he'd go right back out there until bedtime.

Despite not coming home on Fridays until well after his favorite bar closed for the night, he was always up early on Saturday mornings. He spent the day inviting people over to the house and inviting himself over to other people's homes. Instead of going to church with us on Sunday mornings, he worked on the Malibu while singing along to ranchera music on the radio. Our mom hated weekends as much as our dad loved them. With her usually in bed with a migraine as soon as we got back from mass, our dad was free to teach us all he knew about cars.

When we were little, he'd sit one of us on his lap as he drove to The Boys supermarket in Highland Park. He'd leave us in the car with the motor running while he ran in to pick up a six-pack or two and pork rinds for himself and a bag of Ruffles chips and a bottle of Mexican Coke for me and my sisters to share on the drive back to Boyle Heights.

As soon as we were tall enough to reach the peddles, around eleven for me and Claudia and closer to thirteen for Maritza, he taught us to drive stick shift. He'd borrow Mrs. Gonzalez's battered VW Beetle which, by then, was mostly primer and duct tape. It was also the car he'd learned how to drive in decades before.

We could parallel park in three smooth steps in just about any spot without having to use our mirrors—a party trick that only backfired once during a Fourth of July barbecue when one of our jerk cousins set off a cherry bomb just as Maritza began her initial reverse.

Our dad may have not gotten his boys, but he never treated us like we couldn't handle a car due to a lack of a penis. This is why, when we got our permits and then licenses, one right after another and each of us passing our tests on the first try, it wasn't a rite of passage like it was for our cousins and friends. It just was.

By the time Maritza got her learner's permit, our dad had given us the Malibu to share. For himself, he bought a used two-door Ford Crown Victoria that had been custom painted a luminous pearl-gray shade I've never seen since but still dream about.

Our mom thought the Malibu gave us too much freedom—a dangerous thing for girls to have, much less enjoy. She and our dad fought about it. For once, he didn't give in and we got to keep the car. What she got to do was insist we always keep white and yellow striped towels over the seats. I thought it was to protect the pleather upholstery, but after I walked in on her inspecting those towels with a magnifying glass, I realized she was looking for other kinds of dirt.

The older we got and the more ourselves we each became, the less she seemed to want us around. But she also didn't want us to go anywhere. My sisters and I each dealt with this constant push and pull in our own ways. Maritza became our mom's shadow, Claudia excelled at being very smart, and I caused the kind of trouble no one wanted around the house.

When things got especially tense, our dad went with what he knew—cars and driving. He'd put our mom to bed with a cold cloth over her eyes and then order the three us into the Malibu—if one of us was in trouble, we all were. He left it up to whoever was the cause of our mom's migraine to pick a destination after calculating how far we could go on what was in the gas tank.

We'd always stop for ice cream and, as we ate, he'd tell us it was hard for our mom to, basically, be our mom, as if this explained anything. When we asked why, he'd tell us that's all we had to know. Our dad rarely yelled, never threatened to kick us out or lock us in our rooms and he never, not once, raised a hand to us. He expected his daughters to behave, and when we didn't, he called me, Claudia and Maritza on it in his own way and as best as he could manage without making our mom anymore upset than she always seemed to be. As far as he was concerned, we were supposed to be tough but obedient, two traits directly in conflict with each other even if he never saw it that way.

Our mom thought he should punish us, not buy us ice cream, which is why we never told her about it. What she wanted was for him to use his belt on us, then once we were too old for that, to take away the car keys, nail the windows shut, and install a deadbolt on the outside of the bedroom door.

In her mind, we were bad, and even when we weren't, it was just a matter of time until we were. This was especially true for me.

Our mom used to accuse me of all sorts of nasty things, things I hadn't even considered. I would then go out and do exactly what she suspected I'd already done to see if she was right about me. My sisters knew what I was up to, and they covered for me. Maritza always opened our bedroom window to let me back in after I'd snuck out, and Claudia marched me out of parties I shouldn't have gone to and always stayed too long at. They both got rid of the empty cans of Budweiser and cleaned me up after I threw up on myself. Neither of them had any idea how to make me stop, but my sisters somehow understood I wasn't doing it for fun. I was reckless, careless, and a danger to everyone around me. It was Claudia who told me I couldn't drive the Malibu anymore. She was the one who took my keys away.

Somewhere between leaving Boyle Heights and landing at SFO, I developed a fear of not only flying, but driving too. Now I understand that not driving was the only responsible decision I ever made as an alcoholic and addict. Once I got sober, I realized I wasn't just afraid of myself but also afraid for myself like Claudia and Maritza had been.

I'm much braver now, but I am still afraid to fly. This is going to make leaving San Francisco and getting L.A. something of a challenge. With this in mind, I pause by a bus stop for the 14 Mission, which, if I get on it, will leave me a short walk from the Greyhound Station.

"Hey, beautiful lady, going somewhere?" A homeless man in a doorway, as gray and dirty as the pavement underneath him, grins up at me.

"Yeah, getting out of here, old man." I give him a little wave as I start moving toward where I'm heading.

"Take me with you!" he calls out after me.

Just up ahead there's a used car lot and instead of passing it by as I have countless times over the years, I walk in and wander around. A cheerful-looking red hatchback catches my eye. This was the kind of car I wanted when I was sixteen. Maybe it's the kind of car I can have now.

A young guy, dressed as if he just came from an all-night rave, approaches on my right. His mustard-yellow cargo pants have the widest legs I've ever seen. He's also wearing a shirt that's made from some sort of holographic material, and his mustache and chin hair flow into his sideburns. It's a look, but I'm not so sure it's one that sells a lot of used cars.

"That car isn't automatic," he says by way of greeting. "That means it has a—"

"I drive stick, guy. What's wrong with it?"

As well as knowing about cars, I also know how to haggle, another well-learned skill from our dad and his devotion to swap meets. According to him, there's no reason to ever pay full price for something at the mall when the same thing, or something pretty close to it, is being practically given away at a swap meet.

"This one? Nothing! Totally reconditioned 1999 Volkswagen GTI, completely pristine inside and out. Leather seats, top-of-the-line sound system. Really clean. The guy who owned it before was fanatical about keeping it detailed. Just under seventeen thousand miles on it, so it's practically new."

"So the former owner was a music-loving serial killer who didn't get out much?" I'm feeling loose, maybe even a little hopeful about something for the first time in a long while.

"I can check." He looks flustered. Good.

"I'm not sure if I should ask to take it for a test drive or give it an exorcism." He stares at me, unsure of what to say. I nudge his arm. "Relax, guy, I'll take it for a drive. What's your name?

"Derrick. I'll go get the keys. Yeah?" He's no salesman—it's not just the outfit that gives it away.

"Nice to meet you, Derrick. And, yeah, go get the keys."

When he gets back, he takes my duffel bag, opens the hatchback after a little bit of struggle and stows it inside. We climb in, and before he can begin his spiel, I gun the motor.

"Ready, Derrick?"

It's like I never stopped driving, and I forget I'm four hundred miles from where I'm supposed to be. Right now, I'm happy to be with a stranger instead of someone who knows me but has no idea how to talk to me about why I've been sneaking out at night.

"Yeah, you sure can handle a stick," Derrick sighs. He clears his throat, embarrassed. "You wanna go on the freeway?"

"You think you can handle it?" I ask him amused at his expense. He gulps and nods. We hit the on-ramp to the 101 going a steady 65 miles per hour. "You want to give me your sales pitch?"

"Huh? Okay, yeah. I can get you a great deal. Just for you. My dad owns the lot. I'm only helping out until I work some stuff out. Then I'm doing my own thing."

"It's important to do your own thing," I agree with him as I make my way to the far left lane so I can pick up some more speed.

"Dang, girl. Yeah, uh, I . . ." Derrick remembers he's supposed to be a car salesman. "I can get you a good deal. No bullshit."

"That would be great, Derrick." I shrug, my eyes on the road in front of me. This car is a fun drive, but I'm prepared to walk away just as easily as I walked in.

"Car's listed for $7,600. That's already almost $3,000 under Blue Book. And it's been fully customized. Leather seats, sound system, and, uh, other stuff."

"About that other stuff. I can tell the back bumper has been replaced as well as the back windshield. The car's been in an accident, on the receiving end, so that's why the hatch-back is sticky. There's a slight pull to the right too. It's going to need some suspension work. Whoever owned it, loved this car enough to take it to a body shop, but love doesn't make car payments. Does it, Derrick? It's a repo, bought at auction. So three K under Blue Book or not—still a tidy profit for you but hardly a good deal for me. Wouldn't you agree?"

"Uh." He looks at me, defeated but enjoying how he lost.

"I'm not going to jerk you around. My offer is $4,700. Cash." I smile at him. "Do you think your dad would go for it?"

"If you can talk him into it, I'll personally top off the gas tank." Derrick wants someone to stand up to his dad and not only show him how it's done but that it's possible.

I exit the freeway and get back on, this time going toward where we came from. We're both quiet, enjoying ourselves for different reasons. I pull back into the lot, stopping just short of a polished Mercedes. The dad's, I bet. Derrick doesn't even bother to give me the after-test-drive spiel his father probably made him practice until blood came out of his ears.

"What's your dad's name?" I ask, watching as the wind makes Derrick's comically wide pants ripple around his normal-sized legs.

"Derrick." His soft mouth twists around the word.

"Of course it is." I smile at him, feeling as maternal as I believe I ever will. "Guess what, Derrick? Today you get to see your dad get owned. Trust me, both of you are really going to enjoy it."

# ◆ 17 ◆

# MARITZA

IT ONLY MAKES SENSE to have two gift registries for my wedding. The one for my guests is at Pottery Barn, and the other one, for Augustino's side, is at Target. My mother got all upset when I told her about it and I only had to because of the stupid rice cooker. She made a little comment that I was probably going to take the one that's in the kitchen "when the time came," so I commented right back that I was going to put one on my Target registry. Of course, she had to ask, "What Target registry?" I explained to her that as long as no one talks about what they give me, it's all going to be fine. But now she's all worried Auggie's side will think I'm treating them different.

They *are* different! And I'm doing them a favor by having a registry just for them. What my mother can't understand is I'm the one who's making all the sacrifices so his family doesn't have to realize how cheap they are.

Because of my mother's little comment that Augustino isn't involved in my wedding as much as he should be, I invited him to Target instead of coming on my own like I wanted to. I walk ahead of him, pushing the cart—he crowds me and has bumped my ankles one too many times to be trusted with it. I had to take the scanner gun away from him after he pointed it at my privates and yelled "Void!" right in front of the lady who was helping us set up my registry.

"How about this one?" Augustino holds up a yellow place mat. "It's what you're looking for, right?"

He doesn't get why I need place mats. He thinks they're dumb because his mother uses vinyl tablecloths. It doesn't matter what he thinks or what his mother does. Place mats are on my list, which should tell him everything he needs to know. The ones I picked out for myself are from Pottery Barn. White linen with embroidered edges and only for special occasions. The Target ones will be for everyday use or if his family ever comes over for dinner.

"No, not yellow. That will clash with the dining room walls." In my purse, I have my paint chips, but I can only pull them out when Augustino isn't looking. All this double work is giving me a headache. "It's the gray I want. Scan it, the gray, not that one . . . okay . . . and enter in six . . . no eight just to be safe."

"What walls?" he asks with a 'duh' expression on his face.

I look at him and have to see what I've been ignoring— his face is way more rounder than it was just a few weeks ago. He's put on weight. It's his mother's fault because she's always overfeeding him.

"Stand up straight, Auggie." I sound like her. I hate when this happens, and I hate it even more when he stands up straighter. "Let's get this done so we can go get something to eat. I don't care what, but not Olive Garden unless we just get salads. That's what we're having for dinner."

"Who the hell goes to Olive Garden for just a salad? I'm a man, Maritza. I want steak or a hamburger. Let's go to

In-N-Out." Augustino leans on the cart, and it rolls close to my foot. "Then we can . . . you know."

He wants sex. I've put him off for the last few weeks. My mistake. He usually keeps his undershirt on, but I would have noticed the extra weight a lot sooner. There's no way he's going to lose it before the wedding.

He has to fit into the tux that's already been rented. If he has to go up a size, his mother should be on the hook for the fee. But she won't pay it because she's cheap and she wants to ruin my wedding. No, he's going to have to get refitted for a bigger tux. His mother is not going to stop feeding him, and he's not going to stop eating whatever she puts in front of him.

"What do you think of this?" I pull the Pottery Barn catalog from my purse. I've marked the page with the sofa I want. It has a nice, curved back, low arms, and tufted seat cushions. I'm going to get it in the ivory tweed. "It's perfect, right?"

"Perfect for what? That's not the kind of couch you can kick back on to watch the game, and it's not leather." He pushes the catalog away like it's annoying him.

"It's a sofa, not a couch," I tell him, as I lock away all that I feel and don't feel about him in a small space inside of myself. "And not everything has to be leather."

"Lemme see it again." He looks at the page carefully this time and whistles through his teeth. "Forget it. Yeah, there's no way I'd ever spend $800 and change for a couch I'm just going to fart on? Pass."

"It's what a good, quality sofa costs. A real one that you have to order and not buy off a dusty warehouse floor."

I want to say something about his mother's plastic-covered Levitz furniture but hold it in. I don't want to be one of those couples who fight in public. It's so tacky. If I can make myself wait until we're back in the car, so should everyone else.

"Okay, boss." He salutes me. He knows I hate when he does that. "As long as you leave room in this imaginary house with imaginary paint colors where your imaginary *sofa* is going to be in front of my very real massive TV. My cousin Tacho is getting me his employee discount at Good Guys. It's his wedding gift, so no comments about him not bringing a present."

"He could at least give us a card, but whatever." I sigh and then take a deep breath. I can feel the air hissing around inside me, like it's made up of sharp needles. "He's your cousin, not mine."

"Don't be that way, Maritza. It's a really good deal. We're going to have a cherry TV for when we get our own place." Augustino jumps when his phone rings and shoves it at me. We both know who it is. "It's for you."

I move to the other side of the cart to get away from him and his phone. I've given his mother my number about a hundred times, but she always calls me on his when she knows we're together.

"Maritza, babe, don't be like that." Augustino says this like *I'm* the one who's to blame for his mother doing what she always does.

I grab the phone out of his hand. I don't want to talk to her, but I can check his call history before giving it back to him. I have his passcodes, all of them. He can't hide anything from me, but that doesn't mean he won't try to see what he can get away with. He thinks he's so sneaky. He is, but he's not smart. I can always tell when he's up to something. I've caught him before, but he's never caught me catching him because I'm way better at it than he'll ever be.

"Perla? Is everything okay?" I have to bite down on my back teeth to ask her without sounding annoyed.

There's always something wrong with Augustino's mother—it's her normal way of being. If I don't ask her if she's okay, she'll get her big-as-she-is feelings hurt, which just makes more work for me.

"Maritza, I have to ask you something."

She stops talking, breathing into the phone, waiting for me to ask her what she wants to ask me. I look at napkins, prepared to wait her out just like I do with Mamá. She coughs right into my ear. It's really loud and phlegmy, a smoker's cough. I want to scream at her to clear her stupid throat. It's so gross.

Augustino is pretending to be interested in red oven mitts. He puts one on each hand and snaps them at me like lobster claws. Oh, yeah, there's no way he's getting anything from me tonight. Not after that, embarrassing me in front of the registry lady and making me talk to his mother. I have my limits.

"What, Perla? Ask me what?"

"It's just I'm not so sure about this place for the dresses. My sister-in-law, she has a cousin who can get them custom-made. She can get us a good deal."

Her voice is high and whiny. I used to think it was funny that such a tiny voice could come out of such a big person. Now I just wish she would always keep her mouth stuffed with food so I never have to hear her talk again.

"There isn't enough time for that." I want to grab Auggie by the neck and strangle him. She's his mother. He should deal with her, not me. "Claudia's already made the appointment at David's Bridal."

"Oh, is Claudia going to be there?" She's only pretending like she didn't already know this. "Are you sure, Itza?"

"Why wouldn't Claudia be at the appointment?" I'm not biting down on my back teeth anymore. And I hate when she calls me Itza. She only does it to annoy me.

All of Augustino's family thinks Claudia is so special. They're always trying to kiss up to her to get on her good side. Of course, Claudia never notices the fuss she causes because she's so used to people falling over themselves and acting like stupid dummies in front of her. I don't know why. It's not like she's famous, and no one reads the credits on movies anyways. I never did before and there are lots of names on those movies, not just hers. Lots and lots of them.

"We were just wondering, Itza. Gabi and Dani haven't seen Claudia in such a long time," she whines and wheezes into my ear. "Not since Thanksgiving."

Perla never asks about Dooley. No one does. I hate them, all of them, for pretending like she's not my sister and like she doesn't exist. It makes me feel mad at Dooley too. I'm not sure why, but it does.

"And I was just thinking about the dresses," she says. "Maybe it would be better if—"

"Claudia just told me she's really impressed by the dresses at David's Bridal and she doesn't want to even think about going anywhere else." I don't have a problem with lying to Perla especially since she's practically forcing me to. "She already ordered hers *and* Dooley's."

"If Claudia already bought her dress then okay, Itza," she says.

Perla just wants to make sure my glamorous, successful, and sophisticated sister will be wearing the same dress as her daughters. Like some miracle will happen and everyone will be amazed at how much they all look like Claudia when it's obvious Gabi and Dani are basically made from pounds and pounds of raw tamale masa.

"Claudia is planning something special for us," I lie again. Then, because I don't really care, I lie some more. "She told me she can't wait to see all of you."

Monday, when I'm back at work, I'll add the sofa to my Pottery Barn registry. I saw that Chanel purse Claudia was hiding in her tote bag at my dress appointment. Those types of purses cost a lot, probably way more than my sofa. And those boring black Prada heels of hers? At least a couple hundred. Even more, I bet.

"Oh, okay then, Maritza." Perla breathes into the phone, waiting for me to say more, but I'm done talking. She's going to complain about this to Augustino, and then he's going to complain to me. "We'll see you at the appointment then. Unless you want to come for dinner? Tell Auggie I've made his favorite."

She doesn't even bother to tell me what she's making because she knows all of her food is her precious son's favorite. Just look at him!

I force my voice to sound anything but like what I feel about her invitation. "Oh, that's so sweet of you, Perla, but Auggie and I are going to Olive Garden. Okay? Bye-bye. See you soon. Bye-bye."

I point the scanner gun over the barcode of the oven mitt on Augustino's hand. The bright red light sucks it up into my registry and I don't feel anything, not even annoyed. I'll delete it later if I remember. Anyways, what kind of person would buy a single stupid red oven mitt as a wedding gift? Even I don't think anyone in Auggie's family is that cheap.

"What'd my mom want?" Augustino asks. Big liar. He knows exactly why she called.

"Just to say hi." I don't look at him because I might throw something right at his moon face. Instead, I scan a toaster oven, the best one, the Cuisinart. "I told her we'll be out late."

Augustino comes over to me and I let him kiss me. Maybe I'll give him what he wants. It's not smart to keep him hanging for too long. He gets stupid when he doesn't get sex.

He checks out the price and whistles under his breath. "I'd never pay that much for a toaster oven."

"That's the whole point of a gift registry, Auggie," I tell him in my sweetest voice. "It's so we don't have to pay and we still get what I want."

# • 18 •

# CLAUDIA

I PULL INTO THE driveway, stopping an inch or two away from Maritza's back bumper. Mom insists I not park on the street which means part of the ass end of my Audi is blocking the sidewalk. It's like she's telling the neighbors, most of whom I've known all my life, that they can't be trusted around my car. It might also be her way of telling me that my car doesn't belong here on Fickett Street and, by extension, neither do I. Whatever her reasons, she's turned this non-thing into something to worry about, because of course she has.

Still, I park where she wants me to so Mom can pretend there's one less potential catastrophe to agonize over, unlike the two very real ones she's only too happy to ignore— where the hell is Dooley, and why the hell is Maritza marrying a guy she doesn't even like? No, instead, let's focus on my damn car and what might happen if it's just a few extra feet away from the house.

I'll admit, though, she's not entirely wrong about how sketchy Fickett Street is.

Where I grew up has always had more than its share of cholos, dealers, and prostitutes causing a fucking ruckus on the quietest of days, but no one has the balls to jack a car on a Thursday afternoon. Not when there are plenty of neighbors looking out of their windows or hanging out on their porches keeping an eye on everyone else's business. And they all know Maritza has no problem with calling the cops. She's shut down more parties that went past 11:01 PM than she's ever been invited to.

I look over at the house and stick my tongue out at it. Nothing ever changes around here. It's always the same pointless bullshit because everyone is so—

"Stop it, you fucking, petty bitch! Just stop!" I say this a lot louder than I intended to and startle myself into embarrassment. "It's okay. You're okay. No, I'm not."

I haven't set foot inside the house and already it feels like too much to deal with. I don't want to be here, but Dad called me, and he hardly ever does. I couldn't tell him that I need a break from all of them for just a little longer. I certainly couldn't tell him I'd taken the day off from work to spend it having sex with an international movie star, or that I was bare-ass naked, as was the international movie star who was waiting for me in my bed.

No, those details I kept to myself.

Dad's well aware I'm being imposed upon, which means it took a lot for him to call me in the first place. This is why I'm here, to be further imposed upon. He needs me, Mom needs me, Maritza needs me. And Dooley? What does she need? What *doesn't* she need? Where is she?

I lean my head against the steering wheel and take some deep breaths and think about why it was so easy for Ethan to talk me into taking the day off, my first in months.

Since Ethan showed up at my office, I've been the topic of gossip. I can deal with stares and whispers, but what irks me to no end are the unnecessary drop-ins by colleagues asking if I want to grab a coffee, have a minute for a quick chat, and blah, blah, more pointless bullshit.

They act like we're friends, but there's a difference between being a friend and acting like one. The people who I work with can't tell the difference, but I can. This is why there are only a handful of people in my life I consider true friends and none of them are in the movie business.

Ethan's more than my friend, but I can't talk to him about my family and how they make me feel about myself. It wouldn't be fair, not when I'm making him work so hard at the other parts of our . . . whatever this is.

He wants to know if we're fine. It's a fair enough question to ask, but my answer would reveal I'm not sure if I'm fine, good, or even okay. What I do know is Ethan deserves more than what I'm giving him. And what do I deserve? To be happy? Successful? Am I not already both those things? There's no one I can talk to about what Ethan might mean to me because I've tried to keep him a secret. I've been keeping too many secrets lately, and time is running out on my sorry little con job.

I should find another therapist, but I'm so tired of talking, thinking, and feeling. It's twice as exhausting because of all the little games I'm playing with rules even I don't adhere to.

I should just tell the truth.

I had a chance to be honest with Ethan while getting dressed to come here. He asked me if I was okay. He could see I wasn't, but he was careful not to push for an answer. He reminded me so much of Dad at that moment, it filled me with the same kind of sad love I grew up with too much of. I kissed Ethan and let him hold me for a long moment before I rushed out, lying to him that I was late. I'm never late except when I am.

With my dress hiked up around my thighs, I stare down at my legs. They're smooth, long and toned. Mostly what I notice is the lack of hair. I've gladly suffered through the eradication of every strand of superfluous hair from my toes to between my eyebrows.

Next to working, exercising, and therapy, hair removal is also something of an obsessive pursuit of mine. Of all of them, it's never failed to provide me with near instant grat-ification. Hair removal has always done exactly what it promised to do. Whatever the method—first shaving, then waxing, and once I had money, electrolysis and lasers—I've always insisted on keeping a tidy triangle and full eyebrows. I'm a grown woman, a serious one. I earned my pubic hair and strong brows. The rest of it is gone and will stay gone. I'm conscientious about touch-ups and maintenance of all kinds when it comes to my skin, my body, my hair, my psy-che. I take good care of myself even if I'm not always kind to myself. Those two endeavors have never quite lined up for me.

Ethan is kind to me and when he looks at me, he sees . . . me. It's so unnerving.

I run my fingertips from my knees to my thighs and out toward my hips, leaving very slight red marks from my buffed and tastefully shaped nails. No color, not even a clear coat of polish, and they're barely long enough to go past my fingertips. I'll leave the French-tipped talons to Maritza and the chewed-up hangnails to Dooley.

I trace down and up again. This time on the inside of my thighs with the pads of my fingers, following the path Ethan's tongue took earlier today. He started at the arch of my foot, his long, lean body pressed up against the back of my leg as he held my foot up to his lips. The stubble on his chin tickled but I was panting too much to laugh. "You have no idea how much I love you, Claudia," he told me before he put his mouth on me. He made me come again and again before sending me off to fill the bathtub for us with a smack on my ass.

My thighs tingle with excitement even as my heart feels heavy in my chest. I want Ethan. All of him. Now. But he doesn't even know where I am and is trusting enough to not have to know.

"Claudia!"

Mom's voice causes me to yank my head up and my dress down simultaneously. The fabric will snap back into place, but I'm not too sure about my neck.

"Fuck you scared me."

I fumble for my purse to get my hands away from where they were heading. As I do, I realize there wasn't a verbal comma between the "fuck" and the "you." I just told Mom "Fuck you," and it wasn't just because she startled me.

"What are you doing there, Claudia?"

Mom is suspicious by nature. She's always expected trouble from Dooley and selfishness from Maritza, but something more sinister from me. I give her nothing to complain about, which means she can't trust me. I think she hates me for it and for turning myself into someone so different from who she thinks I should be. Sometimes I wonder if everything I've accomplished has been just to prove her wrong without having to tell her how wrong she's always been about me.

"I dropped my earring." A lie. To make it seem halfway true, I pretend to look for my non-missing earring. "I guess I didn't put it in right."

"Your father has a flashlight. I got it at Costco. And one for you and Maritza . . . and Dulcina." She's lying too. There's no way she got Dooley a flashlight—she doesn't think of my sister in that way. "Let me go get it."

"It's okay, I found it. See?"

I show her my ear and take her arm as we make our way up the walkway toward the house. I can feel her looking at the pair of diamond studs Ethan gave me while we were in the tub. I forgot to switch them out for the tiny gold hoops I usually wear. Lately, I've been forgetting a lot of things.

"How's Maritza?"

"Maritza is Maritza," she says. This is as close as she'll ever come to acknowledging my sister and her daughter is, indeed, being a huge Maritza. "You're too skinny."

"Thanks!"

I pull open the front door and step into the dim living room. My parents are forever letting light bulbs burn out. Except on the porch. From the moment I started dating in the seventh grade, Dad has kept a 200-watt bulb firmly screwed into the socket.

When she lived here, Dooley not only never came out as bi, but she also never brought any friends, much less "friends," to the house. Maritza didn't date, preferring fiction and fantasy over reality. The Beacon of Shame was meant only for me. I still remember Mom telling Dad to take the shade off the porch light so there wouldn't be any shadows for me to hide in. This made me laugh so hard, Dooley had to thump on my back to make sure I was breathing.

"Claudia is here!" Dad calls out over the noise of the TV and toward the general direction of Maritza's bedroom. "Your sister has gone super *loca*."

From his neatly pressed and always untucked button-down shirt, Dickie khakis and Nike Cortez sneakers, Dad is what my sisters and I call a wholo, a white cholo. Dad, unlike his brothers, was happy to assimilate as Boyle Heights became primarily Latino. He stayed put not only because he married Mom but because Boyle Heights will always be his home no matter how unhappy he is in the actual house he lives in.

"And hello to you too, Dad." I kiss him on the top of his head, aiming for the bald spot.

I walk through the kitchen, careful not to let my kitten heels—Prada, again—click on the floor so Mom can't complain about me scuffing the linoleum tiles. When I get to Maritza's closed door, I knock. I don't live here and always make sure to announce myself before I open any door.

"Who is it?" She's been crying.

"Oh, for fuck's sake, Maritza. Who the hell do you think it is?" I give Mom a pleading look, but she turns away from me and toward her stove. Since she wants me to deal with her daughter, she's going to pretend I didn't cuss right in front of the dried-out palm frond cross thumbtacked to the door. "I'm coming in. You better have your granny panties on."

I turn the knob, holding my breath. That three of us used to exist in such a small space for so many years never fails to amaze me. How we didn't murder one another has to be a miracle, especially since the whole family also had to share a single Jack-and-Jill bathroom.

The room seems even smaller now that Maritza has crammed in a Pottery Barn whitewashed bedroom suite. She loves that store. I got the email alert about the sofa she put on her registry. It's a very nice sofa, very Maritza, and it makes me wonder if she's forgotten the person she's marrying is in fact Augustino.

My sister is buried under a pile of blankets. There are magazines strewn around on the floor, and a well-thumbed romance novel by Barbara Cartland is on the nightstand. *In the Arms of Love* has been her favorite since junior high. It's the same book too, the one she stole from the library. The cover is held together with careful, overlapping strips of Scotch tape. I'll give her a new one for Christmas. If I can track down a signed copy, she'll like that even more.

"If you're trying to suffocate yourself, Maritza, there are easier ways to do it. Like with a plastic shopping bag. I'll get one from the kitchen and I'll make sure it goes on super tight, no gaps."

"Shut up, Claudia! Don't you have some party to go to? Or some shoes to buy?"

She wants to annoy me, and she sort of does. Good for her. Boring for me. I sit on the foot of her bed and Maritza kicks me, but it doesn't hurt since she's hiding under so many blankets.

"You're squashing my foot! Move!"

"You're going to have to get a bigger bed. Unless you want Auggie sleeping on top of you." My stomach turns over as that image flashes in my mind. "Or is he taking his bunk bed when he moves out? If his mom lets him, you know she's going to call top bunk. It's going to take both of you to hoist her up there every night."

"Shut up, Claudia." Maritza's face emerges from her blankets.

"Oh my God and Jesus as well! What happened to your face? Did you wash your makeup off with battery acid by mistake?"

I kick off my shoes, hike up my dress and straddle her, holding her in place and take her head between my hands. Maritza's skin is red, picked at, and peeling. I flick my hair out of my eyes and tighten my legs around her torso when she tries to wiggle free. I give her a squeeze with my thighs, and she grunts. If I squeeze a little harder, she'll fart. Dooley used to call it playing the Mexican bagpipes.

"I did an enzyme peel," Maritza sobs. "At the nail salon. I needed to relax!"

"It's because of this wedding," Mom says from the doorway in a vaguely bullying voice.

I'm sure there's more she wants to say, but she won't since it would mean actually saying something that needs to be said.

"Augustino's mother and sisters are trying to hijack my wedding!" Maritza starts to cry, but it's mostly wailing without the tears. She's too pissed off to cry, it must feel awful. "She says her precious daughters won't wear the dress I picked out. That the dresses are going to make them look like *gorditas*."

"They'll look like *gorditas* because they are *gorditas*. As for the dress, even I look fat in it, and Mom just accused me of being anorexic. Didn't you, Mom?"

"I said skinny, Claudia," she protests.

"Okay, skinny. I'm not anorexic, but I'm always willing to try if that's what it takes to win your approval." I reach over to the nightstand for a barrette to get my hair out of my face. "You picked out a pretty pink dress—"

"Blush! Not pink. Everyone looks good in blush," Maritza yells up at me. "Everyone!"

I get off of Maritza and scoot her over so I can lie down and stare up at the ceiling. My body and brain just want to sleep. But not here, not in this bed. I want to be in my own with Ethan.

"Yes, not pink. Blush. Sorry."

"Maybe there's a more slimming color?" Mom continues to stand in the doorway, slowly twisting a dish towel to death. She's been itching to say something about the dresses, and she's going to go for it now that I'm here to deal with the fallout. "A more grown-up color than pink, like . . ."

"It's my wedding! And it's not pink! It's blush!" Maritza squeezes some real tears out of her eyes. Her face is red, her skin irritated. Crying isn't making her any prettier.

"It's okay, Maritza," I say, feeling genuinely bad for her. She might be bringing all this grief onto herself, but it's still painful to see her so unhappy. "I have the appointment all taken care of, don't worry. It might even be a fun, bonding thing. That's what it's supposed to be, right?"

"I should just uninvite them, disinvite them, whatever, to be my bridesmaids. I never wanted them to be in my wedding anyways." Maritza reaches to pick at her face. I grab her hand and stop her. "I'm going to call them right now and tell them."

"You can't do that, Maritza." Mom's voice cracks with excitement and anxiety. This is exactly what she wants my sister to do. It's an empty threat on Maritza's part, but it's still the kind of drama they both feed on. "You can't! Tell her she can't, Claudia."

"It's your wedding, Maritza. You're the bride. No one will look more beautiful than you. It would be impossible."

It's always a safe bet to appeal to Maritza's vanity, but in this case it's true. Maritza can outshine anyone with her sheer determination to be the center of attention.

"*Órale, pues!*" Dad's voice booms from the living room where he's done waiting for the latest daughter-centered crisis to pass. "Where's my lunch? *Me muero de hambre!*"

All three of us freeze.

Dad doesn't drink like he used to, but sometimes he sounds like it. This hyperawareness for drunkenness is a muscle memory that is still very strong in me. It doesn't take much to be reminded of how it used to be around here when someone was drunk, and someone always was. Is still drunk. It's all the same but different.

*It's all the same but different.*

I close my eyes around the echo of that thought as my heart continues to beat frantically in my chest. For a moment, it feels as if I'll never get away from this sameness. Logically, I know I already have, but it doesn't feel that way. One of these days, those two things, the knowing and that feeling, will also line up for me and I'll be able to believe it is different. But not today. It's not ever today when it comes to my family.

I open my eyes. Maritza and Mom are staring at my earrings.

"Well, shit, ladies, party's over. Get out of bed, Maritza. We're going to see my aesthetician and hope she can save what's left of your face."

I climb over Maritza and stand up, ready to get on with the work of being who they expect and need me to be while very aware that Ethan has given me more than just jewelry, art, and sex.

$$\bullet \quad 19 \quad \bullet$$

# DULCINA

I'M GOING TO TAKE Highway 1 until I have to decide whether I'm going to cut across to Bakersfield on my way to Los Angeles. This is what I'm thinking about when I realize I'm in Big Sur. There are only trees on either side of me, big ones, bigger than I've ever seen in my life.

Big Sur is beautiful. It's also so quiet and so devoid of the normal sounds I've been surrounded by for all my life, it makes my ears hurt. And there are so many trees, too many. All I can think about is what might be hiding behind them. I keep the doors locked and my window rolled almost all the up to keep what might be out there from getting into my car.

I speed up, keeping an eye on the gas gauge. It's already in the red and only getting redder. After a few miles of white-knuckle driving, I almost burst into tears when I see a Chevron sign. I pull in by the pumps, reach into my pocket and come up with $28.

Trying to remember what types of wildlife are in this part of California, I look around.

All I can see are those trees and the thirty feet or so that separate me from the painfully charming general store. I step out of my car and take in a deep breath. And then another, followed by a third just to make sure. The air is clean and fresh, but heavy with whatever it is those trees have seen through the years.

"Beautiful, ain't it? No other place like this on earth."

A stocky, bearded man in a tie-dye T-shirt, paint-splattered jeans, and suspiciously new sneakers leans against an ancient VW camper van.

"Sure. I guess it's beautiful," I tell him, careful not to make prolonged eye contact. I'm not interested in his pot-head philosophizing, I just want to buy enough gas to get me out of here before it gets dark. "If you're into this kind of thing."

"And you're not? Take a look around you! If there is a God, God is here." He picks at his nails before shoving his hands into his front pockets. He's not a mellow hippie, he's twitchy and those sneakers are too big for him. "You staying overnight? There's a place, down a ways, not too far. Clean rooms at a good rate. I can show—"

"No thanks." I double-check to make sure my car doors are locked and head toward the store. "Just passing through."

"That's too bad. Can't really take it all in from a speeding car."

"I suppose not, but it's also kind of the point," I reply, shifting into bartender mode to better manage my way out of this interaction.

"For some people it is. You looking to score?" he asks pushing himself away from the van to follow me inside. "I got primo Humboldt Kush."

Of everything I did, pot was my least favorite. It made me feel slow and dumb but not dumb enough to slow down my brain so I could forget why I was taking drugs in the first place. Primo or not, I'm not interested in his pot, conversation or company.

"No thanks. I'm good."

I speed up, using my longer stride to my advantage. When I reach the door first, an old screen one with a tight hinge, I don't bother to look back, much less hold it open to make sure it doesn't slam closed on him.

"Hey, Ruth. How's life?" The hippie guy sits at the counter and watches as I grab a Snickers, bag of Doritos, and a bottle of water.

"You know, same old, same old. You bothering this gal, Sean?" She winks at me. "Is Sean here bothering you, honey?"

She looks like a hippie too, in her long skirt, faded men's work shirt, and head full of graying dreads. I can't help but scratch my head, wondering how long it would take for the braids in my hair to get matted like hers. I don't plan to find out, but it still makes my scalp itch.

"Yes, he's bothering me," I answer her, seeing no need to lie to spare either of them the truth. They both laugh. I don't. "He really is."

"Hey, me and my old lady are having a cookout just down the road. You're more than welcome to join us," Sean says.

It takes me a second to realize he's talking to me.

"I have somewhere to be. Thanks, though." I give him a quick, thin smile and set my stuff on the counter and hand Ruth all my cash. "I'll take this and however much gas I can get for the rest of it. Thanks."

Sean keeps talking as she rings up my stuff. I thank her again and hurry out only to stop short when I see my car has been broken into. I rush back to the store and yank the screen door open. Sean is nowhere to be seen.

Ruth looks up, surprised. "You forget something, honey?"

"Yeah. No. It's . . ."

My heart beats like a drum in my chest. I run back outside to my car. My duffel bag is gone. I glance into the

front seat and see the cell phone I got in Daly City has also
been stolen.

"Damnit!"

"It was Sean," says Ruth from where she's half inside
and outside her store. "I know who to call, honey."

I start to follow her but only make it a few steps before
I stagger away to throw up on the trunk of one of those
glorious trees. As soon as I'm done barfing, I'm crying. Hot,
angry, ugly crying. I can't catch my breath, and it feels like
my belly and chest are going to collapse into each other.

Ruth comes out, a cordless phone pressed to her ear.
She hands me a can of ginger ale, some paper towels and
pats my back as she speaks with whoever is on the other end
of the call.

"Deputy Keegan will be right over, honey. You want to
come and sit inside?" she asks after she hangs up.

I shake my head, feeling the weight of all those braids
Velma spent so much time plaiting. Ruth keeps patting my
back, and I don't want her to stop.

"Sean's not a bad guy, stupid as a dried turd, but not a
bad guy. Oh, honey, I'm so sorry this happened to you."

We both look up as a sheriff patrol car pulls in, lights
on, no siren. I force myself to stop crying and tamp all those
feelings down, but just barely.

"It's all going to be set to rights now, honey, don't you
worry." Ruth puts an arm around my shoulder, leads me
toward my car, and gently encourages me to sit on the
hood. "Hey, Keegan. It was Sean and his girlfriend. They're
camped out not too far from here in their usual spot."

The deputy has on a pair of mirrored sunglasses I
thought cops only wore in movies. Despite the uniform,
mustache, and ramrod straight posture, he sort of reminds
me of turdy Sean. I want to laugh at him and cry for
myself.

"Is she okay to talk?" he asks Ruth, who moves off to the other side of my car. "What's her name?"

"She is, and her name is Dulcina Bernal." Standing up, I answer for myself. Anger wells up inside of me, pushing aside what was left of those other feelings. "He, this Sean, came into the store and she, whoever this girlfriend of his is, jimmied my door open, popped the trunk, and took my duffel bag, my money, and my cell phone while I was inside."

"You should never leave your mobile phone in your car. It's safer for a woman to always have it with her." He pulls out a small notepad and jots down notes. "How much cash?"

"Exactly $4,317."

I know how many of each bill I have. Or had. I don't want to explain myself to him, but I know I'm going to have to. Ruth steps back into the store to help a customer. We both follow her with our eyes, each of us wanting her to stay for different reasons.

"You always carry around so much cash?" he asks. "Why?"

"I don't trust banks. That's not illegal unlike what just happened to me." I sit back down on the hood of my car, this time with my head in my hands. "It's all the money I have. All of it. And I need my phone back—it's not safe for a woman around here without one. Obviously."

Deputy Keegan tucks his notepad into his pocket and reaches for the flashlight on his belt. He shines it around the back seat of my car. There's nothing there, not a single fast-food or candy wrapper, sweater, nothing. It was empty before and even emptier now.

"Where is it you said you're heading again?" he asks as he takes a close look at the window where it was jimmied open.

I reach for a cigarette before realizing there aren't any to reach for. Even if I wanted to take up smoking again, I don't have the money to buy a pack or replace the nicotine gum Sean and his girlfriend stole from me along with everything else.

"I didn't say where, but if you're asking, I'm going to Boy . . . Los Angeles."

"What was in the duffel bag?" he asks.

"Tampons, an Uzi, and a pair of tap shoes. What do you think? Are you going to, I don't know, get on your radio and issue an APB or whatever it's called?" I'm annoyed he's interrogating me instead of tracking down skuzzy Sean and his old lady. I need my money and want my monogrammed washcloth back. "He invited me to a barbecue. I just might take him up on it and kick the crap out of him for robbing me."

"Okay now, Miss Bernal, it's all supposition at this point. Unless you have a witness—"

"Are you for real? Listen, this is the way I *suppose* it all went down, sheriff, deputy, sir, officer deputy, whatever. Sean hangs around here all day looking for people just passing through, distracts them with his happy hippie talk about the trees and the beautifulness of God while his accomplice-slash-old lady hides in the van he's parked between the victim's car—that would be me—and the front store window. As soon as the person passing through—that person still being me—steps inside, his old lady girlfriend breaks into my car, robs me, jumps back in the van, and pulls it around the back. Then, they both take off to barbecue themselves a feast of soy hot dogs and racoons."

"Sounds like you have some experience with this kind of thing," he says as he jots down more notes.

"Yeah, I'm a self-confessed reformed hippie criminal. I used to be all about peace, love, and larceny," I snap at him.

From just behind the screen door, Ruth laughs as she pushes through it. "She's got you there, Keegan."

"Hey, now, Ruth, not helpful," he says. He's the kind of person who, when embarrassed, flushes. And he's flushing now. It starts from somewhere below his neck of his shirt and creeps up to his face like an iodine thermometer.

"It was Sean. We all know it," Ruth says. "I know he's your brother and all and is generally harmless, but some people just don't outgrow stupid."

"I knew it!" I shout up to the trees. "He doesn't get a pass because he's your brother. If anything, it should make it twice as easy to track him down. Call your mom! I bet she knows where he is."

"Hey, now, that's neither here nor there, Miss. Bernal." His face is beet red.

I hop down from the hood, ready to get the hell away from here, but I can't without any money. I'm not going to call Claudia. She's bailed me out way too many times for this to be a funny little story we can chuckle over when we're both old ladies. This might genuinely be the first mess I'm in that isn't entirely my fault, but I can't expect her to fix it for me. I'm also more than a little bit embarrassed at having been rolled by a hippie.

"I want my stuff back." I'm angry and there's nothing I can do about it except be angry. "All of it."

"If you come down to the station, Miss Bernal, you can file a report first thing in the morning. In the meantime, I can offer you a lodging voucher while this gets sorted out."

"Already called over to the inn, Keegan." Ruth pats my arm and hands me the paper bag with what I bought while I was getting robbed. "Here you go, honey. It's just about half a mile down a ways, on the left. Doris will take care of you. She's good people."

He holds out his card, then snaps his notepad shut with the other hand. I grab it, get into my car, and tear out of the parking lot, leaving his patrol car in a cloud of dust and gravel. I stop in the middle of the road, reverse, and pull back into the gas station in one, smooth motion. Ruth has filled my gas tank and inside the bag along with the chips, water, and candy bar, she slipped in $40 along with my $28.

Deputy Keegan watches, silent and still red in the face, as I stomp past him to where Ruth is standing on the steps of her store.

"Damn, honey, you can drive," she says.

"Thank you." I reach up and hug her, allowing myself to let go of some of my anger as she hugs me back. "Thank you for being such a good person."

# ◆ 20 ◆

# CLAUDIA

IT'S TAKEN ALMOST FORTY-FIVE minutes to drive the ten miles or so to Burbank from my acupuncturist's office in Koreatown. Despite traffic, I'm not going to be late, but right on time. I switch off the radio and roll down my window so I can clear my head. There isn't much of a breeze, of course, and since I'm surrounded on all sides by cars and one city bus, the air is decidedly unrefreshing on Empire Avenue. I can see the sign for David's Bridal just up ahead. Almost there, but not quite.

If this doesn't sum up what life in L.A. is like, I'm not sure what does.

There's no point complaining about the traffic—there's always traffic, always—but at least I was able to talk Maritza into this location instead of her preferred one in Torrance. It's one thing for her to impose on me and Mom, but she can't expect Auggie's mother and sisters to indulge her geographic whims.

Getting them to agree to meet us here plumbed only the shallowest depths of my considerable well of false flattery, but it was still work. I don't blame them for being the way they are or behaving the way they do. Augustino, his sisters, and their mother have never pretended to be anything but who and how they are. What I do question is Maritza's

THE NEAPOLITAN SISTERS     169

decision to marry him and into his family. Trussing herself
up in a white dress isn't going to change anything, especially not them . . . or her.

Why doesn't she understand this? Why don't I accept
that she can't understand this?

I've always wondered how it's possible for two people
who are essentially identical—genetically, at least—to view
and experience reality in such diametrically opposite ways.
How is it that we can both be right and wrong at the same
time?

In the end, it comes down to what I realized years ago
but still haven't fully accepted—I've had way too much
therapy and no one in my family will ever have enough.
Not even Dooley, and I paid some hefty bills for her to . . .
what? Get better? Be less like herself and more like me? Is
this what I want for my sisters? For my parents? For them
to be like me? I don't like myself most of the time so why
would I want the same for them?

Whatever. Asking these questions when they'll never
have an answer is purely self-indulgent. I should keep my
focus on what needs to get done.

This wedding is going to happen. While I may not
agree with her decision to marry Auggie, I respect it's her
decision to make. No, I don't respect it, but I'm trying
my hardest to accept whatever she decides to do. If she
were to choose to walk away from this farce, I'd applaud
her. I'd even buy her a set of matching armchairs for the
Pottery Barn sofa she had the balls to put on her registry.

But she's not walking away—she's digging in. It's
that jar of maraschino cherries all over again. Maritza is
still Maritza, and for me to want her to do anything other
than be herself is unfair. Just as it's unfair of her to criticize
Auggie and his family for being who they are. She doesn't
see it this way because she can't, not because she won't.

There's such a difference between the two, and it's taken me forever to wrap my mind around this concept.

This, all of it, is just therapy talk. It makes sense in a session, or here in the safety of my car, but not in real life. I'm not Maritza, Maritza isn't me, neither of us is Dulcina but we're sisters. Everything else is bullshit.

I pull into the parking lot, circling around long enough to find a spot for a whole new layer of stress to take up residence in my neck and shoulders. Earlier, my acupuncturist, Dr. Zheng, commented my chi was "very blocked." I'd almost answered back with a "no shit, Dr. Z" before remembering she was in the process of poking a dozen tiny needles into my back.

My cell phone rings, sounding more shrill than usual. It must be Maritza. I answer, holding it away from my ear. "Yeah?"

"Where are you? I'm going to kill her. I swear it. You know what she just said? Do you!" Maritza's voice hisses into the side of my face. "She said it's my fault my wedding won't be at the church . . . because of . . . me and my past. Claudia, I swear—"

"Maritza, it's okay. I'll deal with her. Just take a deep breath and don't . . . just don't."

I get out of my car and immediately feel dizzy. I lean against the open door, waiting for it to pass. Dr. Zheng must be right about my chi being very blocked. I'm also hungry and thirsty, which I'd forgotten about as I tried not to stress myself out over how long it was taking to drive ten miles.

"Get in here! Claudia . . ." her voice goes low, coming somewhere deep inside of her so she sounds like a pissed off alley cat, ". . . I'm going to kill her. I am."

Dooley and I found out the hard way to never take Maritza on in a fight. Neighborhood kids stupid enough to rile her up soon learned why we would step aside when she'd go into what Dooley called "wild dog" mode. It wasn't just that she fought dirty, all three of us did. The difference was Maritza didn't fight to win, she attacked to maim.

Whoever had set her off would soon find themself on the receiving end of the most vicious ass-whipping ever delivered by a bucktoothed, knobby-kneed girl who had "victim" written all over her. We'd pull her off the kid—and it usually took the both of us—after we figured they'd had enough and would then drag her back to the house. In the kitchen, Mom would force a tablespoon of sugar into her mouth and wipe her sweaty and snotty face with a wet dish towel as she held Maritza's head over the sink.

"What happened?" Mom would ask over the sounds of Maritza hyperventilating.

"Just some kid," we'd always answer with a shrug.

There were a lot of kids. Mom plastered her cuts and bruises with a mixture of sugar and Farmer John lard so regularly, Maritza spent much of her girlhood grainy, greasy and wired on pure cane C&H. Word got around that she was someone to be avoided. This warning followed her from First Street Elementary all the way to Roosevelt High. Growing up, Maritza never had many friends. Her dirty fighter reputation was part of it, but there were—are—other reasons why she's always had a hard time with people her own age, especially women.

I turn away from my car as memories give way to familiar anxieties. Maritza hasn't outgrown her tendency to go wild dog on anyone, so if she says she's going to kill her future mother-in-law, I believe her.

"Put Mom on the phone." There's no reason for me to talk to her, but I need to distract my sister by asking her to do something besides seethe. There's a rustling sound as her phone exchanges hands. "Mom?"

"Claudia, please, hurry!" Mom sounds stressed, but there's something else in her tone of voice that makes my skin prickle. "She's going to give herself a stroke!"

"I'm here, in the parking lot. I'll take care of everything."

With a tote bag full of distractions digging into my shoulder, I weave my way through parked cars taking the risk of getting clipped by a distracted driver.

Part of me hopes Maritza will calm down, at least a little bit, before I have to face not only her, but everyone else as well. The other part of me, the part which knows better, tells me I should have stopped for something to eat. Realistically, there's not much more I can do for anyone other than what I can do for myself.

Thank you, therapy speak, and go fuck yourself.

There might come a time when I can put what I've learned into practice, but not right now when it's obvious it should have occurred to me to pack some lard and table sugar along with the couple of bottles of Moët, plastic champagne flutes, and bride-to-be sash in my tote bag.

I walk into David's Bridal like I own the place and find the unhappy homicidal family-to-be squaring off outside a dressing room. I dump my purse—not the Chanel—and tote bag on a chair and put my arm around Augustino's mother, guiding her away from a red-faced Maritza.

"Perla, how are you? Dani, Gabi! It's been too long since I've seen you. Totally my fault. But it's what happens when you let your job take over your life, right?" As I'm talking, I deposit Perla's considerable bulk onto the chair farthest from my sister and pivot around to exchange quick air kisses with Gabi and Dani, who've followed like ducklings. "We have to get a drink and catch up after this. Margaritas, lots of them! Maritza's treat, of course."

I stand between them and my sister, beaming like a game show model who's stroking a jet ski. They stare at me, seeing exactly who they think I am, who I'm pretending to be for all of our sakes. I keep talking, not giving anyone a chance to regain their bearings.

"This is going to be so much fun. Isn't it? So much fun! It already is too much fun. Maritza, I have a surprise for you!"

Quickly, I greet Mom while reaching into my tote bag for the Swarovski headband I bought at Neiman Marcus while my aesthetician worked her magic on Maritza's face. The headband is close enough to a tiara, I'm hoping Maritza will wear it instead of an actual crown. I place it on her head, fussing over her hair, making sure to keep my body between my sister and Auggie's mother. Despite how angry she is, Maritza's eyes flicker over to one of the many mirrors to check herself out.

"You look beautiful, Maritza. Doesn't she?" I address this to Augustino's mother, hoping she'll play nice.

Perla shrugs her ham hock–like shoulders, her mouth pursed tight. Knowing I won't get any more out her, I focus on the next part of my plan—getting all of them just tipsy enough to take the edge off. I grab the flutes and one of the two bottles of Moët along with the sash.

"Why don't we get started?"

I pour all of us some champagne, drape the sash on Maritza, and then perch myself on the chair closest to Perla. Everyone sits down, Maritza next to me, Mom at the end, Gabi and Dani on the other side of their mother. Yup, pretty much how it's going to be for as long as my family and Auggie's are forced to be around each other.

The salesgirl whose gotten stuck with us holds up Dani's and Gabi's choices. I made it abundantly clear to the three of them that this appointment was for fitting the dress Maritza has already picked out. Instead, they want to try on a long A-line dress with a surprisingly deep V-neck and a knee-length strapless sheath, both in what David's Bridal calls "chocolate" but really is just a rich shade of brown. Like the color of the dresses, what they're trying to pull is pure bullshit.

"I like the long one." Dani leans forward to bat her eyes at me. "Do you like the color, Claudia?"

"You copied me," Gabi says. She, like her sister, looks like Augustino but with bigger tits, which either dress will emphasize to comedic proportions. "I picked that color first."

"Great color, great styles, but . . . ." I nod thoughtfully with enough doubt in my voice to make it seem sincere, ". . . it might be too dark for an afternoon wedding. What do you think, Gabi?"

"I like the second one. The top is sexy." Predictably, Gabi goes for crass over style. "Long skirts make me look short."

Maritza snorts. I put my hand on her knee and squeeze it but don't turn away from the three women on my left. "What do you think, Perla?"

"What do you think, Claudia?" she asks me right back, ignoring Maritza.

"The strapless dress is fun," I quickly answer for both of us. Maritza is stone-faced and silent, willing to see how this plays out. I'm just thankful she hasn't stormed out or punched anyone. Yet. "But since we're going to be outside, a long skirt in that material would be too heavy. And the short dress is so cute, but how often do girls like us get a chance to wear a long dress? Why don't we look at something else?"

I nod to our attendant, and she shows us the dress I've already purchased for myself and Dooley. Long, chiffon, one shoulder, in not pink but blush. A true bridesmaid dress and what Maritza wants, and, as far as I'm concerned, it's what she's going to get.

"This dress is feminine but a bit sexy. Perfect for a garden ceremony." I almost stand to hold it up to myself but think better of it. I requested they only pull sizes which will fit Gabi and Dani. "Maritza is going to regret putting her bridesmaids in such a pretty dress."

"We should try it on!" Gabi stands up and starts pulling off her clothes.

I make small talk as they change, taking pretend sips of champagne, while telling Perla a slightly enhanced story about the time I had dinner with Jennifer Lopez's manager, who let slip she was dating Ben Affleck and then swore me to secrecy. I wind it up with an observation about how the blush color Maritza picked reminds me of Jennifer Lopez's massive engagement ring.

I sneak a look down at my bare wrist. I gave Ethan back his watch yesterday. Or was it Wednesday? I'm running on fumes here. I stand to one side of the dressing room, wanting nothing more than to lean against the partition between them and just sink down onto the floor.

"How are you girls doing in there?" I ask through my best game show model smile.

Gabi and Dani emerge from the dressing room. They look like gorditas, yes, but they also look happy wearing the dress Maritza has set her hard heart on. This is what matters, and it's also all I can do for my pissed off sister right now.

"You look so beautiful, girls." Mom sounds like she's lying because she is. "Don't they, Maritza?"

Maritza, wearing her almost-tiara and bride-to-be sash, keeps her mouth shut and glares at the wall opposite her. Not ideal, but I can work with it. I snake an arm around Gabi's tomato-shaped torso.

"Neither of you will be single for long in a dress like this."

"I love it!" Dani squeezes in closer to me wanting some attention. "Say you love it, *Mami!*"

"My cousin, her friend has a shop . . ." Augustino's mother trails off. She's not going to raise much of a fuss, but she can't help herself from at least putting on the appearance of one.

"Perla, you know there isn't time. This is the perfect dress. If you don't say yes, I'll never speak to you again." I laugh but I give her a long, hard look. She blinks, then nods. I turn back to Gabi and Dani, eyeballing Maritza in the mirror to make sure she doesn't ruin my hard work by gloating. "It's the perfect dress and it's going to be a perfect wedding. I just can't wait. Really, I can't wait for it all to just . . . happen."

# ◆ 21 ◆

# MARITZA

I MAKE SURE CLAUDIA has followed me out to the parking lot and slow down so she can catch up to me. I don't want to have to get in my car like I'm going to drive away because then I might have to.

I see my reflection in the window of the SUV parked next to me. My skin is much better than it was on Thursday, but I saw what the appointment with Claudia's skin lady cost. I would never pay that much money for some creams and whatever else she put on my face and neck. Next time I want a facial, I'll go to the Korean day spa in Fullerton Mrs. Kim takes me to for my birthday. It's not super fancy, not like what Claudia is used to, but it's very reasonably priced and the hot corn tea is free.

"Maritza! Hold up!" Claudia grabs hold of my purse strap and yanks it off my shoulder. "For fuck's sake, Maritza, stop! How the hell can you walk so fast in those shoes?"

She's out of breath and sweating. My mother is right, she does look too skinny. But this isn't about her, it's about me, the bride, and how Augustino's family is trying to ruin my wedding.

"You know what she told me? You know what she said to my face?" I start crying. "She's a fat cow."

"What did she say?" Claudia puts her arms around me, and we lean against my car. I can feel her shaking so I hold her around her waist. "Besides 'moo,' bitch. And by 'moo' I mean her. The 'bitch' is for the both of you."

"Shut up, Claudia. This isn't funny. She told me Augustino is so happy we're going to live with her in her house." I wipe my face with my hands, smearing my makeup. "She said she has it all worked out so I can do *my* laundry Friday nights and *our* sheets and towels on Saturday night so none of it will get mixed up with the family's!"

"They have a washer and dryer? I always imagined the three of them around a big cauldron of water over a fire, stirring their dirties with a big stick. Not Auggie's stick, which I hope for your sake is at least not small. Fess up, Maritza. Baby carrot or *pepino*?"

"This isn't a joke, Claudia. This is really serious." It's too hot out here. I shouldn't have had any champagne, and I should have used the bathroom before I left. "What am I going to do?"

"What do you mean—what are you going to do? You're going to get married," she says as if it's obvious. She digs through my purse and holds up a pack of matcha wafers and waits for me to nod before she opens them. "I was wondering where you and Auggie are going to live."

"I bought a house." I need to blow my nose but settle for wiping it with the back of my hand. "In Bellflower."

"You what! Jesus, Maritza!" She's so surprised, the cookie she was biting into falls out of her mouth. I laugh at her. Claudia hugs me, smiling. I'm glad at least she's happy because I'm not. "Auggie must be so excited. Now he can make all the noise he wants when he bones you. I always pegged him for a squealer. Wow, Maritza! You guys bought a house. Congrats, really."

"Auggie doesn't know about it yet." I'm still mad but not as mad. Plus, it's distracting how fast Claudia is eating those cookies, like she's starving. I open the trunk of my car and hand her a can of Vinut tamarind juice. It's warm but I don't think she'll mind because it's tart and she's never liked sweet stuff. "I'm going to tell him after my wedding. I want it to be a nice surprise."

"Maritza . . ." Claudia holds her hand out like she's trying to stop invisible traffic. I notice she's carrying another purse, not the Chanel. I don't recognize it, and I can't see any sort of logo on it. It must be really expensive. "Oh, bunny, how can I put this? A blow job first thing in the morning is a nice surprise and a house is a *house!*"

"Tell me what to do, Claudia." I start crying again. I don't care if people are looking at me as they walk to and from their stupid cars. "Tell me I'm doing the right thing."

"Come on, Maritza, you've already decided what you're going do. Right, wrong or somewhere in the between, you already know." She puts our purses and her snacks on the roof of my car and hugs me again. She rubs my back and kisses my cheek before she takes me by the shoulders and looks me in the face. "But I'm pretty sure Auggie's mom doesn't give nearly as good head as you do. He'll choose you. I'm almost positive he will."

"Claudia! You're so gross." I want to laugh, but I can't. "Don't tell anyone about the house. Okay? Please?"

"I know how to keep my trap shut, trust me. Come back inside, Maritza. They're hemming the dresses right now. You have to be there to supervise to make sure Gabi doesn't ask for it to be raised up to her *chocha.*" Claudia wets her finger with the tip of her tongue and tries to rub my runny mascara off my cheeks. "Everything will be fine. And you don't have to take us out for drinks. I wouldn't do that to you . . . or them."

"You promise?" I ask her. Claudia always keeps her promises. "You super promise?"

She puts her arm around my shoulder. She's still sweating but instead of looking flushed, she's pale. Maybe she *is* anorexic. Claudia always had a thing with food and her weight.

"I super promise, Maritza."

"Then okay, I guess." I let her lead me back into the store. If they've started pinning the dresses, it's too late for Auggie's mom to back out now. "Just keep them away from me."

"I'll do my best," she says.

I believe her. Claudia only accepts the best and has always gotten what she wants. This time, though, it's going to be for me, so I'm fine with it.

# · 22 ·

# DULCINA

WRAPPED IN A THIN, scratchy towel, my skin pruned up and the room filled with steam from the longest shower I've ever taken, I kneel on the edge of the bed and take stock of my recently returned possessions. They consist of my mostly empty duffel bag, a Patricia Cornwell paperback I found in the nightstand, $59 after buying snacks and a toothbrush and toothpaste last night from the vending machine, and my car with a full tank of gas.

Hippie Sean and his girlfriend dumped my bag at their campsite and took off with my money, phone, most of my clothes, including all of my bras and underwear, and even my monogrammed hand towel.

Deputy Keegan personally told me the bad news and gave me another hotel voucher along with $100 out of his own pocket. He was embarrassed but also hurt—a look I've seen plenty of times. He offered to drive me to Monterey so I could file an official report and seemed relieved when I told him I wouldn't be pressing charges. I also declined his money, which I now realize was dumb of me. He thanked me for my cooperation, wished me luck, and promised he would be in touch, but we both know I'm not going to get my money back. I can't even prove I had it in the first place.

I pick up the motel phone and dial Claudia's home number. It's only one of two I know by heart, and there's no help for me on the other end of the second one.

"Hello?" It's a man who answers.

"Yeah, hello? I'm trying to reach Claudia. I don't say her full name in case it's some random pervert I've called instead of her townhouse. "I might have misdialed."

"You didn't but she's not here. Is this her assistant? Sorry, I forgot your name."

"No, I'm Dulcina, her sister. Who are you?" I ask him.

"I'm your sister's boyfriend." There is a hitch in his voice.

"You don't sound too sure about it, guy." I let out a bark of laughter at hearing what I just said. "Sorry, man."

"It's fine, I get it. Your sister is . . . complicated." His voice sounds vaguely familiar.

Claudia has always been closed off about her personal life. Also, I was wasted for most of my life, so she could have told me she was going to marry Walt Disney's thawed out corpse and it wouldn't have registered.

"Glad to hear you've figured that out about her. So, yeah, if you could tell her I'm—"

"Oh, wait, you're Dooley! She'll want to talk to you. Hold on, I'll give you the number to her mobile."

"Nah, it's okay. Just let her know I'm on my way and I'll get there when I get there, but I'll be there in time." I pick at the loose threads on the polyester coverlet. "She'll know what I'm talking about."

"Hey, you okay?" he asks. "It's none of my business, but are you?"

"Well . . ." I have nothing to lose by being honest. If this guy really is my sister's boyfriend, he'll find out about me sooner or later. "Yes and no."

"Tell me about it," he says, sincerely sincere. Oh, man, he must be confusing the hell out of Claudia.

"I'll make it short. Ready? I just walked away from my life in San Francisco, and managed to get myself robbed in Big Sur. Now I'm stuck in some motel while a deputy sheriff tries to track down the guy who did it who also happens to be his brother. I think they're twins."

"That's messed up. Especially the twin part."

"It is, right? But whatever. Now you know what's up with me, but I don't know your name. I'm sure you don't go by Claudia's Boyfriend. Or do you?"

"It's Ethan," he says. It's enough for me to figure out who he is. Hey, even alcoholics go to the movies sometimes. "Can I ask you something?"

"Sure, but I can't promise you'll like the answer, especially if you want the truth." I settle back on the bed, covering my legs with my one remaining sweatshirt, and wrap the Nirvana T-shirt around my neck like a scarf.

"What is up with your sister?" he asks.

"Which one? There are three of us sisters and something is always up with one of us," I admit to him, hiding the truth behind a joke. He laughs but he's just being polite. "Okay, Ethan, I don't know you, but if my sister is leaving you alone at her place, she must trust you—"

"That's the problem, Dooley. I don't think she does, and it's killing me." There's another, deeper hitch in his voice.

I'm all for men crying, everyone should cry when they need to, but I don't know anything about him other than what I've seen from his movies and read in *Us* and *People* magazines. I wait for him to say something else, but all I can hear is his quiet, stuttered breathing.

"You okay, Ethan?" I ask after a few moments.

"I love her. I'm in love with her, and I'm afraid I'm going to lose her because she won't let me love her." Worry and sadness weigh down his words.

"Okay, man. I know what's going on and it is complicated," I tell him. "Once I get to L.A., we're going to talk."

I'm not going to let Claudia use us, especially me, as
an excuse not to be happy because it's what she's always
done and felt she had to do so we wouldn't feel bad about
ourselves. Yeah, those days are done, at least as far as I'm
concerned.

"Let me float you some cash," he offers without
hesitation.

I want to hang up on him, but I don't. Claudia needs
me, and Maritza wants me there for her wedding. For the
first time in a long time, if not ever, I hope I can be the
sister they've always deserved. To be able to do that, I have
to get myself from here to where they are and pride doesn't
gas up a car.

"Dooley? You there?"

He's probably wondering if he's offended me. Maybe
he has, but it's coming from a good place. This much I'm
already sure of when it comes to Ethan Jacobs.

I straighten up and close my eyes. What I say next is not
only going to change my life, but his and Claudia's too. I
take a deep breath and ready myself to say the truest words
I've probably ever spoken in my life.

"I'm here."

## ♦ 23 ♦

# CLAUDIA

ANOTHER DAY, ANOTHER EVENT where my tits and I have to make an appearance for the sake of keeping up appearances. Today it's an industry screening and circle jerk at the Vista Theatre Milty is hosting for one of his "friends." Thankfully, there's no red carpet. Even Milty isn't that pandering. But there are paparazzi outside and a select number of industry reporters on their way in. I avoid them and the clusters of guests who are preening while pretending not to notice they're being photographed while checking each other out.

I don't make eye contact with anyone until I reach the headset-wearing intern who's been put in in charge of the guest list. Ingrid, born and raised in Des Moines by a single mom, is attending UCLA on a gymnastics scholarship and majoring in anthropology. She smiles at me, checks my name off, and waves me in.

Not too many years ago, I had Ingrid's job and it never failed to surprise me how rude people can be to someone who's holding a clipboard. Now I'm colleagues with those same people. They're still assholes who now greet me by name and with big, fake smiles that let me know they haven't forgotten my clipboard-holding days.

Just inside the Vista, I pause, giving myself a moment to scope out the lobby. I need to know who's standing where and with whom, where the bar is, the location of the bathrooms, where the catering staff has set up, and how to get out of here without being seen leaving. Once I have the layout memorized, I'll force myself to speak to the biggest jerk in the room.

Today's jerk king is Austin Ford Taylor—actor, producer, and future director once he loses the rest of his hair and gives in to his gut. This little fete is for the documentary he's made about himself campaigning the UN to pass a clean water initiative. Austin Ford Taylor, who always introduces himself as such, is a selfish, egotistical, insecure man who also truly believes safe drinking water is a basic human right. He's used not only his celebrity but also his own money to fight for this, which makes him being such a repugnant person kind of a huge bummer. He also wants an Oscar for his documentary, and, by the looks of who's here, he just might get it.

He's not going to get anything from me, much less a prize, which makes me wonder why Milty insisted I attend. Whatever the motive, my task is the same. I have to greet Austin Ford Taylor and listen to him talk about the looming water crises, complain about the director of his current movie and wait for him to ask, once again, if my tits are real because he'd really like to touch them. Once I congratulate him on his genuinely good work and acknowledge but don't encourage his advances, I'm free to disengage and speed work the rest of the room. Then I can leave for another contrived event I have no choice but to attend.

Resolved to be as efficient as possible, I walk across the crowded room, mentally rehearsing what I'm going to do once I reach him. I always make sure to extend my hand first and keep at least half an arm's length between myself and whoever I'm greeting. No hug, no air kiss, no touching anything but my hand.

I've had my ass palmed, backs of hands "accidently" brushed against the side of my breast, hugs that lasted too long, and pelvises pushed into mine so many times, it's almost become a game to guess who will try to get away with what. These men are used to getting what they believe they're entitled to, which is my time, my attention, and my body.

When Austin Ford Taylor sees me, a wolfish grin over-takes his face. He's one of those men who wants exactly what he can't have. I pause at the edge of the invisible bar-rier which separates him from everyone else, pretending not to notice when he signals to one of his discreet bodyguards to let me proceed further.

"Claudia!" He holds his arms open to welcome me into his universe before he remembers I don't roll that way. He drops both of them and reaches for my extended hand. "You look beautiful, as always."

"Hello, Austin. Ford. Taylor. You're looking okay." I allow my hand to endure a mauling before pulling it out of his grasp.

The event photographer swoops in. I turn my back to him so he can't get a clear shot of my face and Austin Ford Taylor immediately moves into my space. I can feel the heat of his body and can't escape his expensive, false smell as he tries to pose me for the camera. I can't step back or forward without making it obvious I'm trying to get away from him. He's has caught me, and until he decides to let me go, we're uncomfortably close.

"When are you going to run away with me, Claudia?" he says as his eyes sweep down to my breasts. "Marry me and make me the happiest man on earth."

"Just as soon as your divorce is final," I say through my don't-fuck-with-me smile as I turn my face away from the camera lens. "This is your fourth, right? Or does it count as a gimmie since it's your second wife you're divorcing again."

"Third, sugar, only my third. The first one was annulled so it doesn't count." He runs his hand up and down my back. "It's nice to know you're keeping count."

"A girl has to consider what her alimony payments will be." I tilt my head up and stare at him full in the face and watch as his pupils dilate.

"I could fall in love with you, Claudia. I really could." He sounds like he halfway means it.

"Oh, bunny, we both know I'm too old and too ethnic for you." I catch his hand and set it away from me. "And too smart by half."

He waves the photographer away as his other hand comes up to play with my hair. I push it away, annoyed. He zeros in on someone over my right shoulder and freezes.

"We should get dinner, but I'd prefer breakfast in bed. Call my assistant. She'll set something up." He gives me a fast, full-body hug that forces most of the air out of my lungs before he scurries back to the safety of his celebrity bubble.

"Isn't this a coincidence, Bernal. It isn't, by the way."

Ethan kisses my cheek. Instead stepping away, he keeps his hand on the small of my back as he looks down at me. There's an audible dip in the conversations around us. I know what they see and what they're thinking—we look like we're a couple.

"You left for your flight. That's where you're supposed to be right now. Not here." My voice sounds shaky to my own ears as I struggle to keep myself together.

"Scheduling snafu. Someone is going to get fired but they won't since I'm the boss and I'm the one who snafu'd it.

Here I am, here you are, and Austin Ford Taylor better keep his fucking hands to himself if he wants to keep his hands."

"I . . . Oh . . ." I take a wobbly step back. Immediately, Ethan's hands take hold of my upper arms, steadying me. I feel myself blush as people continue to stare at us. I press the heels of my own hands over my eyes and leave them there longer than I should dare to. "I have to get out of here."

"Let's go."

He puts his arm around my shoulder and guides me to the back exit, a route reserved for those who want to be seen leaving by the right people but not by the public and paparazzi out front. I sway against him as if drunk, but I'm completely sober because I've always been in control. I'm not right now and not anymore.

I let him pull me along down a hallway, past the caterers who do double takes as we pass by them. Ethan tries a random door, and we're alone in a storage room. There's a chair, a trash can, and boxes of paper towels and cleaning supplies on the shelves around us. It's quiet but stuffy.

"Claudia? You look like you're going to pass out." He takes my face between his hands and looks at me closely. "We're going to the emergency room. No, fuck that. I have a doctor on call, he can meet us at the townhouse in half an hour."

"No, no doctor, no emergency room," I say as I try keep from falling into him. "It's nothing. Just a little lightheaded. I had a drink, I guess it was stronger than I thought."

"Bullshit." Annoyance battles with the concern on his face and in his voice.

"I drink." Even to my own ears the protest is too quick. It's an obvious lie and a weak one at that. "I do."

"No, you don't, sweetheart." Ethan embraces me, speaking into the top of my head, his breath warm and steady. "You'll accept a drink and hold it, but you don't drink."

"Of course, I do." I have no idea why I'm lying about this, but I am. I push away from him, and he lets me go but keeps his hands circled around my wrists. "And if that's all you have to complain about, that I don't get drunk as often as you'd like, you can go fuck yourself."

"I love it when you talk all romantic to me."

"Go . . . go . . ." I want to tell him where to go again but his smiling face swims in front of me as my knees give out. Instantly, his arms tighten around me, holding me, keeping me upright and off the floor.

"Claudia?" Ethan stoops down so he can look up into my face, still holding me with one arm against his chest as he tilts my face up to his. "We're going to the hospital."

"No! I'm serious, Ethan. I just forgot to eat." I straighten up and smile at him while grasping on to what's left of my equilibrium. "See? I'm . . . I'm perfectly okay. I'm great."

"Fine. Have it your way. Let's go home." He reaches over and pushes my hair away from my face, the palm of his hand cupping the back of my neck gently. "I'll order us a pizza and we'll have some wine. Or at least I will."

By home he means my townhouse or what used to be my townhouse but now looks and feels like both of us. Ethan folds his laundry, and mine, while watching screeners in the living room. He eats his trainer and nutritionist approved meals in the dining room at the table and chairs he picked out and paid for. In the kitchen, his favorite coffee beans are in the fridge and on the counter, along with his matching Hermès mug, is a vaguely phallic-looking grinder he insists makes all the difference between a good and great cup of coffee. Yesterday, Milty had a kiss-ass gift basket delivered to him there, to *my* townhouse.

How could I let this happen? How could I not only let him into where I live but also become part of it when I've tried so hard not to have a home in the first place? And I like it. I like it so much, I want to burn it all down.

"Let's not go anywhere just yet." I lean into him, pressing my breasts against his chest, my lips on his chin, tilting his head up to trace a small scar that's hidden underneath his stubble with my tongue.

"Here? In a storage room?" Ethan shifts closer to me, his hands on my hips. He's not hard, but with a little more distraction, I can get him there. "Not very ladylike of you."

"I'm no lady." I kiss his neck, touching the tip of my tongue to the flutter of his pulse. "And you like it."

"Come on, Claudia." He tries to keep my hand from snaking its way toward the growing bulge of his erection. "What the hell has gotten into you, Bernal?"

"Claudia?" Milty pokes his head into the room. I shrink into Ethan to hide from my boss. "Hey, Ethan! I was just looking for Claudia. Sorry, I didn't know I was interrupting anything."

Ethan turns me so he's looking over his shoulder at Milty, shielding me from him. "What do you want, Milton?"

"Nothing." Milty steps into the room, letting the door shut behind him. I fold myself deeper into Ethan, hiding my face in his chest. "But it's pretty obvious both of you are up to something."

"Leave. Now." Ethan's voice is cold, hard, a tone I've never heard him use in real life before. He turns toward Milty, setting me behind him as he stares my boss down. "Don't make me repeat myself, Milton."

"Okay, okay. You both come on out when you're done, have a drink on me," Milty says, sounding nervous. It might be his party, but if someone like Ethan isn't willing to show up to the next one, this might as well be his last. "Great cause, great time. Screening is going to start soon."

Milty scuttles out, closing the door behind him. For a few moments, Ethan stands very still as he takes a few deep breaths, still facing the door.

"I can't do this," he says.

"Do what?" Playing dumb makes me feel stupid, but I still do it.

"Sneaking around, hiding from people. Pretending we're not together. Having to show up here and at your office like I'm some sort of stalker." Ethan struggles to gain some control over what he's feeling. "Is that enough 'what' for you, Claudia?"

"We're not sneaking around or hiding. We went out to lunch, in public, together, just me and you. You came to my office, now everyone is talking about it. Milty won't leave me alone. And what you did in there, Ethan? You might as well have laid me on the bar and tossed my dress over my head. That's essentially what you did. Why?"

"Why, Claudia? You of all people have the balls to ask me why? I don't know what else to do. I don't know what to do about you or with you."

He's angry at me and he hates it. He might even hate me for making him angry. This I understand. It's what I've been waiting for and have wanted from him, but it feels wrong, not like I expected it to. I keep my lips pressed together as I glare at him, waiting to see if I can make him say more of what he doesn't want to admit to.

"Because this?" Ethan pauses and takes a deep breath. "What we've been doing, what I've been going along with, is about you. Not me, not us. You. Just you."

We've had a version of this conversation before, but now it's a fight, a real one, and he's calling me out. I am the problem. It's all me, and all of it is mine. I know this, but I can't admit it to him.

"What do you want, Ethan? Do you want me to take out an ad in *Variety*? Do you want me to tell everyone no one has ever fucked me like you have? That I've never come so hard and so much in my entire life? That your cock is as perfect as the rest of you?"

"Fuck you, Claudia. What we do, what we have, is much more than just fucking. And you know it," he says. He sees me flinch at his words, but he keeps himself from reaching for me. Instead, he takes a step back and then another. "If you can't admit it to yourself, much less to me, then I really don't know why the hell I'm here."

I stare at him, unable to say the words he needs to hear from me, and watch as his heart breaks. I've done it. I've pushed him to his limit. Now he has no choice but to accept how fucked up this all is because of me.

"Then go! I don't care." But I do. My fingernails dig into my palms to keep myself from crying, from taking a single step toward him. "Just fucking leave!"

I look away, too ashamed of myself to face him. I keep my eyes down as he opens the door and goes through it, letting it close behind him. I stumble over to the trash can and vomit until my stomach is as empty as the rest of me feels.

# ◆ 24 ◆

# MARITZA

I T TOOK ME ALMOST two hours to get ready, and I look good, really good. Way better than Augustino deserves and now, probably, he's not even going to get to see me. Anyways, I didn't do it for him. I did it to show everyone how lucky he is to be with me.

Agreeing to a party at Augustino's house instead of a rehearsal dinner was a mistake. I said no to Auggie going to Vegas, so I had to say yes to whatever it is that's going on over there. And it is! They started without me, so why should I even bother showing up?

The food is from a taco cart, the music is from Auggie's loser of father's 1970s stereo and record collection, and all their neighbors have been invited, including kids. This is what I get for letting Dani and Gabi to plan it like my mother told me I had to. Everyone is turning my saying goodbye to my freedom into an excuse to get drunk, eat too much, and yell at their dumb kids. Like they all don't do this exact same thing every other weekend.

I've already avoided two calls from Perla. Funny how *now* she remembers my cell phone number. The others went to the living room phone, my mother hovering over it but not letting Daddy pick it up so we all have to listen to her phlegmy, whiny voice on the answering machine. Perla wants to know where I am and when I'll be getting there. It's Augustino who should be wondering where I am, not his mommy.

"I'm not going and no one can make me," I say to my mother, who looks like she wants to have one of her migraines. She better not. I already have way too much to deal with "Why should I? They're more than fine having their *fiesta de* fatsos without me, the *bride*."

"Maritza, please. Everyone is waiting." She wrings her hands. I had to force Mamá to get a manicure this morning and she's going to ruin it if she doesn't cut that out. "Claudia, do something."

Claudia is sitting Indian style at the foot of my bed, flipping through my issue of *Allure* magazine. I haven't even looked at it yet and she tore out all the perfume ads. She told Daddy to throw them away in the outside trash because they were giving her a headache.

But at least she has her shoes off. If it wasn't for the red soles, they could be just any other pair of boring black heels. She doesn't wear polish on her toes or her nails. It's too plain for me, but on Claudia it looks expensive like everything else about her.

"Tell Dad it's time to stop hiding out in the backyard and to meet us out front. We'll be right there. Thanks, Mom." Claudia waits until the door closes behind her before she rolls up the magazine and swats my shins with it. "Get up and get your butt in the car right now, Maritza. This whole thing was your idea, so now you have to show your face."

I have two choices—fight or cry. Tears will ruin my makeup, but yelling at her will only make Claudia angry. I can't afford for her to be mad at me right now. Tears, then.

"No, nuh-uh. Don't you dare cry. It's not going to work on me," she says before I can get started. She goes back to flipping through *Allure*. "I'm wise to your fake tears. Have been for years."

"Fine! But don't expect me to have a good time." I get up and look in the mirror above my dresser to make sure I didn't mess up my hair too much. "Because I won't!"

"Enjoy yourself or don't enjoy yourself. It's all the same to me, Maritza." Claudia keeps reading my magazine as she says this. It's almost as if she's bored by being so nasty to me. "You can't behave like a princess if what you want is to be respected like a queen."

"What does that even mean? You don't understand, Claudia! How could you—"

"Stop. Just cut it out. Unless you're going to call Augustino, his sisters, and his mother and tell them you're not coming, then shut up. I'll support you if it's what you've decided to do. But this? This is pure chickenshit behavior." She yawns, sighs, and then yawns again. "Pardon me. Where was I? Oh, yeah. You either go to this thing and smile or nut up and tell Augustino you're bailing on it. Two choices. Easy. Pick one."

"I already said I was going to go!" I tell her. "Why are you so mean to me?"

"Because it's so much fun." She says this with a smile, but it's confusing to me because she doesn't seem happy. "Now let's go have us some tacos and cake."

Claudia hooks her arm through mine as we walk through the house and out to the porch and down the front steps. We get into the back seat of Daddy's car as my mother locks the front door and then the screen door, checking it a million times to make sure it's really locked.

Daddy holds open the car door, waiting for her, then closing it only after she's buckled in. When he gets behind the driver's seat, he adjusts the mirrors and glances back to make sure Claudia and I are wearing our seat belts before he starts the car. He didn't use to be this careful, especially not when we were kids.

Right before he retired from the foundry, he was in a car accident. A bad one. He was on his way to the Super King all the way over in Cypress Park on San Fernando Road because my mother likes the produce from there. An SUV cut him off and his car rolled over. Insurance covered everything, but now he's really careful and drives a Honda. It's good that happened, in a way, because now he won't drink so much if he knows he's going to drive.

He won't count his beers at the fiesta de fatsos, though. Daddy loves any sort of party, so either Claudia or my mother will have to drive back to the house because I'm also going to do whatever I want tonight. I'll get as drunk as the rest of them and dance on all the tables.

My mother adjusts the radio station away from where they're talking about the Dodgers beating the Expos earlier today.

"So much traffic," she comments.

No one bothers to tell her it's not bad at all, not even Daddy, who I can tell wants to listen to his baseball stuff. Ignoring the presets I put in for him, she goes the long way to her favorite oldies station.

Claudia leans her head against the window and closes her eyes. I reach over and take her hand in mine. She turns her face to me a little and smiles but doesn't open her eyes.

She understands I'm sorry for acting like I was and it's really not my fault. She knows all about how Auggie is and that his mother and sisters are even worse than him. Perla, Gabi, and Dani are freaking out because I'm taking away "the man" from their house and forcing him to act like a real one. They should just go get their own instead of convincing themselves my wedding isn't going to happen. It is happening, period.

Daddy gets on the wrong off-ramp. We end up having to take the 2 to the 134 and back down to the 5 so we can exit on Colorado like we were supposed to in the first place. Mamá is making little noises under her breath but doesn't say anything. She could drive here with her eyes closed.

When we were little, it was a big deal to shop in Glendale. My mother thought the Galleria was the best place on earth, and if we couldn't find what we were looking for there, it didn't exist. When I told her Auggie lived in Glendale, the first thing she wanted to know was how close to the mall his house was. That's all Mamá cared about.

When Augustino first took me to meet his them, he told me his mother had promised no other woman would ever come between them. Of course, I took it as a challenge to make Perla love me like one of her own daughters, to accept me into the family and appreciate all I was doing for her son. I gave her expensive birthday and Christmas presents. I ran errands and did other nice things for her.

I'm embarrassed it took me as long as it did to realize she would never be grateful that I was her precious son's fiancée. That's when I stopped calling her Mrs. Acevedo. She lost that privilege and all the nice things that come with it.

Daddy slows down to look for parking. Auggie didn't bother to mark off a spot for me—the bride—like he should have. I'm sure this didn't even occur to him. If I had thought of it before just now, I would have told him to. Because, of course, I have to do everything.

We get lucky and find a spot a couple of houses down so my mother can't complain about having to walk.

"We're here!" Claudia says in a singsong voice like a preschool teacher. She practically drags me out of the car, through the house and into the backyard.

Augustino, his arm around one of his hundred or so cousins, raises his bottle of beer as someone takes a picture. As soon as he sees us, looking at Claudia more than me, he practically runs over.

"Augustino, your bride-to-be is here," Claudia tells him in that same singsong voice. "Doesn't she look beautiful?"

"Hi! Claudia! Hi!" He's all over her like a horny dog that's escaped from someone's yard. "You look good. I haven't seen you in forever. Man, you're looking good."

"Jeeze, Auggie, you've been smoking some super *foochi* weed." Claudia pinches her nose shut and tries to pull away from him, but he keeps grabbing on to her. It's going to take a blast from the water hose to make him let go. "You reek of it."

"If it's organic, don't panic," he says, putting his face right up next to hers.

"Get your hands off my sister, Augustino." I'm annoyed by how creepy he's acting right in front of me. Him drinking and smoking whatever is no excuse, even if it's the ones he's going to give me tomorrow when we fight about it.

"Yeah, Auggie, we're practically brother and sister." Claudia laughs, but it's not really a laugh. "In our family we keep the fondling to a minimum. Especially in front of witnesses."

"Huh?" he says.

Claudia and I bust out laughing at him, right to his big, round foochi face. We laugh so hard that she has to sit down, and I pee myself a little bit. It's okay, I'm wearing a panty liner and have another one in my purse.

"I don't get it. What's so funny?" he asks, proving he really is a dummy.

"Your bride-to-be will make sure you get it, but not the 'it' you think you're going to get." Claudia stands up, gives me a kiss, and pats my back as she hugs me. "I'll be around if you need me."

I watch as she says more hellos, remembering everybody's name and making it seem like she really cares about who she's talking to, like the sun has come out just for them. I'm the only one who knows it's an act. But still . . . how did she get so good at it, at making people fall in love with her? They don't even notice she's just pretending or maybe they don't care that she is.

"Itza, babe, didn't my sisters do an awesome job? My mom, she's so awesome." He has to be a mama's boy even when he's drunk. "Best mom ever. Hey, do you want something to eat?"

There are tamales from Juanito's, my mother's favorite, and he went to Porto's to get my favorite mango mousse cake along with a hundred potato balls. He only got my cake because Claudia called him and told him I was expecting it. Besides the tamales and cake, there's carnitas and carne asada tacos, rice, beans, fresh salsas, and beer and more beer. No wine, definitely no bottle of champagne that his greedy sisters took home with them from the dress appointment.

"No, Augustino. No, I don't want to eat anything," I tell him.

"Smile, Itza!" He presses his wet lips near my ear when I don't move away from him fast enough. "Another beer, Rafa? Gabi, get your *tío* a beer."

"Augustino, we need to talk." I don't know why I say this, but I do. The drunk smile drops off of his face, and it makes me feel good. "Now."

Holding my hand only because people are watching, he walks through the kitchen and into the living room where it's less crowded. "What is it now, Maritza?"

"Your mother." I take a deep breath, not liking the tone he's taking with me, but I don't have time to deal with that right now. "She told me that you told her . . . Gabi, can you give us some privacy?" She doesn't move. "Augustino. Do something or I will."

"Gabi, I'll be there in a second. So? What did my mom say?"

"She's going around telling everyone we're going to be living here afterward."

"Afterward? You mean after we get married? Well, yeah. We gotta live somewhere. I figured you'd want to get away from all the gang stuff, but, okay, fine." He shrugs. "We'll live over there, on Fickett. Fuck it. Same difference."

It really is all the same to him. Here. There. It doesn't matter to Auggie. He'll get up for work, come out of the shower expecting to find his already-ironed clothes on the foot of the bed, a hot cup of coffee, and a plate of huevos con chorizo on the kitchen table. And when he comes home from work, another hot meal and as much cold beer as he wants drink will be waiting for him.

His mother, his sisters, my mother, or me, it doesn't matter to him who it is. It's exactly how he sees the rest of his life working out for him because it's the way it's always been.

"Jesus, man, it's a party, Maritza! For once, can't you act like you're having fun?"

I look around at the tacky fake flowers and plants, the second and third place trophies, and the framed pictures of Auggie and his sisters. A big portrait of their father hangs on the wall next the dining table like he's some sort of saint instead of a deadbeat dad who got killed in prison because he was a snitch.

Perla has never put up any of the photos I've given her of me, but she's used the frames for other pictures. Even one for the dog they had to put to sleep after it bit Dani. None of their pictures will ever be in my house. They'll be lucky if I ever invite them over.

"We all good now?" He doesn't care about me. He just wants to get back to playing the big shot in front of his family and friends. "Yeah, Itza?

"Sure, Auggie," I lie again. "Everything is all good."

## ◆ 25 ◆

# DULCINA

FOR THE PAST HOUR I've been watching families, couples, and groups of friends go in and come out of the Denny's just off of Highway 178 in Bakersfield. It's been a long time since I've paid attention to something like this, and it feels a little bit wonderful because of how perfectly ordinary it is. Seeing people excited to eat at Denny's so they can be around each other is, to me, fascinating. It's the families I pay most attention to, noting it's usually a dad who's missing.

Our mom would agree to going out to dinner only if it was El Torito. And El Torito was only for special occasions and never on weekends because it was always too busy. For years, even after we knew it wasn't fair, my sisters and I had to share a single birthday dinner at El Torito, never Olive Garden like we were desperate to try. As soon as I got my driver's permit, we started taking our own selves to Olive Garden whenever we wanted.

A guy taps on my window and waits for me to roll it down before he asks, "Dulcina Bernal?"

"Yeah." I nod while having a minor flashback to high school when I used to buy drugs from the driver's seat of the Malibu. "That's me."

"Can I see some ID?" he asks.

He shifts from foot to foot like he's wired on coffee and whatever else he's downed to make the drive from L.A. to Bakersfield. This, too, brings back memories.

"Sure." I hand it to him, wishing he'd move back so I can get out of my car and do this thing while standing on my own two feet.

He looks at my driver's license and hands it back to me along with a clipboard. "I have something for you to sign before I can, uh, release the delivery to you."

I scrawl my name on what is basically a blank sheet of paper aside from the printed letterhead. He hands me a sealed manila envelope and stands there, trying to figure out who I am and how I know Ethan Jacobs. He's also probably curious to see what Ethan had him drive more than a hundred miles to deliver.

"Okay. Thanks, guy."

I wave him off and roll up my window up. I wait until he pulls out of the parking lot and back onto the road before opening the envelope. Inside are a hundred crisp $100 bills and Ethan's business card with a phone number scrawled on the back.

"That's a lot of money," I say out loud as I look around for shifty hippies in rundown camper vans.

Ethan made it easy for me to accept his loan by just asking where I wanted to have it delivered as if I'd already agreed. We never even discussed how much he was going to lend me and neither of us had to tell the other it's best if we keep all of this between the two us . . . for now.

Sending me $10,000 so I can get myself to Boyle Heights pegs him not only as generous to a fault but also as someone who's willing to put his money where his heart is. I'll wait until I meet him in person to make sure he's really on the level, but my gut tells me he is.

Getting robbed in Big Sur almost gave me an out from making this side trip, but now, with more than enough money in my pocket, I can't avoid it. I start up my car, put it in gear, and drive towards the very outside tip of Bakersfield.

I loop through identical-looking blocks of homes, getting lost twice before stopping in front of a newish Spanish-style house. It's painted a peachy pink, and the lawn in front of it is an electric shade of green. I double-check the address halfway hoping I have the wrong place. Nope. I've wound up where I'm supposed to be.

I had no intention of making any friends when I checked myself into the hospital. I told myself once I got out, I was out. Having decided to go it alone, I was sitting in the common room counting the minutes until I could have another cigarette trying not to think of booze, pills and sex. Of course, someone came over to talk to me.

"You're here!" A woman taps on the front passenger side window of my car. "Praise his name for delivering you safely!"

"Joey . . . Joey Ludlow?" I ask.

My friend is blonder and much heavier than she was the last time we saw each other. She looks so normal, I wouldn't have recognized her if she'd done cartwheels right in front of me.

When she introduced herself to me that day, Joey had been half her current weight, her hair buzzed off because of lice. Her right arm was in a cast, both her eyes were black and there was a ladder of stitches that traveled up from her busted lip to the side of her broken nose. She was also the most genuinely cheerful person I'd ever met in my life especially for someone who'd been turning tricks to pay for her boyfriend's heroin habit until he put her in the hospital.

"Listen to you, Dulcina, always joking! And it's Stahl now. Like the news reporter on *60 Minutes*, but she's not a relation." She laughs from deep within her belly and hugs me hard, all soft parts and soapy-smelling like the mom she's become. "I'm so happy you're here!"

Right before she wound up in the emergency room and then held over as a 5150, Joey had found religion at a store-front church in Daly City, but this wasn't why she refused to let me push her away. She just liked me.

We saw each other when I was sober enough to pretend I wasn't wasted and a lot of times when I was. She never lectured me or tried to get me to come to her church. All she wanted was to be my friend. She even visited me at the place Claudia put me in and helped me move into my first halfway house.

Through her church, she met a man, got married, moved to Bakersfield, and had twin girls. Besides Claudia, she's the only person I've ever bothered to let know I'm still alive with semi-regular phone calls.

"Joey, you look, uh, great." I take a step back, only delaying impact for a second or two as Joey slams into me for another hug.

"I just love what you've done to your hair! It must have taken forever. Did you do it yourself? Well, come on in! I just got the girls out from their bath and into their pj's. Roy had to go in for an emergency call—water heater burst or some such thing, but he should be back soon. He's so curious to meet you after all I've told him about you." She wraps an arm around my shoulders and pulls me up the steps, keeping our sides pressed against each other. "You're more than wel-come to spend the night, and I sure wish you would. We can stay up talking, playing cards. Just like old times!"

"You make the loony bin sound like it was summer camp." I find myself relaxing into her, leaning on her just

THE NEAPOLITAN SISTERS 207

like I used to when she was nothing but skin and bones and double her weight in love. "I hated both, Joey, and I've only been to one of them . . . twice"

"Same old Dulcina!" she laughs as she takes my face between her warm, soft hands and plants two quick kisses on my lips and adds a third for luck. "Well, what are you waiting for? Come on in! I apologize about the mess."

The inside is all tall ceilings and big windows. The walls and carpet are both a watered-down beige color with splashes of bold florals on the upholstery and matching drapes. It looks exactly like she used to describe to me what she wanted her home to look like.

"Yeah, this place is a complete pigsty, Joey." Only a woman on something potent could keep a home this spotless. She's not using, I can tell, so she must be powered by pure Jesus. "How do you clean the windows?"

"Once a month with an extension ladder. Inside and out. Isn't it all such a hoot? Roy said it was too big, but I said, bigger is better! Just like me!" She leads me into the living room. "So? Tell me everything!"

"There's not much to tell." I look around, suddenly realizing it's too quiet, especially if there are children in the house. "Where are your girls?"

"Oh, my little angels are in their playroom." Joey smiles and I can see all the work she's had done to give her back the teeth her junkie boyfriend knocked out of her one night when she told him it was raining too hard to go out and trick. "Imagine that? A room just to play in!"

"Does it lock from the outside?" I sit on the edge of the couch, not wanting to indent it.

"Oh, you and your jokes! We'll go peek in on them in a second. I want us to have some girl talk first." She scoots in close to me, taking my hand in between both of hers. "I swear you're still as quick as a whip. You could talk a worm into buying dirt. I tell Roy all the time, 'Roy, honey, my friend Dulcina could sell dirt to a worm.' He's just a peach. I can't wait for you to meet him. He had an emergency call . . .'"

Peach.

Joey is one hundred percent certified Georgia trailer trash whose family considered a move to a trailer park to be a step in the right direction. Her mother, Big Joey, had hoped her daughter would storm the local pageant circuit and eventually provide her with a comfortable lifestyle. Instead, Little Joey grew up plain and sickly with no obvious talent for anything other than getting in the way. Joey told me this all within five minutes of meeting me and with a huge smile on her face.

Joey may have been a victim of various forms of abuse, both self-inflicted and just inflicted, but she never wavered in her belief that the world is a good place full of equally good people.

". . . Look at you, Dulcina!" She drowns me in another hug. "When I first saw you, you were in worse shape than me! I saw someone who truly had no joy in her heart, and it broke mine to pieces. I just knew from the second I laid eyes on you it was my mission to get you to smile again."

"And see how well that's paid off for you." I grin at her to let her know I am joking. I look down at her feet. They're plump like the rest of her, shoved into spangled mules, her toes painted a shiny candy-apple red. "You've done really good for yourself, Joey."

"And I thank the Lord for all of it. I've missed you. I talk about you all the time!" Joey pulls me to her again, almost onto her lap. "So much that Roy says, 'Aww shit, Joey, not another Dulcina story.' I tell him you're about as close to family to me besides my church family and Roy's family, of course. You're like a sister to me."

"Considering what you've told me about your sisters, I should be offended." I hug her back and try to catch the breath she's just squeezed out of me.

"Let's go introduce you to my girls." Joey hauls me off the couch and holds on to my arm as she leads me toward the back of her house. Aside from pristine white tile in the kitchen area, there's nothing but the same beige carpet underfoot.

We get to the playroom, right off what looks to be a family room. There's no door, just a knee-high gate between it and the rest of the house.

"My peaches!"

Joey claps her hands and then waves them both at her girls. She doesn't bother to open the gate but steps over it, and I do the same. The girls crawl over to their mother, who while not letting me go, manages to pick them both up for a group hug.

"Let's show Auntie Dulcina your toys!"

Joey hands me one of the girls and we sit down on the floor. On top of the same beige carpet are bright rubber mat tiles that connect like giant puzzle pieces.

"Now, girls, you keep your auntie busy while I make us all something yummy to eat!"

"Joey? Wait . . ." I try to stand up, trying not to upset the small mound of stuffed animals the girls are dumping into my lap.

"Never you mind, Dulcina, you just sit down and have fun! Roy'll be here any second. I'll fix us a pitcher of iced tea!" In constant motion, Joey steps around me and the twins as she veers off toward the kitchen. "My special recipe, extra sweet. I'm supposed to be watching my sugar, but I like to imagine Jesus would've liked his tea on the sweet side."

I can hear Joey chattering toward us from the kitchen and knowing she's not expecting me to answer, I keep my focus on her daughters, which is why I don't notice when Joey's husband steps over the gate and into the room.

"You must be Dulcina. I'm Roy, Joey's husband."

Roy is older than I thought he'd be. He's somewhere south of forty and looks exactly like the kind of man who prefers his wife to be on the fuller side. He leans down, offering his right hand for me to shake, holding his work boots in his left. His hands are clean and rough, like they are with someone who works with and washes them often. One of his fingernails is bruised so it looks almost black.

"Nice to meet you. Sorry I'm still wearing my boots. I can take them off, but I don't have any socks on. They've gone missing."

"We can find you a pair of Joey's to borrow," he says as he accepts the toy one of his daughters hands him. "So, Dulcina, you just passing through?"

I laugh, startling him. "No worries, man. I'm heading out right after dinner."

"No, it's not—"

"It's okay, Roy. If I were you, I'd make sure I was just passing through too."

"Roy, honey!" Joey rushes into the room wearing what I believe is an actual hostess apron. "I didn't hear you come in. You two went ahead and met without me!"

This is the last time Joey and I will ever see each other in person, and, as the years go by, we'll talk less and less until we just don't. Even so, Joey will always be with me just like Curtis, Wendy, Rosie B., and the handful of other people who I've been lucky enough to meet along the way. I'll miss Joey, but it feels good to know she has someone like Roy to keep her safe and soft for the rest of her life.

"We sure did, Joey. And your Roy is a peach, just like you said he was." I smile up at my friend as a piece of my heart fits itself back into place.

# • 26 •

# MARITZA

M Y OLD DOCTOR HAD a poster of a tropical beach taped on the ceiling of the exam room, but she was a woman doctor. Here, in my new doctor's exam room, it's just boring ceiling tiles with the little holes. I guess a man doctor has no reason to think his patients might like something to look at while he's poking around down there. I feel a little weird about having a man doctor for this type of thing, but I needed an appointment fast and this was all I could get.

My mother doesn't go to the doctor unless she's super sick. Then, when she's there, she won't tell them what's really wrong, and when she gets home, she'll only take half of the medicine prescribed to her. I guess it's sort of understandable why she's so weird about doctor stuff. When I was a little girl, Mamá was in the hospital for a long time. She almost died, but we don't talk about that.

This morning, I took extra time to pick out my jewelry, do my hair and makeup, and choosing my outfit. I'm glad I decided to wear my new burgundy-colored velour hoodie and pants set because it's comfortable and I look really good in it. I got it at Fashion 21 in Highland Park for $23. There's no way I'm going to spend more than that on sweats, not even fancy sweats. That's something Claudia would do.

When Mr. Kim saw me this morning, he knew I was going to be leaving early to go to the doctor or to get a wax. But by now he knows not to ask me about it. I'm supposed to go back to work once this is done, but maybe I'll go to the Glendale Galleria instead. It's not too far from here, so I might as well see if I can find the right shoes for my dress.

I found him, this new doctor, after my old doctor got married and then told me she was pregnant. She was focused on other things, so I figured it was best to make the change before she went on maternity leave. Maybe she wouldn't come back to work, and I would have been stuck with the other doctor who works out of her office.

I never liked her. She was really rude to me once when I had to see her after I had an abnormal pap smear and my doctor was on her honeymoon. She wasn't at all nice about my situation. I complained about her to the front desk, and when my doctor got back, she apologized to me.

My new doctor is way cuter than I thought he would be, in his mid-thirties and not married. I checked for a ring before he put on the examination gloves.

"Everything looks normal, Maritza." He takes off the gloves before he picks up a pen to make notes on my chart. "I'll send these samples out to the lab, and we should have the results back in a few days."

"Normal, like, normal good?" I sit up, feeling the KY jelly run out of me. I want to use the exam sheet to wipe it off, but I'll wait until he's gone. "When I'm ready to maybe get pregnant, is that something I can do?"

"I don't see why not." He looks down at my chart. "It looks like you terminated a pregnancy last year."

"Yes." I stare down at my toes, glad I got a pedicure yesterday instead of putting it off for later in the week. "I had to."

He washes his hands, watching me in the mirror. When he looks away to grab a paper towel, I fix my gown to make it look more flattering.

"And you're currently in a monogamous relationship?" he asks me when he turns around.

"I'm engaged."

I'm wearing my ring, so there's no reason to hide it from him. I saw him looking at my hand when he first walked in. It's looking a little dull. I should take it to Mr. Kim's niece so she can run it through the machine. I'll take her a case of grape Sac Sac because we didn't buy the ring from her like maybe we should have.

"Was your fiancé the—"

"Of course, he was!"

"I'm sorry, I didn't mean to imply anything." He leans his hip against the sink, in no hurry to move on to the next patient.

"Could he be able tell I had that . . . procedure?" This is something I've been wondering about since last year but was too afraid to ask about.

Augustino never said anything about those three months when I hardly saw him. He's never even bothered to figure out when it's time for my period. When I tell him we can't, he assumes that's why, not because I don't want to.

Living with his mother and sisters, he must think women are always on their periods. And when we do have sex, I doubt he's ever noticed much of anything, since he only cares about getting what he wants.

At least now we go to the Double Tree. Before it was in his car, never mine, or in his room when his mother and sisters weren't home. Now it's the Double Tree or nothing. Once I move into my house, maybe we'll still go there just to keep those things separate.

"Have you been intimate with your fiancé since the abortion?" he asks me as he hands me some tissues.

That's a dumb question even from a doctor. I decide not to answer. I accept the tissues but hold them in my lap. I'm not going to wipe myself in front of him.

"You didn't tell him about your abortion?" he asks when I don't say anything.

I guess, maybe he's supposed to for, like, professional reasons ask me these questions. My ex-doctor never said a word about it. I don't know why I even bothered to tell her. She was so distracted by her wedding that she wasn't paying attention to her job.

"I didn't tell anyone," I whisper because it feels like the kind of thing I should say in a quiet voice.

"Is there any abuse, verbal or physical?" He stands up straighter, looking at me closely. "Maritza?"

"No, no." Something flutters in my stomach at the way he says my name and how he's acting. I tuck my left hand under my thigh. "It was an accident, the. . . what happened. I just want to make sure I'm normal and it's okay for when the time comes . . . if it's what I want."

"You've been my healthiest patient this week." He smiles at me, not even pretending to write anything down on my chart.

"You must get sick of talking to women about their, you know, stuff. Your wife must be a very understanding woman."

I'm almost sure he's single, but now he has to admit if he is or isn't. I'm sure he has to follow the same rules like when a drug dealer or a hooker asks a cop if they're a cop.

"No wife," he laughs. "I'm married to my job."

He starts to wash his hands again, before remembering he already did. He turns back to me, embarrassed. He grabs one of the business cards from the desk and hands it to me.

"Call me if you need anything or have any questions. It was a pleasure meeting you, Maritza."

When he's gone, I stand up and carefully wipe the sticky gel off my legs. There's a little bit of blood. I grab a couple of paper towels and press them in there until it goes away.

I wash my hands, get dressed, and put his card in my wallet, behind my AAA membership card. Then I take it out and tuck it behind my bra strap right in front of my shoulder. I'm not hiding it because there's nothing to hide. I just want to keep my personal business private. I press the card into my skin and think about how he said I was his best patient. And said my name a total of nine times.

I should have switched doctors a long time ago.

# · 27 ·

# CLAUDIA

I PARK ACROSS THE street from my townhouse for no reason other than that I just can't deal with the prospect of running into either Megan or Bryan in the garage. Also, it buys me a few minutes before having to go inside where I know Ethan is waiting for me.

He called me at the office this morning, after staying away for a few days, so I had plenty of time to think about the fight we had in that storage room. He told me what he needed to say, or at least some of it. I listened, told him I was sorry, and agreed not only to see him tonight but also pick up dinner from his favorite Indian place.

I spent the rest of my day avoiding Mom, Maritza, Julie, and Milty. With all of them, the less I give them, the more they want to take from me. Ethan seems to appreciate what little I give him even while it frustrates him that I won't give him more of myself. All of it, and everyone, just makes me feel so tired.

I lean my head back, close my eyes, and try to focus on breathing without smelling. Dr. Zheng showed me a meditative exercise to help me relax when she's sticking those tiny acupuncture needles in me. I don't have time to take myself to a happy place. It's already crowded with the random, irritating events from an otherwise unproductive day.

Austin Ford Taylor sent me an obscenely large bouquet and a handwritten note asking me to run away with him. I gave them to Ingrid and shredded the card myself. I don't have to worry about him taking it any further than a hundred red roses and innuendo couched as good-natured harassment. He's just playing, and I'm not playing at playing hard to get. He'll get bored and move on to the next set of tits soon enough, giving me a break before he circles back again.

Like a shih tzu with the case of the shits, Julie spent the day dropping hints that she knows more about me and Ethan than she really does. I'm going to fire her and have to do it before she makes her big move. I caught Julie going into Milty's office as soon as she thought I'd left for the day. I hadn't even made it to the elevators before she hotfooted her USC ass over to his office.

Milty is worried there might be something serious between me and Ethan. If he had walked in on us and found me on my knees with Ethan's cock in my mouth, it would have been more than okay with him. What's not okay is my having ambitions that are loftier than just doling out a blow job to an international movie star at a vanity charity event that's just cover for chumming the water for Oscar votes.

Milty may not think too much of me as a person, much less as a woman and even less as woman who's also a minority, but he can't deny I'm a good producer. His ego can't take even a hint that another, more prestigious if smaller production company might be interested in poaching me. He needs to believe that dropping to my knees is the only way I'll get anywhere other than where I already am and should grateful even to be.

Julie has nothing on me and Ethan, but she could tell him about what I've been doing at work. Or, rather, not doing. For the last couple weeks, I've been cleaning up minor messes on projects that are done or close to it. I've been reading scripts, sort of, but nothing has caught my eye. I'm not slacking but I'm not producing either. What I am is distracted.

I can't blame Ethan, but part of me does. He's not only made my life more complicated, but he's also now a factor in my career. I have to get a handle on this before a blurry picture of me winds up in *Us* magazine along with a few exclamation points and a vague non-denial from Ethan's publicist about his relationship status.

I crack the window open, opting for gas fumes over curry. My stomach turns over on itself, and I take deeper breaths to settle it down. As if to taunt me, my dumb-bunny neighbor Megan peels out of our shared garage, taking my last excuse with her. I count to fifty, press the clutch down to the floorboards with a little more force than necessary, and then make a tight U-turn into the garage. Ethan comes bounding down the stairs as I pull into my space. His bags are already in the back seat of his Jeep for when he leaves later tonight for his rescheduled trip.

"Hey, beautiful. I was getting worried." He opens the car door and helps me out before he leans over to the passenger seat for the food and my purse and tote bag full of unread scripts. "I'll heat this up so we can eat."

"Sorry." I'm late and it's all on me.

"Nothing to be sorry for, Claudia," he says. "Okay?"

I nod, but what I really want is for him to get angry, to yell at me, to call me out for being a bitch and trying to drive him away. I want him to tell me this is exactly what's going to happen if I keep pushing him. But he's not angry or even annoyed which only proves he is going to leave me. If I could, I'd leave me.

He sets the food on the hood of my Audi. His hands on my hips, then my waist and up the sides of my ribs, he stares into my face, concerned. "You okay?"

"Just a headache." All I want to do is sleep until I don't know what day it is. "I might be dehydrated or something. I don't know. It's nothing."

"You should go to the doctor, a real one." Ethan folds me into his arms. I lean all my weight into him, grateful he's here. "Not that needle quack you see."

I asked my quack about the possibility of chronic fatigue syndrome, but Dr. Zheng pooh-poohed it with a jab of a needle, calling it an "unhappy white woman complaint." I'm definitely not quite white, but not so sure about the unhappy part.

"Acupuncture is holistic. Mind, body connection, blah, blah, blah and crap." I talk into his chest, feeling my breath on his T-shirt.

"Crap and blah, blah, blah is right." He lifts my chin and kisses my closed lips. "Come on, Bernal, I'm starving."

Hours later, I wake up confused and blinking into the dark.

I've always been a good sleeper. Even when I had to share the same bed with Dulcina and Maritza, I never had a problem falling sleep and staying that way until morning. Maritza would always be in the middle. Mom was afraid she'd roll out of bed during the night and break her neck. It was up to me and Dooley, on either side of her, to keep her from hurting herself. The two of us would wake up with bruises from Maritza's nocturnal kicking. Sometimes she wasn't asleep and just kicked us out of spite.

Fucking Maritza. And fucking Dooley too. She left me a voicemail with a new number, telling me she was on her way and for me not to worry. Great, thanks, Dooley. Now I can relax and think about how Julie is going to rat me out to Milty. Once she does, Milty is going to leverage Ethan over me and . . . who cares? Things are way more fucked up than any of them realize.

I'm so tired. I just want to sleep. I turn over onto my side and reach for Ethan, but my hand only finds his pillow. I sit up with a gasp. My heart beats like crazy in my chest, my body drenched in a sudden cold sweat. I'm afraid, and I've never felt such intense fear in my entire adult life. I hold my breath and listen. It's not as quiet as it's supposed to be. I reach over and flip on the bedside lamp.

"Ethan?"

Quick memories flash through my mind. He laughed when I called naan ethnic flour tortillas. He carried me upstairs after I fell asleep on the couch. He pulled off the soft gray T-shirt he had on for me to wear after he took off all my clothes and offered to help me brush my teeth in bed so I wouldn't have to get up. He was serious and he did, both of us laughing, as I tried not to dribble on the towel he held under my chin.

"Ethan? Is that you?"

He's not here, but he's somewhere. I made a point of not asking where he was going even though I could tell he was waiting for me to. I don't want to think about this, not now. I don't want to think. My heart rate slows. I sink back into the pillows ready to give in to sleep again. In the living room, one floor below, the smoke alarm goes off followed by the one in the kitchen.

"Fire! Ethan, fire!" I'm so awake now it hurts. "Ethan!"

I jump out of bed, tangled in the sheets, falling onto the hand-tied Alpaca wool rug made by a small collective in Peru. Ethan happily presented it to me the day after he spent his first night in my bed. It must be extra flammable because it's so special. I free myself from the sheets and take off downstairs. I can't see it, but I can smell smoke. Reflexively, I inhale and immediately my head feels fuzzy.

"Ethan!"

I start up the stairs before I remember, again, that Ethan isn't here. He left for the airport after he brushed my teeth and tucked me into bed. He's gone. I run back into the living room. I can see the smoke now, like a faint gray film over everything, but I'm sure it's not from here, from my place. I pull up the neck of Ethan's T-shirt to cover my nose and mouth. It still smells like him, but just barely.

I yank open my front door, sprint down the steps and up the identical set next to mine, and pound on Megan and Bryan's door. Through their window I see nothing but red where their living room is supposed to be.

Suddenly my toes leave the floor. My bare ass is exposed to the cool night air as Ethan's T-shirt is bunched up around my waist. It takes me a moment to realize a firefighter has tossed me over his shoulder and is carrying me down the stairs.

"It's okay! I got you." I feel his hand, heavy and scratchy from the leather gloves he's wearing, yank down on the T-shirt to cover me. "I got you!"

"My neighbors! They're inside!" I struggle against the hold of his arms, but he's really strong. Maritza would give her left nut to have a fireman haul her around like this. "I have to wake them up!"

"We got it." The fireman puts me down, and my feet sink into damp grass. "What are their names?"

"They're the, uh, Bryan and Megan." I'm so used to referring to them as the Beaverless Cleavers, their real names said out loud sound wrong.

"Anyone else in your place?" He peers into my eyes, holding my face between his hands.

"I . . . no." I'm very aware of being practically naked, but I'm not cold. Still, I'm shaking so hard, my teeth are chattering. "No one else. I feel very odd."

"It's the adrenaline. If you feel light-headed, make sure to sit down." He signals over to the ambulance, giving them a thumbs-up. "You got a dog or a cat?"

"God, no. Just me," I tell him. I startle when one of the paramedics wraps a Mylar blanket around my shoulders. I look around to thank him, but it's all just a swirl of figures, lights, and noise. "What about my neighbors?"

"They're going to be okay. Don't go anywhere." He turns around and charges back up the stairs into Bryan and Megan's place. Their front door is on the floor instead of on its hinges. Bryan isn't going to like that.

"Who do you want to call, honey?" the older woman with the small yippy dog who lives in the townhouse next to mine asks me. Her dog is tucked into the crook of her arm. It's wearing pajamas, complete with a robe. I feel bad for it, and I'm not a fan of small dogs. "Honey?"

I stare back at her until she points to my cordless phone. I don't remember grabbing it, much less dialing the first few digits of Ethan's number. It's too far from the base to get a signal.

"Yes, it is, honey. Much too far from the base." Her agreeing with me confuses me even more until I realize I said my last thought out loud. I can only hope I kept that remark about her off-puttingly small dog to myself. "Do you want to come inside and use my phone, honey?"

"I . . . no, thank you. I'm fine."

She steps away to fill in another neighbor about my misfortune. Her dog growls at him, but he goes ahead and tries to pet it. It nips at him. For a moment, this small drama supersedes mine and I'm able to step away.

I set the phone down on the curb and stay there, stooped over, staring at my bare feet. Everything feels fragmented and out of order, but I'm very aware of being inside my body. My car, my townhouse, what's in it, all of it is separate from me. Even the cactus Ethan gave me that I've managed to keep alive by pretending to ignore it doesn't matter at this moment. Despite what could have happened, what's happening, and what might happen, I'm absolutely certain I'm safe.

So why am I still so afraid?

"Stop playing dumb, Bernal," I say under my breath in case anyone can hear me over all the noise. "You know what you have to do, and you know why you have to do it soon."

I stand up, walk over to one of the fire engines and press my hand against it. Underneath my palm it vibrates with energy and purpose as I watch black smoke pour out of Megan and Bryan's front door and wait to see if the place where I live, my home of sorts, will start to do the same.

# DULCINA

I WANT TO LEAVE a message for Claudia to let her know I'm on my way, but her answering machine doesn't pick up. I disconnect the call and lie back on the bed. I went ahead and made it myself after asking for fresh towels from housekeeping this morning. I've booked this room until tomorrow, but I'm leaving today. Or I might stay the night. I could also drive until Ethan's ten grand is spent only stopping wherever I wind up to earn gas money so I can keep going again. These little mind games let me pretend I may not show up at the house even though I know that's exactly what I'm going to do.

I try one more time and let it ring a dozen times like it did a few moments before. I could call Ethan, but this feels a little too much like I'm going behind Claudia's back even more than I already am. When she's ready to tell me about him, she will and I can't blame her for not sharing her personal life with me. Honestly, the only way I was ever going to find out she has a man was by him answering her phone and telling me he's in love with her.

I get out of bed, make sure the door locks behind me, and take the elevator to the lobby. It's a nice enough budget hotel right off the 5 with complimentary breakfast. Today there was a waffle maker along with the usual yogurt, pastries, and dry cereal. I like fresh waffles but it's not what caught my attention this morning.

I make a quick purchase at the overpriced convenience store off the lobby before I browse the rack of tourist attraction brochures by the front doors. The desk clerk watches me pick one up and put it right back. I'm no tourist, but I am here for a specific type of attraction.

He's a pale guy except for where the sun hits him—tops of his ears, bridge of his nose, and back of his neck. He's also young, mid-twenties at most, probably plays in a garage band he hopes will take him far away from Tejon Ranch and Interstate 5. I'm sure the long sleeves of his white button-down shirt are hiding more than a few painfully clichéd tattoos.

"The outlets aren't too far from here," he says in a surprisingly deep voice. He taps out a little rhythm with the tips of his fingers on the countertop. "If you like shopping."

"Who doesn't like shopping?" I bought myself some new underwear, bras, and a pack of Hanes T-shirts, but my jeans have taken on a sweet molasses odor and shapeless texture of being worn for too long between washes. Joey gave me a half dozen pairs of her colorful print socks, so I'm set there. "But that's not why I'm here."

"There's a pool downstairs and an exercise room." He looks me up and down.

His eyes are a watery shade of blue, and they're only going to grow dimmer with age and disappointment. He has good hair, though. Thick, wavy, and dark. Rock star hair. That's probably what the girls around here tell him, and it's true enough for Tejon Ranch.

"I'll pass on the pool." I walk away from the rack and toward him.

"People like to go horseback riding. I can call a place and set it up for you," he says, making no move toward the phone.

"I'm allergic. To people." It takes him a few seconds to process what I said. He laughs a little self-consciously. "I'm going to leave today."

He comes around from the other side of the desk that separates us. He's just about my height, thin, wiry. His black chinos are cinched tight at his waist with a cheap leather belt. His fingernails are cut short, and there's a faint hint of a callus on his thumb. Definitely a guitar player, probably bass. I'll make sure not to ask him.

"I don't blame you. I just listed all the best parts of this place, and you're not interested in any of them."

"I never said I wasn't interested."

He swallows hard, smart enough not to play dumb. "Let me get someone up here to, uh, give me a second. Don't go anywhere."

I wait for him by the brochures as he talks to the woman he's asking to cover for him for a couple of hours. I pretend I'm not listening as he tries not to come right out and tell her why he needs her to do him this favor. When it's settled—he agrees to take her next overnight shift—I go stand between the two elevators and let him press the button. When it opens, he steps aside for me and then stands away until the door closes. As soon as it does, he's kissing me—my mouth, my neck, my ears—and dragging his knuckles across my nipples. He's done this before, and he knows what he's doing.

"Here," I say, handing him the box of condoms I just bought.

"I got my own," he says, and presses his hips into me. He's already hard.

The elevator deposits us on the third floor and he moves his hand from my arm to my waist. I lead him to my room, where he takes the keycard from me to open the door. As soon as it closes behind us, I drop to my knees so the toes of my boots are pressed right up against it. Looking up at him, I undo his belt, unbutton his pants, and pull down his zipper.

"Ouch," I say when I get a look at him. "You could have given me a heads up, man."

Before he can apologize, and there's no reason for him to, I take him into my mouth, or at least what I can manage without causing my complimentary breakfast to repeat on me. He lets me work him for a bit before he hauls me up and strips off all of my clothes except for my underwear.

He likes to kiss and knows how to use his tongue. He does foreplay like I do when I'm with a woman. Once he has me making the sounds I'm used to being the one to orchestrate, he eases off me. He gets naked and rolls on one of his condoms.

"Take off your panties. Open your legs," he says. I do as I'm told, feeling giddy at his words and my own compliance to them. He settles himself on top of me, kissing my ear and neck. "I'm going to fuck you hard and fast. I'm going to come in you, and then I'm going to do you right."

All I can do is moan, and I only get louder when he puts himself inside of me. Another "ouch." It is fast and hard, but he makes sure I come before he does. Once he catches his breath and after he offers me a cup of lukewarm water from the bathroom sink, he's ready to do it again. Just as he promised, he does me right.

He moves around this second time, positioning my body where and how he wants me, not letting me get on top so I can't take over like I'm used to. When I try, he tightens his hold on me to keep me in place. When I try again, he takes my chin in his hand and shakes his head. Sighing with annoyed relief, I give in to him. With a firm, open-palmed spank on my butt, he raises my hips on a pillow before hooking one of my legs over his shoulder, always touching me with just enough pressure to get me to respond. He likes it from behind, his strong fingers trailing from my neck and down my spine to hold my hips in place as he moves his. Goose bumps ripple over my skin and I come, long and loud. The comedown is just as good and feels like I'm very high and just drunk enough.

Facedown and completely relaxed, I hear him snap off the condom and wrap it in a tissue before tossing it in the trash can to join the first one. I'm guessing he used to clean these rooms before he was promoted to the front desk.

"What's your name again?" he asks from the foot of the bed.

I flip onto my back so I can look at him. His torso and arms are a mass of tattoos with no rhyme or reason to them.

I worked at a piercing and tattoo parlor in the Haight after I dropped out of art school, customizing designs for clients who wanted something more original than a dag-gered heart. The pay was good, in cash, but it bothered me to see something from my imagination rendered on human skin. Worse, some people would ask to have their picture taken with me and their new tattoo. That's when I started waitressing for Curtis, who I met when he came in for a Prince Albert.

"Rachel." I never told him my name, just what floor I was on when we were in the elevator.

He gets back into bed and hauls me onto him, my head on his thin shoulder, his arms around me. I'm not used to being held like this, and it makes me a little uncomfortable, but I'll go with it. I close my eyes so I won't have to see his tattoos up close. His hand strokes my back, up and down, in a way I find surprisingly soothing. It makes me feel drowsy, but I'm not going to fall asleep. It's time to go.

"You don't look like a Rachel."

I open my eyes. Whatever drowsiness I was willing to indulge in leaves me in an instant.

When I was eight, some random creep tried to get wise with me and my sisters on our way to the park. He asked my name, I told him it was Rachel. He asked what my sisters were called. I told him they were Rachel Two and Rachel Three. Then I told him our dad was a cop who loved to shoot old perverts in the dick. Claudia and Maritza were red-faced with laughter as he ran away from us.

I doubt we'd find that story funny now.

"There's an okay place to eat not too far from here," he says, making his move with the suggestion and by settling his hand on my ass. He's getting hard again.

"Usually, the going out to eat part happens first, not the other way around, guy."

We're quiet, nothing but our breathing and the hum of the air conditioner to fill the silence. I move my head so I can't hear his heartbeat and stare at my new mobile phone on the nightstand. I'll give Claudia's townhouse another call before I go, but first I have to get him out of here.

"So, Rachel? You still checking out today?" He sounds as young as he is, almost timid—exactly the opposite of how he was during sex. "Because if you want to hang out, we can do that."

I'm flattered he's trying to coax me into staying, but not nearly sentimental enough to consider what he's offering me. I move off his shoulder and hand him his shirt and pants, keeping my eyes off his impressive penis. He more than deserves this small courtesy.

"I have somewhere I need to be." I lay my palm flat on the center of his chest, right over his tattoo of a heart with a dagger going through it. "But I'm really glad I stopped here on my way there."

# ♦ 29 ♦

# CLAUDIA

Dad sits on his blue plaid La-Z-Boy recliner watching soccer on the TV Mom always feels compelled to mention they got at Costco. The chair, wobbly side table, and TV are all slightly off center from the front window. This setup avoids the late afternoon glare from the sun, and allows him to keep an eye on what's going on in the neighborhood.

When he's not in the living room, he's on the front porch sitting in his other favorite chair—a dark green plastic stackable patio chair he buys in pairs from the local hardware store. Inside, his only company is the TV, but outside there's the mailman, the Sparkletts guy, fellow residents of Fickett Street, and anyone else passing by the front yard who might have a moment to shoot the shit with him. He's even on a first-name basis with the patrol cops. Dad is lonely. Not that he'll admit it, much less admit to the reason why he is.

I will. It's Mom.

I wonder if he resents her for narrowing his life into such a small existence. He must have some thoughts on how he spends his days in an endless blur of sameness in front of the TV or on the porch and always where she can keep an eye on him.

Cheating on Mom throughout much of their marriage was one thing, but acknowledging his past infidelity is mutually inconceivable. And since she won't confront him with what he did to her, he never has to atone for what he's done. Their unspoken agreement means Mom gets to resent him to her heart's content, and Dad has to live out his remaining days like an untrustworthy yard dog.

"It was the *gringa's* fault. Tell them, Claudia," Dad loudly suggests.

I wave my hand at him, willing him to be quiet. I'm on their cordless phone, but it cuts out if it's more than a few feet from the base so the Farmers Insurance rep can hear everything he says. My place is okay, the firewall between our townhouses did its job, but I can't stay there until the smell of smoke is taken care of.

"Tell them she was doing *brujerias* with her candles. Claudia, tell them."

Dad's not entirely wrong. Megan had planned a romantic evening of bare genital bumping, complete with a dozen or so candles in the living room. She didn't think to put out said candles before leaving to meet friends for a drink. Stupid romantic gringa.

"Yes, I'll hold. Thank you," I say, even as I resign myself to being transferred to yet another department where I'll have to start all over again.

I stand up to stretch my legs. Catching sight of my reflection in the front window, I have to look twice to make sure it's me. I'm wearing Maritza's Juicy velour knockoff, which is the color of old period blood, her sparkly bebe T-shirt, and a pair of Repetto ballet flats I'd stashed in the trunk of my car and pretended to forget were there so I wouldn't feel guilty about adding yet another pair to my already full closet of unworn shoes.

"Hello? I'm still holding," I say as I hear the muzak cut out only for it to come back on. "Great. Fucking great."

Dad looks over at me, his can of Budweiser hovering between his chin and mouth. He thinks I curse too much, which is true. I think he drinks too much Budweiser, which is also true. I glance away with a mumbled half-assed apology. It's taken less than 24 hours under his roof for me to resort to acting like a kid again.

I showed up here just after 3:00 AM wearing an oversized UCLA sweatshirt, basketball shorts, and tube socks provided by the neighbor who got bit by the other neighbor's tiny dog. I had to sweet talk the fireman who tossed me over his shoulder into retrieving my purse but didn't think to ask him to get my cell, BlackBerry or a change of clothes, much less my laptop.

The lack of my own stuff is an annoying inconvenience, but having to sleep with Maritza in her queen sized bed is what's put my current situation into stark perspective.

My sister still kicks in her sleep, harder than ever. I woke up hanging off the very edge of the bed with a nose full of sooty snot and a bruise on my shin. I should have checked in to a hotel, but for whatever reason, once I got into my car, I drove here, to the house. It was automatic, a reflex I gave in to even as part of me wanted to pull over, look for a phone, and call Ethan. I could call him now, but I can't. I should, but I won't. At least not until I get all this and another thing sorted out. Once I do, everything will be as it should.

Muzak drips into my ear and adds to the other sounds that surround me—boom boxes and car stereos, police sirens, kids making the most of their last minutes of playing on the street before they're called in for dinner and everyone shuts their windows and double locks their doors for the night. In the kitchen, Maritza and Mom bicker over what to have for dinner and talk about me. Dad seems unfazed, which tells me a variation of this conversation is a daily occurrence he's learned to tune out.

"Good thing her dress was here," Maritza says to Mom. She sounds put upon, as if I purposely failed at burning down my townhouse just to ruin her big day. "We'd never be able to get another one in time for my wedding."

"Maritza, that's not nice," Mom tells her a testy voice. "She's your sister."

"So? I'm her sister too," Maritza replies in that ever-injured tone of hers.

"Claudia could have died!" Mom yells, for once calling her out on her selfishness. "Stop eating avocados."

"I'm stressed out right now—my sister was almost killed last night." Maritza sounds more bored than concerned. "I'll go on a diet tomorrow."

"Someone is taking *El Chino's* spot." Dad lets out a low whistle as a small red car is expertly maneuvered into an equally small spot across the street.

"Not so loud," Mom says. Not, "don't say that" but "not so loud."

"He's not Chinese, Dad," I remind him. "The Phams are Vietnamese."

"Okay, college girl," he says, tipping his can of Budweiser in my direction. "Pham, Chang, Chavez. You got it."

It wasn't until I left for college and had the chance to live around all types of people that I realized I should be nothing less than horrified by my parents' attitude toward people of other races and ethnicities. I was raised in an environment of entrenched—if benign and even affectionate—bigotry. When we were growing up, we would squat "rice paddy style" on the sidewalk to play jacks. Mom would always say "*Chino chino combuh combah*" when we saw someone who was Asian. A Black person in the neighborhood would cause everyone to rush out to their yards, where they stayed until that person turned the corner and became another block's problem.

My parents, especially Dad, always have an opinion, usually negative, about anyone who isn't at least a little

Mexican. At the same time, Dad has always been quick to offer help or an invitation to the many people he's befriended, explaining how this particular person or family is different from "those others."

The Phams, who are firmly in the "those others" camp, purchased the house from Mrs. Gonzalez about a year ago. She went to live with her daughter in El Paso this past February after she broke her elbow. She'd forgotten her keys and had tried to climb in through a window because she hadn't wanted to bother Dad. Mrs. Gonzalez had lived on Fickett Street way before my parents moved into this house when Dooley was a baby and I was well on my way to joining the family.

Mrs. Gonzalez was like a mother to him even before he lost his real one when he was 13 and she took him in. When the For Sale sign went up on her lawn, Mom called me at work to tell me the news, but didn't mention Dad was so depressed, he'd spent most of the month in bed. She called me again to tell me who was moving in. *They* were.

*They* are never referred to as the Phams, only as Los Chinos. There's El Chino, the father, La China, the mother, the kids are Los Chinitos, and the grandmother is La China Mas Vieja.

Dad has taken to watching everything they do, and their doings have become a favorite topic of his, after Los Dodgers and the latest episode of *Judge Judy*. He's so enthusiastic about the Phams, he'll answer the phone and update whoever is on the other end with the latest travesty they've perpetrated on Mrs. Gonzalez's house.

Recently, it was their "Chinese Garden" he couldn't stop talking about. The Phams poured concrete over the bare dirt of their front, side, and back yards after stripping the property of every last living green thing except for the massive avocado tree that Maritza helps herself to at her leisure. And, of course, there's the thing about the parking.

"Mr. Pham doesn't own the street, and neither do you, Dad," I tell him. "Anyone can park wherever they want. Except for me. I have to park in the driveway and a little bit on the sidewalk."

Maritza wanders in from the kitchen and stops cold. "Oh my God!"

"Órale!" Dad calls out in alarm as Maritza takes off like a shot through the front door. "Ques tu problema?"

"It's Dooley!" Maritza yells over her shoulder, already unlatching the front gate. "Dooley's here!"

"Dulcina?" Mom rushes to the door, crossing herself, and is joined by Dad, TV remote in one hand, can of Budweiser in the other. "Claudia! Take the beer into our bedroom."

I ignore her and hang up the phone as adrenaline surges through my body. I brush past both of them to follow Maritza across the street. Neighbors are peeking out from their windows, some coming out onto their porches. The news of Dooley's return will travel up and down Fickett Street like a busted water main, dredging up old gossip about her along the way.

Before Dooley has a chance to get the key out of the ignition, Maritza is already reaching into the open window and hugging her so hard, she's practically strangling our sister. Dooley keeps both hands on the steering wheel, a big goofy smile on her face.

"Oh my God, your hair!" Maritza yanks on the door handle, but it's locked.

"Like it?" Dooley smooths back the tiny braids as she gets out of the car.

"No," Maritza says. "You're going to take them out, right?"

"Don't start, Maritza." I embrace Dulcina, signaling to Maritza that the braids will come out.

"We were getting so worried." Maritza links her arm through Dooley's and leads her toward the house. "Dooley, give Claudia your keys. Claudia, lock Dooley's car."

"Yeah, I'll get the bags too." I reach for the lever to pop the hatchback open.

"There's nothing there," Dooley says, with an edge in her voice. I feel myself stiffen. "Just my duffel bag in the back seat."

If she says there's nothing there, I have to accept there's nothing there, which means I have to assume there's something there. This must be how Mom's mind works. No wonder her head always hurts.

"Nice car. It needs a tune up and the tires should be rotated," I tell her as she hands me her keys.

"Did you pay for it?" Maritza asks with complete sincerity.

"No, Maritza, I jacked some old lady outside a senior center," Dooley says with a completely straight face. "I threw her knitting out the window and smoked all her Newports because that's the kind of person I am."

"That would have been my guess," I call after her. "But I'd always hoped you had more self-respect for yourself than to smoke Newports."

I catch up to my sisters and the three of us pause at the front gate. Our parents are waiting for us on the porch—Mom twisting her hands, Dad holding his beer. Their faces show relief but also worry. Nothing has changed and everything is different.

"*Déjà vu*, huh?" I say as much to myself as to Dooley.

She nudges me gently in the ribs with her elbow but keeps looking straight ahead. Mom rushes forward in a burst of anxious energy and gives Dooley a quick, awkward hug.

"Your father has to move your car," she says. "Give him the keys, Claudia."

"It's okay where it is," Dooley says. Her arms are at her sides as if the hug unsettled her. "Why move it?"

"Don't ask," Maritza and I say at the same time.

"Jinx," I yell at Maritza and punch her in the arm but not as hard I'd like to. "Now you have to do what I tell you until bedtime and no bitching about it. First thing I want you to do is stop bitching."

"Daddy's new hobby is fighting with the neighbors across the street," Maritza says, ignoring my rightful jinx. "*Los Chinos* take up all the parking."

"Dad doesn't fight them. He just throws major shade from the porch like he does to the *cholos* to keep them in check. Except the Phams are Vietnamese, so his shade isn't translating, but it's true about the parking," I explain, which just piles onto Dooley's amused confusion. "I'm sure they're lovely people. Just as lovely as we are."

Mom stands back and inspects Dooley. "You're too skinny."

"Thank you," she says.

Dooley looks around at all of us, her eyes clear and bright like they were before things went bad for her. I see this and I see her. A warm feeling grows in my chest, easing itself over the panicky doubt that had filled it just a few seconds before. She's here, she's safe, and she's my sister.

Choke on that, Fickett Street.

# 30

# MARITZA

I POKE AT THE bag, trying to see if I can feel if there's anything besides clothes in there without opening it. Dooley
used to hide her secret stuff in all sorts of places. For months,
after she left, I would pull bottles of gin, vodka, and all sorts
of loose pills out of the weirdest places. I threw everything
away because she was gone and couldn't get mad at me for
touching her stuff.

Dooley has a temper and it won't be fair if she gets mad
at just me. It's not like I'm the only one who wants to know
if she's still doing that kind of bad stuff.

My mother just stands there holding a towel she says is
for Dooley. She already gave her one of the white and yellow striped towels, so I don't know what she's doing with
this second one. She never lets me use more than one, even
from the set Claudia gave me for Christmas. They're practically new, those towels, and I'm taking them with me to my
house when I move out.

"Open it, Claudia," I tell her when she comes to stand
in the doorway. "Super fast, before she gets out of the
shower."

"No, and no one is going to open her bag. There's nothing in there but clothes," Claudia says, but doesn't sound
too sure. "Let's go back to the living room."

None of us move.

"What's going on?" Daddy asks from behind Claudia. It's past dinnertime, and he's been drinking his beer on an empty stomach. "What are you doing with that? It's none of your business. Leave it."

"We can't have her bringing those kinds of. . .of. . .*cosas* into the house." Mamá sounds really stressed out. I'm surprised she hasn't gone straight to bed with a migraine. "She has to get rid of it or leave. Right, Claudia?"

"This isn't my house, Mom. If you don't want her to stay here, then you can throw her out."

"Claudia," is all Daddy says even though she's being disrespectful to my mother.

"You can't tell her to leave, Mamá. It's too close to my wedding." Claudia gives me a dirty look. "What?"

"She's sober." Claudia moves away from the doorway. "What's for dinner? Besides Budweiser."

"Watch yourself, college girl, or I'll take you for a drive," Daddy says, but he doesn't sound serious. They let Claudia get away with so much.

"How can you be sure?" I ask her. I smooth out my coverlet around the bag, trying to listen for the sound of pills or liquor bottles.

"Because I am." Claudia has a stubborn look on her face. She's ready to turn this into a fight, and she won't back down until we agree with her. "She's sober. Period."

My mother twists her hands. She's afraid of Claudia. Not of what she'll do, but of what she might say. Sometimes I am too. Claudia always does what she says she's going to do.

"Good to know," Daddy says, like it's all okay just because Claudia said so. "What's for dinner?"

"Pollo Loco." It's what Mamá always suggests when she doesn't want to cook. "Maritza can go pick it up."

"Me? I'm the bride! Why should I—"

The shower squeaks off, and I race out of my room. I look behind me and see Claudia is laughing, holding the door closed, pulling on the knob so hard she's leaning back. On the other side I can hear my mother knocking on it, fast and nervous.

"What are you doing?" I ask her. I want to laugh at whatever it is she thinks is so funny but not if it's because of me. "Claudia?"

"I'm . . . I'm making sure Mom gives Dooley that extra towel." Still holding on to the knob, she bends over, her cheeks all pink, tears coming out of her eyes. "I'm going to pee my pants!"

"You're going to get in trouble, Claudia," I tell her. "And you better not pee in *my* pants. They're almost new."

She just shakes her head, laughing so hard now, she's not making any noise. I get her away from the door and we go outside to where Daddy is watering the flowers he planted for my wedding. He's smiling, but I can't stop thinking about Dulcina and my wedding plans.

"She is going to take those braids out, right?" I ask Claudia. "She has to."

Daddy and Claudia look at each other and start laughing, this time for sure at me. I get so mad, I start crying. Claudia stumbles away and goes to pee behind the lemon tree, laughing at me the whole time.

## ◆ 31 ◆

# DULCINA

I LOOK OVER MARITZA'S shoulder at the guest list she's put into a spreadsheet. She's color-coded and grouped names. We're categorized in a rather jarring shade of pink, and Augustino and his family are in a puke shade of green. I'm no therapist, but I know enough about color theory to understand this is as close as Maritza will ever come to visualizing how she feels about the people in her life. A name toward the bottom of the spreadsheet catches my eye.

"Mrs. Flores! Why are you inviting that old *bruja*?" I ask as I sit down next to her. The three of us have nurtured an eternal dislike for Mrs. Flores since we were kids. "Honestly, why?"

"*Mamá* says I have to. She moved to Huntington Park but still goes to St. Mary's." Maritza sniffs. She was crying when I got out of the shower and our dad and Claudia were laughing, not necessarily at her but probably because of her. Yeah, nothing new there. "I bet you she brings like a million people to my wedding."

"And only one gift," Claudia says as she serves herself some of the food our mom picked up before going to bed with a migraine. Maritza ignores her, which only feeds Claudia's sarcasm. "Mrs. Flores is a straight-up old-school, *mantilla*-wearing Mexican. She's going to demand to see the bedsheets the morning after your wedding night, Maritza. You better hope Augustino's a bleeder or she's going to come after you with a bucket of holy water in one hand and her *chancla* in the other."

"She's a horrible person," I say instead of laughing, which would make our baby sister cry again. I pull the towel off my hair and ignore Maritza's frown at seeing my braids. "Some things, and especially some people, never change."

"Oh, man, now the only thing I can smell is Vicks and mothballs." Claudia pushes her plate of food away and puts her hand to her mouth, looking pale and green.

"You better not barf because this one," I gesture toward Maritza with my thumb, "can out barf us all. Don't. Claudia. Don't!"

"I'm not," she says, still looking green. "I hope you're inviting her to dump a bucket of pig's blood over her head. I know a guy who can get us fake blood. We're not complete monsters."

"Maybe," Maritza says, not dismissing Claudia's suggestion as the joke she meant it to be.

The summer I was to turn six, our mom started sending us down the street with some fruit, a jar of last night's caldo, and a fresh package of tortillas Mrs. Flores would swap out for her stale ones.

As soon as our mom left, Mrs. Flores would make us do yard work, cleaning the gutters, sweeping the sidewalk, and gathering up the apricots that dropped down from her tree with a thump. Sometimes they'd burst if they were too ripe to survive the fall intact. Those were a pain to clean up from the grass. She only let us inside to use the bathroom and eat. If she caught us so much as stopping to pick our days-of-the week chones out of our butts, there would be a

pinch on the back of our arms, right where the skin is thin-
nest. For Maritza, she'd also yank, sharp and hard, on one
of her pigtails, but only if Claudia wasn't around.

A heavy silence falls over the three of us as we each
decide not to delve any deeper into the reason why we had
to endure Mrs. Flores's sadistic babysitting for those few
months.

I look over at the wall of framed photos our mom fusses
over like a curator at the Met. A glossy photograph of a big-
jawed blond man with bangs and a mustache sits square in
the middle of the wall. A thick black scrawl mars the otherwise airbrushed image.

"Who the hell is that guy?" I ask.

"That helluva guy is Chuck Norris," Claudia says with
a grin. "I gave it to Dad for his birthday. My last assistant
knew a person who knows a person who sells weed to the
person who trims Chuck Norris' bangs."

"Okay, but why is he on our wall?" I can't help but feel
his picture makes it less special.

School pictures never cut it with our mom. She insisted
on a yearly visit to Kremer & Sons Family Portrait Studio
on Olympic. We wore coordinating outfits, curled our hair,
and tried to make her happy. This went on right up until I
left for San Francisco. The three of us haven't taken a picture together since.

"Daddy loves Chuck Norris." Maritza says this as if it
should be totally obvious to me. "I got him all his movies
for his big birthday. Remember?"

"Nope," I shrug. Claudia looks at me. She knows why
I don't remember but won't remind Maritza that we had
to leave his party early because I was so wasted. "I thought
Mrs. Flores was dead."

"We should be so lucky," Claudia snorts. "Oh, don't
look at me like that, Maritza. There are plenty of better

reasons why I'm going to burn in hell, and most of them I've done at least twice. Including butt stuff. Both ways."

Maritza's expression is equal parts displeased and confused by our sister's raunchiness. Poor, sweet bunny. She doesn't know what she's missing. It's probably why she's okay with marrying Augustino—she's never had any better to miss.

"It's her husband who died," Maritza says to me after giving Claudia one last dirty look. "It's why she had to move to Huntington Park to live with her son."

I can guess the answer, but I still ask. "Moses or El Dorky?"

"El Dorky," both Maritza and Claudia answer.

Maritza doesn't call jinx—she's still annoyed with Claudia—and Claudia can't double jinx Maritza without voiding her original jinx. If she was to call it, the next time Maritza jinxes her, it'll count for twice amount of time. Technically, Maritza is leaving both her and Claudia open to my third-party jinx, but I'll let this one slide.

"He's divorced, but he still takes communion at Mass. He's not supposed to," Maritza says in a judgmental tone.

"If that's the worst thing he's doing, then he's doing okay." Claudia shrugs, then shudders. "Unlike his brother."

"Moses is in prison," Maritza tells me, as if this piece of gossip is so expected, it's not even worth sharing. "Manslaughter or murder, one of those, and he's never getting out."

"Neither of them had a chance with a mother like Mrs. Flores," I say just as casually, even as I try to ignore the sudden sour taste in my mouth. "They were doomed from the start."

"Yeah, well, it's not like we got to pick our mother either," Claudia says.

She drops this bomb so matter-of-factly, I almost want to slow clap her. Maritza definitely wants to slap her. Honestly? Claudia probably deserves both.

"Did you invite the mailman too?" I ask Maritza in a lame attempt to steer our conversation back to the wedding.

"Dad invited him." Maritza scrolls up her spreadsheet and shows me his name in the blue category. "He's going to bring his wife and two kids."

"Really?" There are too many traps to fall into when it comes to Maritza's wedding. "Okay, then."

"Hey, Maritza? Have you and Augustino done the deed yet?" Claudia's ready to start teasing Maritza again. "Or is his mommy keeping his peepee in her purse until you put a ring on his finger?"

"Shut up!" Maritza yelps. She's trying not to laugh, which means she's less annoyed with Claudia. "It's none of your business."

"You guys do it here? Or at his house? Your car? Please don't say you've done it on your bed. That thing squeaks if you so much as breathe on it."

"Shut up, Claudia." Maritza is red in the face, but her mouth twitches. "And grow up."

"Don't be embarrassed, Maritza. I did. With Nick. Remember him? God, I do," Claudia sighs. She points toward the couch and our eyes follow her finger. "We did it there once, really quick and real quiet. And in the Malibu for hours. *Hours.*"

"*Cochina!*" Maritza gathers up her laptop and stomps into the kitchen.

"You think they do it?" I ask Claudia. I prop my feet on Maritza's empty chair and start eating off her plate.

"All the time," she says around a yawn.

"All the time what?" our dad asks as he wanders in from the porch.

"Nothing," we both answer. Quickly, before she can beat me to it, I reach over to pinch Claudia's arm and yell, "Jinx!"

# ◆ 32 ◆

# MARITZA

I LOOK OUT THE kitchen window over the sink where my mother usually is and listen to Dooley and Claudia. They always gang up on me and think they're so smart and funny, especially Claudia. I'm not mad at her, just annoyed because she didn't give me a chance to get in on the joke. And I'm annoyed with everything else too. The wedding, who I have to invite, all the money it's costing for things I don't even want like sod and Jordon almonds. Maybe I'm even annoyed with having to go through with it.

This must be exactly how Princess Diana felt.

It's way too late to back out now. Not that I'm going to, and anyways, I have it all planned out. I know what I'm doing. I don't care if everyone thinks I'm being a spoiled brat. Why does getting what I want make me a brat?

They keep talking like nothing is wrong. Daddy comes in from the porch to tell Dulcina why Chuck Norris is a good actor, repeating himself like he always does around this time of night. Claudia makes her little jokes and Dooley laughs. None of them ask me to come back and join them. They don't seem to miss Mamá either.

Sometimes I wonder if my life would be different if I wasn't the youngest, the baby of the family. Maybe if there had been another one of us after me, a little brother, it would be easier for my mother not to need me as much as she does. And Daddy would have someone to talk about Chuck Norris with instead of having to put up with Dooley and Claudia giggling like dummies. He's had too much Budweiser for it to be funny, but it doesn't stop my sisters from cracking themselves up.

I go to my room and open the door extra quietly like I've taught myself to do. I'm not at all surprised when I catch my mother going through Dooley's stuff.

She looks guilty but relieved it's me who's caught her. I knew the second she suggested Pollo Loco she was going to look in Dooley's bag while we ate. She hates Pollo Loco and King Taco. I really like both, but I shouldn't be eating that kind of food so close to my wedding.

"Did you find anything?" I ask her as I close the door behind me. She shakes her head. "That's good. How are you feeling?"

My mother doesn't answer again. She's pretending I didn't say anything, like she always does when she wants to keep playing her little games. Of course, she didn't have a migraine. She hardly ever does, but it's the excuse she gives when she wants to be sneaky or have a break from Daddy. I know this about her, but I won't tell anyone. I have respect for my mother.

Not like Claudia with her comment about us not getting to choose Mamá. As if my mother is anything like Mrs. Flores. That woman used to hit Moses with an electrical cord. One time she made El Dorky put his hand in a pot of boiling water because he tried to steal a dirty magazine from the corner store.

Claudia can be so hard on Mamá and on everyone else too. She needs to soften up, or she's never going to attract a man.

"Where's your father?" Mamá asks as she starts to put Dooley's clothes back into the bag in a way that's obvious someone's gone through it. "And your sisters?"

"They're all in the living room," I tell her. She already knows this, but she just wants to make sure I'm going to keep her secret. "Making jokes and being stupid like always. How's your migraine? Do you feel better now, Mamá?"

She starts fussing with my coverlet, slapping at wrinkles that aren't there. I've made her mad, really mad.

"Mamá?" My heart beats fast and my mouth tastes like I chewed on a piece of foil paper. "I'm sorry, Mamá. I just want to make sure—"

"You better watch yourself, Maritza." She says this in a way that makes me remember she used to have one of Daddy's belts in a kitchen drawer where he never thought to look for it. "I know about you."

"What, Mamá?" I wish Claudia would come check on me or Dooley would do something bad so Daddy has to yell at her. "What are you talking about?"

"I found that card. What would Augustino say if he knew you were seeing a man doctor for that kind of business? Hmm? Do you think he wants his prometida letting another man touch her and see her like that? No tienes vergüenza. That must be what you want, to be nasty with other men. Isn't it? Marrana. You might as well have stayed married to—"

"Please, Mamá, don't! Please don't say it."

Her face is all twisted into itself. She looks so ugly and full of hate . . . for me. I back away from her toward the door.

"Where do you think you're going? Out there? With them? They don't want you there."

"I know they don't, Mamá. Please, I'm sorry."

We both jump when Claudia knocks on the door. I'm too scared to move, even when she tries to open it and hits me on the back of my head.

"Maritza? Come on, let me in. I'm sorry for teasing you. I'll even pardon you from my jinx and take you to Jack-in-the-Crack for a milkshake. I'll get them to layer all three flavors just the way you like it. . . . *Maritza* . . ."

My mother flinches at the change in the tone of her voice. We both know what it means when Claudia sounds like this. Mamá's face gets all worried, and she starts to twist her hands.

". . . open the door. *Now.*"

My mother hurries out through the bathroom and into her and Daddy's room. As soon as I hear Mamá lock her door, I let Claudia come in.

She looks around, standing very tall and very still. "What happened in here?"

"Nothing." My voice is very small just like I feel. "Nothing."

She lets out a deep, angry breath and then she hugs me like she used to, rocking me just a little and letting me twist her hair around my finger. Claudia won't make me tell her what happened because she already knows. I just hope she doesn't say anything about it to Mamá. Anyways, what good would that do?

# ◆ 33 ◆

# DULCINA

CLAUDIA LEANS ON HER car horn—a quick blast followed by a longer one. The sound is an open invitation for the neighbors to pop up at their windows to see what the deal is. Around here, car horns are less common than gunshots, which are casually noted and then, for the most part, ignored.

The neighbors may rarely remark on gunshots, but everything else is open season. Gossip is a sport for them. Every fight, new piece of furniture, even the installation of cable never gets by without notice or comment. On the rare occasions when the police are called, everyone who's not involved gathers on the sidewalk to hash out the details and contribute their own two cents, which are usually worth just a penny.

Knowing I'll have an audience, I hide behind a pair of Claudia's sunglasses and hurry outside before she gets it into her head to beep me again.

"I forgot you're not a morning person," she says. "Actually, I didn't. Say hello to Fickett Street, Dooley. Everyone is talking about you. Give 'em a wave or the finger . . . most of them deserve the finger."

Claudia smoothly shifts her Audi into gear as soon as I sit down but before I have a chance to buckle up. She might want to get gone as fast as possible, but I can tell she's nervous about where we're going.

We wave goodbye to our dad, who's watching us from the porch, drinking his coffee, and already looking bored. He offered to take my GTI into his mechanic, and I didn't have the heart to deny him an opportunity to get out of the house. It's going to leave me without a car for a couple of days, but I'll manage.

I rushed past our mom where she was fussing over their breakfast, oatmeal, always oatmeal. Her nervous energy was as hot as a burner on the stove, and she refused to make eye contact with me. Someone went through my stuff the other night, either her or Maritza, probably both. I can't blame them. It's going to take some time and effort to earn their trust. I hope I can.

"What time did Maritza get up this morning? Wait, don't tell me. It's still way too early now." I lean my head back and close my eyes. "Wake me up when we get there."

"I see you're going to be great company." Claudia turns on the radio, then switches it off. She wants to talk.

"What happened to the corner store?" I ask as we stop for a red light. She lifts her sunglasses and stares at it with a frown. "It looks the same but different."

"Ain't that the truth, sister. But, yeah, some new people own it." She hides behind sunglasses again, her eyes back on the road as the light turns green. "They're Salvadorians, but Dad says they're okay because they make *pupusas* like they're Mexicans. I don't know if he's joking or if he's convinced himself that *pupusas* are Mexican just like he thinks he is."

"What happened to Mr. Bellani? Did he . . ." I try to sound casual, like it isn't even worth asking about, much less finishing my question.

"He had a heart attack a year and half ago." Claudia sounds like she wants to yawn, but I can tell she's choosing her words carefully. She glances in her review mirror at the store as it gets smaller and dingier. "He's in a nursing home."

We're both quiet for a moment as she gives me space to decide where I want to go with this. My fingers start tingling as if they've fallen asleep. That numbness moves up from my hands to my arms and shoulders, then through my whole body.

Claudia smiles at me. It's both a sad and kind smile. The same one she has in most of those studio portraits Mr. Kremer took of us that are up on the living room wall. "Think of your sisters, Claudia," he would coax in his gentle baritone, having given up on squeaky toys and corny jokes when it came to her.

My sister is still waiting for me to say something and, so, I do.

"The Neapolitan sisters."

The words come out in a whoosh as if something or someone very heavy forced them out of me.

Mr. Bellani had fat, sausage-like fingers and always flirted with our mom. He overpriced his meat and sold dented canned goods at a pathetic markdown, knowing people around here had little choice where to shop back then. As kids, Maritza and I spent most of our weekly allowance at his store on grape soda, corn chips, and all sorts of candy. Not Claudia—she saved her money for the school book fair.

"Here they come! The most beautiful girls in the world!" he'd shout as he held out a handful of cheap penny candy when we'd come in with our mom. "Here you go, little ladies. A treat almost as sweet as you girls are."

"Mr. Bellani, the girls must save room for dinner," our mom would say in her careful English.

He used to tease her about her accent, tell her how pretty she looked, and ask her to run away with him. He made her blush and she always made sure she looked nice when we went to his store.

"What a shame, ladies," he'd say as he dropped the candy back into the jar by the register. We all knew he was going to ignore what she'd said. He always did. "Can you girls share?"

Maritza nodded, though she was the least likely of us to share anything. I was never one to pass up a free treat, but I always looked to see if it was okay with our mom, who'd just sigh and start her shopping. Claudia never like Mr. Bellani, free candy or not. She'd stand by the door waiting for our mom to be done so we could leave.

"I have just the thing, Mrs. Bernal," he'd call after her. "A little something that'll leave plenty of room for dinner."

He'd lean over and reach inside the low freezer he kept up against the front counter for a wrapped ice-cream sandwich. He'd cut it into three equal parts, carefully spacing them so they didn't touch. Chocolate for me, strawberry for Maritza, and vanilla, for Claudia, who never ate hers and would throw it away when Mr. Bellani wasn't looking. She preferred to shoplift rolls of SweetTarts, packs of Fun Dip, and Zotz by the handful to give to me and Maritza. Claudia never had a sweet tooth, but she had quick hands.

"Thank you, Mr. Bellani," we would say—even Claudia—because it's how we were raised.

"It's my lucky day! *Tre principesse* in my store," Mr. Bellani would shout at our mom and to anyone else who happened to be there. "The famous Neapolitan sisters!"

"Those fucking ice-cream sandwiches," Claudia finally says. "He'd split it in three parts so he wouldn't have to give us each a whole one. Cheap bastard."

"He didn't have to give us anything. You shoplifted enough from him as it was." I laugh, but it sounds fake. "He was old when we were kids. How old do you think he is now?"

"In his eighties." She yawns, letting the Audi coast for bit so she can cover her mouth with one hand and keep the other on the steering wheel instead of on the gear shift. "I thought you were going back to sleep."

"Yeah, I'm trying, but you just keep talking."

"Pardon me, lady, I'll just chauffer you in silence," she says, sounding more tired than sarcastic. She's quiet for a moment, but she might as well be screaming. When she speaks again, the sound of her low, measured voice startles me. "We never talk about it. About what happened in Mr. Bellani's store or how Mom never set foot inside there again. She's never said a word about it."

My entire body tenses up. I know what Claudia is talking about.

Our mom's miscarriage is one of the many things we had to piece together on our own. We realized much later that she'd been leaving us with Mrs. Flores because she was pregnant and had doctor appointments. After Maritza came early, it must have been a high-risk pregnancy. It was also why our parents had been so distracted during that time. They would have quiet conversations that stopped immediately when one of us walked in on them. We knew something was up but knew enough not to ask what was wrong.

"Why would she talk about it, Claudia? We were just kids then, and she . . . Jesus Christ, man." My voice sounds sharp, angry. Claudia doesn't flinch. She's good at not taking most things personally. "You know, it's not like she decided to have a miscarriage by the canned goods because why the hell not?"

"It happened by the tortillas," Claudia says.

She's right, of course, it did happen by the tortillas. Claudia has a good memory, good enough for all of us.

There was so much blood. Our mom was embarrassed about the mess she'd made and tried to talk Mr. Bellani out of calling an ambulance. Just like with offering us candy and then giving us a third of an ice-cream sandwich, he ignored her. Maritza grabbed at our mom, screaming at her to get up. Claudia tried to calm her down as I ran to the next aisle for a box of C&H sugar. I got back just as Claudia slapped Maritza into silence.

Our mom had been far enough along for it too look like a baby, a very small one, in a big puddle of blood on the polished concrete floor. It was going to be a boy. That's what one of the paramedics said as he scooped it up and put it into a plastic bag.

Claudia sighs and turns on the radio, a little louder than necessary, ending the conversation. I've always loved Claudia's honesty along with her ability to back off but not away from the truth. Right now is not the right time, not for me. I have other things on my mind and other plans I have to see through. First on my list is making sure she doesn't blow up whatever it is she has with Ethan because of us, her family.

We're still keeping to ourselves when she pulls up to her townhouse, slowing down as if she's afraid of what she'll see. She sighs again, parks right in front, and then, with a muttered "fuck it," gets out and waits for me on the curb. We link elbows, and I stop us at the foot of the stairs leading up to her open front door. There's a blond woman standing in the driveway smoking a cigarette.

"Is that *fulana* your neighbor?" I ask, tilting my head in the woman's direction. "The romantic arsonist?"

"Yeah, that's her. She's pissed at me for filing a claim against their policy." Claudia carefully steps over the cords and tubes leading from the humming van double parked on the sidewalk. "We're both with Farmers and it's causing her more than a little confusion as to how insurance works. She thinks . . . Ugh, forget it. She makes my brain hurt."

Claudia tugs me up the rest of the way, holding on tight to my arm as if she's preparing for the worst. Aside from the very slight odor of cleaning solution, noise from the huge whirring fans, and a half dozen people milling in and out in paper suits, her place is fine. We stand, shoulder to shoulder, watching as one of the workers runs the handset of a powerful vacuum cleaner over the couch.

Besides the furniture that wasn't there the last time I crashed here, there are fasteners on the wall where art has been professionally hung and all of Claudia's books are now thoughtfully arranged on built-in shelves. There are even throw pillows and a small solitary cactus in a cream-colored glazed pot on the coffee table. Ethan has made Claudia's townhouse a home. I wish I could ask her how she feels about this and tell her, despite what she might be afraid of, it's a good thing.

"You got some new stuff," I say, looking around. "Even on the walls."

"Yeah, I've made some changes and change comes with . . . stuff," she says with a self-conscious shrug. "It, um, the . . . art had to be professionally cleaned offsite."

"Oh, so it's, like, *art*—not framed prints of the Eiffel Tower from Posters, Etc." I push up my sleeves. I worked as a Molly Maid when I needed a break from waitressing for Curtis. It didn't pay well, but I enjoyed the work. "So where do you want me to start?"

"It's all taken care of. The upholstery is the last of it. The rugs won't be here until next week. There's a guy coming at eleven to bring back some of the art." Claudia starts up the stairs, talking as she goes. She takes shallow breaths out of her mouth, pinching her nose shut. "If you could keep an eye on things and then get my keys back from the cleaning guys when they're done, that would be great."

I follow her upstairs, unsure of what she really needs from me other than wanting me to be here with her. As always, Claudia is sure of what she's doing, but I know her well enough to recognize there's something slightly off about the way she's holding herself.

"You can use my car today. I'm just going to get some more clothes, then you can drop me off at work." She's still holding her nose, looking a little pale. I might be a recent ex-smoker, but even I can tell there isn't any smoke smell up here. "If you could pick me up at six or so, we can get something to eat before we head back to the house. I can't do Pollo Loco or King Taco again."

"You're not staying here tonight?" I ask.

Just outside her bedroom, Claudia pauses in the doorway, debating whether or not she can pretend she didn't hear me. "No. Not until it doesn't smell like it does. I'll be down in a second. Okay?"

"Sure thing, Claudia. Take your time." I head back down and watch the guys work and then tap the one who looks like he's the supervisor on the shoulder. "Hey. Are you guys hiring?"

He pulls off his painter's mask and looks at me like I'm crazy. "Yeah. Always. Why?"

"I have cleaning experience." I gesture to the rest of his crew. "And I speak Spanish."

"I can give you a card and you can talk to the owner." He hesitates as if waiting for me to tell him I'm just joking. "It's not an easy job. We do smoke, flooding, and biohazard cleaning."

"Like after murders and suicides?" I ask. Above us there's a series of thumping noises followed by Claudia swearing. "My sister must have opened the closet where she hides all her shoes."

"Dooley?" Claudia calls from the top of the stairs. "Can you give me a hand?"

"I'll be back for that card," I tell him as I sprint up the stairs, happy to have something to do.

## · 34 ·

# CLAUDIA

SITTING ON TOP OF my desk, next to my barely warm elixir tea, is a copy of this week's issue of *People* magazine with a yellow sticky note jutting out of it. I open it without a second thought—I've never been a snob about where I get my information—and am sucker punched with a series of photos of Ethan diving into the Mediterranean from the deck of Austin Ford Taylor's yacht.

Julie is pretending to be on the phone, but she's watching me, waiting for a reaction. She put this issue of *People* on my desk with its helpfully marked pages and has done the same for Milty. If she has the balls to expense the cost of the magazines, I'll rip her a new one and smile while I do it.

I had no idea Ethan was in the South of France. He hasn't called me, and I haven't I haven't called him either. There's not much I can do except shove the magazine into my purse and begin going through the motions of returning calls, slogging through emails while keeping Julie busy with a series of utterly pointless tasks so I won't scream at her.

The most consequential thing I have her to do is pick up my usual $9 salad when what I really want is a medium rare steak with a twice-baked potato and to punch her face in for dessert.

When Dooley shows up just after five, way too early even for her, I'm not done pantomiming being a busy, hyperfocused film exec. She sits to the side of my desk flipping through magazines, then scripts and does that leg jiggle thing the three of us do when we're relaxed, nervous, bored, or excited.

Watching my sister fidget just confirms how awful it looks. I've trained myself to stop doing it, mostly, but I can't forget how good it feels and how much I miss it. I especially miss how I used to allow myself to slump down in my seat and let loose with both knees.

A few weeks ago, when I forgot myself, Ethan caught me jiggling my knee while we were reading the Sunday paper at the kitchen table. He looked amused, and I asked him why. He pointed to my knee and smiled at me, which made me self-conscious.

"Don't stop on my account, Bernal," he said. "It's like when a dog wags its tail. It lets me know you're happy."

Maybe I was happy and didn't even know it. Maybe that's what being happy is supposed to feel like. Maybe I was happy with Ethan and too stubborn to allow myself to enjoy it with both my knees. Maybe I need to stop asking myself pointless maybe questions.

Thinking of him makes me want to check my messages, but he hasn't called. I don't need to look to know. Ethan is an incredibly talented man, but even he can't dial a phone while doing back flips off the coast of St. Tropez.

"Julie?"

I wait for Julie to stop yakking with Milty's useless intern. She's a Harvard grad who gets drunk on free industry-party liquor and takes pregnancy tests in the company bathroom every Monday morning. Julie told me this because Julie is a malicious gossip.

"Julie." It's a strain to keep the annoyance out of my voice. Dooley looks up at me, her eyebrows raised.

I'm both irritated and numbed by Julie's very existence. Was I this rude at her age? No, I wasn't. I couldn't afford that particular luxury until well after I'd proven myself as someone who shouldn't be fucked with. Julie thinks she can get away with being rude to me. In her mind, there are different rules for different people, and legacy USC always beats scholarship Princeton.

"She sure does jump when you call her, don't she?" Dooley stops fidgeting, curious to see how I'll handle this.

"Julie!"

Julie looks over at me, shrugs her shoulders, and takes her time getting her ass in my office. "Sorry, Claudia, I was confirming some stuff for Mr. Wasser."

"While I'm sure he appreciates your dedication to his *stuff*, my *stuff* needs to be picked up from the dry cleaner. You can leave everything at the valet stand with Mauro."

I point to the envelope with the claim tickets and some cash, not bothering to look up at her. She knows the drill. It's not the first time I've asked her to do this, but it's the first time I've done it out of spite.

"Anything else?" She says this with such derision, I almost admire her for it.

I stare her down. Watching her get nervous, I give into the overwhelming urge to prove no one fucks with me and gets away with it. Not her. Not Milty. Not anyone except for Ethan.

Instantly, my anger turns into a feeling of such heaviness, all I want to do is put my head down on my desk and close my eyes. I would, too, if she and Dooley weren't here to see me do it. This, all of it, just feels wrong, and it especially feels wrong to take it out on Julie. She's not worth it.

"No, that's it for you, Julie." I turn back to my computer. "You can go."

"Okay, thank you, Claudia." She hurries out, cowed for now, but it won't take much for her to get her confidence back.

"You going to fire her?" Dooley asks, setting aside the script she was reading. "Or do you want me to jump her in the parking garage?"

"You can't jump her on company property, liability issues." I roll my head back and forth, trying to ease the tension in my neck and shoulders. "I'll fire her first thing in the morning."

"So what is it exactly that you do?" Dooley asks. "I know you've told me hundreds of times, but I wasn't paying attention."

My email pings. It's from Milty. I shut down my computer without bothering to open it.

"I make people feel good about giving us money they may never see again, and convince actresses it'll be great for their careers to do nude scenes."

I look up at Dooley. She's really listening and waiting for me to keep talking.

"I also get to deal with asshole agents, coked out directors, needy actors who think sleeping with me is included in their contract along with backend profits, and, my favorite, neurotic writers who also do coke but are too polite to make a move on me. And unions, crafts, zoning boards, accountants, lawyers, and local fixers, etc., etc., etc. When it all works out, we manage to make something special happen—a good movie, or at least a good enough movie that earns tons of money. And then I get to do it all over again for the next one."

"That sounds like a lot of work." Dooley shakes her head as she loops her hair into a loose knot at the back of her neck. Maritza has been on me to get her to take those braids out. One more thing for me to do. "Do you like it? What you do?"

"*Pues no hay de otra.* And there's more. At night, I go to parties and premieres where I make small talk with people who think very highly of themselves and wonder whose dick I sucked to get where I am."

"Wow, just like working at McDonald's." Dooley laughs. "Whose dick are you sucking?"

"No one's and everyone's," I lie, but it's only half of one. I should tell her about Ethan, and I will soon, but not until I get everything sorted out. "Some days I feel like a pimp. Except I'm both the whore and the pimp."

"So why do you do it? Why don't you do something else?" she asks.

"Like I said, what else is there? I'm not sure which part of my job I like most or least. The pandering, the hustling, the rare chance to put my weight behind a truly innovative and groundbreaking project or a talented writer. It might just be that I get off on being in control of so many factors at once. I'm so good at this, Dooley, it proves there's something wrong with me."

"You're always going to be good at whatever you decide to do, Claudia," she says. "And you should never have to apologize for being successful."

"The only Latina who doesn't have apologize for being successful is Selena and that's because she's dead," I retort without a thought. Dooley smiles at me, allowing my tasteless joke to blunt her kind and thoughtful observation. Tears come to my eyes. I turn away from her and blink rapidly to keep them from spilling over. "Julie should have left my dry cleaning with Mauro by now."

"Who's this Mauro?" she asks letting me off the hook again. "And why do you trust him with your stuff?"

"He's a good guy, reliable. He used to run with a Lincoln Heights graffiti crew." I grab my purse, and the magazine falls onto my lap. I shove it back in, all the way to the bottom where I can pretend it doesn't matter. "I'll introduce you. I bet you'll like him even though he's from Lincoln Heights."

I leave the tote bag of unread scripts by my desk, shut the door behind me, and walk beside my sister through the office to the elevators. I smile and nod at people but make it clear I have no time to stop and chat. They already think I'm a bitch. There's no reason to try to give them a different impression now.

Except now I'm the bitch who's sucking Ethan Jacobs' cock. Or, rather, I was. They've all seen the pictures. I might be very talented with my mouth and tongue, but I can't be in two places at once. They're assuming I've been dumped, and they very well might be right about this.

The elevator opens to the garage level and were greeted by the sight of a confused looking valet who's holding my dry cleaning in his arms.

"Hi. Is Mauro around?" I ask him.

I don't this guy, he's new. Usually, Mauro hires his cousins and friends he also calls primos. From the eager look on his pleasant-enough face and too-stylish haircut, he'll be leaving his headshot in my car before the month is out.

"Yeah, he's in the back, Miss Bernal," he says with a smile. Good teeth. He won't need them capped, but his hairline looks a little thin for his age. "Do you want me to get him?"

"No thanks." I smile back at him, no teeth. I've already bared them too many times today to be comfortable using them in a friendly manner. "Just my car and my dry cleaning."

"This your stuff? Some girl told me to deal with it. She didn't say anything about letting Mauro know."

Dooley hisses through her teeth, but I shrug it off. I'm tired and just want to get out of here. "Sorry about that. If I could get my car? Thanks."

"Yeah, sure thing, Miss Bernal. I'll put this in the trunk for you. Back in a minute."

We watch the valet sprint away. He's back so fast I don't have time to check my cell phone to confirm Ethan hasn't called me.

He holds the door open for me as Dooley makes her way around to the passenger side. I step forward to get in but stop when someone calls my name. It echoes through the parking structure, startling me.

"Claudia! Claudia!" I look up to where a small pack of paparazzi are furiously clicking their cameras in our direction. "Where's Ethan! Claudia! Did you know he was in France? Have you guys broken up? How long have you been together?"

The valet backs away, holding his hands out. "It wasn't me, Miss. Bernal. I swear."

"What's going on?" Dooley asks, sounding a little scared.

"It's nothing," I tell her. "Don't worry about it."

I put my head down and I'm about to get into my car when I see Julie sitting in her white BMW, blocking the two handicap spots by the garage entrance. She's on her phone laughing and pointing at the paparazzi. When she notices I've spotted her, she ducks down in a lame attempt to hide. It's extra stupid of her since she has the top down on her car.

"Claudia," Dooley calls out when she sees where I'm heading, "don't hit her on company property or in front of the photographers."

I walk over to Julie's car and lean over her, not giving her a chance to sit up or start talking.

"You're done, Julie. Give me your badge. Accounting will issue you a check for what you're owed. It'll be mailed to you along with anything you were dumb enough to leave upstairs. Don't bother using me as reference, but we both know you're going to hit Milty up for one. Good luck with that. Now fuck the fuck off."

I return to my car and drive out of the garage. Dooley looks both impressed and a little shocked, covering her face as we pass the paparazzi, who are still yelling my name. I stare straight ahead, ignoring them, feeling steady and calm, my focus on the road ahead of me. It's not as hard as I thought it would be to give in to being the coldhearted bitch everyone already thinks I am.

I guess Dooley is right. I'll always be good at whatever it is I decide to do.

# · 35 ·

# MARITZA

I'M NERVOUS. MY hands are sweaty and I'm holding the steering wheel too hard as we get closer to my house. Next to me, Dooley is talking about jaywalking, but I'm not really paying attention. I really hope she gets rid of those braids soon. Claudia's asleep in the back seat. Good. She's been in a mood lately.

I heard Dooley tell Daddy her place is okay, so I don't know why she's still at the house. It's so crowded in my room and there's only the one bathroom for all five of us.

My new house isn't ready yet, but I want to prove to Dooley and Claudia that I'm not just pretending at living my own life. I'm sick of their jokes and of them rolling their eyes when I talk about my plans. They think it's just a dumb fantasy, but it's not. I have a mortgage to prove it. And in a little more than two weeks, I'll have my wedding.

It's all real.

I have to make lots of big decisions for my house like ordering new carpet for the living room, bedrooms, and hallway. Or maybe I'll go with wood floors like Claudia has in her townhouse. Laminate wood looks just like wood but is easier to take care of. Then there's the easy stuff, painting and putting in new toilets.

I can't live here until all these things are done. A ready-to-move-in house is a much better surprise than a half-finished one.

I pull into the driveway. The contractor says I should get it replaced, but I can deal with a few cracks. It's not like it's falling apart; it just doesn't look so nice. In the meantime, I'll have him patch it and then paint it. I know this is possible, and if he won't do it, I'll hire someone else. Mr. Kim had to do it a few years ago for one of his rental properties, and it looks okay enough.

Dooley holds up a finger to her lips as she unbuckles her seat belt. She leans in between the seats and gets in close to Claudia's face. "Wake up, Claudia!"

"Ow, you bitch! Fucking damn it, Dooley," she yells as they bump heads.

"The mouth on you, Claudia." Dulcina rubs her eye and the top of her head. "And I'm sorry."

I stay where I am, holding on to the steering wheel, waiting for them to say something nice about my new house. Claudia glares at Dooley, cusses some more, and then gets out of the car.

"She's mad at me," Dooley says. "I shouldn't have done that. I'm sorry, Maritza."

I nod, but now I'm annoyed with both of them. They're acting like this isn't a big deal, like it's not important. I get out of my car and wait next to it for Dooley so I can lock it.

"I really have to pee," Claudia says. There's a red mark on her forehead. "Do you have toilet paper? If it's not two-ply, I'm going to judge you hard for it, Maritza."

I walk past her, my house keys in my hand. I want to cry, but I won't. There's no reason to cry when I'm getting everything I thought I wanted.

"Maritza?" Claudia catches up with me, tugging at my arm. "It's a nice color, your house, but I think I heard you tell Dooley you're going to get it painted?"

"Yeah, a custom color I saw in a magazine. I can get it matched at Home Depot." I let myself relax a little. "I'm going to have shutters put on and painted the same color as the trim."

"It's going to look really good," she says. She smiles at me and sniffs like she's about to cry. Instead, she gives me a hug and squeezes my butt. "I'm really happy for you, Maritza."

I let her hug me for a minute, then I open the door and let us inside. I don't even get mad when she rushes past me asking where the bathroom is.

"You really own this place, Maritza?" Dooley walks around the living room, making footprints on the carpet with her heavy boots. "Legally own it?"

"Of course I do!" I pull out my new vacuum cleaner, following behind her, smoothing out her steps right after she makes them.

Dooley sits down in the middle of the living room and yanks her boots off. She's wearing socks with smiley faces all over them. "Jeez, Maritza. You just have to ask."

"Toilet works." Claudia wanders in, barefoot, holding her shoes, a different pair of the red soled ones. "Points for the nice hand towels in the powder room. Classy move, you classy lady."

"In my bathroom, I'm going to put in a special toilet seat, like Mr. and Mrs. Kim have. It's a bidet and has all sorts of features." It's not cheap, either, but it's easy to disconnect just in case I move or something. "Bidets are much more hygienic. You don't even have to use toilet paper."

"And you can use it to power wash Augustino's baby carrot and grapes," Claudia says. "Fess up, Maritza. When it's magic time, does he announce his wand with *bibbidi, bobbidi, boo*?"

Dooley laughs. It's a little bit funny, so I kind of laugh, too.

"What do you guys think?" I can't keep myself from asking. "It's a nice house. Right?"

I really want my sisters to tell me they like it and that this wasn't a huge mistake. If they say this to me, it'll be easier when I tell Mamá and Daddy and Augustino. Mr. Kim and Mrs. Kim will be proud of me, I'm sure about that, so I'm not worried about them.

"It's really great." Claudia hugs me again.

She's been really touchy-feely lately. Last night she almost started crying when I gave her the Hello Kitty stamper of her name from when we were little. She must be under a lot of stress at work and it's probably why she has no appetite.

"Beyond great, Maritza," she says. "You did good."

"Where's your mother-in-law's room? I'm sure she'd appreciate if you put a ramp up the front steps for her Jitterbug scooter." Dooley likes to tease. Not as much as Claudia, but she still does. "She's going to leave wheel marks all over your carpet."

"She's not moving in here. Ever. Maybe I won't even invite her and Gabbi and Dani over. Maybe I won't even let Augustino through the front door."

"You don't have to decide anything right now." Claudia is staring at me, her head tilted to the side, her eyebrows together. "Unless that's what you want to do. Is it?"

"Well, okay, that's a conversation for another day. What are you going to do with all this space?" Dooley asks me.

"One is the master, of course. I already measured it for my bedroom set. The one near the front of the house is going to be my office. I'm not sure what to do with the third one, maybe a guest room, but I'm not sure." I start to get excited and then I remember I'm still mad at Gena. "It almost didn't happen, me getting my house, because of the real estate agent. She's a big PFC and so bad at her job I can't believe she's been able to keep it as long as she has."

"What's a PFC?" Dooley asks, looking up at me and Claudia, who is choking on her own laughter. Claudia sits down next to Dooley and tries to catch her breath. "Did I miss something?"

"I'm not going to say it." I point at Claudia. "She's the one who made it up."

"Fess up, Claudia. What's a PFC?" Dooley pokes her right under her arm where we know she's really ticklish. Claudia tries to roll away, but Dooley grabs on to her. "No, you're not going anywhere until you tell me."

"Okay, fine. I was a production assistant on Risk Management, the first one, and it was my job to get— ugh, I don't even want to say her name. Either way, I had to get her ass to set on time which she got off on making impossible for me to do. A few days before wrapping, she pissed me off to no end and, in front of the entire cast and crew, I called her a . . ." Claudia cheeks go extra pink. ". . . potato-faced cunt. And not only did I not get fired—the crew gave me a cake that looked like, well, not a potato. Best damn cake I've eaten and you know I don't like cake. I like penis."

"That's so foul, Claudia. Even for you," Dooley says. "You've corrupted our little sister and now me, too."

"You're both more than welcome." Claudia looks around and frowns. "When are you planning on moving in? I know a good moving company if you need one. They're not cheap, but they'll make sure all your *pantaletas* get from there to here without being sniffed."

"There are some things that need to get done first. So don't say anything to anyone, not yet." I wrap the cord around the vacuum cleaner and wheel it back into the closet. "I still want it to be a big surprise."

"Oh, it's going to be a big something." Claudia laughs but stops when Dooley smacks her on the arm. "Fine, sorry. I'm going to go ahead and ruin one surprise—I ordered your sofa. It's ready to ship, just tell me what day you want it delivered."

"Thank you, Claudia!" I kneel down next to her and hug her. I was worried I was going to have to ask my mother to ask her about it and how I would explain to Mamá about my couch without telling her about my house. "Dooley? I was wondering if you could paint something?"

"Um . . . sure. Like what?" she asks.

"Something bright. Like you used to do with the flower paintings. Remember?" I stand up and grab a roll of painter's tape and outline a rough rectangle where the couch will go. I stand next to her so I can see if the size is right. I don't know anything about canvases. Dooley does, she'll figure it out. "And one for over where I'm going to put a gas fireplace and another for the dining room."

"I can do that." Dooley wraps her hand around my ankle and leans her head on Claudia's shoulder. "They can be your wedding, birthday, and housewarming presents."

"It's going to be perfect. Isn't it?" I ask, but this time I don't need them to answer. Like with my wedding, everything is coming together just like I've decided it has to.

## • 36 •

# DULCINA

I CAN TELL THE moment I arrive in Santa Monica by the cars. In Boyle Heights, it was Camrys and Fords. As the 10 gets closer to the beach, there are plenty of BMWs and Mercedes-Benzes with the odd Ferrari and Bentley thrown into the mix of traffic. I don't care what anyone thinks of my GTI, but I did step up my own game.

I'm wearing one of Claudia's blazers, and helped myself to Maritza's large collection of makeup. She's been itching to undo my braids, but I'm not ready to let them go just yet. I've compromised by twisting them into a heavy, low bun. Otherwise, I'm dressed like me in my favorite pair of Levi's, freshly and unnecessarily washed for the second time in a week by our mom, a new white Hanes T-shirt, and my Doc Marten boots that have officially seen better days.

I turned down Maritza's offer to tag along with her to work. Claudia, who has meetings to go to and egos to stroke, plus a new assistant to hire, said I could hang out at her townhouse if I wanted to. I gave them both the same answer—I'm good. I don't need babysitting, but I understand why my family is waiting to see if I start up again.

For a little while before I left for Santa Monica, it was just me and our parents in the house. Both of them were extra careful around me, unsure of how to treat me without my sisters there to act as a buffer between us. I told them I had a job interview and they both assumed I was lying. Our mom certainly did but wasn't going to get into it with me. She'll pass this task off to Claudia like she always has.

She offered to fix me a bowl of oatmeal. I guess she's forgotten how much I hate oatmeal. Or maybe she hasn't which is exactly why she offered. Our dad wished me luck and gave me a twenty along with an awkward pat on the shoulder. He looked like he could use a beer.

I've always hated lying to my family and was never really good at it, drunk or sober. Right now, it's best for all of us if I keep my plans to myself. If anything, it feels good to have a purpose even if one of those purposes is far from good.

Last night, after she tossed it in the trash, I looked at the *People* magazine Claudia had been hiding in her purse and I called Ethan. When Maritza snuck up on me just as I hung up, I pretended to have been smoking. Everyone gave me dirty looks when I came back inside. Even Claudia.

Ethan asked me to meet him at his office in Santa Monica to talk about what's going on. If this guy  thinks he can mess with Claudia, I'm going to set him straight. He looked like he was having a lot of fun in those pictures. If this is all he wants, he has to leave my sister alone or else.

I find parking on the street, avoiding the valet stand right in front of the address he gave me, and walk the extra four blocks. I still arrive right at ten o'clock. I couldn't be late even if someone paid me to.

In the lobby, after waiting a few minutes for my turn, I give my name to the receptionist, who flirts with me as she checks me in. She's blond, petite, early twenties, and not really my type, but from how strong she's coming on to me, I am hers. She hands me a Post-it with her number on it. I nod at her as I pocket it, and she points me toward a couch and chairs right off the front doors.

As people come in and out, their eyes flicker over me, sizing me up. Some smile, a few offer up a good morning, but most dismiss me without a second glance. When I realize I'm looking at them just like they're trying to figure out if I'm someone, I flip through one of the magazines on the glass coffee table to give myself something else to do.

"Dooley?"

People can't help staring at Ethan Jacobs. Including me. And why not? He's gorgeous, very tall, and, oh yeah, famous for more than just being gorgeous and tall, but I'm sure those two things don't hurt. Claudia always has to make things difficult for herself.

He extends a hand to help me up and turns it into a hug. There's no agenda behind his gesture. He's genuinely happy I'm here and, it seems, is the kind of person who expresses himself through touch. He's also got a touch of a tan. That I'm not okay with.

"I'm so glad you're here, Dooley. Can I call you Dooley, or do you prefer Dulcina? How's Claudia?"

I step away from him before he's ready to let me go. I feel overwhelmed at the attention, not only from him. Who I might be just got a lot more interesting for everyone around us.

"Either is fine with me. As for Claudia, she's, you know, Claudia," I tell him with a shrug. He smells good, healthy. They'll make beautiful babies together. I pull away from him and blink the thought away. "How are you, Ethan?"

"Me? I'm fine, thanks. Are you hungry? Thirsty? I can have Christie order something in for you. Anything you want, Dooley. Smoothie, coffee, green juice?"

I look over at her, Christie, and slightly move my head in a motion that's somewhere between a shake and a nod. "I could go for some coffee, if it's not too much trouble. Black, straight up."

"Sure thing, Dooley. You get that Christie? Great. Just send it up to my office." He's oblivious to the stares and whispering. "There's a bagel place not too far from here that delivers. Or did you already have breakfast?"

"I'm good." I can't help but let out a snort that I try to play off as a cough. No wonder Claudia is freaked out. This guy really is a giver and not a taker. "Just coffee, thanks."

"Okay, sure. Whatever you want. So how is Claudia?" he asks again.

"She's fine. For the most part." I notice how people step aside for us, or at least for Ethan, as we make our way to the elevator. "The fire kind of stressed her out, but she's—"

"What fire?" Ethan physically turns my body to face him, the grip of his hands on my upper arms strong and panicked. I can feel him shaking. "What happened? Is she okay? Where is she?"

"Hold on there, buddy. She's fine. There was some minor smoke damage to her place, but it's been dealt with. Ethan, she's okay."

He lets go my arms and runs both of his hands through his short hair. "Okay, she's okay. I'm sorry. Did I hurt you?"

I shake my head and pat his shoulder, but it's of little comfort. Ethan looks pale, stressed, and utterly miserable. Exactly like Claudia. He glances around, realizing how everyone is taking close notice of our conversation. Instantly, his manner becomes protective. He places his hand on my back to provide a barrier between me and everyone else.

"Let's go." He's not asking, but also not assuming I'll automatically do as he says. I'm sure this trait of his rubs Claudia both ways.

It's a short ride to the fourth floor, and we walk down a hall at a quick pace, Ethan waving off people who want to talk to him. As soon as he closes the door to his office, he leans against it and takes a deep breath.

While Ethan is having his moment, I look around. There are a pair of tailored couches upholstered in a dark tweed separated by a solid-looking coffee table that I'm sure cost as much as my car, full Blue Book value. His desk is well made and well considered, as is everything else in his office. The man knows his midcentury furniture as well as his art.

"You want some water?" he asks, his offering of it automatic. Tears well up in his eyes. In a few long strides, he slumps onto one of the couches, his head in his hands. "I'm sorry."

"Nothing to be sorry about. You're not the first guy Claudia has made cry." I walk over to the vintage credenza and pour us each a glass of water from a chilled pitcher, complete with cucumber slices floating around in it. "Here. I didn't mean to freak you out. Obviously, you guys haven't been talking."

I sit on the couch next to him. The wall opposite us is covered with framed pictures. A mix of landscapes and candid shots obviously taken by him, judging by the unintended artsy angles and the fact that he's not in any of them. There's a single framed photo on his desk. It's of Claudia, and it looks like he took it while she was sleeping.

"Fuck!" Ethan leans his head back on the couch and rubs his tears away with the heels of his hands and keeps them there. "I couldn't stand it, being so close to her and having to hold back, so I took off. I thought she would at least call and cuss me out after those pictures got out. I should have been here, with her. She could have . . . I might have lost her."

I prop my feet on the coffee table. It looks like we're going to be here for a while so I might as well get comfortable. "She's not sleeping too well, if that makes you feel better."

"I've watched Claudia sleep through earthquakes." Ethan sits up, concerned. "I'll call her right now. No, fuck that, I'm going to put an end to this bullshit pissing match in person."

"Don't get ahead of yourself." I laugh. A flicker of a sad smile quickly passes over his face. "Sorry, man, this isn't funny. Give it to me straight, Ethan. No bullshit, especially no pissing. What is it you want from my sister?"

"Nothing. Everything. . . ."

He gets up and starts to pace around the room, ignoring the ringing phone on his desk that then kicks over to one in his pocket. I don't say anything, just a nod to encourage him to keep talking. He takes a deep breath, preparing himself to say what he's probably been wanting to put into words for as long as he's known my sister.

"I love Claudia. Not just love her, I'm *in* love with her. From the moment I saw her, I knew it. She's the one. But she pushes me away and comes at me at the same time. It's intense, incredible, but it's not only about the sex for me and never has been. She's trying to distract me from loving her. Claudia wants to be in control. I get it. I may not know why, but I understand it's important to her. What breaks my heart is she thinks she can't trust me to take care of her. That's it, right? She doesn't want to trust me. And what do I do? Act like a total asshole on Austin Taylor Ford's fucking yacht after he was all over her just a few days before. Some boyfriend I am. No wonder she hasn't called me."

"Looks like you got it all figured out. Except she's a lot more complicated." I smile at him. He doesn't smile back.

"I know she's holding back. She's not lying to me, but she's not sharing parts of herself, what she's thinking or feeling. The only reason I know about you is because you get mail, insurance stuff, at the townhouse. She doesn't talk about any of it, and she doesn't want to talk about us." Ethan sits down on the coffee table next to my feet. He brushes at a scuff mark on the toe of my boot. "I'll marry her today or I'll never propose if it's what she wants but . . . most of the time I don't know what she wants, much less what she needs. Man, Austin Ford Taylor is right, I am totally puh . . . whipped."

"Yeah, you are totally puh-whipped, and you might want to rethink who you're hanging out with and getting relationship advice from." I put my glass of water down, careful to set it on a coaster. "Ethan, you seem like a good guy, a good man, which is why we're going to figure out this next part together. After that? It's up to the both of you. Okay? Okay. So why don't you have Christie order us some bagels and coffee for yourself. Or green juice. Whatever you want."

Ethan hugs me lifting me off the couch a little as he gets up to go over to his desk. As he's talking to Christie, he picks up Claudia's picture and stares at it, running his thumb over her face. Oh, yeah, he loves her. Very much.

I close my eyes for a moment and decide it's right to trust not only him, but also my own instincts to do what's best for my sister. It's a good feeling.

# ✦ 37 ✦

# MARITZA

I JIGGLE MY RIGHT knee a little bit, and the heel of my shoe taps on the floor a few times. The woman sitting across from me gives me a dirty look, and I give her one right back. This is the reception area of an insurance company in Pasadena, not the Vatican.

I check the cover of the *Sunset* magazine I'm looking at—it's from March—and put it down next to my purse. I don't think anyone will mind if I take it. I run my fingers under my eyes to wipe away any mascara flakes or smudged eyeliner. There's air conditioning in here, but I'm sweating a little bit.

I'm wearing Claudia's dress. The super dark navy one she wore to the fiesta de fatsos and to my dress appointment. I'll get it dry cleaned so she'll never know I borrowed it. I also have on one of my pretty bras with matching panties. She wore those boring black heels to work, so I couldn't borrow them like I planned to. Doesn't really matter anyways. My heels look almost the same. It's not like Augustino will know the difference between Nine West and Louboutins, but he did mention at that stupid party how much he liked her shoes.

I told Mr. Kim I was meeting with a potential client in Glendale. I don't feel bad for lying to him about the client part because I am close enough to Glendale to make most of the lie almost true even though I would never dress like this to make sales calls. My job isn't one giant cocktail party like Claudia's is.

Mr. Kim doesn't need to know I came to Pasadena to meet Augustino so we can check in to the Double Tree. Even Auggie doesn't know I'm here. This is a surprise for him, a big treat. He always complains I'm not spontaneous when it comes to this stuff, so here I am dressed like this and being spontaneous on a Wednesday. I'll even pay for the hotel this one time, and we can order room service if he wants. This isn't going to be cheap, but if it's what I have to do, I'll do it and get it over with.

It's been a while, and this will make up for the fight we had on Monday. Plus, I want to make sure I'm sure that I'm sure. Today is my last chance before the wedding. I'll be way too busy this weekend to deal with him. It's unfair that everything is happening so fast. I wish I had more time, not a year like Mamá said, but another six weeks would be nice.

I try not to think about my wedding or that my sisters are still in my room and I have no privacy except for when I'm in my car on my way to and from work. On top of everything, I now have something else to worry about.

My new doctor called with the results of my tests. They were all okay except for one he's going to have done again. I offered to come in so he could use a fresh sample, but he said I didn't have to and it was most likely a mistake by the lab technician. He also said I can call him anytime.

I'm almost sure he's single. I'll find out from one of the nurses. They love to gossip.

I look at the door that separates the waiting area from the office part where Augustino is. He always has lunch really late, close to two o'clock instead of at noon. I got here early to make sure I don't miss him. I tried calling him at his desk, and it went right through to his voicemail just like with his cell phone. If he's ignoring my calls on purpose, I'm the one who gets to be mad, not him.

It was just a stupid fight, typical pre-wedding jitters. I'm under a lot of stress and he wanted to go to the park by the house. I told him no, and he got all upset with me. It's me who should be upset! I'm a bride-to-be, and he wanted me to do stuff in his car at the park I used to play at when I was a little girl. That's so not classy, and I don't care if I've done it before. But I can't let him acting all stupid ruin my wedding. I only have ten days before it's supposed to happen, and there's still so much to do.

Auggie hasn't even hired a DJ, and now he's saying his friend's band has to play at my reception. I told him okay, sure, but only if they do it for free. He got all offended. So now, according to him, there's going to be a DJ *and* a band because he's in charge of the music and I should just butt out.

Who cares about stupid music anyways? Band, DJ, both, it's all the same. People will dance to whatever, they don't care. What everyone really wants to see is how I look in my dress. Then it's all about eating free food and getting drunk for the cost of a single red pot holder from Target.

I didn't believe him for one second when he said he was going to leave me at the altar. Like Augustino would really not show up because I didn't go to the park with him, and I won't let his friends play bad covers of songs I don't like at my wedding. Even his mother wouldn't let him do that. He can ignore me all he wants, but she'll make sure he's there.

Maybe I'll ask my doctor what he suggests I do about all my stress. I'll call him when I get back to the office, after I send Mr. Kim home to Mrs. Kim. Then I'll start looking for DJs. I doubt this thing for Augustino will take longer an hour or two even if we end up ordering room service.

Augustino still hasn't come out for lunch.

I'm sweating so much and starting to feel sick to my stomach. I fan myself with my magazine and try not to swallow or else I'll throw up.

"Are you okay," the dirty-look lady asks me. My heart is beating so fast, she must be able to see it from where she's sitting. "Do you need some water?"

I shake my head. I don't know why I'm here, but I do know being here makes me feel stupid. I stand up and walk to the elevator, pressing the button a few times to hurry it up. I need to get out of here before Auggie sees me. If he catches me here, I'll have to give him what he wants and doesn't deserve. I don't care what he says or what he thinks. I'm not a stupid little girl who will do whatever he wants just so he'll like me. He can be mad at me all he wants for all the good it's going to do him.

Augustino needs to remember that I have a great job, a real career even. I make good money and have an investment portfolio. I own my car, and now I have a house. And I'm going to get my wedding. No one is going to care about the food, or the music, and especially not about the groom. He has to accept that a wedding is only about the bride. And isn't getting to be a bride the whole point of everything?

# • 38 •

# CLAUDIA

MILTY GOES THROUGH HIS usual spiel. He's name dropping and ego massaging—both his own ego and that of the director's, who's the reason for this early afternoon lunch—while keeping an eye on who's here, who's leaving, and who's coming into The Ivy.

I'm so over this place. I'm so over Milty. I'm so over smiling through my teeth and pretending I care about any of this.

I'm also a liar and am lying to myself.

I do care, and as much as I don't want to, I'm too good at my job to allow myself to screw up. I can't do that. Not when there are so many other ways I've already screwed myself over. I don't have the luxury of just sitting here looking somewhat attentive, but mostly attractive even if it's why Milty invited me to this thing. We both know why I'm here.

I present well.

That's how someone I had considered a friend and mentor put it to me. Worse, she meant it as a compliment. She was the last friend in the industry I made the mistake of thinking I had.

So here I am, presenting like a sprig of parsley sitting on top of a towering club sandwich—there but only there to be there. I'm decorative garnish, not even a condiment.

Fuck parsley, but a club sandwich sounds good.

I try to catch the waiter's attention, annoyed that Milty waved him off a few minutes ago. This is going to be one of those lunches where my boss doesn't order food. Milty loves lunch and dinner meetings but refuses to be seen eating. The most I've seen him consume is glass after glass of unsweetened iced tea. He always picks up the bill, so I can't fault him for that.

I take a deep breath, or as deep as I can get away with before it turns into a yawn, and try to get my head back into the game. I'm here to work, and this is work. Milty may have asked me here to be parsley, but I want to get something done.

The director, a music video visionary, an honor MTV bestowed upon him at the ripe age of twenty-four, lights up yet another cigarette even after being asked to put out the previous two by the manager. He's closing in on thirty-five, and his star isn't burning as brightly as it once did.

I yawn. I can't help it. I cup my hand over my mouth and try to look apologetic, but what I really want to do is laugh. I also really want a club sandwich.

Milty is glaring at me. If he could, he'd give me a kick under the table, but his legs don't reach that far. Instead, he ramps up his spiel. He's like a shark that has to keep swimming or it will drown in the very water it can't survive without.

"A project like this will bring you into the next level of your career," he says.

There's an edge to his voice. He's pissed at me. I don't care. He can't fire me for being bored. If he does, I'll have no problem setting up interviews with at least half a dozen production companies by tomorrow morning. We both know I check a lot of boxes.

"I'm talking Tarantino, Scorsese, Coppola when he wasn't fat and drunk on his own wine. Right, Claudia?"

There's somewhere else I have to be in a few hours, and it's also why I agreed to come to this foodless lunch meeting. I can't be in two places at one time, and I'll always choose my job over myself.

"Claudia?" Milty stops short of snapping his fingers in front of my face.

"Mysterious Ving . . . or do you prefer just Ving?" I ask him out of reflexive courtesy.

I turn up the wattage so suddenly, it makes my head swim. Milty sits back and lets me take over. He knows what this guy needs to be told is going be easier to take if it comes from me, with my face and my body. He also wants to give this guy the idea he has some sort of chance to get into my pants. He doesn't, but in each of their minds, he definitely does.

"Can I call you Derek? No? Never mind then. I'm going to give it to you straight. No bullshit, no tugging on your chub, just the truth." I tell him, dropping my polite facade. "Ready?"

"Yeah, sure, give it to me any way you want to, sugar," he says with a lazy smile.

That smile. I can imagine him tilting his head back as I reach to undo his zipper, but he'd be sitting in a wicker armchair by a pool and have a mustache. Where have I seen that image before? I remember. I can't forget. That's my problem . . . one of them.

"Your career is in the toilet," I tell him with a smile of my own. "Your last movie was beyond a flop, you have royally pissed off some very important people in this town, and, to top it off, you knocked up what's-his-face's girl-friend . . ."

"Biz Nasty Flash. And she's not his girlfriend anymore," Milty offers up as if on cue. "She's now Mrs. Biz Nasty Flash. Congratulations on your impending fatherhood, by the way."

Mysterious Ving, a prep school–educated stockbroker's son from Connecticut who dirtied up his past just enough so it seems almost plausible he grew up in Detroit proper, slumps in his chair.

"Fuck that shit. My lawyers are all over it, sugar."

"The paternity test her lawyers had to sue you to take also has your DNA all over it. But we all know this gives you some much needed street cred. Eyes up, Derek." I tap on the table before continuing to draw his gaze from my cleavage. "What Milty is telling you in a very nice way is, you need in on this movie more than this movie needs you. If you sign on, you'll have more buzz than you can choke on, and you can double your fee for your next project. Have your agent, manager, and whatever is left of your wannabe posse look over the contract. You won't get a better offer this year or next or ever again, sugar."

I unhook my purse from the back of the chair and stand up. There's a Denny's on Wilshire. I'll have a lemonade with my club sandwich even if it's Minute Maid. I'll ask for lemon wedges on the side to make sure it's tart enough. Wait. Am I not supposed to eat? I forgot to ask. I did ask. I chose to forget.

"Are you always this much of a cold bitch?" Ving asks, his eyes skimming my body. It doesn't make my skin crawl so much as annoy me. "And are you really banging Ethan Jacobs?"

"She is and she was," Milty answers for me. "Now what do you say we get your people on the phone and do this thing?"

I can feel both his and Milty's eyes on my ass as I turn to leave. This does make my skin crawl, but I don't speed up. No. I take my time and walk out like I own the place.

# DULCINA

I SIT ON THE porch steps after parking my car across the
street, my keys still in my hand. It's hot and dry outside
and I've had to peel off my San Francisco layers down to
just my white T-shirt. It's quiet and as peaceful as it gets on
Fickett Street when everyone who has a job is at work and
everyone who doesn't is waiting the heat out.

Sitting behind me, in his usual chair, our dad is going
through the mail. He separates it into piles. If the bill pile
is higher than the junk pile, he'll complain to our mom
until he dozes off in front of the early afternoon news. The
rest of his day will be spent wandering around, looking for
something to do and someone to talk to. This is what he did
yesterday and all the days I've been here except for Sunday.
On Sunday, he spent hours washing and detailing his and
Maritza's cars and was very happy to do the same for mine
and Claudia's.

I understand his restlessness. This is the longest I've
gone without a job, aside from when I was in the hospital
and then rehab. It feels odd not to be working, especially
since I owe Ethan money. He'll never ask me to pay him
back, but he's smart enough to keep from suggesting that
I don't.

I should register with a temp agency. Maybe I'll be a receptionist or a file clerk. It's time to get a grown-up job where I can sit behind a desk, get carpel tunnel, and accumulate a barely manageable amount of credit card debt like a respectable woman. First, I'll follow up with the cleaning company and Ethan's art guy. Work is work, and I like to work, but I'm done with bars, restaurants, and tattoo parlors.

I invited Ethan to to be Claudia's plus-one but told him not to bother with a gift. He's the kind of man who'll buy a person a pony if they ask for one as a joke. And it's exactly the kind of joke Claudia would make. I also made him promise not to do anything stupid like show up here at the house or at her office until it's the right time. He has to trust me to know when this is.

"You going inside?" our dad asks me.

"Nope," I tell him.

It feels wrong to be here a lot of reasons, not just because Maritza wants her room back to herself. Our mom wants me gone too but neither of them will come out and say it. They're waiting for Claudia to take both me and her off of their hands. Our dad is just going with the flow, spacing out his allotment of Budweiser to get him from noon to bedtime. For her own reasons, Claudia hasn't said anything about going back to her townhouse. I don't want to rush her, but she can't stay here for much longer. Neither of us can.

Even Maritza, in her own way, knows it's better for her to leave even if she won't. I have serious doubts about her ever really living at her new house. She'll stay there, of course, but she'll always think of this place as where she belongs. I don't feel the same way about the house and neither does Claudia, but I understand why each of us is here and why we're all here, together, for now.

"Whatever happened to Mr. Bellani?" I ask our dad. He's been relatively quiet for the last few minutes after chatting the mail guy's ear off. "Claudia mentioned he had a heart attack or something?"

"Yeah. His sons put him into an old folks' homes. The one on Eastern and Hubbard. Sunshine Fields."

"Between the freeway and the cemetery? I hope they charge double for a room without a view." I don't mean it as a joke, but he laughs. "Where are his kids?"

Mr. Bellani's sons, Lorenzo Jr. and Mikey, were jerks who only came around on weekends from where they lived in South Pasadena with their mother. Their father always smelled like raw animal fat and their teeth were a mass of cavities from gorging on candy, but they walked around here like they were royalty.

"Junior lives in Gardenia. The other one, Mikey, moved to Colorado. Both of them got married, had kids. Junior is divorced. Big mess with that one." He points at my hair with a piece of junk mail. "You going to take those out?"

"Maybe." I stand up and dust off the seat of my jeans. It's exactly 1:45. "I'll be back later."

I drive over to Eastern and Hubbard and find the place easily enough. It's called Moonrise Meadows, no sunshine there. I let out all my giggles before I lock up my car and go inside.

A young guy with a pot belly and bleary eyes shuffles up to me in the reception area. The air conditioning is jacked up so high, it almost hurts to be in here.

"Can I help you with something?" His eyes flicker down to my overly air-conditioned nipples.

"Hopefully, I'm here to see my uncle . . . Lorenzo Bellani," I say with a bright smile, hoping to distract him a little bit more. "He's my uncle, I'm his niece. His son Mikey, my cousin, on our mother's side, said he'd let you know I was going to stop by. I can tell from the look on your face he forgot to call. Typical Mikey. Right?"

I'm talking too much. I put my hands in my pockets, tightening my T-shirt across my breasts.

"Yeah, no, that's okay. Happens all the time. Dr. Potter is in with your uncle right now. I'll call the room and see if it's okay for you to go in."

He shuffles back to the reception desk and speaks quietly into the phone, staring at me the whole time. He nods and gives me a thumbs-up. He has me sign into the visitor's log and then hands me a "Hello My Name Is . . ." sticker along with fat purple marker for me to write my name on it. His eyes flicker down from my face as he watches as I press it over my right breast.

"Do you live around here, Rachel?"

"Oh, yeah, sure, sort of close to here. Lincoln Heights, so not too far, depending on traffic. I just moved back from Bakersfield. You'll be seeing me a lot now that I'm . . . yeah." I step away from him and point down the corridor. "Which room is he in? My uncle?"

"He's in room 27."

I smile and give him a little wave and step carefully so my boots don't squeak on the painfully clean linoleum. I pass open doors where old people are sitting in wheelchairs in front of muted televisions or are motionless lumps on beds. Outside of room 27, I stare straight ahead at nothing as I wait in the hallway for the doctor to come out.

"Hello, I'm Dr. Potter. You're here to see Mr. Bellani?"

Dr. Potter is an older man, but not exactly old. It's more like he's drained of life. He smells like strong soap, cigarettes, and cheap gin. I wonder what he did wrong to end up working in a place like this. Whatever it was, I hope it was worth it.

"Nice to meet you, Dr. Potter." I shake his hand pulling mine back quickly. I have a good idea of where it's been, and I don't want any of that on my skin.

"You're his niece? Rachel?" He looks at me closely before shrugging off whatever it was that gave him pause. "Your uncle doesn't get many visitors."

"I'm here to visit him." I sound more defensive than apologetic. Dr. Potter doesn't blink but I can't help but try to soften my rudeness with another lie. "I just moved back from Bakersfield. How's he doing?"

"Your uncle's cancer is holding steady, not getting worse, not getting better. It's his heart that's failing. Otherwise, he's lucid and can be handful for some of the attendants. Your cousin, the one who admitted him, signed a DNR."

Not at all sure what my reaction should be, I decide to keep quiet and let him keep talking.

"Given all these considerations, he's stable enough to be moved to a home environment," Dr. Potter says. "With assistance, it's possible to manage his care and keep him comfortable until he, uh, expires."

"I'm living in an apartment right now, third floor, no elevator." Another necessary lie.

"I understand. Your uncle's situation is a difficult one." Dr. Potter looks at me closely again as if he has it in him to care enough to try and figure me out. "Not just his health considerations."

"I'll talk to my husband about it." My lies are getting shorter, but that one was doozy.

"Yes, of course." Dr. Potter nods and pats the pocket of his white coat where he's tucked a box of Newport Menthol cigarettes next to a blue Bic pen. Nasty on both counts. He steps aside so I can go in. "Angh, his nursing attendant, should be in soon with his medication."

"I'll get on my cousins to be a little more involved. In the meantime, I'll do what I can. Thank you, Dr. Potter. "

"Of course," his eyes flicker down to my name tag and back up to my face, " . . . Rachel."

I walk in and stand by the window, away from the bed and the empty chair beside it. There's a view of the cemetery, lots of green, but it doesn't look at all like a park. It looks exactly like what is. Even so, there's more life across the street than there is in this room.

He isn't fat anymore. If it wasn't for his thick fingers and the faded tattoo on his forearm, I would barely recognize him. His teeth are in a glass of water by his bed and his eyes are closed. They were blue—a big deal in our neighborhood when we were kids. They still must be blue, but I doubt anyone on Fickett Street gives him a second thought these days.

I stare at him, all my senses attuned to who's in front of me. He needs a shave and a haircut, but there isn't much of a point for either. He smells old and almost dead. Lucky for me, he's not. Lucky for him, he's well on his way there.

A woman who I assume is his attendant, Angh, flutters into the room. She's tiny, but I can tell she's strong and can flip over the inert figure of someone three times her weight without so much as a grunt. She sprays disinfectant to try to hide the smell of slowly dying old people.

"So nice you came today, beautiful lady! His sons so terrible! Never come. Never call!"

Angh takes my arm and guides to the chair by his bed. It's one of those cushy vinyl hospital chairs with the waxy blond wood arms and legs.

"I go now and get the cart for happy medicine time! You stay. Keep your uncle company. You okay? Your color not good, nice lady. Very hot day. I get you some juice. Be right back!" Angh is out the door before she even finishes her sentence.

I reach for the chart at the foot of the bed. It's not good. He should have been dead yesterday, which is what anyone who has ever known him wants.

"Junior?" His voice is weak and creaky, but I can tell that inside his shriveled body, he's still all there.

"Nope, old man. Junior hasn't been here to see you in, like, ever. Why do you think that is?"

"Who are you?" His eyes flicker open. They're gummy and faded but still sharp. I see them spark the moment he remembers me. "Tell me your name again."

"Rachel. Here, in this place and in this room, this is who I am and it's what you'll call me."

"You're the one with the quick hands," he says, confusing me with Claudia. "Did you bring your other sisters to visit me too?"

My shoulders tense up, but this is all he's going to get from me. If he's stupid enough to mention them again, he's going to regret it.

He tries to pull himself up into a sitting position, but he can't. He's weak now, useless. He used to easily toss a side of beef over his shoulder and carry it in from the refrigerated truck. He used to do a lot of things.

"I don't have any candy." He turns his face toward me. "You always liked my candy. Didn't you?"

He's trying to make me angry. I won't let him. "I don't eat candy anymore, old man. It's bad for you."

"Always a smart girl."

He smiles at me, toothless so it makes his face cave in, but it's the one I remember from when I was a little girl. An innocent scared, and ashamed little girl. He knew I wouldn't say anything. He said I'd get in trouble and the police would take our parents away. And it would be all my fault because what he did to me was all my fault. And I believed him. For a long time, I believed him.

"All three of the Neapolitan sisters were smart." His voice is stronger now, louder. "And they were sweet. One sweeter than the next."

A rush of acid fills my mouth, and everything tilts side-ways. I feel like I'm spinning even as everything around me stays perfectly still. I'm surprised to find the faded lino-leum floor under my knees and the palms of my hands. I stay there unable to move, wanting to yell, to scream, but nothing comes out. Instead, I concentrate on the tube that snakes down from underneath the bleached bedsheet that covers him. I watch as it changes from clear and empty to bright yellow, filling the bag it's attached to.

I pull myself up and focus on slowing my heartbeat until it's strong and steady. Holding my breath, I lean in close, my braids falling into his face. I want to make sure he doesn't miss a word of what I'm going to say to him. He blinks fast, startled, not smiling anymore.

"You just pissed yourself, old man. Is that what you do for fun these days, Lorenzo Bellani? Piss yourself?"

I press my forefinger against his chest. It gives way under the pressure, and it wouldn't take much more for me to hurt him. I press a little harder watching his eyes go wide, his mouth twitch with pain. I pull my finger away and straighten up.

There are lots of ways to make him suffer, but I'll never touch him again. These other ways might be less than what he deserves, but he'll still get a taste of what it feels like to be alone, frightened, and helpless.

From the hallway, I hear squeaky footsteps. Angh, humming under her breath, pushes a cart into the room and bumps the side of the bed. I move out of her way and stand by the window again.

"Mr. Bellani, awakey wakey! Happy medicine time!"

Angh plunges a syringe into what used to be the meaty part of his shoulder. She moves quickly not just because she knows what she's doing but because there are other patients who also need their happy medicine. She hands me a bottle of orange juice and guides me back to the chair beside his bed.

"You see your beautiful visitor, Mr. Bellani? Today is a very lucky day for you."

"It is," I tell her as I turn my face away when she lifts the sheet to check his catheter. "It's a lucky day for both of us."

# ◆ 40 ◆

# MARITZA

I TOUCH UP MY makeup while Mr. Kim and Mrs. Kim yell at each other over the speakerphone in his office. He yells that she's spending too much money and this why is why they won't be staying in a hotel in Jeonju when they go to Korea in September. Mrs. Kim yells that he's just being cheap. Mr. Kim yells that his mother's house will have to do. Mrs. Kim yells she won't set one foot outside of Seoul if he doesn't agree to a hotel.

It's the same fight they had last time they went to Korea. They go every two years and stay for eight weeks. It's the only time it's quiet around here.

"Bah!" Mr. Kim says as he slams down the phone. "She think I made of Money!"

"No, she doesn't, Mr. Kim." I pull my lips tight to make sure my liner goes on exactly where I want it to. I switch to Korean. "She just doesn't like your mother very much."

"What did you say?" He stomps over to me. He knows what I said—my Korean is almost as good as his is. It should be, he's the one who taught me.

"I said you should take Mrs. Kim to Hawaii this summer and then she'll have to say yes to staying at your mother's house in September." I cap my lipliner and drop it into my makeup case. "See? Simple."

"Money. More money. She buys all new luggage for our trip! Not even on sale."

Mr. Kim paces up and down. He glares out the front window, checks the fax machine and then jiggles the water cooler so it stops making that ticking noise. I'll get it replaced when he's in Hawaii so he won't complain about the extra cost of leasing a new one.

"If you use the luggage to go to Hawaii *and* to Korea, you'll get twice as much value out of it." I check my eye makeup. It's a little heavier than usual, but I had some time to think on my way back from Pasadena. "I have to visit another vendor in . . . in Irving."

"I'll come with you." Mr. Kim starts to tuck in his shirt. "In my car. You speed too fast."

"No, Mr. Kim. Someone needs to stay in the office." The phone and fax machine are quiet because I've already taken care of everything. I stand up and walk to the door, holding out my hand to make sure he doesn't follow me. "I'm going now. You stay here. Stay! Make sure the window in the bathroom is closed before you set the alarm."

"Take your phone with you." Mr. Kim wanders back into his office.

"I always do." I close the door behind me, locking it, and walk the short distance to my car.

This time, it takes me almost an hour to get to Pasadena because of a car accident on the 5. It's happened right next to the General Hospital exit so, I guess, that's a good thing.

Mr. Kim calls me. I ignore him. Mrs. Kim calls me right after. I ignore her too. I'm not getting in the middle of their fight. Not even a trip to Hawaii will solve it, but this is how it is for them.

Mamá and Daddy hardly ever fight. They don't even talk to each other that much, except about what came in the mail or what's for lunch or dinner, but not about breakfast. They always have oatmeal, even on Sundays. The rest of the time, my mother listens to her music in the kitchen, and Daddy watches TV in the living room or stays out on the porch until it's too dark to see anything. What do they even have to fight about? Nothing.

I pull into the garage and take the elevator up to the tenth floor. We can leave Auggie's car here and take mine to the Double Tree. He gets employee parking, whereas I'm going to get charged for every twenty minutes. I'll make sure to ask for my ticket to get validated this time. Fiancées are higher up than clients, so it shouldn't be a problem for them to make an exception.

"Hello. I'm Augustino's fiancée, Maritza," I tell the receptionist, pretending as if she's not the one who checked me in a few hours ago and that I didn't tell her my name was Rachel Cartland.

"Okay," she says slowly, like she's confused.

She looks over at the other girl sitting next to her with her eyebrows raised. She needs to tweeze them, or at least the right one. It's thicker than the left and makes her face look lopsided.

"Can you tell him I'm here?" I stand off to the side and wait for her to do her job.

"He's not available," she says without even bothering to check her computer or call his desk.

"Is he in a meeting? I can wait." I look behind me to see if anyone is being nosy.

"He's off-site and won't be back today." She looks at the other receptionist again, like she's not sure what to say. "He must have told you since you're supposedly his fiancée."

No, he didn't and I didn't drive all the way over here twice in one day to waste my time talking to a receptionist about my relationship. It's not any of her business.

"Where is he?" I ask her.

"We can't tell you that," the other one answers.

"You can't?" I'm trying very hard to not get mad, but she's pushing me. They both are. "Why not?"

"It's against company policy," she says, like I'm stupid. "We don't know if you're really Augustino's fiancée. He's never mentioned you and we talk all the time."

I don't believe her, she's a stupid liar. And who do they think they are? They're just pathetic receptionists. I'm the one who is going to be a bride in less than two weeks.

"I can just call him, and he'll tell me!" I yell, but only a little.

"You should do that then," she says, and then goes back to pretending to work. "Sorry, but we really can't help you."

"Thanks for nothing, you jealous bitches." I tip over the bowl of jelly beans, and they spill all over the place.

I walk away fast as they yell at me to come back. I don't care that I made a mess. It's all their fault. I hurry back to my car, pay for parking for the second time today, and drive toward Auggie's house. He's going to be sorry for making me waste my time, money, and gas, and worse, for making me wait for him at his house with his mother and sisters. He has no idea how sorry he's going to be for everything.

## ◆ 41 ◆

# CLAUDIA

I STAND NEXT TO a concrete pillar and watch cars pull in and out of the underground parking garage. I should have gone back to the townhouse and changed out of my dress and heels. I suppose it doesn't really matter. Is there a right outfit for this kind of thing? Sweats, I guess, or yoga pants. Something easy to pull on and off and which can be tossed into the wash or into the trash with little thought.

Maritza's knockoff Juicy. That's what I should be wearing. It would serve her right for sneaking out of the house this morning in my favorite dress. I would have loaned it to her or given her one of the two others I own; she just had to ask. But she didn't, and now she's going to have to—

Dooley taps her horn. It echoes in the parking lot causing people to turn toward us. I ignore them, and so does she.

"Hi," I wave at her, forcing my eyes to focus. "Just park anywhere."

I follow as she neatly fits her GTI into an empty slot a few spaces away from my Audi. It's then I realize I didn't plan this out as carefully as I should have. I have my car, Dooley has hers. One will have to remain behind.

It should be mine. This is my problem, not hers. I'll call Mauro and ask him to come pick it up. He has a spare set of my keys in the valet office. Once that's taken care of, I'll ask Dooley to take me to . . . I don't know. I also didn't think about where I'm going after this. To the house? My townhouse? A hotel? I really don't know. And where should Mauro take my car? Back to the office? To my townhouse? I'll just leave it here and pay for parking until I can come get it myself. But that's not going to work. There's a sign on the pillar that clearly states cars will be towed after midnight.

I start to panic.

"You okay, Claudia?" Dooley asks me.

From the two red splotches high on her cheeks, it's obvious she's been crying. If I remember, I'll ask her about it later. I always remember. I wish I could forget.

"Claudia? Are you okay?"

"Why wouldn't I be?" I nod, not telling the truth without actually lying to her. Before she can get a better look at my face, I slip Ethan's sunglasses back on—a dick move. I'll also remember to apologize for this later . . . after.

She's wearing black jeans, a white T-shirt, the blazer she asked to borrow this morning, and her scuffed boots. The blazer looks good on her. I'll let her keep it by not asking for it back. Dooley's undone some of her tiny braids. Her hair looks messy like it used to when she was a little girl and came in from playing outside. I'll ask her if I can undo some of the braids too. That sounds like a nice way to spend the rest of the day.

"Can you do me a favor?" I ask her, still not able to look her in the face.

My heart is beating so hard, I put my hand over it to keep it from jumping out of my chest.

"Of course." Dulcina links her arm through mine. "Anything."

"Promise not to ask me any questions right now or ever about . . . this." My body is shaking, and I'm glad it's Dooley who's here with me. She feels strong and solid, like my big sister. "Promise?"

"I promise, Claudia."

I believe her. Not because I want to or have to but because she's telling me the truth. Without another word, we walk up the ramp into the elevator vestibule. My phone rings, but I ignore it and it cuts off as soon as we step inside the elevator.

"What floor?" Dulcina asks. I reach over and press it without saying anything to her.

My phone rings again, sounding strangled. It must be Milty calling to say Ving has signed on to direct. I knew he would and so did Milty.

Milty likes the drama, the chase, and getting what he wants. Then he likes to gloat over lobster and steak he won't eat while forcing whoever is sitting across from him to listen while he recounts his triumph. It won't be me. Not tonight. Not tomorrow either. I might even take a vacation. I know a guy who owns a yacht I'm sure he'd be only too happy to watch me do back flips off of.

The elevator pings and then opens. We walk down a hushed, carpeted hallway, me in my $400 heels and Dooley in boots she's going to have to have to let go of soon. There are frosted glass doors on either side of us, all shut and very discreet.

I walk quickly, not giving Dooley a chance to ask where we're going. Directly across from where I have my appointment is the office of a well-known plastic surgeon. I stand between both doors, unable to make myself open the one I'm supposed to go into. Then I do it. I move. Dooley catches my arm as I force it forward.

"Claudia—"

"You promised me!" My words come out in a hiss. I press my hand to my mouth, hoping to get control of myself. She folds me into her arms, and I let myself collapse against her, sobbing, trying to fall apart as quietly as I can. "I'm sorry, Dooley. Please. I'm so sorry."

A nurse comes out. "Is everything okay?"

I recognize her voice, but I'm not sure of her name. She was very kind and answered all my questions when I set up my appointment last week. I hope she's kind to both of us right now.

"My sister needs to sit down." Dooley walks me in, her arms holding me up. "Somewhere private."

"Of course. This way, please."

The nurse leads us into a tastefully decorated recovery room. There's a lot of whispering, but I keep my eyes down, one hand pressed over my mouth and nose, wiping at my eyes with the other. Everything is flowing all together, salty and tasteless.

Dooley helps me onto the bed and covers me with a thin, tightly woven blanket. It's the same type of blanket I remember from when I was a fifteen and had an appointment like this . . . for this. I curl up, turning my back to all of them. All I want to do is go to sleep and wake up in my own bed. Not in Maritza's room or in a hotel where there's nothing to worry about except for leaving the maid a huge tip to make up for having to clean up after me even though I always clean up after myself.

It's what I'm supposed to be doing right now, cleaning up my own mess, not behaving as if it's the first one I've ever made for myself.

"Can you stay with my sister for a minute?" Dooley asks the nurse as she wipes my face with a handful of tissues.

"Of course." The nurse leans over and smooths my hair back from my forehead. I hear the door click shut and startle as if it was a gunshot. "Hush now, your sister is here. Everything will be alright."

She keeps stroking my hair, handing me fresh tissues as my crying turns into hiccups and I start to feel sleepy. I wish I'd taken off my shoes, but I don't like the blanket touching the bare skin of my legs.

There are more voices in the room. One of them belongs to the doctor. He asks me if I'm allergic to anything. For some reason, this makes me start crying again. Big, loud, angry sobs from somewhere very deep inside of me that I've been holding in for such a long time.

"She's not allergic to anything," Dooley says from the foot of the bed.

"We need to make sure because of—"

"For fuck's sake, just fucking give her something," Dooley says, her voice low and gravelly.

If I could laugh, I would. Dulcina hardly ever cusses. It might be the boots, the braids, or just how powerful she is, but the doctor is smart enough to stop quibbling with her. He asks the nurse to prepare a syringe of Valium.

Another nurse helps me sit up and carefully pulls down the top of my dress away from my arm. I smell then feel the tang of rubbing alcohol on my upper shoulder.

"Claudia? This will help you relax," the doctor says. "You're going to feel a pinch."

I make a small noise of discomfort. I feel I owe him at least this much participation in what's happening to me. It burns and then, very quickly, everything gets warm and fuzzy. My overwhelming need to cry just fades away into nothing. I roll over onto my back, my eyes so heavy, I don't know if I'll ever be able to open them again.

Time has passed, but I don't know if it's been a minute, an hour, or a whole day. I don't care, but I do. The last of that floaty feeling I couldn't keep myself from giving in to is slipping away and is replaced with the awareness that someone is close by me.

I open my eyes just enough to confirm I'm still in the recovery room, but my shoes are off. I wiggle my toes enjoying the feeling of them and realize, at some point, a cotton sheet has been placed between me and the blanket. I must have complained about it, but I don't remember. I wonder what else I might have said. After a long moment, I push myself onto my elbows, my eyes still half-closed. Without turning my head, I decide it's time to find out who's keeping watch over me.

"Dooley?"

"She's in the garage with Mauro. They're taking care of getting your car back to the townhouse," Ethan says. "You're coming home with me."

"Oh . . . okay."

I let myself fall back onto the pillow, wishing I had my shoes on. People don't take you seriously when you're barefoot, much less barefoot and on a recovery bed after chickening out of having an abortion. He sits next to me and takes my hand in his. I move over to make room for him. Ethan rolls onto his side so we face each other. He puts his arms around me and gathers me into his chest, tucking the top of my head under his chin.

"I'm sorry, Ethan. I really am."

"I'm sorry too, sweetheart."

"What for? I can't even blame you for those stupid yacht pictures." The tears start again, but this time they don't hurt. It might even feel good to just let them happen. "They make me wish I could hate you, but I can't."

"I wish I could hate you too, Claudia." He holds me tighter. "If that was possible, I wouldn't be your date to Maritza's wedding. Dooley's threatened to serve me my nuts for breakfast if I don't go. Would that make you happy?"

"No, keep your nuts. I like them." I put my hand on his chest so I can feel his heartbeat. "I love you, Ethan."

"I love you, Claudia." His voice is muffled by my hair, but I can tell he's crying. "I love you so much."

He reaches down between us and tentatively settles the palm of his warm, strong hand on my belly. I don't push him away.

# • 42 •

# MARITZA

Augustino's hands are sweaty, and he's holding mine way too hard. I want to let go, but I can't. It won't look right in the pictures. And he did exactly what I told him not to by getting his hair cut a couple of days ago so he looks like he's going into the army. As soon as this part is over, I'll tell the photographer not to take too many pictures of him and the rest of his family.

Now that I see how everything else has come together, letting Auggie and his groomsmen wear tuxedos was a mistake, but the wingtips look nice. Of course, when I decided on the tuxes, I still thought the ceremony could happen at St. Mary's.

I'm still mad we couldn't do this at the church. I had worked it out with the officiant, who was okay with wherever I wanted, even at a park or on a beach, as long as I had a permit. When I asked Father Gabriel one last time if I could have my ceremony at St. Mary's, instead of saying yes, he gave me a lecture and mentioned a bunch of other stuff that's really none of his business. Mamá still made me invite him.

I'm done with being Catholic, and I've only been going to 7:00 AM mass all these years because my mother needs the company. Daddy can start going with her. He's the one who needs to hear some of those lectures, not me.

I can't believe Father Gabriel showed up especially after he went on and on about the sanctity of the church and marriage. I wonder what he thinks of the person doing the ceremony. He's a Unitarian officiant I found on Yahoo by typing "backyard wedding ceremony" into the search box. He's also a notary who charges driving mileage and prefers cash.

No priest and no church, but it still looks like a real wedding, even without the gazebo.

Instead, I rented an arch and a portable dance floor, which is why the heels of the shoes Claudia surprised me and Dooley with aren't sinking into the grass. My shoes are really nice, and I'll see about getting them dyed black so I can wear them again. Dooley decorated the arch with flowers and lots of white tulle. She and Claudia stayed late yesterday to set everything up and got here early this morning to help me get ready.

They both look so pretty in their dresses. Dooley took her braids out, and Claudia isn't wearing those huge diamond studs of hers. She didn't offer to loan them to me as my "something borrowed," and when Mamá asked her to, she said no. Typical Claudia. So selfish.

Dani and Gabi look okay enough, but standing next to the three of us, it's almost mean.

My sisters and Auggie's are arranged in a neat little line, with Dooley closest to me holding both of our bouquets. Mine is all blush-colored roses, a mix of cream and blush for my bridesmaids, and cream-colored rosebud the boutonnieres for the groomsmen. Augustino's is a red rosebud because he says real men "don't do pink." It's not pink, but whatever. Daddy's wearing it, so it's not going to waste. The flowers look just like the picture from the magazine I showed Mrs. Kim's florist. I have no complaints about the flowers. Not one. Not even what they cost. And she threw in Augustino's boutonniere for free, so who cares if he doesn't match the color scheme.

I used most of what was left in the wedding account to cover all the extra guests that ended up having to be invited. The best use of that money was booking a really good DJ who I also found on Yahoo. He's very tall and handsome, but he's divorced. It would be more romantic if he was a widower. Auggie's friend's band is going to play later too. He's charging way more than he should because he shouldn't be charging anything at all.

I glance at Augustino as the officiant starts talking about love, commitment, and fidelity. How they're the three sides of a happy marriage that make an indestructible triangle. Or something like that. He asked me what I wanted him to say, and I told him whatever was included in the standard ceremony package would be more than fine. Once he heard that, he didn't bother to try to sell me add-ons like a unity candle.

Augustino tries to look into my eyes as he begins to repeat his vows. I stare just to the left of his face toward the neighbor's backyard. Daddy invited all of them, even the Phams. They can all go use the bathrooms at their own houses.

Augustino is really sweating now. There are drops of it all over his face and on his scalp. This grosses me out even more than I already am. I wish I could tell him to stop touching me with his disgusting hands.

When my doctor told me the second test confirmed chlamydia, it made me even more sure that doing what's best for me is what's right. I accepted Augustino is a mama's boy, that he only cares about himself, that he thinks Olive Garden is good enough for a special-occasion dinner, and that he always picks really dumb movies for us to see. What I don't accept is that he thinks he's going to get away with cheating on me. I've always found him out, every single time. It doesn't matter if I've never said a word about it. Not saying anything wasn't me giving him permission to do that to me.

When it's my turn, I repeat the vows. They don't mean anything. Not just because there's no priest and we're not at St. Mary's saying these words to each other. There's also no license. I never even made an appointment, and Augustino, dummy that he is, didn't bother to ask if we needed to get one.

With the last of the wedding money, I had Mr. Kim's niece engrave today's date on the back of the fake Rolex. I gave it to Auggie for his groom's gift and he's wearing it now. He gave me a pair of earrings that used to belong to his aunt. I'm not wearing them, and won't ever. Who wants to wear a dead woman's pearl earrings? That's just creepy. I'll give them back to him along with the engagement ring and wedding band when I tell him we're done. I don't want those things either.

He can consider this party an apology for wasting the last six years of my life. If he tries to make me pay him back or force me to stay with him, I'll tell his mother what her precious son has been up to. Not only about the sluts he's been poking his dirty ding-dong into, but also how Auggie made me have sex with him on her bed a lot of times and always told me how glad he was that I'm not fat like her or his sisters.

Auggie's family is probably going to get mad at me, but so what? Some of them didn't even buy me a gift. They're still going to eat, drink and dance. There's even a damn piñata. Two of them! No, I don't really care what anyone will say when they find out this isn't a real wedding.

Anyways, Claudia will let me keep the sofa. I'm sure she will.

# ❖ 43 ❖

# CLAUDIA

I SHIFT SLIGHTLY TO my right and catch sight of Ethan standing next to the lemon tree, having given up his seat for Mrs. Flores. He's trying to be as inconspicuous as possible, but heads are turning in his direction and guests are starting to whisper. Mrs. Flores, in her funeral worthy black polyester skirt suit and just as black lace mantilla, looks like she's about to spontaneously ovulate.

I'll introduce him during the reception as my boyfriend and later, when it's too obvious to deny, as the father of the baby I'm carrying. I have no plans to add any other titles to his résumé. As hard as I try—and really, I haven't tried too hard—I can't see myself marrying Ethan, but I am very much in love with him.

I need a partner, not just a husband. Husbands come and go, as do wives, but someone I can rely on totally and completely to be there for me, the real me, is different. I have my sisters and my sisters have me as proof of this.

I quit my job. Milty was full of promises and promotions. He offered me a bigger office with at least one window and two assistants. I let him go on for a few minutes before I told him no. Just that one word: "No." He'll shit talk me around town, tell people I did my best work while on my knees or on my back. Those who matter to me won't believe him, and anyone who does is also a liar and they know it.

I'm seriously considering Ethan's offer to join his production company, but only as a full-stake partner so it won't be just my name that's tied to projects, but my money too. This way, people can't say I slept my way into the job. Technically, Ethan would be doing the same thing by climbing into my bed every night. That bed is now at his, our, home in Venice. He wants to move us somewhere family-friendly for all the kids—his plural—we're going to have. For now, we're staying put. I'm happy exactly where we are and as we are.

I haven't stayed at the townhouse since Ethan brought me home. I did stop by the other day to decide which art will be making the move with me along with boxes of books, clothes, shoes, and purses I packed myself even after promising Ethan I'd let the movers do it. When I was done, I gathered up all the jewelry he's given me, along with those never-opened bottles of Xanax. There's a safe at home for the first, and I took an embarrassingly full Bloomingdale's shopping bag of the latter to an out-of-the-way pharmacy in the Valley for disposal.

I didn't feel sad or even relived to be leaving the townhouse but was very happy to see a neat pile of Dulcina's sketches sitting on the dining table. I'll put it on the market once she finds where she wants to be. She can't stay here at the house, it's not good for her, but I won't be surprised if she wants to live somewhere nearby.

Boyle Heights was never the source of Dooley's troubles, and it might even be her inspiration. Mauro is plugged in to the Chicano art scene around here and has been introducing her as his prima. This important part of my sister may have already found its tribe. Dulcina has also been hanging out with the receptionist from Ethan's company. A nice enough gal, but not her type. From what I've gathered, it's not serious or exclusive.

They're just having fun, and why not? It's going to take someone who's special like Dooley to be with her while letting her be who she is. I hope she finds this person. It might even be a combination of people. She has a lot of love to give and deserves even more in return.

Whatever else it is that's been keeping her busy for a few hours a day when I can't reach her is also her business. She'll tell me what she's been up to when she's ready.

As for Maritza, I don't expect her to move to Bellflower, but she'll go there. She bought herself a life-size dollhouse. She'll play with it until she gets bored and then she'll rent it out. She's going to be a nightmare of a landlady.

With Dooley at the townhouse and Maritza coming and going, Mom and Dad will have a chance to get to know each other again. That's not true. They never knew each other in the first place. Mom is incapable of such intimacy, and Dad, I suppose, decided a long time ago he's okay with the way things are between them.

Things aren't okay between me and Mom. I took her out for a drive a few days ago and straight up told her to lay off Maritza and not mess with Dooley. If she doesn't or tries to, she and I are going to have a very serious problem, and she better have believed me when I informed her I already know what the solution is.

Telling her what I think, feel, and know without the underlying hope that something I say will magically turn her into a better mother, woman, and person must mean all the therapy I've done is starting to pay off.

I don't think I'm perfect, like she accused me of along with a vile slew of other faults and failings, but I am an ambitious woman as well as a generally decent person who will always cuss too much. I also want to be a true partner

and lover to Ethan and a sister to my sisters instead of need-
ing to be their mother. I'm already a good daughter, better
than she deserves. I made sure to tell her that too.

But really, what do I know?

A lot and very little. Accepting this simple fact about
myself will, hopefully, allow me to live my life in full color
instead having to see everything as either black or white.
I'm going to be someone's mom, and I expect this to be as
difficult as it is wonderful. I'm also going to make mistakes,
but for the first time in my life, I don't have to do it all on
my own.

I want to look at Ethan, but I don't even though I can
feel him watching me. He loves me, all of me. I've never
been more sure of anything or anyone in my entire life. I
blink away tears that anyone who really knows me would
never believe are there because I'm so touched by Maritza
and Auggie exchanging their vows.

I glance over at her, worried that the attention Ethan is
drawing will annoy her, but Maritza's staring off into the
neighbor's yard. She was excited this morning, talking about
the flowers, her dress, Dooley's hair and how she wants to
grow hers out, not as long but longer than mine, how nice
her patched driveway is going to look. Not once did she
mention Augustino. I can't blame her—there's really not
much more to the guy other than that he showed up like
she told him to. What a dumb bunny he is.

Maritza is not dumb, just greedy, stubborn, and a little
delusional. She got her wedding, another one, and showed
us all up, especially me. She won. Now she can stop being
such a sore loser.

I already talked to a lawyer about an annulment. It's a
pretty straightforward process, especially with cause. The
antibiotic prescription and pamphlet on chlamydia she
has in her purse along with those matcha wafers I've been

craving looks to be grounds for cause to me. I'll bring it up with her in a few days. She'll be crashing from her wedding high pretty fast, and her window of logic will be open just enough for me to talk some sense into her.

I'm okay with pissing Maritza off, but I'm not okay with her being married to someone like Augustino. She deserves better, even if that better is a romance novel hero who would never dare suggest butt stuff or a Disney prince who can sing and dance and will never get old. This time around, she'll have to agree to an annulment. If she doesn't, I won't let her keep the sofa.

This isn't a threat, it's a fucking promise.

# • 44 •

# DULCINA

I'VE GOTTEN TO KNOW all the nurses and attendants at Moonrise Meadows well enough to ask about their children by name. They like me enough to share gossip and tasteless jokes, two things that make their shifts go by a little easier. They also appreciate any help I can give them so they can catch up on the endless amounts of work they have to do.

Mostly, though, I just sit in room 27 and consider the various ways I could kill its occupant. I've already decided I won't do that, he's not worth it, but it's my right to think about it as much as I want or need to. Those thoughts sometimes distract me from my memories. One in particular, though, is very strong and vivid.

Our mom needed a can of peas and was yelling at me to go get it from the corner store. I hid on the roof so Maritza was sent for it because Claudia was in the bathroom. I watched from up there as Claudia ran out after our baby sister, still yanking up her pants. She looped her arm through Maritza's and together they walked into the store. Claudia always tried her hardest to not let us go there by ourselves, and sometimes she even went in our place. And I let her. We all did.

I'm not angry at myself for what I did as a little girl. I've already punished myself more than enough for it. In the last year or so, I've earned some measure of forgiveness for what I did to myself and learned I'm deserving of forgiveness from others. The one responsible for what happened, for what he did, is Lorenzo Bellani. All of the fault and the burden of the wrongness of it is on him.

I made sure to mention to Dr. Potter, Angh, and Oswaldo at the front desk how he's more and more confused and how sad it is that he insists my name isn't Rachel or that I'm not his niece. I told them I would understand if the door to his room has to be closed when he gets too loud. I also made sure I'm the one they'll call when he takes a turn in either direction. I want to be there when he dies so mine is the last face he sees. I also want to be there in case he feels better so I can make sure it doesn't last for long.

Just before I left his bedside yesterday, I adjusted the morphine dose on his chart again. He'll only be receiving a quarter of what's barely keeping him comfortable. And he's not. He's in pain, but it's been so gradual, it's snuck up on him. Just like I did. Until someone catches the change, which will be difficult as I used the same blue Bic pen as Dr. Potter, whose handwriting is easy enough to mimic, Lorenzo Bellani's remaining days might not be for long, but they will be more and more painful.

When it's over, I'll tell Claudia. She'll be mad at me for not letting her take care of it. From going through his records, I'm not the first Rachel Neapolitan that's taken interest in Lorenzo Bellani's decline. The last time Rachel Two stopped by Moonrise Meadows was a little over six months ago, just before she met Ethan.

Good.

My sister is going to be a mom and has a man who loves her. Claudia has every right to move forward with her life without old burdens weighing her down. Besides, I'm strong enough to carry this one for both of my sisters.

I'm grateful Claudia is letting me stay at her place, but I don't plan to be there for too long. I'm not coming back to the house, that's a given. Mom washed my clothes even after I asked her, more than once, not to. I found Wyatt's card crumpled into a linty ball in the front pocket of my jeans even though I'd left it in my jacket on purpose. She's getting sloppy in her old age, and I'm still testing her like I did when I was a kid.

It doesn't matter—I memorized his number. Once I'm done with what I need to do, I'll let him know how nice the weather is. Just like it is today for a backyard wedding in Boyle Heights.

Maritza gives Augustino a closed-mouth kiss, holding her face to his just long enough for the photographer to snap a couple of pictures. She pulls away from him and poses for all of us. She's much too beautiful for Augustino. It's what we're all thinking, and she knows it. This why she looks so happy.

I hand Maritza her bouquet, and she guides him in between the folding chairs that make up the aisle. She stops to hug her boss and his wife, who hug her back just as hard. Whatever happens next, Maritza is going to be okay. She has me and Claudia to make sure she is.

I notice Claudia's shoulders are shaking. Her cheeks are pink, and her eyes are watering. I reach for her hand, ignoring the groomsmen we were paired up with. Auggie's sisters can have them.

"What's so funny," I ask, tugging on her to slow us down so we don't step on Maritza and Augustino's heels.

"There's nowhere for them to go but into that damn kitchen," she manages to say.

I laugh with her, not bothering to hide how funny this all is. Maritza glances back at us and winks. Claudia and I laugh harder.

All around me I see faces I haven't noticed in years. There's curiosity, of course, but there's also kindness in their eyes. I hold on tight to Claudia and keep Maritza in sight, my heart filling with so much love, it almost hurts.

# ACKNOWLEDGMENTS

THE NEAPOLITAN SISTERS TOOK a long time to go from idea and first draft to the novel it now is. What never changed was the title, the beginning and ending chapters and my hope that someday I'd be brave enough to tell this story as it needed to be told. After reading that early and stalled version of the book, my sister Martha called me out on holding back and told me I was capable delving much deeper into Dooley, Claudia and Maritza's story. "Don't be nice," she said. "Be honest, even if it is fiction." When she'd ask me about The Neapolitan Sisters, I'd tell her the truth—life wasn't where it needed to be for me to be able to focus on writing. After many years of waiting, on March 29, 2021, I was finally ready and able to commit to this novel. I'm glad I had the chance to tell her I was able to finish The Neapolitan Sisters as best as I could the night before she passed away on February 1, 2022. Martha was a difficult, complicated, smart, and charming woman and she was my sister.

As for me, lots has changed since the story of the Bernal sisters occurred to me so many years ago and I'm glad and grateful life has led me from there to here. I'm especially grateful for Elias, Justin, Adrienne, Alex and Ali, Anne,

ACKNOWLEDGMENTS

Bonnie, Emma, Danny, Dennis, Jaynee and Jodie, Jeff, Jim, Kim and Mike, Laura, Lily, Lisa, Maria, Marta, Martin, Monique, Nicolle, Reyna, Sulay, Tim, Theresa, Toni, Veronica, Whitney and Yvonne. One is my son, another is my nephew, and all are wonderful people who have made my small part of the world a better place. I'm thankful for all your help, humor, encouragement and kindness.

Publishing a book is not an easy process and a lot of work goes into making one happen. Thank you to the fine people at Alcove Press for all the time and effort that went into making The Neapolitan Sisters a reality, not just a Word doc that existed on more than a few laptops, hard drives and, even, a random thumb drive. And thank you to Niege Borges for designing such a vibrant, energetic and compelling cover.